ACCLAIM FOR

The Fearsome Particles

"Trevor Cole has masterminded a densely layered tale that sensitively peels away the complex facades of the individual members of a small, excruciatingly contemporary family, to reveal their (and our) most intimate fears and vulnerable desires."

— Governor General's Award jury citation

"[A novel] laced with subtle black humour, a sprinkling of pathos and large doses of human failing. . . . With writing like this, Trevor Cole is quickly gaining a reputation as a major talent, deservedly so."
— *Edmonton Journal*

"Impressive – funny, absorbing. . . . Beautifully authentic."
— *Winnipeg Free Press*

"Humour that comes from a deeper, more satisfying place. . . . The book soars."
— *Quill & Quire*

"One of the most entertaining novels I've read this year. . . . In its intimate examination of the inner lives of its characters, however, it becomes something greater, opening the door to fundamental and significant human truths. Its power comes from its narrowing of focus, and from Cole's significant strengths as a writer."
— *National Post*

"In very precise and skilled prose, Cole gets us very close to these characters, and the story consistently holds our interest. The book's not easy to put down."
— *NOW* magazine

"Cole is an ongoing contributor to Canadian letters who is worth watching."
— *Toronto Star*

BOOKS BY TREVOR COLE

Norman Bray in the Performance of His Life (2004)
The Fearsome Particles (2006)

TREVOR COLE

THE

FEARSOME

PARTICLES

EMBLEM EDITIONS
Published by McClelland & Stewart

Cloth edition published 2006
First Emblem Editions published 2007

LIBRARY AND ARCHIVES CANADA CATALOGUING IN PUBLICATION

Cole, Trevor, 1960–
The fearsome particles / Trevor Cole

ISBN 978-0-7710-2260-9 (bound)
ISBN 978-0-7710-2283-8 (pbk.)

I. Title.

PS8605.O44F42 2007   C813'.6   C2007-902015-1

We acknowledge the financial support of the Government of Canada through the
Book Publishing Industry Development Program and that of the Government of
Ontario through the Ontario Media Development Corporation's Ontario Book
Initiative. We further acknowledge the support of the Canada Council for the Arts
and the Ontario Arts Council for our publishing program.

SERIES EDITOR: ELLEN SELIGMAN

Cover design: Terri Nimmo
Cover image: Yoni Zonszein / Getty Images
Series logo design: Brian Bean

Typeset in Fournier by M&S, Toronto
Printed and bound in Canada

ANCIENT FOREST
FRIENDLY

This book was produced using ancient-forest friendly papers.

EMBLEM EDITIONS
McClelland & Stewart Ltd.
75 Sherbourne Street
Toronto, Ontario
M5A 2P9
www.mcclelland.com/emblem

1 2 3 4 5   11 10 09 08 07

For Krista

ONE

1

An animal that small, that dextrous, could be anywhere. An animal that *silent*. There was no defining its limits. What troubled Gerald was not the threat of the threat per se, but his sense of helplessness in the face of it.

In his imagination, in those thoughts that lay just beyond his control, the cat he called Rumsfeld was stalking him. It was an absurd idea, but as he stood in his slippers at the foot of the bed, with the new light of April stealing across a floor of cinnamon cabreuva, Gerald could not quite reach the absurdity and smother it. So he was forced, in the sense that addicts are forced by their addictions, or invalids by their infirmities, to picture the cat mincing through the cavities and recesses (what interior design people liked to call "dead spaces") of the sprawling turreted house on Breere Crescent. He was obliged to see in his mind's eye its white whiskery face peering around the pants press and shoe trees of his closet, looking more resolute, more purposeful, than a cat's face should be capable of looking. He was compelled to imagine it – ludicrous as it might sound to the great majority of people who weren't him and didn't live at 93 Breere – planning.

All Gerald Woodlore could do, and so did with conviction, was curse himself for thinking about the cat. Because this was not the time to be getting cat-fixated; this morning there were other things of far greater importance to be addressing, mentally. His son, Kyle, was returning home from a hostile territory with an uncertain injury. His wife, Vicki, was edging toward madness. Work entailed its own many, many challenges. For these reasons there was no force in the world worthier of invocation, in Gerald's view, than the will to ignore the cat's presence in their lives. And if there had been a way to call forth the will, and impose it on his thoughts the way he imposed plastic wrap on a freshly lopped lemon, to keep its spiky lemoniness contained, of course he would have. But Gerald had to acknowledge, unhappily, that he wasn't built to ignore sneaking threats to normalcy, to order, to the way things were supposed to be. He was much too conscious; he was conscious to the point of affliction. And so to him, the black-and-white cat, which a neighbour named Lorie Campeau had brought to the door in a wild panic three weeks before –

LORIE CAMPEAU: It's my mother. They've taken her to the hospital. She fell. She lives in Vancouver and she fell! So I have to fly there today, and of course I have to take my daughter, Jewels. But we just got her this cat. *Literally just got it.* And we can't give it back because

Jewels is completely in love. And I don't know what to do. We haven't even named it!

— the cat that Vicki had taken in without consultation though he, Gerald, was in the nearby den, listening and perfectly consultable, was a threat. It was a rogue presence. It was their own small, fluffy insurgency.

Gerald had named it Rumsfeld.

It was definitely skulking somewhere, at this moment. Preparing to effect cattish havoc. There was no point in looking over his shoulder. Peeking under furniture. The cat, Rumsfeld, was never seen until it wanted to be seen, until it was too late. Until you were walking through the dining room at midnight, naked, with two glasses of your wife's selected Youngerton Pinot Noir in your hands and a kalamata olive poised between your back teeth. Then it was there, ready to . . . trying to . . .

But see? This was what happened in his head. Reveries of menace. This was surely what rabbits felt like as the talons of eagles dangled overhead, the danger inescapable. This was what field mice felt like, when they scurried. This morning Gerald refused all rabbit–rodent associations. People were counting on him, a company needed him, his son needed him, his wife . . . He gripped his face with both hands and pressed until the flesh no longer gave.

What he needed was the distraction of concerted activity. He had already breakfasted, he had already rifled through the paper, looking for the latest references to Kyle's war (he thought of it as that, though some still refused to call it a war; and Kyle was not a soldier and he was no longer there, so it, whatever it was, was no longer his and thinking of it as "Kyle's war" was just another good reason for Gerald to shake his head at himself). Now he needed to get showered and dressed.

He stripped off his robe and flung it over an armchair. The diodes of the clock radio on his side of the bed emitted a calm, blue 8:06, which was the real time. On the small table by his wife's side, near the window, an old-fashioned enamel carriage clock pointed a thin brass hand at the thirty-first minute, because it was Vicki's recent notion that she was likelier to meet her early obligations if she believed the time to be twenty-five minutes later than it was. She had worked this out, that she could no longer rely on herself to respond to time in a rational, fore-sighted way but needed to fool herself to the tune of nearly half an hour. And the fact that she could rise, breakfast, shower, dress, and *avoid looking at his clock* so as to enter the day accord-ing to a deliberate misconception, and yet could not apply this same resourcefulness to functioning in the actual present, was, frankly, incomprehensible to Gerald, and deeply worrisome, if he allowed himself to think about it.

Soon enough, after his shower, he was standing wet at their bedroom window, looking out at the signature landscapes and century-old stonework of Breere Crescent, the midtown clois-ter of tumescent property values they'd called home for just over a decade. He stood there with a warm towel draped over his shoulders, letting trickles of water pool at his feet.

He did this knowingly, for three reasons: first, because the specially sealed cabreuva flooring, which Vicki had chosen two years before to have installed throughout the main and second levels, promised stability and imperviousness, and as a general rule Gerald believed in holding products to account; second, because he remained convinced that at some point in the future the cabreuva, whatever its claims, would let them down on the imperviousness front, and he wanted to be the marshal of that moment of disappointment and not its astounded victim; third, because despite the fact that it no longer seemed to irritate Vicki, as it once had, to see him slapping around their bedroom floor leaving small, foot-shaped lagoons, Gerald still held out hope that he could provoke a bit of the old exasperation, and so reassure himself that things were not as bad, regarding Vicki, as he feared.

A pale wash of daylight stretched across the foot of the bed to the far wall, where the wedding pictures hung, and outside the window, against a malt vinegar sky, the huge shagbark hickory that belonged to the Linders next door took on a majesty that to Gerald seemed unwarranted. Other people, he knew, admired the hickory; the Linders were particularly smitten and often held lawn parties beneath it. But Gerald was aware that the hickory provided food and haven for the squirrels that wanted to ravage his cable and telephone wires, and so he was denied the pleasure other people took for granted. Still, he had to admit, it was impressive. And with Vicki gone to her house assessment and the day's adversities ahead, Gerald sensed this might be his only moment to enjoy. So he stood there in the glistening nude, letting the water puddle around his feet, trying to admire the Linders' hickory, and dwelling as little as possible on the squirrels.

Kyle was due at the military airport in Trenton in six hours. He was already in the air.

Gerald began towelling off.

The previous July, as Gerald and Vicki were sipping coffee in the breakfast nook, Kyle had come to them and announced that he was going overseas. Canadian troops deployed in dangerous regions apparently needed civilian support services and he was going to do what he could to provide them, as part of something the government called the Canadian Occupational Forces Assistance Program, which sounded to Gerald like welfare for subjugators but evidently wasn't. Kyle was going to be a water treatment technician, meaning he would operate pumps and valves and read meters and gauges and handle chemicals, presumably dangerous, so that soldiers could have clean drinking water. The contract, which he had already signed, was for a year. How he had found out about this program, what had possessed him to apply to it and become legally bound to it without telling anyone, why the combined brain power of the government and the military and this COF-AP group thought a nineteen-year-old boy one year into his undergraduate chemistry studies was appropriate for such an assignment, they didn't know, and Kyle, who was six months into a phase of living his life as though no one else had any say in the matter, wasn't inclined to illuminate them.

KYLE: (laying the COF-AP folder on the breakfast nook table in the space between Gerald's Fil-Tru mug and Vicki's Wedgwood cup) This is what I'm going to be doing for a year. In Afghanistan.

Although Vicki had seemed resigned to the situation, Gerald had done what he could. He had taken steps. Because at the time his belief in himself, as someone who had a hand on everything handle-able and a way to steer clear of everything not, was still pure. And he was certain that this plan was not only lunatic but fully reversible. A boy could make his choice, a mother could accept it as such, but that didn't mean a father should let it happen. Gerald was sure that someone with power, a decision-maker, would agree no child should be allowed, in the twenty-first century, to put himself in harm's way. It wasn't a war zone over there, not officially, but it was hostile. For what other reason were there troops? And so this action of going overseas to live and work in a place where men held guns and mines lay under the sand and the water was not fit to drink, this machine of consequences that chugged to life when Kyle signed a piece of paper, could be shut down, Gerald knew, if only he could locate the switch.

But before he could find and flip that switch, Kyle was on a plane. The machine had taken him. And now he was being returned, three months before the end of his contract, because something had gone wrong.

As he walked to the ensuite to re-hang his towel, Gerald checked the time (8:17, just enough leeway) and stabbed the radio button with a finger to get the NEW1020 traffic reports. While he listened through the reliable cycle of NEW news and NEW sports and NEW weather and NEW traffic that pinwheeled through the hour, he monitored his sense that the cat and its trouble were edging closer.

That Lorie Campeau had called yesterday from the west coast to tell Vicki she would be another two weeks, that her mother was recovering but needed time, and that Vicki had not told the woman that her cat was ruining their lives, *had very nearly cost Gerald his life*, was merely background irritation. More tormenting was his belief that by now he should already have dealt with this problem – called an exterminator, or whatever sort of company you could pay to remove unwanted semi-domesticated animals – because now Kyle was coming home and who knew what the presence of an all-but-feral cat might contribute to the distress of a young man who was mysteriously damaged? This was what happened when you didn't take care of a problem crisply; another factor entered the picture and made the problem worse. It was a simple equation, A+B=C, in which A and B could be any separately manageable issues but C invariably stood for Catastrophe. He'd based his whole executive career on his grasp of that basic math and now here he was having to relearn it.

Five days ago, someone from COF-AP operations, a man named Oberly, had reached Gerald as he was driving home on the 407. All he'd said, after Gerald had pulled over to the side of the highway and turned off the radio, was that Kyle was "unable to complete his contract" after an "off-camp event." When Gerald, being shaken rhythmically by the cars speeding past, asked what kind of event, Oberly had told him that couldn't be "opened up," as if the troubles of his son were a Christmas present Gerald had been angling to get a peek at.

OBERLY: I'm afraid I can't open that up, sir. We're only able to discuss what's been approved for release.

What had been approved was the news that something that shouldn't have happened had happened, and that Kyle was coming home, ahead of schedule, and needed a family member to meet him at the Canadian Forces airport in Trenton. What had been approved was the bare reassurance that he was "physically sound." Nothing beyond that, despite Gerald's protests, was allowed out of the box of facts.

In the flattering bio-pink light of the ensuite, Gerald hiked up a bare leg and placed his foot against the edge of the marble countertop. This was the new post-shower ritual, checking his shins and calves for gouges from his wife's suddenly ragged toenails. For the past few months, the toenails had been a growing component of Gerald's Vicki-related concerns. All the years they'd been married, Vicki had taken inordinate care of her toenails. It was an important professional matter; just about any day of the week, Vicki could count on having to walk barefoot, or in stocking feet, through the pristine home of some wealthy person. There was no telling what media or corporate celebrity might get a glimpse of her pink toes. Consequently they never went more than a day, two at the most, without being sanded, buffed, and lacquered at enormous expense.

But those days were over, apparently. For whatever reason – if not madness then certainly some kind of mental malaise, connected to the clock nonsense and the dripping inattention, that could hardly be less timely – Vicki now allowed her toenails to descend into anarchy. It was an armed rebellion down there. And who was paying the price? For weeks now Gerald had been waking up in the middle of the night to stabbing pains, and had to spend time every morning surveying the damage and applying liquid bandages to the worst of it with a tiny brush. And whenever he raised the issue of her toenails, or, for that matter, the disturbed cat she had welcomed into the house, Vicki simply stared at him in the way of someone reconsidering her dinner plans. As if the toenails problem, the cat crisis, the discomfort each of these things caused him, deserved only that part of her attention devoted to finding him wanting. Gerald sighed and wondered if this was what twenty-one years of marriage had wrought, that you could now inflict injury on a spouse without care, except to wish that he wouldn't complain.

As he reached with one hand for the liquid bandages bottle, he ran the other up the inside of his thigh and dealt with an itch in the scrotal region. He could imagine himself being happy, having a job that supplied endless opportunities for satisfaction, living in a house where all clocks showed the same time, with a wife who cared enough not to wound him repeatedly, and a son who had not gone to Afghanistan and was now, therefore, more than just "physically sound." He could imagine himself coming home, opening the door, and not checking for surreptitious movement before stepping inside. But that was someone else's life, obviously. It was his once, but it wasn't any more. Which is why it didn't surprise him when he felt another itch at his dangling testicles, sent a hand to quell it, and encountered something other than his own fragile self. Why it wasn't shock he felt, but a mixture of horror and sweet vindication, when he looked down and saw between his legs the whitish reality of Rumsfeld, the cat, reaching up with a five-clawed paw.

2

Vicki still treasured moments like this, when out before her stretched the possibility of perfection, and she could already see it taking shape.

"Is that going to pose any challenges, do you think?" Avis trilled. They were on the second floor of the Lightenham Avenue house, standing at the top of a small mountain of polished stairs, and Avis Nye was slowly circling her manicured finger to indicate a vacant, apparently purposeless area south of the fifth bedroom, about a hundred square feet of iroko wood, gleaming as if it had just been stripped from the west African coast, bound on one side by a wall of closets and on the other by a burnished chestnut railing.

"Not at all," said Vicki, smiling her reassurance, for Avis was a silent agonizer and would soon, if Vicki was not convincing, need to take a series of pills. "We'll make that an 'open den.' I'll use the Turkish prayer rug and the Georges Jacob set. You know, the one with the chairs in cross-hatch blue?"

"The Georges Jacob set, of course." Avis adjusted the rose-petal scarf riding her shoulder and let her fingertips trail over the lapel of her blazer in a way that suggested profound relief. "You haven't used the Georges Jacob in a very long while."

"Not since Roxborough Drive," said Vicki. "I've been waiting for an opportunity."

"It will be wonderful to see it again."

Well, really, thank God for Avis. When she'd called last week, moments after Gerald had reported the unexpected but happy news that Kyle was coming home, she'd said the builders of 146 Lightenham were nearly finished and would love for her to begin staging on Tuesday. And Vicki had felt a noticeable and somewhat confusing spear of discomfort, just there, under her rib cage. It would have been difficult to name the sensation, but it was almost a feeling of dread, as if the assignment to bring to life the largest home on Lightenham Avenue – fifteen rooms on three levels, nearly eleven thousand square feet – were anything but a privilege. It had made her wonder, briefly, whether she should accept.

But what she loved about tiny Avis Nye, besides her patrician centredness and the sweet, flutelike music of her voice, was the way she, more than any other luxury realtor, made her feel appreciated. Avis understood and respected the service she offered – Avis never said *fluffing*, she always said *staging*, she accepted that even very wealthy buyers lacked a certain imagination when it came to looking at a collection of empty rooms, could not picture themselves or their things in a new, unadorned space, and needed a not-so-subtle nudge in the direction of fantasy – and this awareness was certainly a contributor to Avis's status as number one in dollar volume among luxury realtors in the city's central core, to say nothing of Vicki's own success.

Now that she was here in the Lightenham house, Vicki could tell she'd made the right decision. This was where she was meant to be today; here she felt completely sure of things. She gazed around at the cornice mouldings and wall details made of a pressed-fibre material that, having been painted, looked ceramic to the casual eye. Even the best builders engaged in small deceptions to save cost, or time. Vicki knew just how to work with such falsehoods, to aid the effect.

"So what are you planning in terms of price, Avis – about six three?"

"Six seven five, I think," said Avis. "There was a quite plain Georgian resale several doors east that sold for six two in March." When Avis said *six two*, her mouth moved exaggeratedly, from a kind of smile into a kind of pucker, as if to suggest the absurdity of such a figure. "The moment I heard that, I decided ours warranted the extra five hundred and fifty thousand. Or it will, once you've applied your particular spell."

Oh, Vicki was feeling so much better! The new Lightenham house was a great big blank French Country canvas, and with her warehouse space full of collected antiques, draperies and linens, rugs and fixtures, mirrors, prints and porcelains, she was going to create a month-long vision that would be worth every bit of the $50,000 she would charge – $35,000 for an extra month if the vendors wished to extend.

"I can always count on you, Victoria," Avis cooed. "Buyers can spin like maple keys in the wind, not knowing what to think, not knowing what to do. But then they come to a house you've done, and they see." She moved to the top of the staircase, which curved slightly and cascaded to the bottom like the gown of a Hamptons bride. "You have a way inside their heads I don't fully understand. It's not just exquisite taste. It's something much more, I don't know, sympathetic." She smiled in the light flooding through the bevelled glass windows and set out two veined hands in front of her. "You're like a sturdy marble cornerstone, propping up the wavering spirit."

Avis touched her palms together, seemed content in the moment, then began to descend the stairs in her queenly way, setting one small stocking foot carefully on each glossy tread. "I hope," she said, her voice escaping into the entrance hall's bright-lit air, "those two fortunate men in your life are as appreciative of you as I am."

Vicki caught the railing with a hand and held on as she watched Avis go, following her strawberry blond head as it moved down through space like an ever so slowly bouncing ball. When the agent got to the bottom, she turned and seemed surprised not to find Vicki immediately behind her. She looked up.

"Is there something else you wanted to see, Victoria?"

The question welled for a moment as Vicki thought, and shook her head.

"Did you want to check some measurements?"

"No."

Avis continued to gaze up at her. Though her face betrayed nothing, was as smooth as a river stone, she was clearly puzzled as to why Vicki was not, like her, headed toward the front door of the house. Vicki was almost as mystified, although it was possibly connected to the sudden return of the discomfort under her ribs, at about the spot where Vicki imagined an important organ should be. It was a very unpleasant feeling. And it made her not want to rush out the door just yet.

She resisted the urge to place a hand on the spot and wondered what to tell Avis. "I think I just need to visit the bathroom," she said, wishing instantly that she had thought of something else, as the word *bathroom* seemed to travel over the unadorned surfaces of the upper and lower floors and grow until it became vibratory and immense.

"Oh," said Avis, a surreptitious hand reaching down for her small black purse on the floor. "Is anything wrong?"

"Avis, it's all right. I'm fine." Vicki smiled as warmly as she could at the top of the stairs, though not warmly enough to prevent Avis from picking up her purse and rooting around for something. "I just need to . . . use the facilities."

Of course, this was all very strange, and Vicki understood why Avis would be unsettled. Use of a client home's facilities was usually considered an emergency-only matter. And this was not something that could be called an emergency. Although it was not *not* an emergency, either.

"You go," said Avis, pulling a small silver case out of her purse. "I'm just going to get a glass of water."

The master bedroom's enormous ensuite featured the Carrara marble vanity and tub surround, the intricate basket-weave floor inlays and the Milanese fixtures that Avis, in consultation with Vicki, generally stipulated among the list of appointments that were necessary for her to agree to list a builder's property (luxury builders, or perhaps their architects, were not as attuned as one would naturally assume to the tastes and needs of the wealthy home buyer; thus their habit of placing compact laundry appliances on the second floor, for the "convenience" of the very people who did not do the laundry, a feature Avis and Vicki were constantly having to purge from their designs). In the comfort of this environment, Vicki sat on the lid of the toilet, smoothed her fine taupe skirt over her knees, and tried to clear her head.

Now, just what was going on here? What was this dreadful feeling? It was a physical sensation, but not entirely physical, so she couldn't quickly put it down to having eaten something off. And anyway she hadn't eaten this morning, she'd been in such a hurry. Sitting on the toilet, Vicki listened to Avis take a call on her cell phone and considered the possibility that the feeling had something to do with Gerald, because he was very agitated about Kyle's homecoming and when Gerald got agitated, nothing and no one in the house could really settle. You wanted to put a blanket over everything, a thick, heavy quilt, and make every-thing just *be calm*, but that wasn't possible. Years ago, when this Gerald sort of feeling pervaded the house she grew up in, her mother used to say, "We're all in an upset!" which didn't help, but must at least have given her the satisfaction of being able to label the feeling. It was an upset, and they were in it until they managed to get out.

Was this "an upset"? It seemed like such a paltry term next to the whirligig of Gerald's anxiety. Something serious had hap-pened in Afghanistan, that was obvious, but it was a mystery to Vicki why Gerald needed to get into such a state about it, since it was equally clear, thank goodness, that Kyle hadn't been hurt. "Physically sound," he said they had told him. After all of Gerald's uproar before Kyle left – and all her assurances that their son was ready to make such decisions – everything seemed to have turned out so well: Kyle was coming home from his adventure, early (delightful surprise), and he was *sound*. If anything, it should have been a cause for celebration. She wished she'd thought of that before; she would have told Gerald.

Vicki sat up straight, tried to take a deep breath, and brought her hand to her stomach. She slipped two fingers between the pearl buttons of her blouse and pressed them delicately into the soft tissue under the rib cage, not certain she wanted to find something unusual, but no less troubled when she didn't.

Of course, she considered, it could be that unfortunate cat. What a mistake that was! She should never have agreed to take it in, although that was not something she could ever admit to Gerald, especially since the olive incident. But Lorie Campeau had been in such a panic, and there were so many other things on her mind at the time, the decision about the cat seemed to make itself. She'd just found herself holding out her arms. Really, though, if she had it to do over again, knowing what an annoying little creature it was (and how irrationally Gerald would react to its every move), she would slam the door in Lorie Campeau's face.

But no, it wasn't the cat.

"Victoria, darling," came Avis's whisper from beyond the door. "Are you at all ill?"

Vicki shut her eyes and pressed her lips tight. Avis was not a young woman, and because of her she'd had to once again climb all those stairs. "I'm just freshening up," she called brightly. What she needed to do was simply stand and walk out the door with Avis, into the rest of her day. And yet, just now, it was the last thing she felt up to. "You must be busy, Avis. If you need to go ahead, I'll be fine."

"No, no, it's quite all right. I'll just . . . have a peek at the western view." Avis's voice, which tended to travel the scale unpredictably, and sometimes seemed designed to keep a two-year-old entranced, offered no indication of the anxiety she was undoubtedly suffering. Vicki, scowling at herself, gave the spot under her ribs a firm press, and sipped a breath.

"I'm almost done."

"Don't rush, don't rush." Avis was still there at the door; she hadn't gone to look at any view.

"I'm so sorry about this."

"Victoria, apologies are hardly necessary. Although, now that I look at my watch, I do see that it's past nine-thirty." All over the place, Avis's voice, like a swallow in the wind. Up, down, up, down. I am not, Vicki said to herself, a child. "And I seem to remember that I have a showing in Forest Hill at ten. For which I have to pick up brochures. Let me just make a call."

She felt herself wanting to sigh. She closed her eyes, took in as much air as she could, and let it out silently. *Enough.* The feeling wasn't going away, and soon she was going to put Avis in the terrible position of having to postpone a showing. And for that Vicki could never forgive herself.

As she opened the door, she beamed. "I think they got the inlays just right," she said. "And I love that grassy green."

"Isn't it gorgeous?" agreed Avis. "It makes me think of Burma for some reason."

"I wish we'd done that in ours."

When they had descended the stairs and slipped on their shoes, the two women clipped through the foyer and out the door, into the fair metropolitan spring. "It's going to be a very good season, I think," said Avis, picking her way along the flagstones that twined through the just-seeded grounds. "It's been very good already." She pointed her keys, causing the bronze Jaguar sedan parked in the drive, next to Vicki's purposely unshowy Camry, to blip. Then she turned to Vicki, took her hand, and gently pressed it between both of hers. As the agent looked up into her eyes, Vicki could feel a large key ring digging into the heel of her palm.

"You'll call me if you need anything."

"Of course."

"I'd be very angry if you didn't."

"I'm fine."

Avis squeezed her hand, then released it, and the women were in their cars.

3

I mostly keep to myself. But nineteen hours, including the stopover in Dubai – it was asking a lot. If I could have slept, that would have helped. But sleep wasn't happening. And reading didn't work either. I needed visuals and sound. Otherwise stuff I didn't feel like thinking about started to climb in through the cracks of my brain like those lizards and cockroaches you get in your hotel room in Mexico. And I was so stupid, because what I should've done was buy some game thing off somebody at the camp before I left. But I didn't think of it in time. Anyway the batteries would've died pretty soon, and then I would've been in the same situation, stuck on a plane, surrounded by soldiers, with nothing to focus on. So, under the circumstances, what else could I do?

I leaned out of my aisle seat and looked back. "Lieutenant Jayne?" Lieutenant Jayne didn't need batteries. Legg used to call him a windup toy. "Lieutenant?"

He was four rows behind, sitting in his pixilated CADPAT

camouflage, reading a Stephen King novel (a lot of military guys like Stephen King; I don't know why). He said something to the sergeant next to him, which I couldn't hear because of the drone of the airplane, then he unbuckled himself and stepped into the aisle.

"What's up, Kyle?"

I waited until he was hulking over me – he's a big guy, he could've played football – gripping the back of the upholstered seat to keep steady. "I'm worried about my tattoo," I said.

"Your tattoo?"

"Yeah. I got it in Dubai, at this place near the airport."

The buzz of the plane seemed to be making his squared-off glasses slide down the bridge of his nose. He narrowed his eyes at me. "What about it?"

"I'm thinking I mighta caught hep C or something."

Jayne studied me for a second and shoved his glasses back up with a finger. "Why?" he said. "What's wrong?"

"It's all puffy and red."

Lieutenant Jayne glanced back in the direction of his seat as if he wished he'd never gotten out of it, then he frowned down at me. "Well, I dunno. Did you want me to look at it or something?"

"Sure," I said. "It's on my ass though. Don't you have to be, like, a captain before you can look at a guy's ass?"

The muscles around the lieutenant's jaw clenched and unclenched, and his eyes went kind of squinty. "You don't even have a tattoo, do you?"

"Yeah I do! It's on my ass, I swear! If you were a captain I could show you."

Lieutenant Jayne bunched up his mouth as if he had bees in there trying to escape, and he stared at me for, like, half a minute, holding back the bees. Then he leaned down to murmur into my ear. "Don't go turning into a dickhead, Woodlore." I could feel the breath from his mouth tickling my earlobe. "See a chaplain when you get home."

I blinked at him as he straightened up. Soldiers sometimes forget things aren't the same outside the forces as they are inside. "You only find chaplains in institutions like the army, Lieutenant," I told him. "I'm not in an institution."

Lieutenant Jayne clenched his jaw again, three times. Clench. Clench. Clench. "I could say something," he muttered. "But I won't." He turned away and walked back to his seat, shaking his head.

I just had to lean back and grin. Not because I'd wanted to give Lieutenant Jayne a hard time for the fun of it (although it was fun), but now I had his big, red face, looking all pissed-off and confused, in my mind, and I figured I could focus on that until they got around to running a movie or something. I knew I could count on the lieutenant. Because guys like Jayne, they have no idea they're sitting ducks.

The problem with these guys, and you don't have to look hard to find it: They haven't given in. Do you know what I mean? They haven't said, "Fuck it." They still care about stuff. And, I'm sorry and everything, but that's trouble.

It's hard to explain to people, because when they hear "give in," they think you mean "be lazy," or "take the easy way out." But that isn't it at all. Giving in is hard. It's caring that's easy. Because caring about things is wired into us, just like jealousy and anger and lust and all the stupidest parts of human nature. It's all selfish survival shit and most people can't help themselves. Imagine not eating for a whole day – how could you not care about food? But what I'm saying is, what if you were stuck in Africa during a famine? You'd have to learn how to not care. It's the only way you could live.

Same thing here. You go along in your job or your life or your marriage and it's fine, but the minute you start caring about it, you try to control it or protect it. And right then you're screwed. Because as soon as you care about *this* thing, you turn your back to *that* thing. That thing you don't expect, that thing nobody ever warned you about. As soon as you want one thing to happen, some other thing happens, and it's never good. People won't admit I'm right. They nod and look worried, but they don't believe me. I try telling them what Legg told me: The world moves randomly, the survivors are the ones who just go along. If I had to pick one word for it, it'd be *whatever*. I'm telling you, if you keep repeating that to yourself, if you keep that idea in your head, you'll be fine.

There's fragmentation mines all over the place. *Whatever*.
People are washing their clothes in the ditch. *Whatever*.
Some friendships aren't meant to last. *Whatever*.

As long as you give in and don't care, you'll make it through. It's kind of a Zen thing. But fuckin' try and tell that to people.

Jayne can't hear it. (I mean, I never tried to tell him, but he's one of those guys, you just go, Why bother?) The big thing for him – there's no missing it – is he's a lieutenant who wants to be a captain. Sure, that's normal for somebody in his position, but it means that, sorry, he's screwed. He's big, right? He could've

pounded me in a second. But if he's going to make captain, he
has to keep everything under control, stay on the path, check off
the rules. One of them being: Don't pound the COF-AP kid
they're sending home, because he can't help himself. He's
Officially Fucked Up. And now Jayne's so full of rules, so tied
up in protecting and caring, he can't even let loose when he has
the chance. He can't even yell at some jerk who's pissing him off
who he's never gonna see again for the rest of his life.

I have to feel bad for him, because it's only his natural human
inability to give in that makes him an easy target. Not everybody
gets the lesson they need, like I did. Most people wouldn't want
to. But it's really the only way you learn. Even Legg, he talked
about it, and he sounded like he could do it. But when it came
right down to it, he couldn't. And then look what happened.

Some people might think that's my fault. Maybe I would
too, if I cared.

4

Bishop wasn't paying attention, you could tell.

In the bruise-blue light of the darkened boardroom, Gerald saw his boss fold his arms, rest his wattley chin in his hand and act as though he was watching Trick Runiman fumble around with his projections. But Gerald could read Bishop well enough to know he wasn't in the boardroom at all – he was in Cincinnati. *Bishop*, he wanted to say, *you can't be in Cincinnati right now, you have to be here, listening to Trick*. Bishop's wife, Susan, was in Cincinnati, costing Bishop a fortune seeing specialists. Gerald didn't know what Susan's difficulty was, because his boss hadn't confided details about her trip, but it was obviously a grave matter because Bishop's eyes had the faraway look of a man with troubles.

Gerald regretted that Bishop had troubles. Partly because Bishop was a good and significant man, the founder and protector of Spent Materials Inc., who had hired him and after only two years promoted him to Chief Operations Officer, and who had told Gerald that he saw in him a detail man capable of bigger things ("COO with CEO potential" was how Gerald, in a splurge of self-confidence, had taken it). But Gerald also regretted Bishop's troubles because this meeting was important. The trends for Spent Materials were not encouraging, and up at the front of the room Spent's sales and marketing director was saying things, however ineffectually, that Bishop needed to hear. A sales and marketing meeting was like a foreign film; it had the threads of a plot but you had to keep up or you could miss the climax altogether. That this was a Trick Runiman meeting, featuring a sequential progression that bored in on itself like a freakish sea creature, just made keeping up all the more vital.

Sitting at the side of the long rosewood veneer table, Gerald leaned forward on an elbow and reached his free hand deep, deep into his pants pocket. It was a delicate, painful matter exploring one's injured testicles, made all the more difficult for having to be done surreptitiously. But he felt an itch that worried him. Probably it was nothing, but possibly it was leakage. There was a thumb-length gash there that hadn't seemed deep at the time (more of a scratch, really – an agonizing, ridiculously unnecessary scratch), and of course he'd slathered on the liquid bandage as if he were buttering Brussels sprouts, but who knew what happened down there in a situation like this? Maybe it was like a piñata, and once a seam was created all it needed was a whack in the right place to get the whole parcel of contents spilling out. What he had to do was check for leakage through the lining of his pants as if he were reaching for a piece of gum. At the same time he had to keep an eye on Trick's slides.

Watch the slides, reach for the gum.

Thought there was gum in here.

Find that damn gum.

In the seat behind Gerald, Doug Allsop, VP of business development, leaned over and whispered, "You okay?"

"Gum," muttered Gerald.

"You look like you're in pain."

Gerald realized only then that he was grimacing. He tried to make his face go smooth. "No, I'm fine."

Doug leaned in further. "Fruit or mint?" he whispered.

"Hmm?"

Doug held out a furtive hand. "Doesn't matter; I'll take whatever."

Gerald, watching the screen, pulled his hand out of his pocket and shook his head at the same time. His testicles were fine as far as he could tell but there was something about Trick's slides that confused him.

"Excuse me, um, Trick," said Gerald, loud enough to be heard at the front. "Sorry, but on the last slide you gave us market share projections for the third quarter, and now we're looking back at product positioning from Q-one. Is that right?"

Trick, who'd been holding his remote control to his chin like an electric shaver, now established two blocks of air with his hands. "*Where* we're going. *How* we get there."

"But we're in Q-two now."

"Yeah, I'm getting to Q-two." Trick was now making an impatient cranking motion with his remote hand. His meeting was an antique truck, apparently. "I'm getting us there. This is all preliminary. You know, just —"

"Could you take us back to the percentages, though? That one went by pretty fast and I think we could use another look." Gerald turned to include Bishop. "Is that all right? I don't mean to stop the flow."

Bishop dropped his hand from his face to the edge of the table and blinked like a man rising out of water. "No, that's fine." He smiled sheepishly at Gerald. "I wouldn't mind seeing it again myself."

Trick's head seemed to roll on his shoulders and he began to study the remote in his hand. "Well," he said, "I don't know if this thing goes back."

Near the front, Phil Barbuda, VP of finance, who'd been slumped with his arms draped over the sides of his chair and his legs crossed ankle on knee, as if he were watching the Red Sox in his rec room, now started waggling his elevated foot. "It goes back."

"How?" said Trick.

"Red button."

Trick aimed the remote, pressed a button, and the projector shut off. "Nope." He jabbed the remote at the projector again and the light came back on.

"Sorry," said Phil, foot stilled. "On mine it's the red button."

"I could just tell you some of it," said Trick, letting his remote hand drop from view. "What it said, basically —"

"You don't have to use that, you can do it with the computer." This was Sandy Beale, Trick's second in sales and marketing. Since she had started at Spent Materials Inc. ten months ago just about everybody, Gerald especially, had come to the conclusion Sandy was smarter than Trick and should be Trick's superior. Reaching out with two fine-boned hands, Sandy drew the computer toward her across the table. "You just have to hold down shift-control and hit the left cursor button." She did this. The percentages slide came back.

"Hokay!" said Trick, stopping traffic. "Don't do anything else."

"Good work," said Phil, slappa-slapping the sides of his chair. "That's definitely not like mine."

"So." Trick hooked a thumb into his waistband and hoisted the listing side of his pants. "These are the Q-three share numbers we can expect. Like I said, it shows some boost from the ad spending that . . . I was going to be getting to."

What the slide showed was an ugliness that made Gerald's chest hurt. In dark green, on the left, was an orderly stack of company names; in berry red, on the right, a stack of corresponding numbers. Trick Runiman was fond of Christmasy colour arrangements – silver and gold was another favourite – and seemed to hope that jaunty hues could obscure numeric horrors. But in this case there was no missing the truth: Spent Materials Inc. could look forward, during the three-month period beginning in July, to occupying 3.9 per cent of the national residential wire window-screen market. This would be, as far as Gerald knew, the worst third-quarter share in company history, good for tenth place out of eleven companies producing residential wire window screens. According to this slide, Spent would avoid last place by a margin of only 0.3 per cent over Nu-Snap Screens, a company that had officially gone bankrupt last June and was now, through receivers, simply selling off whatever wire screen inventory remained in its warehouses. They would barely surpass in market share a company that had been dead nearly a year – and this was presuming Trick's ad boost happened to kick in.

Gerald glanced over at Bishop in the gloom to make sure he was absorbing Trick's holly-themed atrocity. Because these were numbers no materials executive could allow. Numbers no board could accept. Gerald knew, because Bishop had told him, that over the past year Spent's more activist directors had begun to make dissatisfied noises. The company's stock price was half what it had been the previous decade, and after a long stretch of indifference, attendance at board meetings had started to become more consistent. There seemed to be a certain heightening of interest in Spent's year-over-year performance. Bishop had even mentioned to Gerald once or twice that the board was looking for "new initiatives" and "new energy." Yet nothing ever seemed to materialize, and though Gerald – busy after all with matters like plant operations and distribution networks, not sales or strategic planning – had at times felt a worming in his stomach that warned him of trouble, he hadn't until this moment fully registered the extent of the decline. But there it was.

Spent still had some heft in the other end of its business – washable residential furnace filters – something close to a 9 per cent share. In washable furnace filters they remained players (marginal, but at least in the game). However, no one thought of Spent as a "furnace filter" company. It was window screens in which Bishop Spent had made his fortune, window screens that established the company's place in the world. If you were talking about Spent Materials, you were having a wire window-screen conversation. And yet in the past five quarters its market share in window screens had slipped slowly, incrementally, like a toboggan on wet snow, to the point where the company was now as close to comatose as it was possible to get in the residential wire window-screen industry without somebody starting to look for a plug to pull.

Bishop stared for a moment at the image projected before him, with his hands sliding along the arms of his chair. Then he nodded.

"That's good, Trick," he said, from somewhere in Cincinnati. "Thank you."

Gerald noticed that Phil Barbuda, near the front of the room, had both feet on the floor and was sitting more or less vertically, watching him. Sandy Beale, across the table from Phil, was sending up one eyebrow like a flare. Doug Allsop, his mouth half open and his eyes squinting through his glasses at something invisible to everyone else in the room, appeared to be closing in on a thought he might want to express.

No one said anything, however, and before Gerald could figure out a way to politely countervail Bishop's "Thank you" and get the director of sales and marketing to address these numbers, Trick Runiman had taken up his remote with a two-handed grip and wielded it like a light sabre to slice through every percentages slide that stood between him and his Q-three ad spending forecasts.

"Ho*kay*," he said then, a little winded, "here's the direct-mail budget we're looking at."

In his office, twenty minutes later, Gerald was at his desk studying computer maps, calculating the time it would likely take to get to the CFB airport in Trenton to pick up Kyle at two. He'd been warned that the arrival time was approximate, that military flight crews, having no need to keep to a commercial schedule, did things at their own methodical pace. Nevertheless, he'd been told two, it was all he had to go by, and so he was calculating. This was the sort of thing other executives would get an assistant to do, but Gerald no longer had an assistant. He'd given her up willingly – she was working with Doug Allsop now – because he'd never been able to trust her with any task beyond the most menial. It's not that Monik wasn't able, she was extremely able, but Gerald couldn't count on her to take all the nuances into consideration, and he didn't always have time to explain the nuances. For instance, the drive to Trenton was an hour-and-fifty-minute trip, according to the site he used most, but none of these sites took traffic into account. Traffic out of Metro, even at noon, could be crushing. It could also be good; there was no way to tell. (This was what Gerald hated most about traffic, its caprice.) And there was no being sure, without constant, hostility-creating interrogation, whether Monik or any assistant had factored in the traffic uncertainties. By doing it himself he was able to know, with the highest degree of confidence, that the travel time of one hour and fifty minutes did not factor in traffic, and that it was therefore necessary to build in an extra half-hour for the trip, which meant in this case an eleven-forty departure, fourteen minutes from now. And although his need for these layered reassurances wasn't something Gerald took particular pride in, each certainty was itself a comfort.

With a small window of time to play with before he had to leave, he began to shuffle through sales reports for January through March with an eye to starting his own market share analysis, because during the meeting it had become apparent that he needed to review all the numbers so that he could advise Bishop, and he could no more trust Trick's projections than he could expect to stand, unmolested, in his own bathroom. When someone knocked on his door he considered saying he was busy, but the thought that it might be Bishop, come to confer over the market share crisis, made him call out, "I'm here."

It was not Bishop but Sandy Beale who entered briskly, slipped the door shut behind her, and came to a halt halfway between it and Gerald's desk. She stood at quivering attention, with her feet together and her arms at her sides, holding a large yellow pad in one hand and a black pen in the other.

"Gerald," she said. "I think I have a solution."

"A solution?"

She chopped out a hand. "Nothing against Trick, all right? He's my boss. But." She stood there silently, green eyes riveted on him, as if to let their shared appreciation of the *but* and its implications coalesce and drive them forward to a frontier of mutual Trick understanding.

"But," said Gerald.

"*Well*," she started, "there is a problem, don't you agree?"

Gerald motioned toward a small round table and two chairs by the window. "I have a minute. Did you want —?" She was already sitting.

He came around and eased himself into the seat next to the low shelf of blue binders holding product specifications and operational reports going back to 1973. The company had moved four times since its founding year, to lower leases farther and farther out on the edge of the city, and each time, someone had packed up these binders, shipped them with the rest of the furniture, and reshelved them in the COO's office. Though he had never more than glanced at their spines, Gerald liked having them there, a kind of bulwark against flux.

Sandy Beale sat at the table in an attitude of fierce sincerity, arms straight out and hands clasped prayerfully. She smiled at Gerald as he settled into his seat and seemed to be awaiting his cue. Good, he thought.

"This is about the market shares?"

"The market shares, yes. I was hoping, *hoping* you would say something to Trick about that because I knew Bishop wasn't —"

Gerald shifted abruptly. He hated to do it, but he had to pull on Sandy's reins a bit. "I think we should probably leave comments about Bishop out of this."

Sandy looked horrified. "Of course!" she said. "No, no, that's not what I — this isn't about him. At all. It was just, I was so glad when you stopped Trick and made him go back to that slide because he's —"

"Trick too," said Gerald, leaning forward. "I think, Sandy, if you have an idea, that's what we should be discussing."

She was already nodding. "Right," she said, "you're right. I'm sorry." As she looked down at her pad her head vibrated slightly. The small features of her face seemed to cinch. She was, in a moment like this, everything Gerald wanted in a subordinate — someone who cared about her job and wanted to do it well, someone whose aspirations were balanced by propriety, someone who attended to his signals, respected his position, followed his lead. Unfettered ambition was always bad news, in Gerald's view; it was a wild, bucking thing that could do as much harm as good, and witnessing it made him queasy. But ambition with restraint, that could take a company places. It wasn't a matter of control; he didn't want her to think like him, he wanted her to think *with* him.

"You think there's a way to improve our market share?" he said. "Let's hear it."

Sandy took a deep breath, took one last look at her pad, then fixed her eyes on Gerald's. "We aren't crazy enough."

Gerald started nodding, as if this were a reasonable idea.

"Do you think we're crazy enough?"

Gerald stopped nodding. He made a hand gesture to indicate that Sandy should keep going, and quickly get to the part that would make sense.

"We don't take any chances, Gerald. We don't take risks! I was looking back through the files in Trick's office the other night. We haven't launched a new product – I mean something really exciting – in like, four years."

Gerald glanced down at the spec binders. It was an involuntary motion. "What about Teflon-coated screens?" He shifted in his seat. He wanted to reach for the spec binders, for the comfort they promised, but that was just an urge, and he could handle it. "Just around when I moved into this office we were launching Teflon screens for easier cleaning."

"Right," said Sandy. "Well, that's what I'm saying. That was four years ago, and there's been nothing since." Her thin, creaseless lips turned up into a thin, creaseless smile. "And it's not like Teflon screens went huge or anything. I mean, who cleans their window screens?"

To Gerald, the dearth of new product initiatives after the failure of the Teflon screens had always seemed a tidy cause-and-effect package that required no explanation or apology. "So I take it," he said, "you've got some new craziness in mind?"

"I do." Sandy smiled, almost seductively. It was a look, Gerald calculated, of ravishing confidence, fed by aspirations powerful enough to cause her, an assistant sales and marketing director ten months out of university, to stay late one night, or perhaps many nights, in order to examine old files in her boss's office. "I think it could change everything."

Gerald was just about to pick up a spec binder, was actually touching the plastic-cool spine of one of them with an index finger, when his office door opened and Bishop appeared in the doorway. The older man had his hands sunk into his trouser pockets. He looked rather dolefully over at Gerald and Sandy sitting at the small table in the algae-dyed light of the tinted window, then sighed and seemed about to turn away.

"Bishop?" called Gerald. "Did you need something?"

His boss stood there for another moment and drew a flattening hand down the length of his blue and silver tie. He shrugged.

Gerald rose from his chair. "I think, Sandy —"

She snatched up her pad and pen. "I'll come back."

"I don't want to interrupt anything," Bishop said as his lean, six-two frame made its way into the office. Bishop's was the kind of body that in 1958 would have made a high school kid a basketball star, though he'd stopped moving like one long ago. "It's not that important."

"Not at all," said Gerald. A soft, soapy breeze hit him as Sandy moved past with her yellow pad filled with crazy, world-changing ideas tucked snug against her ribs. "We'll pick this up later, all right?"

"Oh yes," she said, with a glance back that promised, not trouble, but something that Gerald thought would probably feel like trouble.

"I didn't mean to barge in on you," said Bishop, once Sandy was gone and Gerald had led him to the small round table.

"Is it Susan?"

Bishop was turned toward the window. Outside, one storey below, a twenty-foot cube truck was pulling away from the loading dock. Bishop watched, and Gerald watched too, as it swayed over the speed bumps and then rumbled off toward the South Service Road that would lead it to the highway which would take it east to Montreal, because according to the schedule in Gerald's head this was the shipment of two hundred thousand square feet of .03 gauge screening bound for Deschamps Fenetres Inc. As Gerald turned back to Bishop, it was these schedule thoughts that made him seize on the image of Kyle, and the realization that he should probably be on the road at this very moment to pick him up.

"I just got off the phone with her," said Bishop. "They can't seem to figure out what's wrong."

Gerald nodded and sighed with a sympathy for Bishop that was heartfelt, though his mind was congested with images of his son waiting, alone and forgotten on a gritty, windswept tarmac because he, Gerald, had failed to leave when he should have. What time was it? How late was he? It was difficult to know. Other offices had clocks on the wall in full view. Not Gerald's. He cursed the day, four years ago, when he'd moved into this office and, in the course of introducing a few decorative touches, such as the framed pictures of the Nova Scotia coastline that he found calming, had passed so blithely on the wall-clock option.

Bishop was slowly shaking his head. "If those doctors in Cincinnati can't solve the problem," he was saying, "I don't know who can."

Over on his desk, Gerald's computer screen had the time. Right now, the time was displayed in blue 24-point type and he couldn't see it. His desk with its computer screen was like a mainland of wealth and abundance, and he was trapped on an island of scarcity with no boat. And whose fault was that but his?

"Those people down there are top-notch," said Bishop wistfully.

There was always his watch. Bishop was still looking out the window, though the cube truck had long since disappeared, and Gerald's own left wrist lay below the table, against his thigh; he could swivel his wrist and glance down in one smooth motion. But it was a dangerous operation, because when a man was telling you about his wife's medical problems, you stayed engaged and involved; nothing was more important. Looking at your watch when a man was sharing his troubles was the kind of thing, if he happened to see you, that could shake the foundations of trust. You didn't screw around with trust. Especially when it was the sort of hard-earned trust produced by six dedicated years of ambition-restraint.

On the other hand, there was the matter of unpredictable traffic.

"What's *wrong* with me?" Bishop demanded.

Gerald had just begun to turn his wrist and glance down – his gaze had made it to the edge of the table – and now Bishop was looking directly at him.

"I haven't done a proper day's work in a week!"

Gerald kept his gaze fixed on the table edge, as though only the seam in the laminate could help him address Bishop's concerns, until it seemed safe to relax and look up.

"Bish, no one expects you to stop thinking about Susan."

"I'm here, but I'm not here, if you know what I mean." Bishop looked away to the window and sighed. "I should have gone with her."

Eleven. That's all he got. He looked quickly and caught the liquid crystal eleven. Which was, of course, useless to him, because he knew it wasn't as late as twelve. But he caught the wrong digits and now he would have to look again.

"She's got family in Cincinnati, doesn't she, Susan?"

Bishop nodded. "Her sister's in Cincinnati." He pursed his lips thoughtfully. "Martha."

"I'm sure she's fine then." One more glance down would get the second set of digits. He knew the procedure now, it was just a matter of shifting his focus. "Just as long as she has family with her, that's the important thing."

Bishop swallowed, and his expression turned sardonic. "Martha," he said, "is a hopeless alcoholic. Her husband left her

years ago. The woman is a complete mess. So, you know, for all
intents and purposes –" he passed a hand over his face and mas-
saged his eyes "– Susan is down there taking care of *her*." Fifty-
nine. It was 11:59! Gerald was so shocked by the second set of
digits that he couldn't help staring at them. Soon only luck
would get him to Trenton on time.

"Guess I'm keeping you from something, am I?" Bishop
was looking at him, one half of his face paled with aqua light,
and his eyes had a new heaviness that told Gerald he was
offended.

"I'm sorry, Bish, that was – it's just I have to pick up Kyle
pretty soon."

"Oh."

"Please. Go on."

"No, it's fine." Bishop leaned forward and pushed himself
out of his chair like a man twenty years older than he was.
Gerald rose with him.

"When do you expect Susan back, end of the week?"

He was making his way to the door and didn't turn. "Something like that." At the entrance to Gerald's office, Bishop put a
hand on the painted metal door frame and looked back. "Your
son's home from Afghanistan, is that right?"

"Yes."

"That's a hell of a place, Afghanistan. Your son see any
trouble over there?"

Gerald tried to smile. "Not sure, actually."

"Guess you've been worried about him. Guess you'll be
glad to have him home."

Gerald worked hard to return Bishop's steady gaze. "Yup." The urge to look at his watch again was almost overpowering; he barely felt man enough to resist it. "Let me know if there's anything I can do to help with Susan, okay?"

Bishop frowned. "What could you do?"

Gerald hesitated, shrugged, drowned. "I don't know. Anything."

His boss nodded slowly and let his hand drop. "Right." He rapped a knuckle against the door as he walked away.

5

Do you know how sometimes you get yourself into a situation, and even as it's going on you're thinking, "Huh. This is pretty crazy. How did I get myself into this?"

I had one knee the size of a pumpkin pressing down on my chest, cutting off my air. That belonged to Lieutenant Jayne. One of my wrists was being pinned down against the nubby carpet of the airplane by Sergeant Leunette (decent guy), the other wrist was being held by the COF-AP deputy project manager, Mike Oberly (asshole). And as you could expect, it was Oberly doing the shouting.

"You will not be getting up, Woodlore! Not until I see some self-control!"

One of my legs was jammed against something, but the other one was loose, so I tried to swing it to wrench myself free, but I only ended up hitting the hard plastic corner of one of the seat arms and that hurt like shit. They don't give you much room for wrestling in the aisle of a CC-150.

"I can't breathe! I can't breathe!"

"Ease off him," said Leunette. He pushed Jayne back with a forearm.

As the air started to come back into my chest – now that about six hundred pounds of military force wasn't trying to turn me into some kind of pressed flower – Oberly stuck his thorny white eyebrows in my face.

"You don't go into the cargo area. That's a regulation. The cargo area is off-limits. You hear me?" It was only when he repeated the last bit even louder than the first that I realized he was actually waiting for an answer.

"I heard somebody," I said, looking up into Oberly's upside-down face. "I thought maybe it was God, so, that's kinda disappointing."

I tried to get my left arm free but Oberly leaned down on it with two hands and his face went fierce as if it was his own personal mission to keep me pinned. There seemed to be a smile in there too, but Oberly was the type to look grinnish when he was exerting himself, so I didn't take that too personally.

"We can stay like this for the rest of the flight. Have no concerns there."

"Well no, now, you can't." Behind and above me I could see a flight attendant corporal, with straight, tied-back hair, slashing a line in the air with her finger, meaning the aisle. "I need to get through here."

So how did I end up getting pinned to the floor and causing all this trouble? It comes down to military planes being different from regular passenger jets. In military planes, at least the ones I've been on, only part of the interior is for passengers; the front

third or half is used for cargo and supplies. A bulkhead keeps the
two areas separated, but there's a narrow hatch you can open
and step through if you're a pilot or a flight attendant. For the
first couple of hours of the flight home I watched people go in
and out through that hatch, so I didn't realize it would be such a
big freaking deal if I did too.

All I'd wanted was to find a movie to put on. I kept asking
the corporal: What about the movie? When's the movie starting? Are you going to show a movie? She wouldn't give me a
better answer than "soon," and when "soon" never seemed to
arrive, I figured I'd go look for one myself. I mean . . . Shit!
Planes are supposed to have movies, aren't they?

So, after the corporal just stopped responding to my questions I turned to my seatmate – this dark-haired COF-AP woman
I didn't know who I sat beside just so I wouldn't have to sit next
to Oberly and listen to him lecture me on "paths" and "organiz-
ing structures" – and I asked her, "Is that cargo area up there
where they keep the DVD player?"

She just shrugged. "I don't know. It might be." And she
studied me for a second as if she knew something. "Boy, you
really want to see a movie, don't you?"

"Yeah."

"They'll get to it eventually, I guess." Then she reached
into the canvas bag at her feet and pulled out a couple of old
Chatelaine magazines. "You can read these if you want."

"No thanks," I said. "That doesn't work."

Believe me, I held off as long as I could. I really *tried* not to
care about the movie. But I'd been sitting there for, like, two

hours, staring at the stupid little screen, waiting for it to give me something else to look at, and my chest was starting to cinch up, and finally it just seemed like it was time to go look for those DVDs.

I opened the hatch door and got one foot over the lip in the bulkhead when somebody grabbed my arm from behind. Of course I tried to shake him off, as you'd naturally do if you weren't thinking about regulations. But, of course, this is the military, so there are always regulations. And when you're on an armed forces plane, and you're Officially Fucked Up, and you're heading toward an off-limits area in the direction of the flight cabin, shaking off a soldier is a pretty stupid thing to do. I mean, that's clear to me now. And when a couple of guys try to grab you and pull you back, it's not the smartest thing to start wrestling with them and swinging at them and shouting at them to fuck off, fuck off, fuck off. All things considered, I have to admit that. I mean, I'm not an idiot.

Obviously I wasn't adhering to my own *whatever* plan, so I have some work to do on that front. I even tried to get some practice in right there on the airplane floor. They were hurting my wrist, and I was doing my best to give in and let it happen. But it's not easy. It's not. So I finally said, into this huddle of hard-breathing men, "I think my wrist is probably crushed enough now."

Oberly leaned down on me, and some of the white hair he kept slicked to his head flopped over, which just added to his standard, marginally crazed look. "I want some kind of signal from you, Kyle, that you get what happened here, all right? You went someplace you're not allowed to go. Then when somebody tried to stop you, you became violent. That's the kind of thing gets charges laid on people, all right?"

"Sure."

"This isn't funny."

I'd only smiled to show him I was surrendering. Now I rubbed the back of my head against the hard carpet as a nod.

"Behave, Kyle," said Lieutenant Jayne, "or you sit on my lap the rest of the way."

"Aye-aye, captain."

Sergeant Leunette was the first one to get off me completely. He had one boot and a foreleg still caught in the cargo hatchway from when they'd first wrestled me to the floor, but once he shook his foot free and found his cap he smacked Jayne on the back – "Let him up" – and Jayne grabbed the blue seat arms on either side of the aisle and wedged himself vertical. Oberly was the last to get off and he held out a warning finger at me until I was sitting up on the floor with my back against the partition. When the flight attendant was finally able to make it past, she exhaled through her teeth and disappeared into the forbidden realm of cargo.

I sat there for a while breathing in the dry airplane air, feeling the engines' hum against my spine and looking at the knees of the people sitting in the first row of seats – there were three dancers coming back from entertaining personnel some place in the Middle East (a big secret where, because they weren't saying) who'd had to connect through to Canada at Dubai. Two of them were wearing jeans and one a sort of flowy skirt. I didn't look up at their faces – probably they would have been a bit upset by what happened – but they had some pretty nice knees.

"I just wanted to see what kind of movies there were," I said.

"What movies?" said Oberly, standing in the aisle with his long arms noodling down from his hunchy shoulders. "What are you talking about?"

I tilted my head back and pointed at the tiny screen above me, embedded in the partition. "Aren't they supposed to show movies on these?"

Oberly shook his head, which made his loose hair wave around. "This is a military plane. If you were military you'd know they don't always show movies. Just like you'd know not to go butting into off-limits areas and to stop dead when you're ordered to!" See, Oberly was ex-military. I think he got as high as Chief Warrant Officer. He was always talking like he was still in the loop.

From partway down the aisle, Leunette called up, "Oberly. Go tell 'em to put on a friggin' movie."

"It's not our decision, Sergeant; it's the crew's. They might not even have any."

Leunette shook his head in disgust. I liked Sergeant Leunette. I didn't know him that well, but he felt a bit like a friend because Legg had liked him. They used to play poker all the time and I got invited to play a fair bit. He smelled like a chimney from spending a lot of his off hours in the smoking tent outside the kitchen at Camp Laverne, but the way he dealt with people seemed clean. "They must have some sorta shows up there," he said. "The kid's just trying to get through the friggin' flight. What's the problem?"

Oberly's arms went all cockeyed. "We just had to tackle him to keep him out of a restricted area, and now you want to reward that behaviour?"

Leunette waved him off like gnats. "Whatever, he's your guy." He yanked a thumb at Jayne to get him out of his seat so he could slide over to the window. "Just seems to me like the decent thing to do."

"Yeah, well, I'm sure we'd all like to see a movie. But it'll happen when the flight crew wants it to happen." Oberly swept his hair back into place with one hand and pointed me to my seat with the other. "Go sit down, son."

The hiss of air in the plane sounded like sand blowing across a field, and Oberly kept pointing to my seat as though the seat had done something horribly wrong and he was making an example of it. It's seats like this one causing all the trouble! I stood up with my back to the cargo area door and my hands in my back pockets. And that's when it occurred to me that it wasn't just movies that were entertaining — all the commotion of the past twenty minutes had managed to keep my mind off things pretty effectively.

I slipped my hands out of my back pockets and found the door latch behind me. "Fuck you," I said to Oberly, and then I opened it again.

6

There were few things worse than a jumbled inventory. Vicki, conscious of the fact that by now Gerald had probably arrived at the airport to pick up their son, but keeping that fact in an anteroom safely off to the side of her attention, made her way, clipboard in hand, around the sharp cabinet corners, past the stacks of boxed linen, and through the upturned chair legs sprouting like river reeds. Thankfully all her country oak and pine furniture (useful for filling out those three-thousand-square-foot finished basements) was exactly where it should have been, including the nineteenth-century fruitwood lambing chair she adored, the useful three-panelled oak settee, and the four small pine pot cupboards that did such admirable work as pedestals for large topiary and the occasional Carpeaux bronze. She was relieved to find as well that the dining sets, mirrors, and drum tables were all properly stored. However, four of the bedroom suites were stationed along the east wall, not the west, the salon pieces were in the wrong corner, the bureaus and credenzas were in each other's places, and the boxes of pewter, ceramic, and miscellaneous accent pieces were catastrophically misarranged.

This was what came of leaving things to Hella, her part-time assistant, which she had had to do this morning during the disassembly of the Gainsmore Road house because it had been necessary to meet with Avis at Lightenham Avenue. Not that Hella wasn't good at many things – she was a true godsend when it came to the assembly phase, taking a firm hand with the moving crews when Vicki was elsewhere engaged and showing real talent with window treatments and linen layering (anything that required spreading or smoothing seemed very much up her alley). But she had proven herself untrustworthy in dis-assembly and pack-up, not seeming to appreciate the importance of being able to lay hands on a given item in the warehouse at a moment's notice. If it was discovered, for instance, one hour before a showing, that because of some subtle shift in a new home's foundation a thin vertical crack had appeared in the plaster seam between the wall and the fireplace mantel, then it was vital to be able to immediately locate and install the taller set of Flemish fire irons and perhaps even the Tunbridge ware bellows as an attractive camouflage. Hella didn't seem to under-stand that it was this sort of taste-appropriate response upon which Vicki's clients had come to rely, and which had con-tributed to Vicki's status as one of the top real estate stagers in the city. Vicki, of course, accepted some of the blame for Hella's lack of awareness in this regard, because she was loath to make Hella feel anything but loved; although in itself, this was hardly a failing.

For twenty minutes she rummaged among the warehouse shelves, through the boxes of accents. She was able to check off the soft toys and the equestrian accessories (the helmets, boots, whips, and riding trophies that she used in the Ralph Lauren-look guest bedrooms). She found the barometers and hearth clocks, and everything to do with the dining room (decanter sets, tea sets, the silver milk jug, the George III mahogany table cellaret with spirit bottles, and so on), the decorative kitchen fruit pieces (a dozen rustic pears and seventeen apples, formed in high-gloss papier mâché at 150 per cent scale), which she displayed in bowls and placed on open shelves to bring colour and culinary intimations to white or off-white kitchens – these were safe and sound. And the boxes of everything silver and everything treen were eventually located. But though she searched the entirety of her accent collection, and then the remainder of her eight thousand square feet of warehouse space, with all the lights on, she could still not find her Meissens.

When she called Hella at 2:08 p.m., about the time she imagined Gerald would have begun to drive back with Kyle, the hand that held the phone to her ear was shaking as if she were cold. "Hella, sweetheart," Vicki purred, "I'm here at the warehouse and I can't seem to find the Meissens."

"Which?"

"The Meissens, darling. They were in a grey box all to themselves." She always treated the Meissens with extra care, because the porcelain tureens with the blue-onion pattern and the two candlestick figures represented the beginnings of what she had made of herself. Her mother, Patricia Dealing, had loved antiques and built up an impressive collection, much of which was now incorporated into Vicki's inventory. But her mother's job, in a very real sense, had been her marriage to Marshall Dealing, the airline executive; antiques had been merely a hobby. It was Vicki who had seen the potential in what the antiques, in their ideal arrangement, represented – an accomplished past, an appreciative present, the clarity of mind and the contentment of spirit that came from all things happily in their place. This was something, Vicki sensed, that people would pay money for, and the Meissen candlesticks were prized as her first find with that objective in mind, bought twenty-three years ago with her mother's approval as a bargain at $285 for the pair.

"Oh, you mean the china bowls and all that? They're in with the treen now. I thought it would be good to pack the wood and the porcelain together, for safety."

"So," said Vicki, turning around to survey the boxes arrayed on the deep shelves before her, "in the box marked *treen*, I will find the Meissen porcelain?"

"Yes."

"And that includes the two candlestick figures?"

"Yeah . . . I think so."

"All right. Now" – she located the box marked *treen* – "I want to say that was a very clever idea, to think that the treen bowls could act as an extra layer of protection, in case the Styrofoam and bubble wrap wasn't enough –"

"Well, wood's a lot stronger."

"Of course, yes." Her heart thumping, Vicki shifted the heavy treen box to the edge of the shelf, eased it to the floor, and crouched down to open the flaps and begin lifting out the contents, item by item, as she shrugged the phone snug to her head. "But do you see why that might not be the clearest way to package things? I mean, if I'd needed to find the Meissens in a hurry —"

"I should have written Meissen on the box too, I guess." Vicki could tell by the turn in Hella's voice that she felt terrible about the mistake. And perhaps Hella was thinking too about having not used enough Styrofoam packing chips around the Meissens, because that had been obvious to Vicki as soon as she'd opened the box. "I don't know, it was just, like, we only had the movers for three hours, remember? For both floors!"

She lifted out the four treen bowls first (these she was using less frequently lately because modern treen bowls had become so popular at crafts fairs her two-century-old walnut antiques were too easily confused for something just carved out of a stump of maple). The ingenious little Meissen inkwell was next. And by the time she had set the two blue-onion Meissen tureens carefully on the worn plank floor, it was obvious that the thing she feared had happened had, in fact, happened.

". . . I don't know whether I'm going to be able to make it on Tuesday," Hella was saying.

The two Meissen candlesticks, each with its own cherub-like putto standing upon a mound of leafy green seaweed, embracing a long, vertical eel-like fish whose tail splayed over the putto's raised knee and whose mouth opened wide to accept the base of a taper, were laid on their sides at the bottom of the box. Each of them, at least 150 years old and now worth $740 apiece in the unlikely event Vicki would ever sell, was wrapped in a single, inadequate layer of bubble wrap. And each of them, precious thing, was snapped in two.

". . . Wednesday should be fine, though," Hella was saying.

"Hella," said Vicki, light-headed and reaching down to the dusty floor for support, "when you packed the Meissen pieces with the treen bowls, did you happen to lay the candlesticks on their sides?"

There was silence on the line as apparently Hella was sending her mind back to the hurried moment of packing, and Vicki, sitting tilted on the floor now with one leg bent underneath her, laid the top halves of each of the candlesticks on the floor and slid the useless bubble-wrap blankets from the bottoms.

"I think so, yeah. I thought it would be safer."

"Hum." Vicki pressed the heel of a hand against one eye. "Well, that's my mistake then." She spoke through a roughness in her throat. "I should have told you it's always better to keep tall, fragile things standing upright. I thought I had."

"Why? Is anything wrong?"

"Hum," said Vicki. Her voice felt squeezed; she found it hard to catch her breath. "Well, it's just that" – she held one of the candlestick bases in her lap, and she folded herself over it, pressing the putto, the child, against her stomach – "they seem not to have survived the trip."

Nothing came from Hella for a moment, until she offered a soft "Oh, no."

7

The Trenton airport wasn't much of an airport, as far as Gerald could tell, and he regretted that nine months ago, when Kyle had been heading out, he hadn't driven his son here himself. He'd wanted to, but Kyle had insisted on finding his own way because he wasn't a child who needed to be driven around by his parents any longer.

KYLE: I'm not going to a school dance or something, Dad; this is a life decision. I don't need a lift to my life decision.

If Gerald had managed to convince Kyle to let him drive, he'd have had a chance to see the Trenton passenger terminal and know that Kyle was about to place himself in the hands of an organization, the military, that invested no effort or attention whatsoever in moments of transition. Kissing one sort of reality goodbye, heading off to another – it was no big deal, apparently, as far as the military was concerned. Gerald didn't know what exactly the components of a transition-friendly passenger terminal would be, but a gathering area with a dozen or so anchored seats, a grey departures counter the size of a lectern, a lone conveyor belt for luggage, a beefy, unhappy-looking man standing with his foot propped up on the rung of a stool, in a building imbued with the character of an unused garage, clearly missed the mark. He was looking for decorous. He was looking for grateful. This wasn't a place for honouring the decision to put everything you held dear at risk, this was a place for slipping in and out unannounced.

That it was small, though, with a minimum of doors and passages, made it hard to miss whatever new arrival – soldier, government official, casualty – one might be looking for, and for this Gerald was thankful. He'd managed to make the trip in just under two hours; not bad given the consecutive slowdowns on the highway east of Bowmanville, the first caused by a man changing the rear tire of a Toyota, the second by a dark-blue van stopped at the side of the road for no discernible reason, which made people think it a speed trap and slow to an ooze. (It wasn't a trap, though; Gerald had made a point of staring into the window as he inched past and saw the driver, mouth open, asleep. He'd banged on the horn out of frustration at that point and the driver hadn't moved, so there was a chance, Gerald realized, that he was dead. Which didn't lessen his irritation.)

Once he'd arrived and determined that Kyle's plane had not yet landed, he'd staked out his waiting area, at a broad window with an unobstructed view of the tarmac, not far from the door through which the deplaning passengers would come. There he stood as one quarter-hour passed, and then another, and a jumble of images, snatches of Kyle as a child, flew past him like brown, blown leaves. He saw three-year-old Kyle building a castle with flowerpots, twelve-year-old Kyle peeing algebra into the snow, Kyle in a bulky diaper dipping his cookie in mud, and his child at eight, motionless on a swing, pondering mysteries. He saw scenes unfold, and felt his body seize at the memories, as when, at the Elora Gorge, one of Kyle's cousins snatched the pebble Kyle had been examining out of his hand and hurled it into the chasm and Kyle, five, tried to chase it over the edge (not dying only because Vicki's brother Arthur caught him with an arm as Gerald, vitrified, watched). He re-witnessed his six-year-old son absorbing the horror of his baby rabbit, dead from over-feeding because Gerald, not trusting his son to feed the animal as instructed, slipped it carrot sticks in the night. And, finally, as a grounds crew worker in short sleeves drove a stubby vehicle across the tarmac in front of him, he saw his son at seven, on the ground, not moving.

Gerald had come home from work on a seething mid-August day to find Kyle lying at the edge of the lawn, near the sidewalk, his legs still wrapped around his bicycle, as if he were a plastic soldier on horseback, knocked over to signify death. He was half whimpering, half talking to himself, in a voice too soft to make out, and it took a while for Gerald to piece together what fragments he could get. It seemed that after day camp, hoping to play, Kyle had biked alone to the house of his sole friend, Li Wen. This was something Gerald would never have allowed, yet Vicki had given her permission – it was only a block – and so Kyle had trundled off. When he arrived, Li Wen's parents told Kyle the boy was playing with another friend just down the street; go and find him. Li Wen, however, was nowhere to be seen; he was inside, out of the heat. And Kyle had pedalled desperately, for more than an hour, down one sidewalk, up the other, until his legs had finally given out.

Gerald stood at the window of the Trenton airport, looking out toward the tarmac, defenceless against the leaves, until a drab-green Polaris jet that surely held his son screamed down onto its haunches. And there he continued to wait, telling himself this was how military flight crews operated, as the plane sat in the middle of the runway, unmoving, with no one coming off for what approached six minutes. Seven.

At eight minutes, Gerald went to look for someone.

He found only the unhappy man behind the counter in the departures area. "Is that the plane coming from Dubai?" Gerald asked, pointing at a wall but in the direction of the tarmac. The man, whose flat features suggested to Gerald an unfathoming density within, though he knew that was probably unfair, looked first at the wall and then at a small screen in front of him.

"Uh-huh."

"Why is it just sitting there?"

"What did you want it to do?"

Gerald stared at the man for a moment, reassessing, then reached into the breast pocket of his suit, pulled out his wallet and from his wallet a business card.

"My name is Gerald Woodlore," he said, showing his card. "My son is supposed to be on that plane."

"If he's s'posed to be then he probably is."

"Oh?"

"That's generally the way it works."

"But he's not getting off," said Gerald, pointing again. "No one is." He backed up and out of the way so that the man could go and see for himself. When the man failed to move Gerald made an usher-like motion with his hand. *This way to the inanimate plane.* Still the man stayed at his counter. His counter was his protection against the intrusions of the outside world's needs for service, and he was not about to let go.

Gerald straightened. "Is there anyone else who could help me?"

The man shrugged. "We're short-staffed at the moment."

"Are you?"

"Unfortunately."

Gerald nodded.

He returned to the window.

One evening nine months before, as Kyle was packing to leave, Gerald had tapped on his bedroom door. Given permission to enter, he'd sat at the end of Kyle's bed and watched as his son stuffed his two bags. The military had e-mailed a list of the things COF-AP employees were advised to bring, among them a certificate of vaccination, a wide-brimmed hat for sun, a warm hat and gloves for winter, sturdy walking boots, hiking socks, shower sandals, ear plugs, sunglasses. Gerald drew his thumb down the list of protective barriers looking for anything the military might have missed. He didn't see any mention of bullet-proof gear. Bulletproof gear, presumably, was supplied as a matter of course, like a bed, but he would have preferred to see at least some reference to it. He was the father of a boy who liked watching complicated movies and subtle chemical reactions, whose chief threat should have been some unnatural resurgence in the career of David Spade, and he was worrying about whether his son would, in two days, be supplied with armour. "Sunblock," he'd eventually said, looking up at his son. "Did you pack sunblock?" Kyle said yes, he'd packed some SPF-30. And when he sighed as if he were impatient for Gerald to leave, Gerald had pushed himself off the bed and toward the hallway, moving through a sense of something-left-undone that hampered his feet like snowdrifts.

At the door, he did the only thing he could think of. He handed Kyle a business card with his office number and asked him to put it in his wallet. The inadequacy of this effort made him sick.

In the first days after Kyle had told them about his plan to spend a year as a water treatment technician at a Canadian Forces base camp in Afghanistan, and then in the months after Kyle had left, Gerald's main concern, after his concern for Kyle, had been for Vicki. He sensed, though there was no way of knowing, that a mother's attachment to her son rendered her somehow fragile and therefore vulnerable in the event of some all-too-imaginable misfortune. And he was worried about that for her sake, and for his own. Because after twenty-one years of marriage and a quarter century in the workforce, Gerald was becoming attuned to the limits of what he knew to be his character; it was obvious to him that he was a man incapable of dealing effectively with calamity or any of its serious repercussions. And so there was a moment, after he'd received the news of the "off-camp event," when he had considered its implications. And one of them had to do with Vicki, and whether he'd be up to managing whatever there would be to manage, re: her.

"Mr. Woodlore?"

Gerald looked away from the window and the motionless plane to see that the man from the departures area had left his counter and was headed toward him.

"Excuse me, sir. You're Kyle Woodlore's father, correct?"

"Yes."

The man came right up to him and leaned in close enough for Gerald to detect the lunch-remnant smell of onions. "You're asked to go out onto the tarmac to meet a COF-AP manager by the name of " – the man checked a scribbled note in his hand – "Michael Oberly."

"Oberly."

"That's right, sir."

"Is something wrong?"

"Mr. Oberly will explain, sir."

Gerald headed out the incomer's door.

"Mind that you keep wide of the wings, sir."

The sudden preponderance of sirs, like machine-gun fire at his feet, sent him hop-walking toward the plane. And as he made it into cool air, and sunlight that seemed absurdly bright, Gerald watched a mobile staircase being wheeled up to the rear door of the plane. By the time he was halfway there, the door had popped open and a white-haired man in a flapping blue windbreaker had started down the steps.

One of the grounds crew started waving and pointing and shouting over the whine of the turbines and it made no sense to Gerald until he realized he was being told again to keep clear of the wing. And so he had to divert from his arrow's path toward

Oberly and go wide, wide – each extra step a delay – around an invisible no-tread zone, as if the threat to him from above was greater than any other.

He met Oberly at the base of the stairs.

"My son," he said.

"You're Mr. Woodlore?"

"What's happened? Where's Kyle?"

Oberly held up his hands; his arms seemed to be an incorrect length for his body. "I'm sorry, sir, can you confirm that you are Mr. Gerald Woodlore?"

"Yes!" Gerald pulled out his driver's license and held it for Oberly to see.

"All right then, well, your son has been involved in a situation on this airplane." Oberly gathered in his hands and zipped up his windbreaker.

"Is he hurt?"

"He is not hurt. But we have had some difficulty getting the situation under control."

Gerald was beginning to eye the metal stairs behind Oberly. "What situation? What are you talking about?"

"Mr. Woodlore, I need your full attention on this matter."

Gerald took a step sideways. The COF-AP man moved to block him. "Why won't you let me see my son?"

"We are bringing him off the airplane." Oberly had small grey deep-set eyes, an acorn-sized nose, and thatches of white bramble for eyebrows. The sun sparkled, the air swirled and smelled of fuel. Gerald took in everything. If he needed to recall the facts of the day he was delayed in seeing his son, he would be able to do it. "I wanted you to come out here, Mr. Woodlore, so that Kyle could see you immediately, and so that you could take him directly to your car. You have a car here?"

"Yes, of course."

"I do not want him going into the terminal. I want our official liability for your son to end and I want you to take responsibility from this point." Oberly jabbed down with an index finger. "Is that understood?"

"Yes."

"You can take him around through there." Oberly pointed toward a gate to the side of the building, leading to the parking lot.

"But what's happened?" Gerald pleaded. "What happened over *there*?"

The whirling air on the tarmac kept pushing Oberly's hair onto his forehead and he seemed to be getting frustrated. He pushed it back again as someone appeared at the door above, a burly man wearing glasses and military fatigues who came out and leaned over the stairs.

"All set?" he called.

Oberly held up a forestalling hand; his arm, as it lifted, seemed to unfurl in sections. "I can't tell you about what happened over there, sir. As soon as it's approved, but not until. That's the way the military works. There are procedures and they will be followed."

Gerald stared up at the soldier on the stairs, and at Oberly, and tried to imagine his son among these men, or others like them. He reached out and touched Oberly's elbow. "Give me something."

The COF-AP manager squinted and his face twitched a bit. He looked suddenly to the ground, and then seemed to gather Gerald with an arm and move him off to the side, as if to make their conversation more private, though there'd been no one close enough to hear. When he spoke, his voice was no more than a murmur. "I'm not an expert, sir, but it's my understanding that when young people are in a state of . . ." He hesitated and Gerald watched Oberly's mouth shape itself around a word. ". . . when they're in a state of, uh, grieving –"

"Grieving. Someone's been –"

Oberly talked over him. "When they're in that state, sir, they can – sometimes – become, uh, erratic. In their behaviour."

"Erratic."

"In their thinking."

Gerald, with jet fuel perfuming the bright, wild air around him, tried to grip the two motes of information he'd just been given, erraticness, and the other. "Kyle," he said, "is acting erratically."

Oberly nodded. "One thing, his work habits slipped. Tasks weren't being completed. We'd find him in the kitchen tent playing cards for money, any hour of the day. We tried talking to him. Tried fining him. Didn't work. He was a different kid. We gave it some time but after a while we thought it best to get him back to his family. This sort of thing, we're not really equipped."

The large soldier high at the door banged the side of the stairs. "Mike?"

Oberly signalled *come* with a wave. There was motion on the stairs above him and Gerald looked up as his son appeared.

He was smiling. He seemed healthy. His hands were tied behind his back.

Oberly jerked the zipper of his windbreaker as high as it could go and gave Gerald an apologetic look. "He went a little berserk on the plane."

TWO

1

For a week, until she cornered him by the photocopier, Gerald had been tenacious in avoiding Sandy Beale. He had more than enough flux in his life at the moment and to him, since the aborted meeting in his office, Sandy Beale had come to represent "crazy change." You could have asked Gerald to entertain all sorts of accelerated efforts and focused initiatives on behalf of Spent Materials and he would have been happy to do it, any hour of any day. But to "crazy change" Gerald said, "No thank you."

Then Sandy rounded the corner of the photocopier station and happened upon Gerald making copies of the latest Materials Girl column in *Sheet and Screen*, in which the Girl (actually a fifty-something woman wearing the sort of maniacally happy expression Gerald associated with bake sales) offered a helpful checklist of measures for combating humidity in metal fabrication systems. He had intended to deposit copies of the "Put the Clamp on Damp" article in the mail slots of his three shift supervisors with an eye to minimizing the inventory losses that Spent suffered due to unchecked corrosion every summer, and then he planned a follow-up meeting featuring some fairly pointed questions a few days later. But all of that blew from Gerald's head when Sandy stamped around the corner clutching a black folder and came to a sudden, hair-flying halt.

"Well, hello there!"

"Hi, Sandy, I'm just about done." Gerald yanked out his copies and then, realizing there were only two, positioned a hand down by the output tray to receive the third. He had his body tilted forward, his face toward the hall, he was exit-ready. No one in Sandy's position would think to waylay an executive so postured.

"I've been hoping we'd meet."

Gerald was forced to glance up. "Have you?" By now the copy should have fallen into his hand. He should have been gone. By now.

"I think it's jammed," said Sandy, as the copier gave a sigh.

He straightened and looked at the panel of lights. Where all should have been green, one was yellow. "Well, it's not important. I'll get it later." He started to leave.

"Wait!"

"Yes?"

Her eyes ballooned at him. "You're not going to leave it jammed are you?"

"Actually, I –" He pointed vaguely down the hall.

She squinted. "What's that on your neck?"

He touched the skin above his collar. "We have a cat. I have to go."

"That looks nasty. She must not like you." Sandy grinned. "I assume it's a she."

Gerald, backing his way down the hall, shrugged. "It's not our cat."

He made it as far as the framed poster for the International Window-Fittings Conference (hosted by Spent Materials Inc., 1989) when Sandy raised her hand and dangled an index finger over the copier like mistletoe. "I don't know how to fix this," she crooned.

Gerald felt his desire to flee crumble under duty's oppression. He reversed course and walked back to the copier with head bowed. It was unbelievable, really, the bind he'd gotten himself into; he doubted anyone would even *read* this humidity column.

As he swung open the copier's flimsy door and reached in amongst the inner workings, Sandy laid her folder on the top of the machine and lifted out a typed sheet. She rattled it at Gerald as he was bent over. "*This* is what I wanted to talk to you about. I thought, while I was waiting, I'd get everything down on paper."

"Your crazy idea?"

She rose up on her toes. "My crazy, earth-shattering idea."

"You were going to make copies of it?"

"Well" – her expression turned pert – "I was anticipating your enthusiastic approval and I was getting ready for the meeting with Bishop."

He pulled the offending sheet from the copier's entrails and tossed it, crumpled, into the recycling bin. "Jumping ahead a bit maybe." As he smudged black toner dust off his hand, he assessed his options and the punishments each entailed. He could hear Sandy out for a few minutes and bear the pain of her disappointment when he said no, or he could let her go around him and drag Bishop into a headache he didn't need. He considered that there might be value too in being seen to be open to new ideas, and that this might serve to instil a little useful fear in Trick, whom he judged to be floating these days like a goose on a warm thermal breeze. "Why don't you come to my office after five and we'll talk about it," he said, then punched the reset button and pulled his issue of *Sheet and Screen* from the glass. "There you go."

"Five-fifteen?"

"Make it six."

From his office, Gerald called Vicki's cell phone. She wasn't answering, most likely because she was setting up the house on Lightenham and had stored her purse under a sink somewhere. Why she didn't keep the cell on her belt or in a pocket so that people could reach her when they needed her was a great, impenetrable mystery to Gerald. "Vicki," he said when her voice mail kicked in, "hope things are going okay over there. I'm just letting you know that I have a meeting at six, which shouldn't go too long, and so I should be home around seven. As long as the traffic cooperates." He was about to hang up but brought the phone back. "By the way, I am sorry about this morning."

It had been bothering Gerald most of the day – to be accurate, since 11 a.m. – that he had, in the night, set Vicki's bedside clock to the correct time. This was his admittedly petty response to being woken, from the best sleep he'd had since Kyle's return, by an attack from one of his wife's more savage toenails, which had dug a finger-length gouge out of his left calf. It was a wound so deep he couldn't let it wait until morning, although part of him had wanted the satisfaction of showing her the blood on the sheets. While he'd padded into the ensuite and repaired himself with a generous daubing of liquid bandage, he'd let his mind run with a visual loop that had him flinging off the duvet before Vicki's horrified gaze to reveal a *Godfather*esque level of gore. (*See? See?* his expression would say. He wouldn't even need to speak. *See? See?* and she would shrink back, ashamed.) By the time he was finished painting over the damage, he'd come to feel that he'd shortchanged himself somehow, that it wasn't required of him to be so saint-like in letting Vicki sleep through yet another of her assaults. She was like one of those split-personality murderers, the evil done by the bad side while the good side lived on, oblivious and guilt-free. He'd decided it was time she suffered some consequence for her crimes, and that he should enjoy some taste of revenge. So for several minutes, in the darkness, he'd fumbled around with Vicki's three-thousand-dollar antique carriage clock until he'd figured out how to slide off the glass front, and then he'd eased the minute hand back until it showed 2:58, the time it was *supposed* to show. And when, at eight in the morning, Hella had called to find out where Vicki was — because the moving trucks were waiting outside the ware-house — Vicki, looking at her clock and realizing that it was not 7:35 a.m. as she'd thought but actually 8 a.m., had glanced over at Gerald, who was in the midst of knotting his tie, and adopted such a withering nonchalance that he'd felt completely cheated.

It was at this point that he'd hoisted his trouser leg and ripped down his sock to reveal the divot in his leg and shouted, "Look at *this*. This is *your* work right here!" as she made her way out of the bedroom, and the house.

He'd been fuming about it until an hour before lunch, when Bishop had stopped by Gerald's office to ask if he knew anything about the medical system in Denver. Susan had called, he explained, to say that the doctors in Cincinnati were recommending she see some specialists there, and Bishop was wondering whether Gerald had any views.

BISHOP: Good people down there in Denver, Gerald, do you think? I'm sure they wouldn't recommend it otherwise. But it makes you wonder what Denver doctors might know that Cincinnati doctors don't. I mean, does medical knowledge really float around like that, settling in some places and not in others? I guess I'm supposed to accept that it does, but why the hell should it? Don't all doctors have a duty to be good?

Gerald had been determined to listen intently for as long as Bishop wanted to lean against his filing cabinet and talk, ignoring his phone, going so far as to slide his left wrist, his watch wrist, into the crevice between his leg and his chair, so that he wouldn't glance at it inadvertently. And when Bishop was done talking, and put a hand out to lightly brush the back of the chair sitting in front of Gerald's desk with the air of a man who wanted some advice, Gerald had told him that he'd heard good things about the hospitals and the specialists in Denver, *very* good things (though he'd heard nothing at all). He told Bishop that if the Cincinnati doctors wanted Susan to see specialists in Denver, then that was the best thing for her, and he knew she'd be better off because of it. And Bishop had brightened considerably at this and then turned the attention around (because he was a gracious man and it was what gracious men did) to ask how Gerald's own family was; how was Vicki, how was young Kyle?

And Gerald had lied and said, "Fine, Bishop. Great. Thanks for asking."

And he'd been thinking about his lie ever since.

It wasn't as if he knew, for a fact, that his wife and his son were not fine and great; they might have been either or both of those good things, and as his own mother had often said (in a whisper, while in the den his lumber merchant father sat in a whisky-scented plume of ire and spat at newspaper pictures of the mayor), there was nothing wrong in hoping for the best. But in truth, he couldn't be sure. Since Kyle had returned, Vicki had become hard to read. For years, Gerald had happily relied on Vicki's certainty about things, such as her environment, the things she bought and touched and admired, or chose to disdain. Certain tile borders, for instance, or a particular kind of cabinetry, or a seldom-seen relative he might have fretted over regarding an invitation to Easter dinner (because his cousin Sonia and her husband were coming and therefore shouldn't he include Sonia's husband's sister Gini?). What Gerald experienced as small, gripping agonies of decision troubled Vicki not at all. (No, was the answer on Gini, because the last time they had invited her to a family event, she'd brought a man who opened their fridge and helped himself to pickles, then laughed about it in the aftermath. So, no.)

And yet now, Vicki no longer seemed as fixed in her world view. She seemed, instead, hazy. It wasn't just the toenail trouble or her skewed grasp of time; she lacked clarity in other ways. Was Rosary, their cleaning lady, doing enough to remove the cat hair from the furniture? Vicki was undecided about this. How long should they allow Kyle to stay closed up in his room? She was unsure. Reports of bombing in the Middle East no longer elicited a crisp *tsk* from Vicki; nor did catching televised antique experts in absurd errors bring her bitter joy. It was as if she had stopped paying close attention to her own sensibility. Gerald happened to have his own views on some of these questions (Rosary was *failing* with the cat hair), but he was able to relax more when Vicki did too.

As for Kyle, since he'd come home, he had spent most of his days and nights sequestered behind his bedroom door. In the context of a recent "off-camp event," this constancy had seemed right enough, and certainly better than the alternative suggested by Oberly's use of the word *erratic*. For much of the week, Gerald had embraced Kyle's quiet isolation as the antithesis of *erratic* and therefore proof of his son's good mental health and Oberly's suspect judgment. He looked on it as a kind of quarantine period, during which whatever infection of anguish Kyle had picked up in Afghanistan could be cleansed out of his system.

He wanted to talk to his son, of course. He wanted to hug him, wanted to hold his ear to Kyle's mouth and hear all the ways the world had become harder for him, less accessible, more vicious. On the drive back from the airport, he'd tried to get Kyle to tell him what happened. Overseas, on the plane, wherever he wanted to start. "What went on, Kyle?" he'd said, glancing away from the road to look at his son, his wrists freed but his body hemmed in by the seatbelt. "They wouldn't tell me," he said over the tire hum, "but you can." Kyle, though, had only smiled. And it had frightened Gerald. Because all his life Kyle had seemed to Gerald to be a boy you could reach, a boy who was more than usually receptive to the appeals of logic. Did it make sense to scream and throw food in a nice restaurant, Kyle? he would ask as Vicki took Kyle into her lap. Did it make sense to scare the waiters away so they wouldn't bring us nice dessert? No, it didn't. What a smart boy. Very good.

Yes, Kyle had had his childhood moments of extreme focus, when it seemed as though he experienced the world through a long, narrow tube. But that was nothing unmanageable, that was almost a skill. And when Gerald witnessed the trouble other parents had with small children – the tantrums, the recklessness, the uncontrollable will – he had known that he had the keys to something special. And it remained his, through Kyle's toddling years, his rambunctious years, into his teens.

Did it make sense to throw the cordless telephone and break Mommy's nice things?

Did it make sense not to take notes in class?

Did it make sense to call a girl's house seven times and repeatedly hang up before anyone could answer? Or join after-school clubs that you never attend, or drive Mom's car until it runs out of gas?

No, it didn't, Kyle. Now you're thinking. Very good.

All the years of Kyle's growing up Gerald had managed to take his son by the figurative hand and pull him toward sound choices. It had only been a few months before Kyle left that this had changed, like a shift in barometric pressure, and the logic message had no longer been able to get through. Which was why *Did it make sense to drop out of school and go work in Afghanistan?* had never reached him.

And it was why Gerald had watched Kyle's face in the car, on the way home from Trenton, and felt scared, because his son hadn't smiled in a comforting way, but in the shiny, dislocated way of someone on drugs, or unhinged, someone beyond the range of his signal. And why he thought that Kyle spending a quiet, uneventful week in his room was perhaps the best thing.

Until he realized it wasn't uneventful at all.

At 5:58, according to Gerald's watch, Sandy Beale appeared at his door and knocked on the door frame, producing a thin clack which apparently dissatisfied her because she was reaching her knuckles toward the door as he looked up.

"Are you in the middle of something?" Sandy asked.

"Nope."

"You said six, right?"

"I did." He tapped his computer keyboard a couple of times and shut everything down. "Come on in."

At the chair in front of his desk, she hesitated. "Did you want me to sit here or . . .?" Her gaze drifted over with a kind of longing to the small round table.

Gerald rose. "There's fine, if you're more comfortable."

She claimed her seat and laid her folder open in front of her. With a glance out the window as he sat, she said, "It's nice to see it's still light out at this time of night."

"It's only six."

"You're right." Sandy nodded and smiled. "I guess it just feels later. Everyone here, well almost, leaves right at five."

"Most of them have a long commute."

Sandy rolled her eyes in an expression of great empathy. "The traffic just *kills*. Especially when people have to get home to their families." She shook her head. "I'm lucky I'm single. I can work as late as I want. And I don't know about you" – here she made fervent eye contact with Gerald – "I find I get a lot more done after everyone's gone."

It was Sandy's mention of working alone that made him aware, just then, of the silence. Without the constant whirr of his computer's fan next to him and the usual drone of ringing phones and hallway chatter from the twenty-seven staffers on the second floor, the offices of Spent Materials had taken on an ethereal air, the apprehensive quiet of something forgotten, left behind. As he became conscious of it, Gerald's thoughts wafted off until they settled, again, on Vicki.

As much as he'd been worried about her lately he was aware of a doubt in the back of his mind, faint, like the slip of smoke from a dud match, as to whether his concern was wholly authentic. He had to admit the possibility that being concerned *for* her really wasn't the same as being troubled *by* her. Being infuriated, in fact, that none of his qualms or issues connected to Kyle, to her, to the house, to the cat, seemed to register with her. It was one thing to think, Oh, my wife is becoming strangely distanced from reality and maybe I should do something; it was another to think, Where the hell is my wife when I need her? And it was at times like these that Gerald, with as much guilt as resentment, wondered whether he was really the man Vicki should have married. Whether, ideally, she should have found someone more . . . lighthearted. If it was an issue of character, that universe of a man's own, unique promise as a father and husband, then the question was whether his was expanding or contracting. If it had ever, once, seemed limitless, Gerald feared that the elastic gravity of his potential was now snapping back on itself, and that if it continued as it was, it would one day be nothing more than a hard, dense nut of miserableness.

There had been a moment during their wedding reception at the Glenbridge Yacht Club – it was a panicky moment triggered by a flash of disappointment on Vicki's face as word came that his best man, Milt Landrow, typically drunk, had fallen into the marina – when he wondered whether they were truly suited to each other and he found himself asking why she'd agreed to marry him.

"Because," she'd told him, "I am hopelessly optimistic."

Would she be happier now if she'd spent the last twenty-one years with someone less inclined to think of that as a failing?

"So," said Sandy. She had freed some pages from her folder and held the topmost sheet by its corner, ready.

"Yes."

"My *crazy* idea."

He crossed his legs tight and leaned back. "I can't wait."

She ran the fingertips of one hand down the side of her face, her clear-painted, elliptical nails drawing away unseen stray hairs. "Well, let me start by saying the fact that I'm here, talking to you, shouldn't be any kind of reflection on Trick. I mean, he's really busy." She emphasized "busy," and in so doing, Gerald noted, seemed to de-emphasize it. "He's going non-stop with details, all day, every day, putting out ad budget fires and trade show fires and sales meeting fires. He doesn't have the time to play around with 'what-if' scenarios like this. But that's okay because – between you and me? – this kind of big-picture strategic development thinking is what I really enjoy doing." She'd been bearing down on this last phrase the whole time, Gerald realized now, and her voice rode up when it hit the word *enjoy* like a ski jumper leaping into the frosted mist.

"So," Sandy said again. She glanced briefly at her sheet, then frowned up at him with sudden intensity. "As a man, not as an executive at Spent Materials, but as Gerald Woodlore, what do you worry about?"

He brushed at a knee. "Many things."

"Let me put it this way, *who* do you worry about?"

He kept his gaze steady; he knew what she was getting at now. "My family."

"That's exactly right. Of course you worry about your family. You worry about them for all kinds of reasons. You worry about them getting hurt in an accident, you worry about them getting sick." She seemed to be trying not to smile through her seriousness, but she obviously felt things were going well, the smile was creeping through. "And you worry that there's nothing, absolutely nothing you can do to prevent something bad from happening to them."

"I guess that's true."

"It *is* true!" In her enthusiasm she slapped the table, which startled both Gerald and, apparently, herself, because she drew back, blushing. "Sorry," she said, clearing her throat, "it's just I'm really excited about this idea."

"That's okay. Take your time."

She looked at her sheet for a moment; her fingers seemed to be trembling and this was perhaps why she laid the paper flat. "But Mr. Woodlore," she began again, "Gerald, what's not true is that you can't do something to keep your family safe." She pressed her eyes shut, and opened them. "A better way to put it is that there *is* something you *can* do."

"I'm glad to hear it."

"One of the major sources of human illness – and you could probably say the main source – is bacteria, dust, pollution, and other foreign particles in the air. Would you agree with that?"

"For our purposes, all right."

"If we include viruses?"

"All right."

She moved to a second page. "Now, our premium washable furnace filters do a pretty good job of collecting a lot of those particles as they go through the heating and cooling systems of the typical family's house."

"Down to half a micron anyway."

"Better than most, certainly. And we promote that by advertising the particle-capturing ability of our filters with the slogan, 'Fil-Tru gets what gets in.'"

Gerald hoped that Sandy would soon move away from telling him what he already knew. He wished for that, and signalled his yearning for that by shifting in his chair and blinking like a man struggling to sustain his interest.

"I can tell you want me to get to the point."

Oh, she could be a dream employee.

She pushed the first two pages aside. "The point is, we're not struggling to sustain market share in filters, because there we have a defined image. Our customers see our filters as helping them keep their families safe. Where we're struggling is in our window screens, because what do our window screens actually do?"

"Keep out bugs."

"Do bugs make us sick?"

"Mosquitoes can."

With her eyes closed she nodded very rapidly. "Yes, yes, you're right. Mosquitoes."

"Flies. Flies can spread germs."

"Yes, all right, but every window screen on the face of the earth keeps out flies and mosquitoes."

"Well —"

"I mean that keeping out flies and mosquitoes is no big deal. It's nothing! The stuff that hurts us, hurts your *family*, is way smaller than that, right? Exhaust from diesel trucks, fatty soot particles from your neighbour's barbecue that mutate genes in mice, atmospheric dust whipped up from Outer Mongolia or some horrible nuclear test zone somewhere – all these tiny particles you can't even see just zoom through that screen as if it wasn't there. They come inside. You can't stop them! You can't control them!" She was sawing the air with a flattened hand, her hair flying. "They come in, like they're on some covert operation, and who knows for sure that viruses like SARS or *worse* aren't riding some of those particles like terrorists on a bus? And once they're inside, what's our defence? All we can do is hope that one day, eventually, they'll get caught in the furnace filter. And until that day, *who knows* what harm they could do."

She stopped to catch her breath. And turned the page.

"But those tiny invaders can only hurt us if they get inside, right? So what we need, what *you* need to help your family stay safe, is some way to keep those particles, those deadly, fearsome particles, out."

"How do we do that?"

Sandy took a deep breath. Looked right at him. "Put filters on the windows."

Gerald gave nothing away. "Filters on the windows."

"That's right. Instead of window screens, you cover every window in the house with a great big air filter." Her thin mouth moseyed into a smile.

"The whole window?"

"Yes!" cried Sandy. "No half measures, no compromises! Every window, completely covered!"

"But, there's no such thing as a transparent filter."

"Doesn't matter."

"Well, I think it does matter, Sandy. If you put filters over the windows, people won't be able to see outside."

She slapped the table again, deliberately, and leaned toward him with a volcanic glare. "What matters more to you, Mr.

Woodlore, the health and safety of your family or . . . a *nice view?*" Then she sat back, aflame with triumph.

The deserted offices of Spent Materials seemed to ring, church-like, as the passion of Sandy Beale hovered o'er all. Gerald's mind was working on myriad fronts. To Sandy, he said, "What about natural light?"

She didn't hesitate. "They'll be translucent."

He scratched his chin. "Our furnace filters are too thick to install in windows."

"Compress them."

Here's where he had her. "But compressing the filters would diminish their filtering ability."

She smiled again. He was starting to not like it as much. "So, you agree," she said, "that you would want the best possible air quality protection covering your windows."

"I think –"

"You accept that a high-density air filter, made of woven translucent fibres, would be a more effective safeguard against particle invasion than even the best window screen."

"What we –"

"And you admit that without such protection, the family you love is vulnerable."

He put his hands up. "Okay, Sandy, this is a really interesting idea, all right? And I'm impressed with your willingness to, not just think outside the box but, you know, crush it."

Her heat subsided a little, and her expression turned demure. "Thank you."

"I think, though, as a product" – he reached out and patted her papers lightly – "it has some big issues."

"But —"

"I just don't see the retailers and the contractors and the window manufacturers we work with accepting the principle that people are going to give up the ability to look out their windows in order to breathe cleaner air."

Sandy huffed. "I *gave* you the rationale. You make people choose — health or beauty." She snatched up a piece of paper and waved it in the air. "You show people enlarged pictures of the stuff that's coming into their houses. Humungous ugly alien-looking things. Then you say, 'Do you want your new baby breathing this just so you can watch the sunset?' Okay, so some people will choose the sunset, but you know what? If we do this right, they'll feel guilty about it."

Gerald sighed as he shook his head. "It's too out there. It's too big a risk."

She studied him for a moment, and then her gaze fell to the table. "Look, you're absolutely right" — her voice had taken on the palliative texture of a cello — "it would be a big gamble. I mean, it's an opportunity to take ownership of a value, like Ford tried to do with 'quality' and Smith Barney did with 'hard work.' Spent Materials could own 'protecting your family's health, above all.' But there's no doubt, it's the kind of risky, go-for-broke move that would only be made by a company with nothing to lose."

Sandy lifted her face toward him, and Gerald feared then that he knew what she was getting at. He feared that he had received exactly the message she intended to convey. He hadn't had a chance to finish his own analysis of the market share

percentages, and now Sandy's expression told Gerald he didn't
need to.

"We're at the bottom," he said.

She held up two fingers, then spread out her whole hand.
Two . . . five. Two and a half per cent.

"You know this for a fact?"

She nodded solemnly. Two and a half per cent. Gerald felt
the acid in his stomach foam up like beer in a warm bottle. He
did everything he could, paid attention to every operational
detail in order to keep the company running smoothly, and it
galled him that it wasn't enough. It galled him that Trick
Runiman would attempt to slip this leper of a number by him
and imagine he could do it. But it galled him most of all that his
instincts had warned him a problem like this was developing,
and he hadn't done a damn thing about it.

In his frustration Gerald pressed back in his chair and
craned his neck so that he faced the suspended ceiling, and was
not surprised to see, in the amber light of evening, a few, brazen
motes of dust larking in the air. To be aware of a thing was, he
well knew, to be plagued by it.

2

The Lightenham Avenue house gave off whiffs of banking. Or perhaps more specifically, international finance. Vicki wanted to be sure, though, and she still had an opportunity to change her mind. Showings wouldn't begin for another ten days, and though she'd selected and had delivered many of the necessary furnishings based on her early banking/finance impressions, few of these pieces were in place. She could order back the movers tomorrow morning and make wholesale replacements if she deemed it necessary. If at the last moment she picked up something, say, insurancey.

For Vicki, staging a house was a process of graduating insights. It wasn't, as too many people believed, simply a matter of pushing around hunks of furniture according to some mythical decorator's code, distributing a few tasteful knick-knacks and calling it a day. Her work was more serious than that. She was dealing in the representation of ideal lives, creating precedents for contentment. And to do that, Vicki felt, she needed to understand whose happiness she was bringing to life.

Her first step was to suss out the character of the house she was staging, and thus the category of its likely buyer. In this case, she had already ruled out media ownership, which was a big one always to be considered, and anything to do with professional sports. No hockey players, in other words, would be buying the Lightenham Avenue house. There were two reasons for this: first, Avis Nye had few hockey players among her clientele (or, as Avis pronounced it, "clee-on-tell"); hockey players were the province of Vanrey & Donlan's honey-haired Meredith Patrick. And second, Meredith would not be traipsing hockey players through the Lightenham Avenue house because it was not made of big blocks of stone. Hockey players might be content to let their wives rule over a home's interior, but they would drive their throbbing Humvees and Ram trucks past any house that from the outside failed to look sufficiently hewn. It was the sweet distinction of 146 Lightenham Avenue to be constructed from carefully aged Portuguese brick of a warm, mustardy hue and it was this, Vicki felt, that pointed toward ownership more rarefied than men who wielded long sticks or large satellite dishes. It said to her money, in one of its less adulterated forms.

She stood in the circular foyer, at the foot of the sweeping stairs, looked around at the conjoined hoops of the guilloche in the moulding above her and in the tile inlays beneath her feet, and tried to detect any hints of insurance (a predominance of greeny-greys, a slightly static flow, though the traces were generally less tangible). She walked from room to room, from dining to living to family, making her way around the chairs, tables, cabinets, and boxes that had been delivered earlier in the day. She briefly visited the library, with its wall of built-in cabinetry and its Crema Marfil fireplace surround, and wondered for a moment whether that was *consultancy* she was sensing. But by the time she had made it to the second level and spent a moment under the coffered ceiling of the master bedroom, she was confident that with international finance she had it accurately pinned. And she spun lightly on the balls of her stocking feet and clapped her hands together, because she was free now to do the thing she most enjoyed, and the sound of her hand clap glanced off the polished woods around her.

She was free to create a happy, loving family.

Her gaze fell first on the Empire dressing table with its shaped kneehole drawer and conforming columns holding erect a large square mirror which was original and nearly unblemished. She'd bought this dressing table ten or eleven years ago in Quebec City, had used it half a dozen times a year in various installations, but now stood before it as if it were new to her. She drew her fingertips across its cool, glassy surface and let her eyes focus on the fine chocolate grains in the wood until a name . . . Margeaux . . . came to her. This was Margeaux's dressing table. She lingered in this thought for a while, in this idea of Margeaux, like a visitor in an anteroom, until she came to know some things. Margeaux, she decided, was forty-one years old. She was the owner of a small publishing company that specialized in fine art catalogues. She had dark, almost black hair that she wore in an abrupt 1920s bob that she had seen once in an early Robert Redford movie and found amusing.

Vicki liked this about Margeaux, that even as an established woman, with a husband in international finance, she made impulsive choices about her personal appearance. And what else? She was well-educated in art history and philosophy. She was romantic but not to the point of losing her pragmatism. For instance, she had an affection for nature and a fierce determination to protect the environment around her – the ravines, the Carolinian forest along the escarpment – but considered efforts to preserve threatened habitats in third-world countries, however well-intentioned, sadly doomed. She enjoyed music, had years ago taken cello lessons, considered the operas of Rossini her particular favourites. *L'Italiana in Algeri*. She had a lovely sense of humour.

As she stood next to the Empire dressing table, Vicki gathered and assembled the fragments of her understanding of Margeaux until she had a complete enough picture in her mind to know, without guesswork, that Margeaux would want the dressing table placed on the east wall of the master bedroom. It would be the east wall, because the morning sun coming through the windows would fall across the western half of the room, and that was where Margeaux would want the bed. Margeaux was a woman who rose early, Vicki realized, and enjoyed waking up to the feeling of sunlight on her face. And for this reason Vicki knew that the Victorian mahogany four-poster bed that lay in unassembled pieces in the middle of the room would have to go back to the warehouse. The heavy canopy would make Margeaux feel too sheltered and so it would, instead, have to be the French rosewood bedstead.

She took up her clipboard and made a note.

The husband. Was named . . . nothing fancy. Was someone who fit snugly into the world of international finance and drew notice for only the right reasons – his extreme competence, his integrity, his dignified bearing. He was a . . . Robert. Yes, he was indeed a Robert, and Vicki smiled to herself. She had never known a Robert before and she liked him instantly. He was a man of forty-six. Good natured – he laughed a great deal, which caused small lines to fan out like spokes from the corners of his eyes. And she saw that he ran before breakfast, every morning, because he was very trim and had slightly recessed cheeks that accentuated his strong cheekbones and narrow jaw. His blond hair was faintly thinning at the top, and it didn't concern him because it wasn't a matter of health. It was good health that motivated Robert to get up at five-thirty every weekday, seven-thirty on weekends, and run an eight-kilometre loop through the tree-lined neighbourhood, even in winter. His father had probably died of a heart condition at a relatively early age, and Robert was determined not to let it happen to him. He was a man of decisive action.

His work? The specifics weren't important, but Vicki knew that Robert handled complex cross-border transactions in the hundreds of millions of dollars, that he enjoyed the interplay of different cultures, and that he was looking forward to making great strides in China. He was shrewd when it came to risk and he was deft with debt. He established clear plans of action and trusted his team to execute them. That was a good word for Robert – trust. He hired the right people, and he delegated. And he did not let the small mistakes of others shake his confidence in them. Robert – here was a good example – would not be the sort to dwell on the inability of his wife to deliver the Heimlich manoeuvre if he was choking on an olive. First of all, Robert wouldn't put himself in the position of *needing* the Heimlich, because he would never walk through the house naked, his hands occupied with wine glasses and his mouth filled with kalamatas, presenting an open invitation to catastrophe. And if it so happened that he did find himself needing the Heimlich, he wouldn't expect his wife to have prepared for the occasion by taking lessons in the procedure. And he wouldn't hold it against her for reacting to the broken glass and red wine all over the Hamadan runner and not instantly noticing his hands around his neck and his face going purple. Robert let things go. He had balance in his life, and at six o'clock almost every evening he was on his way home, free from worry. Sometimes he called Margeaux from his car, just to hear her voice. And he left her blessed clocks alone.

When Vicki knew all this about Robert, and a few other things besides, she was able to relax about the Carlton House desk with satinwood inlay that was at this moment sitting in the library downstairs. She'd selected it on a whim and it had been a worry because it was not a very big desk, and with its narrow legs rather than pedestals, not terribly masculine. But Robert was too secure in his own skin for it to matter to him whether or not his desk was conventionally mannish. Robert was, in a phrase, at ease.

Vicki went to her purse and pulled out her phone. "Hella," she said when her assistant picked up, "would you be a dear and

find the two Chinese folding chairs and put them out for me?
I'm going to need one or perhaps both of them."

"You mean the curly-back chairs with the sort of footstep
things at the bottom?"

Hella was so cute. "Yes," said Vicki, almost chuckling, "the
curly-back chairs. We're going to need them for the library."

Hella hesitated. "I think one of them has a split in the seat."

"Oh?" Vicki pictured the pair of two-hundred-year-old
Chinese folding chairs in her mind and tried to see the split Hella
was referring to. The seat of a Chinese folding chair was little
more than a wide leather sling and a split would render it unus-
able. One had to expect that on occasion a buyer would see one
of her chairs or couches and find it irresistible and want to touch
it or sit in it – the Chinese folding chairs were particularly
intriguing – and one couldn't have prospective buyers crashing
through the furniture. But a split in the seat was the sort of thing
she'd remember. "No, I don't think so, Hella."

"Um, I'm pretty sure there is."

Vicki was still scanning the picture in her mind. "No. No. I
think we're fine. Anyway just put them out for me. And also
we're going to need the French rosewood bedstead so I'll have
you get that ready as well if you would, and there may be one or
two other things so – are you at home now?"

"Yes."

"Well, be sure to keep your phone on." Hella had a habit of
turning her phone off at inopportune times, which made it
impossible for Vicki to get hold of her. "I'll see you at the warehouse about three."

"Sure, but, would four-thirty be okay?"

Vicki, making her way from one bedroom to another, smiled into the shiny emptiness of the corridor. "Of course," she said, and returned the phone to her purse.

And back to the Lightenham family. Having introduced herself to the wife and husband, it was time for Vicki to meet the child. There was always a child to be considered in a staging and frequently two, depending on the bedroom configuration. In the case of the Lightenham house there was one child – the third and fourth bedrooms, lacking walk-in closets (unconscionable builder's mistake), were strictly for guests in Vicki's view and could be furnished generically with two nineteenth-century walnut suites that suited the purpose (one of these rooms would get the Ralph Lauren horsey treatment; the other, botanicals); the fifth bedroom, barely seventeen feet in length, was ideal for live-in staff and Vicki had already installed a lovely Victorian brass bedstead there with a very serviceable mahogany linen press and a nice caned-back bergère tucked in one corner. But the child demanded special attention. As children did.

It was a boy, obviously. As much as Vicki would have liked a girl, because her collection of fine girls' linens was more extensive, the room was a boy's and there was no avoiding it. It was a large room of awkward angles with a sloping ceiling that rose to an off-centre peak. And in the middle of the wall below this peak, at one end of the room, was an *oeil-de-boeuf*, which some people called a bull's-eye window, that looked out over the backyard and its nearly treeless landscaped plateaus (the tree-lessness made Vicki a little sad because she was fairly sure Robert would have enjoyed drinking his morning coffee in the summer on a patio shaded by a spreading burr oak. Perhaps

Margeaux had insisted on unfettered sunlight and he had
indulged her. Yes. He was generous that way). It was this
window more than anything that said "boy" to Vicki. It was a
concession, really, on her part. Boys were rabid about a bull's
eye; depending on their age it became the portal of a submarine
or a spacecraft, or a time-travel conduit, or some other threshold into fantastic scenarios that invariably involved explosions
and death. From the slightest provocation the minds of boys
could conjure up horrifying things; they seemed to lust after
opportunities to imagine the worst. And as they grew older their
fantasies evolved into grotesque adolescent hallucinations – the
spaceship portal that looked out became an eye peeking in, the
room became a display cabinet and the boys were the gruesome
exhibit, something carved open, pinned, and observed – which
made them ecstatic in some unfathomable way, until it happened
that, sooner or later, the boys became men, the fantasias dis-
solved and an *oeil-de-boeuf* returned to being merely a strange
round window, an element in an architect's design. This, at
least, was Vicki's understanding, from growing up with broth-
ers and cousins who were disturbingly normal, and from Kyle.

  The afternoon sun warmed the southern face of 146
Lightenham Avenue, and the house creaked with the musical
yearning of new wood. In the boy's bedroom, Vicki padded
around in an aimless circle, letting her stocking heels thud
against the new iroko flooring, and waited. Inspiration had
usually rushed up to her by now. In all the years of doing stagings – beginning that first summer in 1989 with the pile on
Inglewood Drive that, even including the pieces from her

mother's estate, she'd barely had enough furniture to fill – she'd always managed to skirt the disquieting aspects of exuberant young boys and find expressions for their happier enthusiasms, which she could incorporate into the general scheme. What she did was think of Kyle (in 1989 he was already three) and equip these rooms for the childhood she wished for him: pennants and paraphernalia artfully mounted (a Cooper's hockey stick and a Louisville baseball bat, crossed like swords) to suggest his nascent love of sports; a brass refracting telescope at a window, pointed to the sky, to connote his searching mind. Even, occasionally (because pretending was something to be encouraged), a cowboy hat and a pair of cap-gun six-shooters in their holsters, draped over a bedpost (though she had not used the guns for years).

As Kyle grew older, the boys of Vicki's stagings grew with him, always keeping a few years ahead, to suggest the great times that were surely to come, when he would dive into mystery books with pristine jackets, when he would play a Martin acoustic guitar with an ebony fingerboard, when he would reel with his first crush, go on his first date, and kiss a girl with long, straight hair (estate sales often had a few pictures worth framing, and Vicki found the straight-haired girls prettiest). Every boy's room in Vicki's stagings offered the burnished life that Kyle or any boy should have wanted, a life of milk-white teeth and exercise, high spirits, and limitless possibility. It was easy to furnish this kind of happiness: she had most of it ready, in storage. And when she lacked some small thing, some final touch – a crystal radio set the boy could have fashioned himself, a twin-lens

Rolleiflex camera to showcase his developing artistic eye – it was quickly found at one of the Yorkville antique shops she visited on Mondays, Thursdays, and Saturdays.

A very few times, as Kyle matured, Vicki felt her confidence waver. No one ever told her that a boy's life was not like this. Not once did Avis or any other agent suggest, in so many words, that clients found her boy's room stagings unrealistic. But every so often, Vicki could see a hint of doubt behind their eyes, and their muted approval seemed to insinuate that she was not taking certain grim realities into account. When that happened, when the uncertainty of others threatened to become hers, she reminded herself that her boy's rooms were as realistic, as possible, as any other room she created. The articles she used and the pleasures they represented were absolutely real; that her arrangements were precise and ideal made them no less true. When a woman and her husband admired the dining room she had summoned, complete with pooling drapes, a festooned sideboard, and a six-branch Viennese chandelier suspended over a Belleek tea service on a Gillington table, it never occurred to them her taste was unachievable – this was exactly the life they imagined for themselves. When they looked in on the girl's room, they never thought Vicki's pastels and scalloped-edge sheets, her dolls and porcelain fixtures could not be things a girl, their daughter, would love. Why couldn't this be true for a boy? Why should a son be less deserving of a parent's best intentions?

Her responsibility, Vicki told herself, was to offer clients a vision of the life they wanted for their children. For wasn't this life, or the hope for it, one of the reasons they were house shopping at all?

Some of these thoughts came back to Vicki now in the Lightenham house, because although there was no doubt she knew what a happy boy's life was supposed to look like, just at the moment, the ideas weren't coming to her. That was strange. When her mind drifted to Kyle she saw the possible cause; it was because he'd just come home from abroad, a man of travels now, no longer the handy boyish reference he'd been. She would have to work harder. She would have to cast her mind back. Still, Vicki stood in the middle of the room, surrounded by the mahogany sleigh bed with scrolling at the head- and footboards, the matching dressing table with swinging mirror, the revolving Edwardian bookcase and the charming mahogany *bonheur du jour* with its hinged front and padded writing surface. She saw these things, chosen by her and delivered only this morning, and felt troubled by them. The problem was she could not see the boy who belonged here, did not even know his name, and without a child to represent, these things were just furnishings. That was not the service she offered.

As she paced around the room, touching the corners of antiques that provided no clues, a slight burning sensation made Vicki look down to where she had tucked her hand between the buttons of her blouse. She undid two of these buttons and found she had been rubbing the spot under her ribs so hard the skin was beginning to turn raw.

The sunlight drew her to the *oeil-de-boeuf*, and when she got close, she could see a faint layer of drywall dust clinging to the glass. Vicki placed her lips near to puff it away, but she had no breath to do it.

3

The cat was obviously equa-mouse. Which won't make any sense, but I can explain.

I'd been sticking to my room for about a week, mostly sitting in front of my computer, locked into this site I'd found, just watching the screen, listening to the blips, clicking when I was supposed to click. (After a few hours it kind of felt like floating, which was perfect.) When I wasn't looking at the screen I was watching this cat my parents got while I was away. Which was a weird thing in itself because my dad hates everything about cats ("sociopaths of the pet world" he calls them). But after watching it for a few days, it seemed to me this cat had the exact quality Legg used to call "equa-mouse." It was his version of "equanimous," which was a word he'd found in one of the reports they handed out to the guys in the D&S platoon (Defence and Security) on the state of relations between soldiers and the warlords that were carving up Balakhet, where the camp was located.

("After a period of hostility, exacerbated by the actions of Mullah Takhar Dashti, now under ISAF custody, the temper of interactions between CF personnel and the local Afghan community appears, for the moment, to be equanimous.")

Legg made quick decisions on which things to take seriously and which to make fun of, and to him using "equanimous" in that report was mockable for two factors: (1) its total ignorance of the antagonism the D&S guys felt from some of the Afghan locals during the presence patrols they conducted around Balakhet; and (2) its "ass-licking-lieutenant-typed fuck-headedness" (classic Legg). But he liked the sound of "equa-mouse," I guess, and to him it came to identify a quality he valued pretty highly, which was the quality of not giving a shit. As far as the future went, he told me, as far as having a career, having a family, worrying about anyone else or even about his own personal safety, he was equa-mouse. I didn't know what to make of it the first time I heard it, but I came to understand. I got the whole better-off-not-caring lesson.

The cat made me think of all this because the cat really seemed to be guided by the same principles. Food didn't interest it, or people; its behaviour seemed totally disconnected and arbitrary. One day it might jump from the top of the refrigerator onto Dad's neck, and the next day, not. It didn't seem to have any needs or aims, not even enough ambition to become a regular menace. And the more I watched it, the more I figured out it was this carelessness that gave it a kind of power in the house. And so I just figured Legg would've liked the cat, and would've thought it was okay that I used his word.

Legg's full name and title was Corporal Marc Sebastien Leggado, rifleman, which he never allowed anyone to use. I met him just a few weeks after I'd arrived at Camp Laverne.

I knew zip about the military before I signed up for the COF-AP program, but it turns out that in a few sensitive areas around the world they keep sustainment bases that hardly anyone knows about. When people talk about the Canadians in Afghanistan, they think of Camp Nathan Smith or Kandahar Airport, or before that Camp Julien. Nobody ever mentions Camp Laverne because they don't know it exists. But it's there, unofficially I guess, sitting on the outskirts of a place called Balakhet, a really messed-up old city in the central Wardak province. Legg said we were there "killing two birds" – the camp was about an hour away from Kabul, so it was close enough to get troops and supplies there fast if they needed to; and Wardak was also the site of the Taliban's last stand in 2001 and now, he said, "the shit was bubbling again." Rival militias were fighting each other and the jihadists were getting noisy. He figured the coalition wanted to beef up its presence before Balakhet went all Kandahar on them.

From what I understand about military camps, Camp Laverne is a sort of small-scale, necessities-only version, dug into the desert. It's ringed by tall, thick bastion walls, which are like stiff, ten-foot-high bags filled with sand and topped with razor wire, and it features all the usual flat-painted G-Wagons and LAVs (light armoured vehicles) that are either being driven or repaired. Most of the buildings are canvas Quonset huts called weather havens – big ones for common areas like the kitchen and the messes, smaller ones for the sleeping quarters for officers and soldiers. (Civilian support staff like me generally slept in smaller tents that weren't as insulated from the heat.) There's also a bunch of ISO units, which look like those long steel boxes that get loaded into ships, but they can be stacked or lined up and turned into offices or washrooms or storage units or, in my case, the portable water treatment facility I worked in.

I spent the first few weeks in camp pretty much the way I'd spent most of my life up to that point: keeping to myself, eating whenever they let me, focusing on the work I had to do, and just watching other people go about their lives. I've never been too good at making friends; it's like there's a trick to it I couldn't figure out. Part of it, I think, is people consider my sense of humour a bit off, somehow. Obscure. I tend to say things that make them go "Huh?" And I guess "huh?" is hard to get past. The more trouble I had making friends the less work I put into it. By about grade six I decided it wasn't important.

Before I even met Legg, I heard him. There was this faint, high whine coming through the dead afternoon air as I walked through the compound, across silt the colour of milky tea. I was headed for the ambulance, the closest Camp Laverne ever got to a proper medical facility while I was there, parked under a big tarpaulin to try and keep it out of the August heat. (That heat — the first time it hit me, when I stepped off the plane, it made me think of grade four recess when a big kid named Gary Millson used to sit on my stomach until I almost passed out so he could watch my eyes roll back in my head.)

I was going to the ambulance to get my hand treated for burns. Somebody had set a bunch of metal filter canisters down by the door at the treatment facility, right in the way. And when

I came on duty, after they'd been sitting in direct Afghan sunlight for a few hours, I tried to pick one up, which it turns out is something only a fairly new arrival would do.

The whine was coming from the ambulance, and I knocked on the door and waited in the shade of the tarp so I could breathe. Finally a short female medic in white shirt and pants opened the door for me and I squeezed inside.

They had a generator running a small air conditioner, so it was instantly cooler in there. Once my pupils adjusted to the blueish light I saw there were three other people besides me: the medic, a doctor, and a soldier who was lying on a pad, gripping its edges and making a sound like the steam whistle of a kettle.

In the middle of pressing and prodding around the bubbled skin on my hand, the medic glanced up and saw me staring at the soldier. The doctor was bent over his face, so I couldn't see what was going on, but the guy was obviously in a lot of pain. "Sand devil," she said. "A little whirlwind, whipped sand into his eyes. Happens all the time here." She leaned toward the soldier. "Which is why soldiers on patrol are supposed to wear their *goggles*."

The soldier stopped whining and ground out a few words through a clenched jaw, which sounded like "Hate those fucking goggles." The doctor shifted and for a second I could see through a space under his arm. He seemed to be prodding the solider's left eyeball with a Q-tip, which made the soldier stamp his foot on the platform.

"Don't!" said the doctor.

The medic seemed mildly amused. "Just try to breathe evenly, corporal."

"Can't stand shit in my eye!"

I mentioned my sense of humour? As much as it seems to put people off, it's probably the only thing I like about myself. Generally, when it comes to my positive qualities, I prefer to reject someone else's list rather than come up with my own. At home I'd be heading through the foyer on my way out the door and my mother would introduce me to some client I'd never met as "our lovely, intelligent boy" with "a real passion for the sciences." She'd push the hair off my forehead with her soft fingers and say, "We think there's medicine in Kyle's future." And through all this I'd have to chew on my tongue, literally crush my flesh between my molars until I tasted blood, to keep from screaming at my mother how fucking wrong she was, and how she sounded like she was writing a newspaper ad about some completely different person. She'd smile this proud little smile and I'd have to force my way past her and get out before I started yelling at her, "Who are you talking about? What's his name? Where does he live?"

But I do notice ironies, and absurd juxtapositions, like the professor with dandruff who talks about "precipitating insolubles," or the politician who stands behind bulletproof glass to tell viewers not to let the suicide bombers win. And I think it's good that I notice them, because somebody should. And since they always hit me as funny, I usually can't stop myself from saying something about them.

So when the soldier on the pad talked about "shit in my eye," I immediately said, "I think you mean 'mica *shists*.'" The medic was spreading ointment around my palm and I was kind of hypnotized by that and not really thinking about what should or shouldn't be coming out of my mouth. "But that's an easy mistake," I said. Then I laughed.

"Who's that?" breathed the soldier on the table.

I jerked up straight. "Um." Usually, after I say something that confuses people, I feel a wave as though I might throw up, and I was feeling that now – "I'm the water tech. Kyle Woodlore. I run the water treatment –"

"Fuck you, asshole."

The medic *tsked* and shook her head. "'Fuck me, fuck you.'" She winked at me. "How'd all this hostility squeeze in here?"

The doctor straightened and tossed his Q-tip into a can, and I could see the white of the soldier's left eye was meat red, which made me feel worse. "All right," said the doctor, "I think we can try irrigating again." He held a hand out behind him. "Lieutenant?"

"Yes, sorry." The medic held my bandage in place with one hand, twisted around, and passed a banana-sized syringe to the doctor with the other. He bent over the soldier again and soon I could hear a trickle of water hitting the metal floor. After a second I realized, hey, that's my water; I made that. Normally I wouldn't have thought anything of it, but I guess at that point, in terms of my self-image, I was in take-anything-I-could-get mode. So the idea went through my mind that maybe this was something good I'd done . . . maybe the only thing. Which made me feel good and bad at the same time. Which is sort of typical.

The canvas that covered the kitchen tent was the same arid-region beige that covered just about everything else in the camp

– what my mother might have called "a drought motif." Inside it featured a steam table for hot food, a bread table, a couple of fountain dispensers with orange and purple pseudo-juice, a place where you could get coffee and hot water for tea (which I didn't see too many people drinking), a salad and fruit bar that was always stocked up, and enough long tables and chairs for ninety diners at a time to eat and not think about all the things they'd been told in the orientation briefings about the IEDs (improvised explosive devices) the jihadists were busy making and the disease-bearing sandflies everywhere and the Russian PMN mines, Bouncing Bettys, and "green parrots" that were sitting out there just beyond the walls.

I was in there taking my lunch hour early, and I saw Legg getting a glass of Tang. And maybe because it seemed weird, after we'd been in an ambulance together, to sit on opposite sides of the room, we ended up grabbing two chairs at the same table near the entrance. He told me his full name and said there'd be "negatory consequences" if he ever heard me use it.

"I was in B-H for Roto five," he said, rubbing the back of his neck hard as if scraping away dried sweat or boredom. He brought his hand up and through the cropped hair of his head and every movement he made seemed to carry a vehemence.

"B-H?" I still wasn't used to the whole military acronym thing.

"*Bos*nia-Herze*go*vina," he said, mocking me. "Stationed up at Camp Casa Berardi in Drvar, this old bread factory they cleaned out. 'Castle Greyskull' we called it. Looked fuckin' spooky in the fog. And they was all'ays moving us out into weather havens 'cause of the bedbugs." Legg brought his drink

halfway to his mouth. "Roto five, that was pretty fuckin' hot."
He took a noisy swig and gave a long gargley sigh of satisfaction. "Not as hot as this though."

I nodded and tried to think of something to say that he'd
consider relevant. "How long have you been here?"

"We was prob'ly on the same flight, so, pretty much same as
you," Legg said. "'Cept you get to stay a lot longer." This I
knew; soldiers' rotations lasted six months, but support personnel were contracted for a year. Before I signed I was warned that
a lot of people found it difficult being away from home and
family that long; I told them I was looking forward to it.

"After that I had to wait a few years, got shipped around, and
they sent me to V-K for Roto twelve." Legg gave me a glance.
"That's *Velika-Kladusa*. No patrols, nothin', just bureaucracy.
Human resources and public relations." Legg shook his head.
"Total fuckin' waste."

There was movement around us while he talked, soldiers in
CADPAT fatigues soaked in sweat and embossed with grit
coming back from patrols, others heading off to drills or illegal
weapons searches. Some of them would lift a hand to Legg or
nod or say something and . . . it was weird. In chemistry there
are certain molecules that like to cluster – in the treatment facility we used a process called "flocculation," where we'd inject
polymers into the water to pull the contaminant molecules
together so they could be swept away – and, when I was talking
to Legg, I had this sense that these bodies moving around us
were trying to catch him and drag him off somewhere, to pull us
apart. I couldn't have explained why I didn't want that to happen
just yet, but I didn't. Thinking about it, what I'd probably say is

that talking to this soldier, who was so different from anybody I would normally have met or talked to in my life, felt like I'd won some sort of prize or something, like I'd graduated into a whole new level. And I felt this need to counteract the pulling action of all the soldiers walking around us, and the only thing I could think to do was ask questions.

"What do you mean, a waste?"

When Legg grinned, which he did just then, I couldn't help noticing his right eye. His face was already . . . I guess vivid is a good word. He was tanned, with curved creases around his mouth that looked whiter than the rest of his skin. He had a snub nose over a dense, dark moustache that looked like it might be hiding a faint hare lip scar (which I figured was not something I could ask about). And now over the left eye the doctor had taped a square patch of gauze, which Legg kept worrying with his blunt fingers. And it had the effect of making the right eye seem unnaturally big and round and alive, because it was doing the work of two.

"Waste of *me*, for fucksake. You got a guy who's equa-mouse, you should fuckin' use him properly, put him in the right situations. But these assholes don't know what they're doing." He glanced around, spreading scorn over the uniforms sitting nearby.

That was the first time I'd heard him use that word. "Sorry, what's that you said? Mouse something?"

Legg's eye lit up – questions seemed to work for him – and he explained the meaning and origins of equa-mouse. "A situation like up at V-K, you know, no shit happening. Everything all fuckin' ruled out, planned out. This here, that there. Nothin' to worry about. That's fuckin' boring for a guy like me. That's actually dangerous. 'Cause, the thing is, the world moves random, right? It's the survivors that move with it. You can't stop the fuckin' storm from blowing, you know? It's gonna fuckin' blow. And if you try and stand still you're just gonna get hit with shit. So you move with it. You with me so far?" He waited.

"Uh, yeah."

"Okay. And why do people try to stand still in a fuckin' storm?"

I shook my head.

"Because they got shit they're trying to protect, that's why. They got a house or kids or career plans or whatever so . . ." For a second Legg seemed to lose his train of thought. "Fuck, I dunno."

"So they . . . shouldn't have those things?"

Legg leaned back in his chair, looking depressed. "Something like that."

I hesitated. "Is it —"

"It's bullshit, I dunno, it's bullshit!" Legg waved the bullshit away. "Alls I'm saying is like with me, I don't want shit all planned out. It's like" – he stabbed the table with two thick fingers – "that's like strappin' me down in the middle of the storm. And I gotta be able to move."

Legg downed half the drink in his glass and stared off.

"Kinda weird you're in the D&S platoon then, isn't it? Protecting people?"

He looked at me with his eye half closed. "That's just my job, asshole, not my life. Life's a totally fuckin' different thing."

He shook his head as though he was fed up with all the idiots in the world.

"Right," I said.

"Look." He leaned forward. "Some people hate surprises, right? But me, I like 'em. 'Cause that's all the real world is, just one surprise after another. And that makes me good at my job, because if you're a guy like me, you stay cool when shit's happening because you don't give a fuck, you just do what you need to do. Right? But you put me in a situation where surprises are like, what, like artificially removed, and that's when it's fuckin' dangerous. 'Cause then you get lulled." He held his hand up as if it were floating, and his voice went soft. "And if you're lulled, you're not movin'. And the thing is, you can't keep the surprises out forever, 'cause the storm's still fuckin' blowin'. And sure enough . . . one day . . . *bam!*" He brought his hand down as a fist and rattled the cutlery of two captains half a table away.

"Hey!"

Legg leaned away from the table, visibly contrite. "Sorry, sir!" He gave me a clandestine look and let a smirk lift the corner of his mouth. Then he leaned back in. "So you tell me, asshole, why don't I wear my goggles on patrol?" He waited.

I tried to process everything as fast as I could. "Because then . . . you'll think everything's under control, and you'll get lulled, and –"

"And then somebody shoots me through the eye or I step on a PMD or some fuckin' thing. You got it." He nodded like he approved. "And then I'm like all those Pashto assholes out there walkin' around on one fuckin' leg." He brought a hand up and pressed the edges of the patch.

I took the opportunity to change the subject. "How long do you have to keep that on?"

"Doctor says forty-eight hours. 'Cause I have a 'corneal abrasion.'" He rolled his eye.

"Are you gonna keep it on?"

"Nah. Take it off tonight." He looked around with a juicy leer. "Take it off now 'cept I'd scare all the ladies." He motioned to the bandage on my palm. "What about you? How long you keeping that thing on?"

"They said a week."

"A week!" Legg let his eye roam the canvas roof, apparently overcome with disdain.

I thumbed the plastic medical tape at the heel of my hand. "I dunno, maybe a few days."

Legg pursed his lips and spoke with motherly precision. "You don't want to get an infection."

A group of five or six soldiers came into the kitchen at that moment laughing and pounding desert dust off each other's backs – the grit got into everything, after half a day you could feel it in your shorts – and Legg shot a hand out to take a glance at his watch. He crossed his arms and the intensity in his eye dimmed a little. It seemed like he wanted to leave, and I couldn't think of anything else to ask.

"So," he said, "what's your story?"

I just shrugged. "I was in school," I said. "First year chem. Then I heard about this COF-AP thing and applied for the water tech job, 'cause I knew a lot of the stuff already, and I wrote the test for the certificate, and they signed me up."

Legg seemed to be studying me, gauging his investment of interest. "You quit university?"

"Yeah."

"Why?"

"I, uh, I guess because I knew it'd piss off my parents." I looked up at Legg. "Because to them it wouldn't make sense."

It was subtle, like a ripple over dark water, but Legg's eye seemed to come alive again. "Huh," he grunted. "That right, eh?"

Water treatment at Camp Laverne was handled through a portable filtration system about the size of an ISO container, which they'd helicoptered in and hooked up long before I ever got there. It was a system designed to be able to take water straight from a sewer and turn it into something safe to drink, but in this case it was drawing from an army-drilled well. It took me about half a day to learn my job, which was basically to keep my eye on flow meters and follow a standard routine to put clean water through a gauntlet of purification, just in case. All the steps were detailed in a checklist from the Supervisor of Camp Services:

1. Chemical Mixing, Stage 1 Clarification

To soften the water and kill off the first possible batch of bacteria on its way from the well to the clarification chamber, I had to dump lime and soda ash from fifty-pound sacks into a chemical mixing box that fed into the water.

2. Flocculation

Once the water passed into the clarification chamber, my job was to pour in a positively charged liquid polymer that dispersed and grabbed whatever negatively charged impure molecules were there and dragged them to the bottom.

3. First Filtering

From the clarification chamber the water passed through a media filter of silica sand to clean out the flocs. Every night I had to backwash all that gunk out of the filter bed.

4. Final Polishing

Here the water got fed through a wound fibre cartridge to strain out "bad organics" that might affect the water's smell and taste. I had to replace that filter about once a month.

5. Chlorination

Once the water was made super clean, by dumping all this stuff in and taking it all out, a metering pump fed in chlorine at a rate high enough to prevent bacteria from getting any more ideas but low enough to keep officers' eyes from stinging. Every morning, at the beginning of the shift, I had to prepare the chlorine solution, which meant pulling on rubber gloves and dumping enough caustic calcium hypochlorite tablets into a fifty-gallon tank to get to 200 ppm.

During the shift I did tests for turbidity and pH at regular intervals and made a few measurements of the five-thousand-gallon holding tank to determine rate of water usage. Other than that, and the odd time I had to help bottle hundreds of litres of water for the presence patrols and the occasional American or European unit passing through Camp Laverne, there wasn't much to do. Which was fine with me because in those first few weeks it felt too hot to do much of anything. At night, when it got a bit cooler, a few of the COF-AP guys from my tent who worked in vehicle maintenance liked to play ball hockey on a big concrete pad with spare kitchen tables tipped over for boards. But sports never were my thing. Sometimes I listened to CDs and read paperbacks that I pulled from the bookshelf in the junior ranks mess. But for the first while that I was there, what I mostly did was think about the contrasts between life back home and life in the camp, because in nearly every way, life in the camp was better.

It's true that the heat and the dust could get on your nerves — a lot of people stored their clothes in these big tin chests spattered with plastic jewels, which you could buy for six dollars at the weekly markets that set up next to camp, but even then the grit got inside. And it's true that living on a military base meant you had no privacy at all — every environment was shared and even your bathroom moments were communal experiences. And except for visits to those markets near the gates, COF-AP civilians like me were never allowed to leave the camp. You had to stay "behind the wire," which meant being stuck in the same beige world day after day with two hundred people you didn't know, most of whom had such different expectations from life that they thought living for six months or a year next to temporary bomb shelters was just a natural career progression.

But even factoring all those things in, I liked it better there. Because it was cleaner, somehow, despite the dust. Because it was free of all the tensions and issues I took for granted at home. Things like the way Mom and Dad edged around each other all the time as if there was something they wanted to say but couldn't quite bring themselves to say it. Things like the worried way they smiled, as if whatever happiness they felt was loaner happiness that was already piling up late fees. Things like – this was a big one – nervous expectation. I mean, you can take that in small doses. But at my house on Breere Crescent, the walls practically ran with it.

Here's one example: yogurt. Mom, whenever she was working on a house, always woke up really early. And every morning, before she left, she'd set out breakfast items for me to eat – a fruit, a grain, and always a dairy in the fridge, which was usually yogurt. Then she'd call up the stairs, "Darling, there's yogurt in the fridge." And if I didn't answer right away, because maybe I was half asleep, she'd call again – "Darling? . . . Kyle? . . . Yogurt." And then . . . "Creamy Peach" . . . which I'd once said I liked. I'd wake up hearing her voice reaching up with its searching fingers, until I'd have to say something – "I heard you, Mom! Fine!" – because if I didn't say anything, she couldn't leave. And later, when I was sitting in the breakfast nook across from Dad, I'd eat the fruit and the cereal, and Dad would wait seven or eight minutes, sometimes nine, while he listened to the news and the traffic reports, and then, always, every time, he'd remind me.

"Don't forget about the yogurt in the fridge."

It's like there was this unspoken fear in the house, this huge, worrisome possibility that the yogurt Mom left for me might go . . . un-eaten. Not because I was deliberately defying them – that was never suggested – but because of, you know, crossed signals, static in the transmission, an accident of fate. Somehow, nobody's fault, *the yogurt would remain*. And if that happened then, holy shit, Mom's attempt to feed me a complete breakfast would be ruined, and her love for me would go unexpressed, and Dad would have failed in his duty to help his wife fulfil her most fervent hopes! And I knew that, if both Mom and Dad left the house before I did, which happened a lot when my classes began late, then for the whole day they'd be wondering . . .

Did Kyle eat the yogurt?

That was just my mornings, okay? So from that, maybe you can figure out what my lunches and dinners were like, and the expectations around my school marks, and my career choices, and my driving habits, and my sleeping patterns, and my clothing decisions, and my friends. And maybe it won't seem quite so weird that I'd prefer spending a year in a dry-as-dirt, hot-as-hell military camp in Afghanistan surrounded by uncleared minefields and angry private militias to living in a luxury five-bedroom home on a street lined with big trees and SUVs.

It was a few weeks before I saw Legg again. I figured that was because our shifts were different – COF-AP employees worked pretty normal hours but soldiers were on duty for twelve hours at a stretch, so lunch and dinner times didn't always match up. I looked for him, though, a few times while I was standing in line, getting my plate loaded up with rosemary-roasted chicken thighs or steak and potato pie or ground-beef burritos topped with Monterey Jack cheese (they had fish and pasta most nights too, and they served curries for the Kurds and the Turkish units that came through). A few nights, when the junior ranks' mess opened up after seven, I looked for him among the soldiers shooting pool or playing "Call of Duty" on the communal PlayStation. But he'd never be there and sometimes these guys would ask me if I wanted to join in one of the games they were playing. I guess because it looked as if I was waiting or hoping for something. It always surprised me, when they asked, and I always said no. And then I'd just end up sitting at the end of a couch for a while, staring up at the blue and gold Afghan rugs that somebody had wired to the roof of the tent. The designs were so intricate, there was lots to look at. (It didn't seem so loserish at the time.)

Then came this one day when I'd had to spend pretty much my entire shift draining and flushing the whole treatment system – including the five-thousand-gallon holding tank – because one of the senior officers thought he'd caught a faint whiff of gasoline in the water he'd gotten from a tap. Which wasn't possible; it was likely just an old Iltis vehicle with a fuel leak driving by, but that didn't matter. After that shift I really felt like I deserved a beer (we were allowed two a night, although there was some talk of shutting even that down like they did in Kandahar, out of respect for the Muslims) so I walked into the mess and headed straight for the makeshift bar at the back and found myself standing in line right behind Legg. I could tell who it was from his dense brush of hair and the slope of his shoulders under his T-shirt. And the way he was griping.

"Fuck me! Fuckin' wogs."

He spun away from the counter empty-handed and began to push past me. I had to kind of wave my hand in his face.

"Hey, uh, hi."

He stopped and stared at me like he didn't know who I was.

"It's me, from . . . remember? Kyle, from the —"

"Oh, yeah." His glare cooled off and he shifted his head back as if he needed to get a better look. "Yeah, right, I remember. Water guy. Howsa hand?" He was half grinning and I couldn't tell if it was because he was glad to see me or because he thought I was a joke. There was a loud clack and a shout from the pool table on the far side of the tent, and other soldiers and a few COF-AP types were pushing past Legg to get to and from the bar. He seemed ready to move on.

"Good," I said, holding up my palm. "Your eye looks okay."

Legg blinked. He seemed to be thinking. "Oh, yeah, fuck. I was done with that shit the next day. Hey, you gonna be needing both of those?" He thudded a finger against the laminated punch card hanging by a chain around my neck. Two punches on the day's date and you were done drinking for the night.

I hesitated and looked down at my chest. It was strictly against the code of conduct to let someone else use your drink allowance.

"I dunno," I said. "I guess."

"No, see" – Legg ran a thick finger under his nose and then pointed off – "I gave my buddy over there one of mine because he lost his card, right? Fuckin' asshole. And this piss-head" – he waved a hand in the direction of the bartender – "I tried telling him but he won't listen to fuckin' reason. So whaddaya say?" He grinned. "You're prob'ly a water man anyway, right?"

I sort of shrugged. "Sure, okay."

"Thanks, man." Legg pounded me on the back. "Hey, if you want you can play some cards with us later."

At the counter I asked for two beers. The bartenders rotated from night to night between a thin guy about my age who might have been Kurdish and a bored older woman with dyed black hair. Tonight it was the young guy.

"You want two?" he said with a frown, looking from me to a space over my shoulder.

"Yeah," I said, "just 'cause, you know, so I don't have to come back." I waved my arm back and forth to indicate what a big hassle that would be.

The bartender hesitated for another second, then leaned forward with a shiny hole punch in his hand, plucked up my card and snipped twice. A minute later, when he set the two tall cans on the counter, he looked into my eyes. "These for you, yes?"

"Yeah!" I smiled, easing the cans away. "Of course."

When I turned from the bar one of the maintenance guys from my tent (at the time I wasn't sure whether his name was Joe or Joel) came up to me with this freaked-out grin on his face.

"Hey, do you know that guy, that corporal?" Joe/Joel was one of the ball-hockey players, a bit older and bigger than me. He'd never bothered talking to me before and now he had this look like he was trying to figure out if he had to take me more seriously.

"You mean Legg?" I had to shout over the Stones music coming from the far end of the tent, and this guy leaned in as if he didn't want anybody else to hear.

"Is that his name?"

"Well, Leggado. Why?"

"He's one of the D&S guys, right?"

I nodded.

"Do you know what they're doing?" Joe/Joel scratched the side of his neck furiously. "I don't know if it's true. But some guys are saying that you can, like, rent one of the watch towers on the wall from them for a couple of hours."

"Yeah?" I said. "What for?"

Joe/Joel looked at me as if I was missing some important features on my face. "To be with a girl."

"Oh."

In the briefings, they'd more or less spelled out that hooking up in the camp was a firing offence. If there was a girl you really liked, maybe you could touch elbows in the dinner line. By accident. That's what they said.

"Do you think you could ask him for me?"

I looked down at the beers in my hand, and then back. "I don't really know him that well."

As I walked away, I could tell Joe/Joel was mentally scratching me off his list of significant people.

There were about three dozen bodies in the tent, so it took a minute to locate Legg. I found him seated at a table in the corner with four other soldiers, including a pretty female master corporal with a head of mousey curls. When I got there Legg shot an arm out.

"Hey, there's my new best bud. Grab a seat!" He kicked out a chair at the end of the table.

As soon as I set the beers down, Legg grabbed both and slid them away. "Two! Even better; Tanner here was gonna ask you but now he don't have to." By Tanner, Legg seemed to mean a big, moon-faced warrant officer with his foot propped on a chair and his forearm on the master corporal's shoulder. Legg started to slide the second beer over to him across the plastic tabletop and Tanner leaned in for it before I could remember how to speak.

Then suddenly Legg swept the can out of Tanner's reach.

"Fuck off, you! This is my buddy's beer." Legg grinned at me and slid the beer back. "Just kidding, eh?" He turned on Tanner again. "You woulda too, wouldn' ya! Huh? Just take his fuckin' drink without askin'!"

Tanner shrugged, helpless. "You were handing me a beer. Am I supposed to say no?"

"No fuckin' manners!" shouted Legg. "You're a disgrace!" He leaned back toward me, his jaw hanging loose and playful. "Don't mind him, eh? It's Kyle, right? Yeah, you gotta watch this one. All these assholes, really. 'Cept Zini. She's pris*tine*." He raised his voice. "Right, Zini?"

Zini, the master corporal, was talking to a sergeant across from her. Now she stopped and showed us a resolutely peaceful face. "Are you causing trouble again?"

By the end of the beer I'd found out why I hadn't seen Legg around for a while: he was being disciplined. On a Friday, two days after his ambulance visit, he'd been on Op Shield duty as one of the armed soldiers assigned to protect a group from CIMIC (Civil-Military Cooperation) who were out looking at possible project sites around Balakhet, things they could help fix up as a way to improve relations with the locals. At the eastern edge of town, near one of the community wells, they looked at a bombed-out school that needed a roof. And there were a lot of Afghan men gathered around, which always made the military guys edgy because crowds could turn hostile pretty fast. So Legg was supposed to stick to the CIMIC group and stay alert.

Instead, he'd dropped back, because he'd noticed that all these people were actually spectators watching a strange event – a bunch of bearded men running across an open field, fighting with bright coloured kites. Legg said they were "goodprans" but Zini corrected him; *gudiparan* they were called. The object seemed to be for a man flying a kite to cut his opponent's string before his own could be cut and his kite was sent flying off into the distance. The strings, Legg noticed, glittered in the sun.

"Ground-up glass," he explained, jumpy like a kid who'd just found money in the street. "They smash up Coke bottles and shit. They grind 'em till they're almost like sugar. Then they gum up the strings with some kind of sticky paste and roll them in the glass to make 'em sharp."

"It's called glue," said Tanner.

"Huh?"

"That sticky paste is some kind of flour glue."

"Yeah, whatever you fuckin' – like you know shit about it."

Tanner smirked as he lifted his glass. "I know enough not to go watching it when I'm on guard duty."

Legg rose up and swung his arm as if to hit Tanner in the side of the head, but making the big man flinch seemed satisfaction enough. He sat back down and leaned in toward me.

"A lot of 'em wear gloves, right? 'Cause these glass strings'll cut you up. But this one Pashto fucker didn't. Guy's all decked out in his baggy pants and shirt, he's got his beard down to here, right? His head's wrapped up, he could be like fifty, who knows? So I'm watchin' what he's doin', and he holds out his hand for me to see, and it's all scarred like it's been ripped up a hundred or maybe a thousand times. He's been playing this game his whole life, so this hand's like almost solid scar." Legg was holding his own hand out and staring at it. "But thing is there was still blood all through here." He traced with a finger where he'd seen the blood, where the little shards of glass had found a way into the skin.

"Guess he was equa-mouse," I said.

Legg knocked a forearm against my shoulder. "You got that fuckin' right." He stared at his hand, closed it and opened it as if imagining it covered with scars. "Yeah, I'd like to see all that again. They bet money on it too, you know; I'd like to get a piece of that." He played with the tab on his beer can, apparently lost in visions of fighting kites. "Anyways," he said, pulling out of it, "one of the CIMIC motherfuckers reported me for dere*lict*ion and they put me on fuckin' gate duty for two weeks."

"Is that bad?"

"Ha!" Legg swelled up with glee. He shouted at Tanner. "Tanner! Hey fuckhead! Guy wants to know if gate duty's bad."

Tanner made a moon face of contempt that could've been a comment on my cluelessness regarding gate duty, or on the misery of gate duty itself.

"Gate duty?" Legg said to me. "Fuckin' boring as shit. Twelve hours of this." He dropped his hands to his sides and stared ahead zombie-like with his tongue lolling out. "They made me eat rations, too. You ever eat rations?"

"Uh, no."

"Don't bother. Then at nights I had to do kitchen prep. Which was okay because it's the only way I got any decent fuckin' food."

Legg snickered at me and I snickered back. And in that perfect second I decided I should get up and leave. I should just say goodbye and go back to my tent before I said or did something stupid and ruined everything. I was about to push my chair back when I looked up and saw Joe/Joel.

He was slowly angling up to the table the way you see dogs figuring out their path to a squirrel. He glanced over at me, then grabbed a free chair and pulled it to a space across from Legg, and as he sat down I could feel my stomach going sour.

"You're a D&S guy, right?"

Legg was slouched back in his chair fiddling with his beer can and he frowned across the table at this guy.

Joe/Joel glanced around nervously at Tanner and the others in conversation, then leaned in toward Legg. "I was wondering" – he dropped his voice to a whisper – "who do I talk to about getting one of the watch towers for a couple of hours?"

"Hey!" Tanner turned back to Legg. "I just put it together – it's 'cause of you the mashed potatoes were shit this week."

"What're you talkin' about?"

"You were on prep, and the potatoes were all lumps."

"Yeah," grumbled Legg. "And you don't wanna know what those lumps were, either!"

The table laughed and Joe/Joel seemed to think he hadn't been heard. He tilted his head to try and get Legg's attention. "I'm serious," he said. "Who is it I'm supposed to talk to?" He pressed his chest into the edge of the table trying to get closer. "There's this girl in the —"

"Who the fuck are you anyway?" Legg was squinting at him, his mouth bunched up with distaste. Joe/Joel started to glance toward me and I shot my eyes down at the table.

"Aren't you in D&S?"

"So?"

"So I heard you guys could, you know, arrange for some privacy."

"Somebody's feedin' you shit." Legg waved him away with his beer can.

"He'll vouch for me."

It was hot as anything in the tent, but as Joe/Joel pointed at me, my face went cold, like I'd stepped into a meat locker.

Legg began eyeing me. Suspiciously. "You know him?"

I looked from the guy to Legg and gave a feeble shrug. "He's . . . in my tent."

"You hang out with him?"

I made my frozen head move side to side, but that didn't seem to be enough; Legg was still watching me. "No," I said. Across the table Joe/Joel hated me now, I could tell. But I had no choice.

"Okay, fuck off." Legg waved the guy away. When he didn't move immediately, Legg stretched a foot out under the table and gave his chair a rough shove.

"Hey!"

Legg traced a circle in the air with his beer can to indicate the people sitting around him, who were watching now, and me. "This is a private fuckin' party. Get lost."

When Joe/Joel had stalked off, Legg leaned toward me. "Don't get mixed up in any'a that shit, eh? That's just a quick way home."

That night when I got back to my tent, three of the eight beds were already filled with snoring men – in the summer months a lot of the vehicle work was done before nine in the morning, because later in the day the metal parts and tools got too hot to touch. So these guys were due to get up in a couple of hours and you had to be quiet when you were coming in late. Joe/Joel was there too, stretched out on his top bunk, but he wasn't asleep. He'd clipped an LED flashlight to his bed frame and he was reading a motorcycle magazine.

"Hey, Woodlore," he muttered when I'd stepped inside, his voice just loud enough to be heard. "I had a bottle of your water and it tasted like shit. I had to dump it out."

I didn't bother to answer him. Not even when I figured out he'd poured the water all over my pillow and mattress. I just got into bed. Normally, I would've been pissed off, maybe gone to get fresh sheets, but for some reason it didn't matter to me. I guess this was part of the storm and I was moving with it. A few bunks away Joe/Joel was flipping the pages of his magazine and hissing a little laugh about what he'd done, but I didn't mind lying in the wet; that night, it just seemed kind of cooling.

For the next few months I hung out with Legg a fair bit, eating most meals with him and having drinks with him and his friends in the mess whenever I could. A few times I played poker with them in the kitchen, long after the mess had closed. Legg liked to shuffle and riffle the deck with a snap and then pound the table with each card he dealt. And he liked to give advice on how to play ("Ten-jack? Don't fuckin' throw ten-jack away! What, are you waiting for straight fuckin' aces or are you gonna play the game? Fuckin' live a little, asshole!"). At dinner he liked to snow his meat with pepper and excavate reservoirs for gravy in his mashed potatoes. He always gripped his fork like a shiv and shoved chairs around as if they offended him. But the thing I noticed most was the way he insulted and abused the people he liked best and turned wary around those he didn't know. And when he spoke to officers and others who'd lost his respect, I heard the way the undersides of his words were coated with contempt, like rot.

There were times when I'd arrive at the kitchen tent late and he'd already be seated with other soldiers, mocking them and swearing at them. He never saved a seat for me and I never expected him to; soldiers generally didn't spend much time with civilian support. So those times I just grabbed my food, found a seat a few tables away and tried to listen in, I guess to see if there was any real difference between the way Legg treated them and the way he treated me. The next time I was sitting with him, I'd spend the first few minutes worrying that something would seem different, that maybe he'd decided it was strange that I was always around. I only relaxed once he'd fired that first "fuckin' asshole" my way.

Then one day Legg entered the kitchen after patrol, still

crusted with grit, and he walked past a bunch of soldiers he could've sat with and came up to me.

"Looka this shit," he said, reaching into his pocket. He pulled out two small, olive-tinted eggs.

"Fuckin' partridge eggs," he said. "We're on the north side doin' our route through all the mud buildings, right? And this guy comes up and gives 'em to me." He looked up. "You want one?"

"You mean, to eat?"

"What else?" He tipped his head toward the cook tent. "Come on, they'll do 'em up for us."

Inside the small cook tent, holding our elbows in tight to avoid all the blackened pots billowing meaty steams, we watched as the tall Afghan chef, who'd been trained in England, hefted the eggs with a suspicious look. "Where did you get these?"

"North end, I told you!"

"From who?"

"This fuckin' guy!" Legg looked over at me in the dim light, exasperated. "How do you want yours, fried or what?"

Before I could answer, the chef cracked the eggs against the edge of the stove with one hand and opened them into a bowl. What plopped out of the shells seemed more like oysters than eggs.

Legg's face twisted as he pointed at the bowl. "What the Jesus fuck is that?"

"Embryos," said the chef. "These were fertilized eggs."

Right then I braced for some kind of explosion, but Legg only peered in closer.

"That man," said the chef, "he is one of those who has partridges for fighting, I think. He was not giving you eggs to eat, he was giving you some babies to raise."

Legg was still staring at the phlegmy lumps. "Fuck me, eh?" he said, with a kind of reverence. He jabbed a finger at the eggs. "That's what I like, right there. Shit that keeps you guessin'." Then he straightened up, slapped me in the gut, and yanked a thumb at the bowl. "Whaddaya think," he said, half serious, "scramble 'em for Tanner?"

As the months went by it got dark earlier, and the evenings turned pretty cold. Most nights, after the mess closed, somebody would light a fire in a sand pit that had been dug out behind the tent, a few metres from the bastion wall. There was a corkscrew of razor wire strung along the top of the barrier, and the light from the flames would dance across it and make it stand out orange against the black sky. I'd hang out there for hours while Legg subjected his friends to indignities. Some nights, the best nights, he'd try to push me into the fire.

I didn't have any more problems with Joe/Joel, but I guess he kept at the D&S guys. One day in October, just before lunch, somebody banged on the wall of the water treatment ISO, and, when I looked outside, Legg was there acting jumpy and wearing a big grin.

"What?" I said.

"You busy, asshole?"

"Fuck, yeah," I said. "I have to set up a new batch of polymer." The guy on the shift before me usually did it, but for some reason that morning he hadn't and I'd just figured it out.

"Can it wait?" He couldn't stop moving around.

I shrugged. "Maybe half an hour?"

"Come on!"

He charged off in his heavy boots across the compound and I followed him, around the supply tents and through a parking area for LAVs, jumping over the large black basins set on the sand ready to catch the oil drips from the vehicles when they came back from patrol. When he got within about ten metres of the southeast watch tower, he stopped and pointed up at the tower.

"Fucker's up there."

"Who?"

"That jerk-off from your tent."

It took me a second to figure out who he meant. He pushed a finger to his lips and waved me closer, until we were in a sliver of shadow under the platform.

"Is he with somebody?"

Legg frowned as if he disapproved and squinted out at the hard sun. "Some stupid-ass girl private," he muttered. "Dunno what the fuck she's doin' with him."

"How do you know he's up there?"

"I arranged it."

He watched my reaction — I must have looked confused — and the corner of his mouth twisted up. "He kept buggin' everybody, right? So I told 'em, 'Let him use the southeast tower. Nobody's gonna walk in on him there.'"

I couldn't tell if I was missing something. "That's nice of you, I guess."

He spat a gob of phlegm into the dust. "Not really." He looked at me, his eyes like flares, and I smiled even though I didn't know what for.

"It's infested," he said. "Fuckin' sandflies."

We pressed in and listened. The sandflies couldn't kill you, but they could give you a boil like an orange. We watched some LAVs and G-Wagons roll by leaving tracks in the dust, and then it was quiet until a captain came out of the nearest supply tent on his way to the latrine and looked over. He kept going for three, four steps, his eyes on us, then he turned and came our way.

"Fuck," Legg muttered.

The captain stopped in the middle of the road and set his hands on his hips. "Are you on duty, corporal?"

Legg straightened up. "No, sir." He tried to keep his voice to a half whisper. "Not till thirteen hundred."

"Why are you skulking around in the shadows?"

Legg quick-marched over, murmured something to the captain that seemed to satisfy him, and jogged back looking happy as the officer carried on. When he got close to me he leaned in.

"Told him you were thinkin' a gettin' your dick pierced and I was talkin' ya out of it."

I was still choking on that when Legg smacked me on the shoulder and held a hand up like he'd heard something, and pretty soon I heard it too: a kind of rumbling sound that seemed to be coming from deep inside the tower, almost from its foundation. And pretty soon it was clear that what we were listening to was Joe/Joel's pounding boots, and maybe the boots of his girlfriend, trying to fend off the invaders. And then, over top of the fervent rumbling, from the windows high above, came one loud and desperate "Holy *fuck!*"

Legg was doubled over against the wall, killing himself trying to keep quiet, when Joe/Joel exploded through the ground-level door. He was beating himself with one arm and had half his clothes bundled under the other. As he stumbled away, barefoot, he left a trail of personal effects – a sock, a pen, his underwear. Seconds later the private came down. She was pretty in that stark, sincere way of a lot of army women. Apparently Joe/Joel hadn't gotten her too warmed up because she was still in her fatigues with her boots laced tight. She paused near the entrance, shaking a sandfly out of her cap, then bent down to pick up something small and shiny. As she straightened she eyed Legg and me, giggling by the wall, and flicked Joe/Joel's unopened condom at us.

For a long time Legg was stuck on basic foot patrol duty in the quietest sections of Balakhet. It wasn't until one of the other D&S guys broke his leg falling through some weak floorboards during a security sweep that they put him back in OP Shield rotation. By then the roof of the school, near the open field where he'd seen the fighting kites, had been built. But you could tell he never stopped thinking about the kites, or the Pashtun with the scarred hand, because he never stopped talking about them. "I wish you coulda seen this asshole," he'd say. "His hand ripped to shit, for fuckin' *years*, and he doesn't care."

His only hope of seeing the *gudiparan* again was to get assigned to a patrol that passed near the field at the right time on a Friday, the day the fights happened, but he never had that luck. By December, as the Afghan desert took on the colour of ash, he'd pretty much given up hope.

One day at lunch, when Legg was out on patrol, I loaded up at the sandwich bar like usual and carried my plate through the crowded kitchen to a table near the salad section. After I'd pulled in my chair I noticed I was sitting a few seats down from Zini, the curly-haired master corporal. I'd found out she worked in the command office, and I'd seen her move in and out of Legg's circle of friends almost like she had diplomatic immunity; he showed her respect, but he spared her the cruelty that went with it.

She saw me and smiled the way she usually did with me, kindly, with some pity. "So, Kyle," she said, "when are you going home for Christmas?"

I stared down at my kielbasa on rye. Going home hadn't even occurred to me. "I guess I probably won't," I said.

"What? Why not!"

I shrugged. "I just prefer it here."

"Wow." She looked astonished. "I thought most of the COF-AP people were going." There was a fork in her hand and she stirred the air with it to include the soldiers she was eating with. "Most of us would kill to eat some Mom-made Christmas turkey."

I dipped my sandwich in the puddle of mustard on my plate, thoughts lining up in my head. "You mean you're not going home?"

"Nope."

"Is that true for . . . all the soldiers?"

Zini's face went wry. "You mean guys like Legg?"

I picked at a piece of crust and shrugged.

"Yup," she said, "everybody's staying here through the holidays."

A female lieutenant seated near Zini began singing, "I'm dreaming of a beige Christmas, just like the ones the mullahs know . . ."

"So," I said, "what happens in a camp like this around Christmas?"

Zini speared some feta-flecked rotini spirals and lifted them halfway to her mouth. "We'll probably have a tree. But it'll be a busy time too."

Everybody around her nodded like bobble-head dolls.

"How come?"

"Because . . ." Her mouth was full and she twirled her fork like a conductor until she could swallow. "Our roto ends in January. We have to get ready for the transition."

The smear of mustard on my plate pulsed in front of my eyes for a minute, maybe longer, until I heard Zini say, "What's wrong?"

It wasn't something I could explain. Part of it, sitting there, was just feeling stupid for only figuring out now that Legg would be gone in a few weeks, and that that would be it. Part of it was realizing that for the next six months I was going to be stuck here like a prisoner with a bunch of strangers and people like fucking Joe/Joel.

"Kyle?"

My sandwich was making me sick so I laid it on the plate and pushed my chair away from the table.

"Excuse me."

The men's latrine was full except for one stall with an unflushed toilet. I went in there and rattled the flimsy door shut. I closed my eyes and tried not to breathe and tried not to think. Then I thought maybe I should pee, because other people might think it was weird that I was standing there in a stall doing nothing, not making a sound. But to pee I had to open my eyes, and I couldn't open them. I tried but I couldn't. So I gave that up and just pressed my arm across my face while a lot of soldiers and men I didn't know, and never would know, jostled and joked around a few inches away from me. And as long as I was in there I just kept standing and kept silent as best as I could.

At the end of lunch, I caught up to Zini on her way out to the compound. She stopped and touched my arm.

"What happened to you?" she said. "Are you sick?"

"No, I'm okay. But I was thinking – can I ask you something?"

"Sure."

While I was in the latrine I'd gotten this idea of something I could do. But I was going to need help and she was the only one I trusted to ask. I pulled her off to the side, away from every-body streaming out of the kitchen to go back on duty.

"Do they ever let any support guys like me outside the camp here?"

"Outside the camp? Civilians?" She seemed startled. "Why would you want to?"

"Just – could it ever happen?"

A curl of hair had come loose at her temple and Zini tucked it under the edge of her cap as she thought. "Maybe if we're trying to do some CIMIC thing for PR and somebody has skills that are needed?" She thought. "Last roto there was that awful

disease people were getting from sandfly bites, and they took a
German specialist out to look at them. God, I saw pictures of
some of those people and it –"

"Okay! That's good. That's what I was thinking. So is there
any chance I could do something like that? Like maybe if
there's a well someplace that's polluted, and they need somebody to fix it?"

She squinched her face up. "There's probably a lot of wells
out there contaminated in some way. I don't know of any one in
particular." Then she studied me. "What's up with you, anyway?
I haven't seen this much action out of you since you got here."

There was nothing I could say to her that wouldn't sound
pathetic, that wouldn't make her think I was trying too hard to
be Legg's friend, even though that wasn't it at all. I just wanted
to do something for him; I wanted to thank him. And that wasn't
something I could ever say out loud. I wonder sometimes if I'd
told Zini then everything I was thinking, whether she would've
said don't bother, don't waste your time, and everything would
have turned out differently. But at that moment I just shrugged.
"I was thinking I could do something helpful, you know, for
Christmas. And you're in the Command Office, right?"

She kept looking at me. "If we did get you outside, there'd
have to be extra security."

"Okay."

Her mouth pulled sideways, like she was looking at a car she
might buy. Then she reached up with two hands, shaped her
beret, and nodded. "Okay, let me think about it."

For two days I hardly saw her, and when I did she just smiled and passed right by me. So I started to think she'd forgotten, or decided it wasn't important, and I hated myself for going to her. Then on the third day, as I was filling my cup at the coffee machine, she came up and stood beside me. She had this air about her, something sparkly.

"Christmas," she said.

"Yeah?"

"It's a time of giving."

When I looked at her full on I could see she was smiling.

"Oh, yes," she said, "I'm very good. I had to wait for the right moment, because Colonel Hister, our CO, he has certain times when he's receptive, and certain times when he's not. And when Hister's vulnerable, you have to jump on him." I think she said that louder than she'd expected to, because she looked over both shoulders. "Anyway, he's always hunting around for ways to decrease tensions with the city, and he's a man who appreciates a holiday gesture. So I told him there's a COF-AP employee here who wants to give up his Christmas trip home so he can do something nice for Afghanistan." Her face went serious. "You still want to, right?"

"Uh, yeah. Absolutely."

She gave a crisp nod. "He wants to hear your idea."

At three o'clock that day, I was sitting in the Command Office. On the outside it was a ramshackle combination of three white-painted ISO units joined together. Inside it was divided into two rooms. The one you entered first was cluttered with storage

shelves and desks for two military assistants – Zini and Lieutenant Bob Jayne, who I'd seen around because he's hard to
miss but I'd never met before. The inner room featured a big
Canadian flag, a map of Afghanistan and the surrounding territory, two potted palms, three upholstered office chairs, an
impressive oak desk, and a whiteboard. And right at that
moment Colonel Raymond Hister, a tall, fit guy who seemed
more like a math teacher than a soldier, was standing at the
whiteboard drawing circles on it.

"This is you, Kyle," he said, tapping in the middle of an
apple-sized circle he'd just drawn with a black marker. He looked
back to make sure I understood I was the apple-sized circle.

I nodded.

Off to the side, halfway between me and the whiteboard,
was another man sitting in one of the upholstered chairs with his
arms tightly crossed. That was Mike Oberly, Camp Laverne's
COF-AP deputy project manager. I recognized him from the first
support personnel briefing I went to after I'd arrived, when he
gave us a long speech about following rules and being professional and representing all the good things about Canada in this
poor, screwed-up country, when all most people cared about
was were they going to get shot at. Since I'd been shown into the
Command Office, Oberly hadn't said very much, and he seemed
a little annoyed. But right now he was extremely focused on the
whiteboard, as if what the colonel was drawing up there might
be an important national secret.

Colonel Hister finished off another, larger circle, higher
than the first, and he tapped it. "This is me. Or we could say, the
Command Office." He looked back. "You're following?"

I nodded again. "Yes, sir."

Hister put down his black marker, picked up a blue one, and drew a line connecting the two circles. "This," he said, thudding the board with his middle finger, "is the path of your idea." My idea hadn't been discussed yet, other than to acknowledge that I had one, and that it had something to do with Camp Laverne, the people of Balakhet, and Christmas.

Hister turned partway toward me. "Seems like a good path, doesn't it?"

"Yes, sir."

Hister shook his head. "It's not."

Over in the armchair, Oberly still had his arms knotted up and he was shaking his head too, as if he was right there with Hister in thinking the path of my idea was crap.

Now Hister picked up his black marker and drew a third circle.

"That's me," said Oberly, jabbing his head toward the third circle, as if his arms were useless, or shackled.

"Mike Oberly here" – Hister tapped the circle and turned – "is the COF-AP DPM, as you know." He capped the black marker, picked up the blue one, and drew a line connecting the circles representing me and Oberly.

"That's the good path," said Oberly.

Hister extended a hand toward the DPM. "Mr. Oberly is familiar with how we do things, Kyle, so he's absolutely right, this is the good path. But is it complete?" He raised his eyebrows.

"Um. I don't think so?"

"No, it's not, because in this scenario, I haven't heard the idea yet." He set the blue marker back down. "Now" – his voice turned cheerful – "look at this . . ."

This time he reached for a completely new marker, a red one, and he used it to draw a line between the Oberly and Hister circles. He turned toward me with a smile that was half charitable, half triumphant, and tapped the red line. "Here's where the action is."

Then he set the red marker down and began drawing a huge circle in the air with his finger. "What I want you to understand, Kyle, and as I've already explained to Zini – ideas are like fuel and need to flow in a certain direction, like gas in a car. Now in a car, you have fuel lines to govern the flow, but in a camp like ours, we have a process. It's a process that we like, that we feel works for us, and that we want our support personnel to follow as religiously, if you will, as our military personnel. Because it keeps everything running in an orderly, efficient manner."

Hister stopped drawing a circle in the air and turned to Oberly. "Did you have anything you wanted to add, Mike?"

Oberly stared at the board with a reverence you might give to something in a museum. "Not other than that there is the path we've used every day since day one."

"Right."

"And it's a frigging good one."

"No question about it."

"Well" – Oberly shifted in his chair – "as long as he understands."

"I think he does," said Hister. Then the colonel rolled out his chair, sat down at his desk, and smiled into my eyes. "Now that that's cleared up, and since we're all here, let's talk about how we're going to bring a little Christmas joy to our Afghani friends."

"Wake up, asshole."

It was five-thirty in the morning, the Friday before Christmas, and Legg was standing over my bunk dressed for patrol in full gear, including the flak vest he sometimes called his "Kabul dinner jacket." He was holding his C7 assault rifle in his left hand and punching me in the shoulder with his right.

"Get up if we're gonna do this fuckin' thing."

Right away, Colonel Hister had seen the community-relations value in my idea. The first part was to take twenty thousand litres of our filtered, treated water and distribute it in fifty-litre jugs to the hospitals, mosques, and orphanages of Balakhet (we had to get the jugs flown in, which took a week, and for twenty-four hours after we emptied the holding tank to fill them, nobody in camp could have a shower). The second part – which required me going outside the camp – was to check the water quality of five public wells and, where necessary, treat the water with chlorine. Hister agreed that one of the wells I should look at was the one near the school, where the roof had been fixed, because it was good to remind people about other good things the military had done. He approved the extra security detail, which meant Legg would be involved for sure. And he agreed that the Friday before Christmas was the right day for what he named "Operation Slaked Thirst." He was obviously, Zini told me, "in prime receptivity mode."

The community relations and military procurement parts of the operation were given to Lieutenant Bob Jayne, in the Command Office. I was put in charge of water handling and treatment, which meant I was the one who had to fill up all the jugs. Only once, after about six hours of killing my back, when a jug slipped out of my hands and spewed water all over a bag of calcium hypochlorite tablets, which meant evacuating the ISO unit until the toxic air could be cleared, did I stop and think about all that was going on because of me. And how strange it was that I was going to so much trouble to make something happen, and to be part of it, for somebody who claimed he didn't care about anything. But then I remembered I'd quit school and gone to Afghanistan just because it was the last thing my dad would want me to do. So I figured maybe I was just a guy who went to extremes.

In the tent, Legg sighed and clomped around while I got dressed. There wasn't much light, but he must have seen Joe/Joel asleep in his bunk because he grabbed the guy's leg and shook it. Joe/Joel sucked in a breath and levered up off his pillow.

"Wha' the fuck?"

"Checkin' for sandflies. Go back to sleep."

It was cold outside, colder than I'd expected, and the light was soft and sort of pink. Out by the water treatment ISO, three canvas-sided HLVW trucks were already lined up with their engines rumbling – each of them had to be loaded with about a hundred and thirty water jugs – and in front of them stood Lieutenant Jayne with a sheaf of papers in his hand. When he saw me jogging toward the ISO, he came right for me.

"What the hell, Woodlore," he said. "You working on Central Canada time or what?"

"Sorry." I got to the ISO and swung open the wide door.

"This whole show was your idea."

I knuckled the sleep out of my eyes and pointed inside. "There's a hundred jugs in here, plus that bag of chlorine tablets. And there's three hundred more jugs in the supplies tent."

"Okay," said Jayne, glancing at his papers. "So who's loading it?"

I just looked at him. "Well . . . I thought –"

He jabbed his glasses up his nose. "You thought I'd get some soldiers to do the grunt work, so you didn't arrange for any COF-AP people to be here."

At that moment it seemed possible the whole thing could be called off, and it felt like everything at the edge of my sight was receding.

"Is that right?"

My throat was closing. "Yes."

Jayne looked fierce for a moment, and then his expression shifted, like a coin catching light. "Yeah, that's what I figured," he said. "So you can thank me for rostering up six men to do your work." He began to stalk off and as he did he waved his papers toward a military photographer who was standing near one of the trucks, rummaging in a green canvas bag. "Guess we can't have pictures of one skinny civilian hauling twenty thousand litres on his back."

With six men plus me working, the trucks were loaded and rolling within an hour. Lieutenant Jayne sat up in the lead truck because he had the maps and the names of officials, and with him, besides the driver, rode a language assistant named Nila. She was a tall, quiet woman, a former schoolteacher, and the red and gold hijab she wore didn't quite cover the scars and blinded eye she'd gotten in the days of the Taliban. (She'd allowed her ankle to be seen, according to the story I heard, and for that she'd been beaten with a camel's bridle by her fourteen-year-old nephew.) I sat in the second truck between the driver and one of the guards, doing my best to protect the testing kit from the dust being churned up by the first truck and coming into the cab. Legg was stationed in the third truck with the photographer, and I had a good idea how much swearing was going on back there in the grit cloud from the two trucks in front.

In addition to the five wells I had to test and treat, there were twelve stops on the route, which took us through the poorest neighbourhoods of Balakhet. I'd seen pictures of some of these sections during the first orientation briefing, but that was nothing like being in them for real. We drove past crumbling clay buildings that had been bombed by the Soviets and bombed again by the Americans until the walls that were left looked like they'd been scraped up from the earth. Old bearded men squatted at the side of the road, wrapped in blankets. The air smelled like open sewers.

The driver glanced over at me. "You get used to it," he said.

At each stop, with the photographer snapping away, Lieutenant Jayne and Nila would meet with the grateful doctors, clerics, or orphanage directors who were waiting in the doorways, while the men climbed out of the backs of the trucks and unloaded thirty-three water jugs. The Afghan officials seemed eager to hug everyone from Lieutenant Jayne to the men hauling the water, so there was a lot of hugging and a lot of pictures being taken of the hugging. At one point the photographer, whose name I never found out, made the mistake of suggesting the lieutenant wear a floppy red Santa's cap he'd brought along in his canvas bag, but after that things went pretty smoothly and we didn't see the Santa's cap again. Everywhere we stopped, Legg kept to the fringes of the action with his rifle in hand, staying sharp and mostly silent, although at the third well, when I was on my knees checking a sample for turbidity, I heard him asking Nila about a ring of men that had formed in the square and about the wool-covered domes that were sitting on circles of rock.

"A partridge fight," she explained, and pointed to the domes. "In these they keep the birds." They watched as a short, turbaned man tilted back one of the domes — under the wool was a cage made of sticks. He grabbed the partridge inside by the neck and tossed it into the ring. When the men began shouting and gesturing excitedly, Nila said, "The Taliban hated this. They are betting on the winner."

At the word *betting*, Legg rubbed the crumbs of grit from his face and gave the group a long, wishful look.

Our caravan rumbled for hours through the ruined districts of Balakhet, and took so many turns I lost track of which direction we were headed. On one road, as the windshield wipers cut swaths through the dust, the guard in our truck started twisting in his seat, checking out the windows. "We shouldn't be on this road," he said, shaking his head. A few weeks before, he told us, patrols along here had found caches of ammunition and anti-tank rockets in two of the abandoned buildings. "Honk the horn," he told our driver, and he rolled down the window, pounded on the side of the truck and shouted through the dust for the lead driver to get us off that road. We turned down a street that took us into a busier area with shops and signs painted with Pashto symbols, and after a few minutes he relaxed. The dust settled enough for us to see women in pastel burqas floating along beside the parked cars like ghosts, turbaned men pulling carts humped with sacks, or watching us from alleyways. And teenagers with one arm. I'd heard soldiers talk about this once in the kitchen, about how, a few years ago, children in the desert would see bright-painted butterfly mines scattered from Soviet helicopters and think they'd found a toy. By the end of a day of swaying in my seat, I'd seen enough one-armed teenagers that I no longer paid any attention.

And then there was one more well to treat. It sat on the eastern edge of the city, near the school with the brand-new roof, at the end of a boulevard where the buildings gave way to sand.

By now we were pretty exhausted as we climbed out of the trucks. It was late in the day; the sun sat just above the rooflines of the eroding shops and disintegrating houses. Nila, holding her hijab to keep it from being taken by the wind, motioned toward a blank space in the street. "A hotel was here once, three storeys tall," she said. "Very modern." There was nothing left of it; maybe the foundation was still there, but if so it was hidden by the sand the winds had pulled in from the wasteland that stretched to the mountains. I smiled to show I was interested, but I couldn't really picture the hotel – I was too busy watching the kites.

There were six *gudiparan* fighters, running with their kites across a flat field that nudged against the beginnings of the desert. Each of the men was dressed in a long tunic, called a *chapan*, Nila told me, and billowing pants that fluttered and snapped in the wind. They were battling in pairs of two – green against orange, gold against white, red against blue – and around the field there were thirty or forty spectators, mostly men but a few small children too, who were waving their arms and shouting words I didn't understand.

"Kyle!"

I was by the well with the testing kit and the bag of calcium hypochlorite tablets, and Legg was yelling at me from where he stood with his rifle near the trucks.

"You see that?"

He was pointing at the strings. In the yellow light from the sinking sun, they seemed to be burning. I waved back to show him I saw.

Lieutenant Jayne was standing near Legg with his papers flapping in his hand. "Steady, corporal," he said. "Remember the briefing." Then he shouted over the wind to the men getting out of the trucks. "Everybody stays on the hardpack!"

It didn't take long to figure out the well was like most of the others, drilled probably sixty years ago, maybe more. It had a lever pump on a wood platform raised on old grey bricks a couple of feet off the ground. I pulled my beaker out of the kit and gave the arm of the pump a few strokes to fill it up. Jayne walked toward me and motioned around at the trampled ground. "Stay on the hardpack, all right, Kyle?"

I nodded and set down my beaker. "Lieutenant Jayne?"

"Yeah?"

"You think once I'm done here we could watch the kite fighting for a while?"

"What do you mean, 'a while'?"

"I dunno, a few minutes anyway. Did you see the strings?"

Jayne checked his watch. He sighed. "Ten minutes. That's all." He waved over the corporal who had a radio set on his back and made a call to the camp.

I fiddled around with the testing kit for about a minute. All day I'd been opening the kit and going through the motions of testing water samples, but really the whole testing thing was a lie. Away from camp there wasn't anything I could find in a test that I could do anything about. Poor turbidity wasn't something I could fix, neither was deliberate contamination. All I had was a bunch of calcium hypochlorite tablets, like corrosive mints, and all they could do was kill bacteria. The only tricky part was figuring out how much I needed, but that was something I'd done before we left camp. Because there was no way to flush out the wells, and no way to control how quickly people would start drinking from them, I figured I needed to get the chlorine level as close as possible to 200 parts per million – high enough to do some good, but not high enough to make people sick. And because there was no way to check the precise depth and volume of each of the wells, I'd come up with a formula based on a rough guess of the average.

Basically, with the math done, it meant measuring out half a pound of tablets at each well and dumping them in. And anybody could have done it. I never told Colonel Hister that because if I had he'd never have let me come – and then I never would have seen the kites with Legg, and what came next never would have happened.

When I was finished, I stood up and shielded my eyes from the glare.

"You done?" called Jayne. Most of the men were huddled by the trucks, keeping out of the wind, but Jayne was with Nila off to the side, near the spectators, and one of the kite fighters was kneeling in front of them. Legg was there too; maybe he was supposed to be standing guard. But everybody including Legg seemed to be focused on what the kneeling kite fighter was doing.

"Yeah," I shouted, and Jayne motioned me over.

I walked around the well and made my way across the open field toward Jayne and the others, staying out of the way of a shouting Pashtun with a green kite who ran right in front of me. When I got close to them, I saw they were gathered around a kneeling kite fighter – his name was Chari, according to Nila – who looked to be about forty-five, which I guess is old for Afghanistan. Like most of the other men I'd seen that day, he wore a wool scarf wrapped tight around his head with one end falling loose at his neck and shoulders. On the ground in front of him were two large clay bowls. One was messy with a grey paste that had slopped over its edges, and the other was filled with sparkling grains of glass. He was working on the twine of his pale yellow kite, methodically dipping a length of it in the glue, cleaning off the excess, then burying the sticky string in the glass until it was covered with sharp fragments. Then he draped that length over the ground and worked on the next.

Legg reached over and hit me on the arm. "This is the guy! Look at his hand!" He leaned down and touched the old kite fighter on the shoulder. When he looked up, Legg stuck out his hand with his fingers splayed. "Show him!" he said, pointing to me. "Show him your hand!"

Chari seemed confused and he turned to Nila with a hard look. When she translated he smiled wide, with teeth that were tea-coloured from chewing tobacco, and wiped his right hand on his clothes. Then he turned up the palm for me to see.

His hand looked like it was made of wax, like somebody had spent hours pouring drips from a candle over his palm and fingers, until the hand was completely hidden by hard, criss-crossing ropes and ridges. Chari watched my reaction and he seemed happy, his lined face broke into a grin, and for added effect he leaned over and pressed the palm of his hand into the bowl of ground glass, then lifted it out and showed it around, as if his hand was now made of diamonds.

Shouts were coming from the spectators around us and arms went up, pointing, and I tried to follow and see what they were seeing. There were two fighters on the field, one pulling a red kite and the other an orange, and seconds after I looked up their strings came together and the string of the red kite snapped. Everyone started laughing and spitting tobacco juice into the dirt as the wind carried the kite across the field. Some of the older children raced off to chase it, and some of the younger ones were lifted up onto their fathers' shoulders for a better view. And as I watched, the winning fighter, a younger man whose beard was darker than the others', and who wore the flat, felt *pakul* cap of the mujahideen, approached us with his kite in tow like a flying orange pet, his gloved hand wrapped tight around the string. He didn't appear to be smiling.

Legg nodded toward him. "What's this fucker want?"

"We're done," said Jayne. "We should get going."

But no one moved and as the fighter came close it became clear that he wanted to offer one of the people in our group a chance to hold the string of a conquering *gudiparan*. And as he got very close I realized he was handing it to me.

"No, thanks," I said, shaking my head. "It's okay." But inside my blood was racing because I realized that this was the reason I'd brought us here. I turned and squinted against the sun and the wind, and I pointed at Legg. "I think he wants to try."

Legg's eyes went wide and he looked immediately at Jayne. "Sir? That okay?"

I could see a knot rolling at the turn of the lieutenant's jaw but finally he gave a sharp nod. "For a minute," he said, and held his hand out for Legg's rifle.

Legg passed it over and began to reach out for the string. Before he could touch it the man yanked it back and said some words that sounded like a warning.

"He says the string is sharp," said Nila.

The man shook the leather glove off his right hand, held it out for Legg, and Legg took it. Then he looked down at Chari, still at work on his twine, and he glanced over at me, and he winked. He passed the glove back to the Afghan and grabbed hold of the string with his bare hands.

"Corporal," said Jayne, "you rip your hands up and you're on gate duty until we ship out."

"Yes, sir," said Legg, beaming. He had the string in both hands and he wrapped it carefully around his right. "This part's not too bad," he said. A hundred feet up, the orange kite dove and curled in the wind and Legg had to work hard to keep it under control. He walked with it some ways out, away from our group, but stayed clear of the four fighters on the field.

As he eased out, the wind swirled suddenly and the kite dove as if it might crash. Legg reached up with his left hand to steady it but immediately whipped it away – "Fuck!" – and shook it as if he'd been stung.

"I'm serious," shouted Jayne.

For a second, after he got control again, I dropped my eyes to look at the men in the crowd. They were all lined and worn, like they'd personally been through a century of being fucked around, and they were watching this spectacle – a foreign soldier handling a *gudiparan* – almost greedily, like they were hungry for some kind of comedy relief. So there was a lot of pointing and laughing when Legg showed off the bright stripe of red on his left hand, running from the base of the fingers to the heel.

"That's enough, corporal."

It was getting dark, and part of me started to worry. Even though the look on Legg's face said he'd happily trade a month of gate duty for what was happening, I had this feeling that if things went on too long, what had been good might turn sour. I waved my arm to get his attention.

"Hey, Legg?"

He heaved on the string and made the kite swoop. "Whoa! I'm getting the hang of this fucker. Who wants to bet on me?"

"Legg!"

He turned and looked at me. "What, you wanna try now?"

"No, but—" I didn't bother to finish because Legg wasn't listening. He was leaning back, into the wind, holding the kite steady. Then he started motioning with his thumb, trying to tell the Afghan something. Once it seemed like he'd made the man understand, he slowly walked the kite in.

When he got close, he held his hand out for me to see. "Looka that!" he said, elated. "That mother's gonna scar up!"

"Gate duty," said Jayne. "Count on it."

Legg didn't hear him, or didn't care. He held the string out for me with stiff, struggling arms. "Take it here," he said. "It gets bad higher up." Behind and high above him the gusting wind was making the orange kite spiral like a fish around a lure and I could see what Legg couldn't – that the kite fighter was getting anxious.

I reached out tentatively. I didn't want to take the string, not just because I was worried about getting cut, but because I wanted it all to end right there, with Legg getting what he'd wanted, thanks to me.

But Legg was waiting, insisting, and I didn't want him to think badly about me. So it didn't end when it should have. And I reached out for the glittering string.

I can't describe everything that happened after that. What I mean is, I can't describe everything at once. Maybe that's what happens when you try so hard to fence out stuff that means to get in; it still finds a way, but it comes in pieces, different parts at different times.

So as I sit at my computer and watch the cat, in our house on Breere Crescent, what I remember of what happened is the sound.

I hear the moan of the wind to start with, like a groaning over the field and through the remnants of buildings. And then other sounds, one at a time, join in.

I hear Legg trying to egg me on, to get me to grab hold. "Come on, asshole, don't be a pussy! Put your hands on the fuckin' thing."

I hear my own sharp breath, and then shouts, and Legg –

"Aww, fuck! What didja – shit!"

I hear a roll of laughter and cheers from the crowd, that in my memory sound mocking, even angry.

I hear Lieutenant Jayne shouting. "Corporal, get back here!"

I hear the wind and cheers and laughter swirling up together, then rising and fading as another sound enters – a steady wail, painful, coming from a different direction.

I hear my breathing stop, and the laughter disappear, so that only the wail and the wind are left. And over these sounds I hear the boots on my feet, pounding, pounding across the dirt and sand.

And then that sound stops too; there's only the wail, and the wind, and the hush of blood in my ears.

4

Gerald drove home that night, after his meeting with Sandy, cataloguing for easier reference the various ways he had failed.

He had failed Bishop, by not staying alert to the slippage in market share percentages. It had been there for him to see, like a gargantuan sinkhole opening up in the highway ahead, a great harrowing blackness, and all he'd needed to do was keep his eyes open and not drive the company straight off the crumbling asphalt edge of it. But that was beyond him, apparently.

He had failed his wife, by assuming she was capable of withstanding the lead-weighted, gilt-edged pressures of her world, whatever they were. All an attentive person needed to do was look at her, at the cloud of her face, to know that pressures were on her, nameless and unknowable, and that something should be done to help. But such responsiveness was suddenly a feature of his past, not his present. Now he just went merrily along, attending to trivia, while the woman he'd loved and wedded lay right there in bed beside him being crushed.

And he had failed Kyle most of all. Gerald drove through the tunnelling dusk, watching the street lamps overhead flickering to a kind of greenish half-life, not fully lit, not dead, and he thought of Kyle's eyes. Since he'd arrived home, his son had looked at him with eyes like these street lamps, and whatever had happened in that distant desert place, whatever "off-camp event" had taken his fully lit son and replaced him with a dimmed one, Gerald knew with the faith of the religious that it was no one's fault but his own.

No amount of calling and hectoring could cajole the facts of what Kyle had undergone out of the military or its pillowy layers of bureaucracy. They shrouded the information as if it were poison, or gold. He had found names of some of the high-ups, people in Ottawa, and when they'd resisted him, he had gone higher still. An assistant deputy minister of defence, he was told, was the only person who could help him. An assistant deputy minister of defence became, for Gerald, the peak of the mountain he sought to climb. And when he had finally reached one of these rarefied beings, a woman named Neula Van Wick, she told him he had gone too high, and his call should not have been put through.

VAN WICK: It may be little consolation to you, Mr. Woodlore, but the fact that your call has reached me is going to trigger a serious procedural review.

Gerald had employed language he rarely used to make clear to Ms. Van Wick what little consolation it was. And without insight into the cause of his son's troubles what was left to him was the bare effect, and that alone had taken him far too long to figure out.

The night before, he had come home from work, knocked on Kyle's door, and called to him against the hollow, polished wood as he had every night for a week: "How are you doing in there, son?"

And from behind the door, Kyle had said, "I'm up." And Gerald had been relieved. Because many times over the previous nights, when he'd knocked on Kyle's door and called into his room the same way, his son had replied, "I'm down."

The first few times, Gerald hadn't been overly worried. After enduring a trauma while in the military's faulty care, after coming home with his wrists bound like a felon, of course his son was down. Oberly had also said something about "grieving," and though the man had been mistaken, laughably so, in describing his son's behaviour as "erratic," Gerald was willing to give "grieving" the benefit of the doubt. And so it had made sense, the first night, when Kyle had said he was down. And the second night too. Three nights of being down were not implausible. Four nights, however, were a concern. The fifth and sixth nights, Gerald had begun to wonder what sort of professional he should call. He'd gone to Vicki and asked her opinion but, of course, Vicki had only said, "I'm not sure."

And then, last night, came: "I'm up." And Gerald had nearly punched the door in joy.

"That's good, son," he'd called with his palms pressed against the wood. "That's great!" He'd been so encouraged, he'd done what Kyle had told him never to do: he opened the door without asking. He'd meant only to give his son a hug, a kind of welcome back squeeze. But when he cracked open the door, he saw instantly what Kyle had meant when he'd talked of being "down" and being "up."

He was gambling.

It was there, on his computer screen: StarfishCasino.com. His son was gripping his mouse and clicking . . . clicking . . . clicking the gold "BET MAX" button beneath a virtual slot machine of a suburban luau theme with spinning hams and pineapples and cherry colas.

Gerald had inched farther into the room. "What are you doing there, Kyle?" And his son had simply looked around at him with those half-bright eyes until an electronic bell on his computer went *ding*, and then he turned back to the screen.

Gerald had let that *ding* and that look in his son's eyes roll around in his brain while he scanned the room for other insidious elements. Drugs were on his mind; was Afghanistan not the opium capital of the world? "Now, Kyle," he'd said, keeping his voice low and approaching his own son the way he'd once seen a television trapper come up on a wounded elephant seal. "I notice you're clicking on the Bet Max button there. And I was just wondering how much money – is it real money you're betting, son?"

And his sweet, logical, chemistry-studying son had turned to look at him once more, and this time he spoke.

KYLE: Of course it's real fuckin' money, Dad. Whaddaya think I am, a *pussy?*

And it was after that, when he'd been staring at the back of his son's almond shell hair, trying and rather pathetically failing to make sense of what he'd just heard, that the cat, from somewhere high above, had leapt onto his neck.

Which reminded him, that was another thing he had failed at.

And all of his failures, Gerald told himself as he sped home, were the product of inattention and inaction. He hadn't lost the ability to prevent these disasters from occurring, he'd lost the impetus and the will. Somehow he had become still, as if anxiety alone were initiative, and by becoming so he had opened his house to blights that had no business coming inside. So tonight he was resolved – he was taking back control, and all the avenues for ills would start being closed.

Gerald saw the highway-side doughnut shop that he passed every night approaching on his right, and as if to make concrete the notion of a material change in his character, he decided to not merely watch the doughnut shop go by and *wish* he had stopped for a Honey Glazed or a Cinnamon Strizzle, but to turn onto the exit ramp and go in. The decision came upon him with such force that he began to twist the wheel and change lanes without signalling, which he realized only when the silver minivan lodged in his blind spot blared a protest that went far beyond what was warranted, in Gerald's view.

"Don't sit in someone's blind spot!" he shouted at the mini-van as it passed. It was never satisfying for Gerald to yell at a driver who'd done something stupid; it was a demonstration of impotence, nothing more. But he yelled it out all the same as he squeezed the wheel and made it across two lanes just in time to catch the ramp.

In the doughnut shop, still bristling, he stood third in line behind a stooped grandmother holding the hand of a small pig-tailed girl about four, her hair sown with plastic daisies, and a man Gerald assumed to be a truck driver by his unshaven face, dark-blue work clothes and astonishing obesity. Unlike the grandmother and child, who seemed to be pointing at and discussing the merits of each variety of doughnut displayed on the pull-out shelves behind the counter, the truck driver seemed to know exactly what he wanted, because he spent his time staring out the window and rummaging in his pants.

Gerald had in mind something with icing. He'd always been an icing-doughnut man, much to the chagrin of Vicki, who for as long as he'd known her had considered doughnuts of any kind, and icing-doughnuts in particular, to be gauche. Anything gauche was, to Vicki, a great malevolence. It was why he'd never stopped at the doughnut shop on his way home from work, because he couldn't bear the arm's-length shame, and the thought that he had allowed Vicki's snooty sensibilities to interfere with his enjoyment of icing-doughnuts all this time made Gerald even more infuriated than before.

With no thought for Vicki's apparently fragile state or his contrition over the carriage clock skirmish, he pulled out his cell phone and dialled her number. "Vicki," he said into her voice mail, "I just wanted to let you know that I've stopped at the doughnut shop on the way home from work, and I'm having an icing-doughnut." He made eye contact with one of the women behind the counter and nodded, just to let them know he was coming and looking forward to it. "Probably a chocolate icing one, if they have them, I can't see at the moment. But that's what I'm doing. Really going to enjoy it." He was about to hang up, but added, "If you'd like me to bring one or two home for you, just give me a call on the cell. It's" – he checked his watch – "just after eight."

He folded up the phone and let it slide into the silk sheath of his pants pocket.

The huge truck driver turned and gave Gerald a sheepish look. "My wife and kid are expecting two dozen Boston creams and I can't find my goddamn sticker card."

Gerald smiled.

"You collect the stickers?" said the truck driver.

"No," said Gerald. "But maybe I should."

"It's a good deal. After a dozen dozen you get a dozen free." He was checking his shirt pockets now, rooting around the buttons with parsnip fingers. "Goddamn thing, probably left it on the seat."

"Going a long way, are you?"

The truck driver, reaching for the wallet in his back pocket, frowned up at him, apparently confused.

"I mean" – Gerald motioned out toward the truck parking area – "are you in the middle of a long run?"

The man sniffed, rifling through his bills and receipts. "I look like I run much to you?"

"No," said Gerald. "I mean – sorry. I was just thinking of your truck."

The truck driver knotted his brow. "What truck?"

I am killing myself with assumptions, thought Gerald.

"Hey listen," said the large man, "would you mind saving my place in line? I just gotta go back to the car and see if I left that sticker card on the seat."

"Not at all," said Gerald, happy to help someone he had mentally damned to a life of trucking. "I'll wait here."

The man winked and gave him the thumbs-up. "Be right back."

Gerald watched the man hurry out the door and across the parking lot as fast as his enormity would allow and toyed with the idea of getting a sticker card for his own family. Kyle wouldn't object; he ate just about anything. And the horror on Vicki's face would be priceless.

"Sir?"

Gerald turned to see that the grandmother and child had finally gone, and the counter girl was waiting for him.

"I'm not next," said Gerald. "There's someone in front of me."

A shimmer of bewilderment glided across the girl's face. "But there's no one here," she said.

"He's just gone to his car; he'll be right back."

The girl cast a searching gaze out the window and back at Gerald. "He's gone to his car?"

"He's gone for his sticker card. I'm saving his place in line."

Someone behind Gerald coughed.

"There's people waiting," said the girl, whose orange-and-white paper cap sat square on her head, suggestive of someone who took pride in her work, which Gerald would normally have applauded. She smiled insistently at him and Gerald smiled back.

"He's just going to be a minute." Gerald turned and saw three people in line behind him. "It'll just be a minute," he repeated.

"What are we waiting for?" said a wind-breakered woman at the end.

"Some jerk gone to his car," said a middle-aged farmer-type behind Gerald.

A brokerish-looking man in the middle looked at the ceiling and sighed.

"This is ridiculous," said the woman.

Gerald began to feel hot, and a little damp. He wanted to take off the jacket of his suit but he feared these people would mistake the movement for some sort of capitulation, and he had given the obese man his word.

"He was in line before us," said Gerald, addressing the queue. "He's trying to treat his family. You would want the same courtesy."

"No, I wouldn't," said the farmerish man, who seemed farmerish to Gerald because he was wearing a mesh-back cap. "I wouldn't have fucked off to my car in the first place."

Had none of these people ever tried to do something nice for the people they loved? Could a man not want to bring home doughnuts *and* invest in doughnut treats to come? Was it not something that forgave a two-minute delay? Gerald turned back to the counter girl for no other reason than he needed moral support.

"We don't even do the stickers," said the counter girl. "That's the other place."

Now he understood that he was standing in defence of a lost cause. A false hope. He was a bleeding and beaten tomato can of a prize fighter unwilling to go down, noble to a degree but mostly pathetic and cringe-making.

The broker tapped the farmer on the shoulder. "Just go ahead," he said.

"I should," agreed the older man.

"Do it."

Gerald was about to make a last desperate gesture and block whoever tried to move in front of him, but before he needed to, the obese man reappeared.

"Sorry! Sorry! I'm here!" he wheezed, cramming himself between unmoveable chairs and the people lined up. "Thanks, man," he said to Gerald when he made it to the front.

"Unbelievable," muttered the woman in the windbreaker.

The fat man, out of breath, slapped his sticker card on the counter. "Give me two dozen Boston creams."

Behind the counter, the girl in the paper cap offered a small fixed smile. "That card doesn't work here," she said. "It's for the other place."

For a second, the fat man seemed in shock. "No way," he said. "Really?"

The girl, in response, merely seasoned her smile with pain. "Do you still want the Boston creams?"

Looking up at the signage, as if for help, the man sighed. "Nah," he said, turning. "Forget it."

"Infuckingcredible," said the woman.

At the counter, Gerald reached for his wallet and smiled in a way he hoped was sufficiently apologetic. "One doughnut with chocolate icing, please."

The girl looked blankly at him for a moment. "Sorry," she finally said. "We're out."

For the remainder of his drive home, Gerald blinked against the fatigue of his day and did what he could to revive his debilitated sense of purpose. A few self-righteous cranks lined up for doughnuts were not going to dissuade him from taking the actions he knew needed to be taken. He steered his GS 450 into corners with precision, he accelerated out of them with resolve, he proved to himself over the final twenty minutes of his commute that he was every bit as focused and determined as he'd been when he wrapped up his meeting with Sandy Beale. And by the time he pulled into the driveway at 93 Breere Crescent and pressed the dashboard button to open the two-car garage, he had come nearly all the way back.

He slid his sedan into its slot to the left, well clear of Vicki's Camry (which was as usual parked too close to the middle for comfort) because he didn't trust her in her current state not to open her door into his side. It meant leaving barely enough room on the driver's side to get out, but Gerald willingly put up with a tight squeeze against the poured concrete wall if it meant not having to worry about Vicki.

In the darkened house he set his briefcase on the breakfast nook table and listened for sounds of life. There were none. Kyle was no doubt in his room, betting away the money Gerald and

Vicki had set aside for his tuition, and didn't it strike Gerald now as the purest folly to have given his son access to the account. Gerald hit his forehead with a balled fist for not having thought of that detail before – a whole day of luau-slot losses could have been averted. Well, that would be solved in the morning. First thing. And before then other measures would be taken.

"Vicki?" he called and waited. "Vicki!" he called again.

From some distant part of the house, a soft voice answered. "I'm here, Gerald."

"Where?" he shouted.

"Up here," came the barest reply. It sounded as if it had come from upstairs.

Gerald grabbed his briefcase and swung through the kitchen and centre hallway toward the foyer, paused to drop his brief-case inside the door of his den, then continued up the stairs.

"Vicki," he shouted as he climbed, seizing and pulling on the banister every few steps as if he were hauling fire hose to the scene of a blaze. "I noticed, darling, that once again you parked too close to my space in the garage." On the second level he hesitated outside Kyle's door, listened for a moment and considered going in. But he felt it was only fair to make his wife aware of his intentions before he took any decisive steps.

"Vicki?" he called.

"Up here," she called back, using the same soft voice she had used years ago when she had laid Kyle in his crib and didn't want to wake him.

She was on the third level, probably, Gerald thought, in the turret room, where she sometimes liked to sit and look out over the ravine. "It's really the smallest thing I'm asking for," he continued as he made his way up. "Ten inches more, a foot at the most, is all I need. Then we can both get in and out of our cars with no problem."

He grabbed the baluster near the top of the stairs and pulled himself up the last step. The turret room was at the end of the short hallway, past a small bathroom and a guest bedroom that was never used. Its door was open.

"Vicki?"

"I'm here," she said with a voice low and quiet enough to have suited prayer in church.

He walked down the hall toward her. "Vicki, what are you doing? Why do you sound hypnotized?"

When he arrived at the door of the turret room, he saw exactly what he'd expected: she was sitting in a wingback chair, by the window, in the manner of a woman retreating from the world and into her thoughts. But she wasn't looking out the window, she was staring at something on the floor, next to the door.

"It's kept me here for the last hour," she said, staring.

Gerald looked down, next to his feet. Against the wall, by the brass-plated heating vent, sat Rumsfeld with its tail wavering behind it in the air like the head of a snake.

"I wouldn't make any sudden moves," said Vicki. "Every time I try to get out of this chair it hisses at me."

"Why didn't you warn me?" said Gerald. "I could have brought some sort of weapon."

"I wasn't going to have a conversation with you across three floors."

"Well, we have to get rid of it."

"I know. Get something to shoo it away."

"I mean completely. Out of the house."

She had been leaning with her elbow on the arm of the chair. Now she lowered her head into her hand. "We've talked about this, Gerald. We can't just get rid of the Campeaus' cat."

"Look what it's doing to us!" The cat hissed and Gerald pressed against the door jamb. He dropped his voice to a whisper. "It's causing us incredible amounts of stress."

"Not for me," murmured Vicki. "I haven't had any trouble with it until now."

"Isn't that enough? Look at you! You're being held captive in your own home. How many times does that have to happen?"

"Keep your voice down."

Gerald used a minimal, non-sudden gesture to indicate the floor below. "If you won't think of yourself, think of Kyle. What about him? Have you talked to him? He's in no condition to deal with something like this."

"Kyle hasn't said a word about the cat. I think you're most worried about yourself."

"How dare you!" Gerald found the strain of trying to express his anger and frustration through a whisper hugely taxing. It reminded him of their quarrels years ago in the bathroom, where Vicki had insisted they lock themselves away, whenever little Kyle was awake. "And if I were thinking of myself, which I'm not, I wonder why that would be? I'm only the one constantly under attack."

"Gerald."

"It's not as though I can count on *you* doing anything to help," he croaked. "You had your chance when I was choking to death."

She was rolling her head in her hands. "Do we need to go over this now?"

"I wonder how many husbands can say they were choking to death on an olive, while trying to bring a late-night snack to their wives, and their wives couldn't even administer the Heimlich manoeuvre to save them."

"I said I was sorry!"

"How many choking husbands have had to climb a set of stairs and throw themselves, stomach first, onto the end knob of a railing –"

"It's called a finial."

"– while their wives stood there, worrying about a stain on the carpet?"

Vicki stood up suddenly. "Good work, Gerald."

"I still have the bruise!"

She motioned toward the floor by the heating vent. "It's gone. You've scared it away."

He didn't care about the cat. He was unbuttoning his shirt. "Look at this. Look at this purplish area, right here, under my breastbone." He realized the light was bad. She couldn't see. But he opened his shirt anyway. He spread his shirt the way Superman did, and his bruise from throwing himself on the finial to save his life was his own Superman emblem. "Look!"

She walked by him and out the door.

"This plus my legs!" shouted Gerald. "And this!" He pointed to the scratch on his neck as she continued down the hall. "I'm being killed!" he shouted. "I'm being killed in my own house!"

Recovery came with a generous glass of Youngerton Pinot Noir. Gerald drank it alone, in his den, while Vicki prepared herself for bed. She had left dinner for him on the island in the kitchen, the same dinner she had been delivering to Kyle in his room at around the time he was phoning her about doughnuts. Under the citrine halo of his desk lamp, he spread the cloth napkin across his knees and lifted utensils weighted with lead and his own sufferance. For a while he made an effort to chew through the asparagus spears and slices of lamb leg pasty with congealed fat, but he decided he didn't have the appetite for it. When he laid down his knife and fork, and pushed the plate away, he realized it was the most effective action he had taken all day.

He returned to the kitchen, searched the rack, and found another bottle of the Youngerton. The cork of this one seemed fused to its green glass neck and for a time someone coming into the kitchen would have witnessed Gerald kneeling on the floor with the bottle between his knees, applying the critical leverage. Cork released, he stood in a splay of light from the range hood, listening to the machine-like scouring made by the base of his glass as he swirled it over the island's marble top, and reviewed again, as if worrying a bad tooth, the special futility that had come to define him. In a field of snow, he was the man who huddled naked, without the courage to lift his arms and reach for a coat.

What had he said to Sandy Beale, who'd taken the great risk of approaching a superior with an unquestionably lunatic, but possibly brilliant and salutary, idea? He'd think about it. He'd apply some mental energy to considering it. He'd stand back and assess it, presumably while scratching his dimpled chin. A small purse of the lips, a contemplative nod, a "hmm" – what great decisiveness! What execution of executive power! No wonder Vicki ignored him when he asked her to park in a certain way, or keep the medicine cabinet in a particular order, or please never wash the salad spinach in warm water, only cold. No wonder his son had defied him, to his own great detriment. No wonder his director of sales and marketing had never bothered to inform him of the imminent market share doom. No wonder his puerile bleating in the turret room had fallen on such indifferent ears. He was a weak, ineffectual man. In the feeble glow from the range hood, Gerald took a deep swig of the Youngerton and rued his weakness as it went down.

By the time he was two-thirds of the way through the second bottle, he knew what he needed to do.

He climbed the stairs and moved as noiselessly as possible down the hallway to the door of the master bedroom. Vicki had shut the door, as usual – the nightly event of having to face that barricade and turn the knob in order to enter his own bedroom had always been a small humiliation for Gerald. He'd felt like an exiled citizen submitting to bureaucratic process in order to re-enter the country of his birth.

But not tonight. Tonight he was grateful for any reminder of how marginalized he had become in his own home. It fortified his sense of purpose. When he saw the closed door, he smiled.

Inside the bedroom, the only illumination came from the LED hum of his digital clock radio, the pallor of Breere Crescent's solitary street lamp against the sheer drapes on his wife's side of the bed, and the custardy glow of the night light plugged into the electric shaver outlet of the ensuite. Gerald surveyed the scene and decided it was more than enough.

Vicki lay shrouded in the cadaverous inertia typical of her first few hours of sleep, a coma-like state that had always struck Gerald as creepy, especially in their first few years together, when he would roll over and lay a tender arm across her stomach, and startle awake at the stillness of her breath. He would poke her arm with a stiff finger, or tweak a nipple, and nothing would happen. The thought occurred to him, even then, that she was simply ignoring him. But the thought never stuck because that was back in the days when Gerald truly believed himself to be CEO material, and he couldn't imagine how his wife could sustain such a steadfast indifference toward him. A few times, in the dark, he had made himself hard, climbed on and pressed himself against her, and on one of these occasions her lips had actually parted, so that he thought perhaps, subconsciously, she approved. But the next morning, when he had slipped in a mention of their "shared moment" of the night before as she was sipping coffee, her eyes held him with such fear over her cup that for days his skin crawled at the thought of himself. After that, he did it only once more. And though knowing she would be horrified had made the whole procedure, from beginning to end, intensely exciting, his remorse the next morning had clotted up so thick that he had immediately booked them a three-day Manhattan weekend.

Gerald glanced over at his clock. Around two in the morning was when Vicki began to show signs of life – he had been jabbed awake enough nights to know – and if a noise or a movement was ever likely to rouse her, it was then. But his clock told him it was only 12:33, so he knew he had plenty of time.

He stood at the end of the bed, looked down at the twin crags of her duvet-draped feet, and folded back the duvet's edge. Now the crags were aged cathedral spires hiding beneath protective sheeting of the kind that concealed extensive restoration work, the sandblasting and replastering meant to return great monuments to their former glory. And Gerald, staring at his wife's spires through the veil of six or seven rotund glasses of very fine Pinot Noir, managed to convince himself, at least partly, that he was about to render a similar service to her.

The sheet came untucked in one smooth tug. He left it draped over her feet, against the slight chance that a cool draft could touch the tender ankles and cause her to stir, because he wanted her toes exactly as they were, upright and accessible. There was a spryness to his step, a vivacity, as he made his way across the cabreuva flooring and into the ensuite. And though the nail clippers weren't in the drawer they were supposed to be in, that didn't surprise Gerald in the least. He was used to nothing being as he wanted it to be.

He pressed the door to the ensuite shut and turned on the light, but no amount of rooting in the drawers or in the cabinet behind the mirror could unearth the clippers. There were small zippered makeup bags belonging to Vicki made of the kind of high-tech materials that might once have been vital in aerospace applications and Gerald admired the micro-fibre texture and tensile strength of these bags even as he pawed through the lipsticks and brushes and eye pencil shavings they contained.

When he had exhausted the clipper potential of every drawer and shelf and countertop receptacle in the ensuite, Gerald sat on the edge of the bubble-jet tub and let his mind roam to other options. The clippers were probably at the bottom of one of his wife's umpteen purses, and for a minute he entertained the thought of finding all umpteen and dumping out their contents onto the duvet beside her, and after finding the clippers, filling the bags back up with indiscriminate handfuls of purse effluvia, to see whether she would even notice. But as engaged as he was by this idea, as delightful as he thought it would be to watch his wife reach into one of her bags expecting to find a certain key or card, only to discover that it had by some mysterious force been misplaced – like so, so many of the things to which he tried to attach permanence and order only to have them redistributed by others like a graceful snowdrift attacked by a gas-fuelled blower and turned into flying smithereens – Gerald couldn't accept the image of himself as a purse-rooter. So there had to be some other way.

For the next twenty minutes, his search for an alternative to clippers took him through most of the main and lower levels, rummaging through every household-implements drawer he could think of. It became clear to him that his pleas for Rosary to for God's sake apply some logical order to the implements – to, for instance, centralize the scissors – had had the unintended effect of making the scissors disappear. Somewhere in the house that seemed logical to Rosary, there was a drawer or a box choked with scissors, and he was incapable of finding it. As he made a second pass through the main level of the house, rifling drawers he had already searched, rescattering the spatulas and spoons, Gerald felt sure that he was entering a period in his life of change and flux in which incapacity would be his only constant. Then he thought of the garage.

In the garage, rejoicing.

Amongst the gardening tools, beneath a coil of rubber hose, he found a small pair of red-handled pruning shears, for cutting grapevines and rosebush stems. The curved blades were coated with black grime but he was able to get most of that off at the kitchen sink with dish soap and paper towelling. When the blades were clean he held them up to the range hood light and snipped the air with approval. To make sure they worked, he tried the shears on his own longish thumbnail and found that, if he positioned the nail at the very crux of the curve in the blades, like the tip of a tongue poking through a smile, he could manage a remarkably precise, if short, cut. There was no gap between the blades, as there often was in regular scissors; it was metal on metal, edge against edge, all the way. It seemed plausible to Gerald that, other than actual nail clippers, there existed no better tool for cutting toenails than a pair of pruning shears like these. He snipped the air again and breathed in with a sense of control he hadn't felt in months.

In the bedroom, he knelt at the end of the bed and pulled back the sheet. Against the faint light of the street lamp coming through the drapes, Vicki's toes stood up like short, plump fence posts following the arc of a hill, each crowned by a bit of savagery, like the spiky armaments used to keep pigeons from roosting. He decided to attack the nails of the right foot first, and just to make sure his wife was as deeply asleep as he hoped her to be, he took the middle toe between his thumb and forefinger and wiggled it. She didn't move.

Gerald held the shears against the nail of her pinkie toe, but something about the size and vulnerability of the pinkie, next to the severity of the shears, made him hesitate. Better, he thought, to start on the big toe, and work largest to smallest. He got a firm grip of the big toe, his thumb against the fleshy oval pad, and set the blades of the shears against the nail.

He needed more light. There was no sense in taking chances. He got up and opened the bedroom door just wide enough to let the light from the hallway fall across Vicki's legs, up to her shins. On his way back to the end of the bed, he picked up a chair cushion and placed it on the floor for his knees. Then he went back to work.

His first snip was invisible. He'd been afraid of cutting too deep so he removed the merest sliver, the thickness of a fine pencil line, and even that little took considerable courage. But he realized there was no point to the exercise unless his clipping made some demonstrable difference. He slid the shears down until the blade closest to him was pressed lightly against the soft tip of her toe, where a cut would take off a three-millimetre swath.

That seemed like too much. Being so close to the toe itself meant there was no margin for error, it would be too easy to cut into the quick and then what? Dark images of exactly what flashed through Gerald's mind and he shuddered. He tried to ease the shears up off the skin of the toe, about a millimetre, but he was finding it difficult to keep the blades steady; he had nothing to brace against and his elbows were hovering in mid-air. His pulse was also racing more than he'd expected, which made his hand, and therefore the shears, waver. He needed some kind of purchase.

Gerald forearmed the sweat off his face and tried to calm his breathing. Part of the problem, he realized, was attempting to work over two feet at the same time; one was always going to get in the way. He pulled the sheet and the duvet back farther, lifted up Vicki's right foot by the heel and swung her leg out forty-five degrees.

In this position, she looked like a tightrope walker putting a foot out for balance, which was faintly absurd, and now Gerald found that although he could set his elbows securely on either side of the foot, he was forced into a half-kneeling-on-the-floor, half-lying-on-the-bed position, like someone swinging a leg up to mount a horse, which was far too awkward to manage. He stood up, took Vicki's left foot by the heel, and swung this limb an equal distance away from centre. Now she looked vaguely wanton, her legs spread for him, which caused Gerald his first twinge of guilt. He'd begun by trying to correct a problem that had gotten out of hand, and here he was debasing his unconscious wife! He quickly pulled her right leg back to its original position.

On his knees once again at the foot of the bed, he glanced over at the clock, cursed himself for having wasted so much time, and looked one last time at Vicki's serene face. Then he grabbed hold of the toe, positioned the blades of the shears two millimetres down from the top of the nail, and began to cut.

The nail, he found, was incredibly tough. It was like wood. No, not wood, laminate, the kind used for countertops, made to stand up to the sharpest blades. Whether this was the effect of years of painting the nail with alternating coats of varnish and varnish remover he couldn't know, but quickly what should have been an easy snip became more like gnawing. Gerald began to have his first doubts about the efficacy of the shears. Somewhere in the garage was a sharpener for blades like this and he realized now he should have used it. Trying out the shears on his thumbnail was one thing, but evidently a woman's hardened toenail was something else. By the time he'd made it halfway through the nail of Vicki's big right toe, Gerald was using both hands on the shears.

He paused again to wipe his face and felt the first parasitic tickle of panic. Somehow the great plan of trimming his wife's ten shabby toenails in the middle of the night while she lay naïve and asleep was starting to lose its allure, much as colonialism, thought Gerald, must have struck General Gordon as a bad idea around the time of the fall of Khartoum. He considered abandoning the whole operation, prying the shears from where they were now wedged, dumping them back into the box in the garage, getting into bed beside Vicki and shutting his eyes as tight as he could. Nothing would have been sweeter. But thanks to him the half-cut nail, its sharp flange sticking out like a tusk, had become more of a weapon than ever, and the idea of having to sleep in proximity to something that threatening made Gerald forge on.

With repeated squeezes on the red-handled shears he made incremental progress across the breadth of Vicki's big nail. It had been wrong to attempt the big nail before all the others, he saw that now; it was like trying to climb Everest the first time out. The lesser nails would have given him practice, would have filled in the knowledge gaps. Did you try and land a make-or-break client before you'd learned how to service smaller, less demanding customers? Of course not. What kind of idiot COO let himself get sucked into taking on the big boys before all the systems and processes were honed? Gerald would have pounded himself on the forehead, but he still needed two hands on the shears.

As he girded himself for the last push, the final third, when it should have been getting easier, a shadow fell across the bed, near Vicki's feet, and Gerald saw that opening the bedroom door had let in more than light. On the arm of a stuffed chair that sat near the doorway perched Rumsfeld, its rope-trick tail a twisting silhouette above its head.

"Shoo," whispered Gerald. He lifted one hand off the shears and waved it feebly in the air between them. "Get lost!"

Except for its tail, which never stopped twirling, Rumsfeld didn't move. Gerald couldn't see its face in the dark, couldn't gauge the cat's mood, but he took disdainful as a given. He cal-culated the risk factors and chanced taking his eyes off the cat long enough to give a glance at the digital clock, and he felt his heart freeze at nearly the precise moment Rumsfeld alighted on the edge of the bed. It was 1:52.

"Fuck off," Gerald wheezed.

The cat nestled in a duvet gorge, out of his reach, bullying him with its presence, apparently fascinated by what was going on at the foot of the bed. And what was going on, Gerald could see now, was lunacy, a breach of the bounds of normalcy so clear-cut he briefly considered the possibility that he was ill.

How short it was, he marvelled, how astonishingly straightforward, the path from cohesion to chaos. Gerald took in the dim-lit scene before him – his wife, asleep; her bare foot, exposed; his hands applying gardening shears to her toe – and with clarity of a sort he supposed unique to damned or married men, he knew that his only hope was to finish the nail off in one clean slice. He leaned into the shears with everything he had.

When he recalled the moment later, Gerald was able to picture the slice of Vicki's toenail as it flew. The shape of the arc it followed seemed less parabolic than he might have expected, the path it took to its destination more direct than, say, that of a volleyball lobbed over a net. He was able to picture, too, at the edge of this remembered vision, the head of the cat, Rumsfeld, as it turned and, with eyes able to track the darting movements of small birds, followed the flight of the toenail as it sped toward, and lodged in, the corner of Vicki's sleep-slackened mouth, so that she looked a bit like pictures of that old Hollywood movie star, Edward G. Robinson, sporting a tiny, scythe-shaped cigar.

How he made his body move as quickly as he did is a thing Gerald was never able to fathom. But somehow he managed to spring from where he knelt on the floor toward Vicki's head and at the same time block Rumsfeld's apparent attempt to pounce on and kill the toenail fragment. He flicked the nail from between Vicki's lips in the same motion that he knocked the cat off the bed.

Gerald's momentum, however, sent him shoulder-first into the still mound that was his wife's shrouded torso and, in the midst of the tumult, Vicki came to. "What's happening?" she gasped, her eyes wide and searching in the dark.

"The cat," said Gerald, as he slid the shears under his pillow and kicked the duvet to cover Vicki's bare feet. "Fucking cat was on the bed."

She sat up against her pillows and tried to focus on the cat, which was now bouncing and tumbling on the floor in the light from the hallway.

"What's it playing with?" she asked.

Gerald made his head move side to side. "I don't know."

At 6:45 in the morning, real-world time, Gerald forced himself out of bed so that he could meet with Vicki in the breakfast nook before she left for the Lightenham house.

Downstairs, as he sat in a tannic haze thumbing the serrated edges of the news pages, he watched his wife at the counter. He saw her pour the entire contents of the coffeemaker's utilitarian carafe into a tall porcelain pot decorated with blossoming trees and blue pagodas, then pour coffee from the porcelain pot into his mug and her Wedgwood cup. This was something she had done every morning, so far as he could remember, for the last six or seven years. And whether he was afraid of what the answer might reveal, or the question, he had never been able to ask why.

She took a spoon from the drawer and set it musically in the Wedgwood saucer, then paused at the counter, apparently looking down at her stocking feet.

"I'm worried about Kyle," Gerald said.

She lifted her head and brought the cups to the table. "Just give him time," she said.

With the sharp clarity of guilt, he saw Vicki now more keenly than he could remember seeing her before; he saw the silver hairs threaded into the gold, the softness of her jaw, and the etching around her eyes, like the faint fossil impressions of evergreen needles. It was as if time had been sped up, unannounced, and its effects cruelly focused.

"You're probably not aware," he said, unable to stop staring, "what Kyle has been doing in his room."

"What are you looking at?"

He dropped his gaze to the table. "He's in there gambling, Vicki. On the Internet."

His wife lifted her cup with two hands – her fingernails, he noted, were in reasonable shape – and pushed its fine edge against her lower lip. When she took it away, it had left a piping of moisture between her lips.

"I'm sure," she said, "it's just a way of relieving tension."

"No, it's not. It's a way of creating tension, by losing thousands of dollars."

She smiled serenely. "Kyle would not bet that much money, Gerald. He's not like that. How do you even know he's betting?"

"I saw it, on his computer screen."

The toaster popped, and she rose out of her chair. "I've done two halves," she said. "Do you want one?"

"What is it, one of your poppy seed bagels? No thank you." The little seeds always ended up in his teeth, looking like bits of rot. "We should never have allowed him to have a computer of his own."

"Every student needs a computer, Gerald."

"Now it's in there and he's being corrupted by it."

He heard Vicki, at the counter, sigh.

"We shouldn't have given him his own ensuite, either. He never has to come out of his room! He's like a tenant!" Gerald was aware of flitting waterbug-like from worry to worry. "And you exacerbate the situation by taking him his food. He might as well still be over there, for all we see of him. For all we can help him."

Vicki came back to the table with a plate bearing two buttered bagel halves. She checked her watch as she sat down. "I'm going to need to leave soon."

"What time do you have?"

"It's a little after seven."

"No, what time do you have, on your watch?"

She looked at him with her back straight, her shoulders square, and breathed very deeply. Gerald had a sense of himself being scattered; he was not one waterbug but many, he was rays of light broken up by leafy branches. It came with a physical sensation, a fluttering in the middle of his chest. He needed to focus on a single issue at a time, and the gambling was the biggest concern right now; the computer was the problem.

"We need to get rid of that computer," he said.

She was spreading her bagel halves with raspberry jam. "That's ridiculous."

"I think it's necessary."

"How is he going to study, Gerald? How is he going to write his papers?"

"He's not in school any more, Vicki. He quit school."

She sniffed. "I'm sure he will go back. He's very talented." Her teeth made a careful incision in the bagel's raspberry layer.

"I want you to support me on this. I want you to go up there with me, right now, and be supportive."

Vicki set down the bagel and rubbed her fingertips together over the small china plate, as if salting it with crumbs. "A great deal depends, I think, Gerald, on what you are planning to do."

What he should have done, after he got home last night, was ride his profound sense of purpose right into his son's room. The computer had come inside and, while not dangerous in itself, it was a carrier of danger. Who was there to deal with it but him? He should have seized the computer and pulled it out of the wall, no matter what Kyle's objections.

He looked at Vicki now, working her lower jaw, brushing crumbs from her fingertips to the plate, and he knew that she would not support the removal of the computer unless she saw the danger first-hand.

"All I want to do is talk to him," said Gerald. "Come upstairs with me and let's talk."

She appeared to study him as she chewed. She took a sip from her cup and considered him further. "All you want to do is talk? A proper talk, that is, not yelling."

"At the moment, that's all."

She gave him a small smile. "I would enjoy that."

At Kyle's door, Gerald knocked. "Son? Are you up? It's your mom and I." He waited. "We'd like to come in and chat for a minute." He looked at Vicki to confirm that she was still onside and as ready as he was to confront hard truths. Vicki was adjusting her blouse. "Son?"

From behind the door, they heard the creak of a chair, and Kyle's lazy voice: "It's your fuckin' house."

Gerald shot Vicki a did-you-hear-that? look, and couldn't be sure that she had. "Hear that?" he murmured. "That's very odd."

"Oh, Gerald." She rolled her eyes. "He's a young man. Young men sometimes speak coarsely."

Not Kyle, he wanted to fume at her. Not Kyle. He turned the knob of the door and gingerly pushed it open. As he had expected – as he had explained – Kyle was seated at his computer, and he was clicking the BET MAX button of StarfishCasino.com.

"Kyle?" said Gerald, motioning for Vicki to look at the screen, *look at the screen*. "Here we are, son. Both of us, your mom and I, together."

Kyle turned away from the screen and passed his gaze over Gerald. His eyes shifted to the right, where Vicki should have been, but Gerald could see that he had not opened the door wide enough. He reached in and pushed it farther.

"Hello, darling," said Vicki, as she was revealed.

Gerald began to ease into the room. He tried to catch Vicki's elbow and bring her along, but she lifted her arm up and out of his grasp. A *ding* came from the computer and pulled Kyle back to the screen. "How long have you been going at it there, son? Since you got out of bed? How long have you been up?" He glanced around his son's room for daylight signs of disorder, for typifiers of a pre-dawn struggle between anarchy and reason. But aside from the rumpled bed, it looked the way Kyle's room always had. Nothing had changed on the walls; the black and white picture he had taken of Kyle at age seven, cupping moist garden earth in his hands, still hung between the two leaded-glass windows. The three framed periodic tables still sat over his desk, all of them gifts from Vicki, antiques showing the table's evolution from Mendeleev's version in the 1860s, when the world knew of fewer than seventy elements, and so many perils had yet to be introduced.

"I'm not up, Dad," said Kyle. "I'm down."

Gerald turned and flung his eyebrows at Vicki. *You see?* He said, "Your mother wants to know how you're doing too, son." He prompted her with a jerk of his head.

Vicki smiled at the back of Kyle. "You're doing just fine, aren't you, dear."

He stared incomprehensibly at his wife. Everything, *everything*, was up to him. Outside Kyle's window the ravaging squirrels skittered along stone ledges, looking for tender new wires, and Gerald knew he was the only one who heard. "The thing is, son," he said, "I have some concerns." He laid his hand lightly on Kyle's shoulder. "You seem to be spending a lot of time on that particular site. You seem to be betting a lot of money. Am I right there?"

"You're right, Dad."

Gerald nodded. Over his son's shoulder he watched the hams and pineapples and cherry colas spin. He watched rum bottles and lime wedges line up with coconuts, and nothing good ever came of that. Beyond his general unease over Kyle's betting spree lay a more specific distress: slot machines. Why, he wanted to know, was his son genuflecting before aimless chance? At least a game like poker required some skill, at least it offered a semblance of control. And the father-son opportunities – he could teach Kyle how to calculate pot odds! But his son was in trouble and this was no time to be drawing fine distinctions.

"Where's this money coming from, son?"

"It's coming from my fuckin' bank account, Dad."

Gerald nodded and as he nodded he turned and tried to include Vicki in the envelope of parental concern. Vicki smiled. "Is this your tuition account or some other account?" he said, turning back. "I'm just wondering."

"Gerald." Apparently Vicki had something to contribute. Hurrah. "I don't know whether it matters which account, does it? It's Kyle's money, either way. I'm sure he knows what he wants to do with it."

He took a very long, very deep breath. He found that pressing his lips together while doing so mostly quelled the urge to rave, and as he waited for the sudsy fury that filled the space behind his eyes to subside, he looked again at the periodic tables, framed and mounted over Kyle's desk. On the far right, in a table printed in the 1950s, he could find the metals and gases that used to fascinate his son – Pm for promethium, Am for americium, Np for neptunium and others. He heard, as if it was fresh, the delight in his thirteen-year-old son's voice when he'd detailed the insanities of an age that equated radioactivity with the miracle of sliced bread.

KYLE: You wouldn't believe it, Dad. See the Rn? That's radon. They used to put that in bottled water, 'cause they thought it made you healthy, until everybody who drank it, like, *died*. The Th is thorium. They put that in camera lenses and in those cloth things in camping lanterns, because it made everything brighter. And polonium, that's Po, they used that for anti-static brushes to get the dust off vinyl records. All this stuff can kill you, Dad! And people just treated it like nothing!

And when Gerald had told Kyle that as a boy he had worn a watch with a face that glowed in the night under the blankets of his bed, because it was painted with radium (Ra), his son's mouth had opened and his forehead crinkled with such astonishment at the news that this stupidity had touched his own family, Gerald had felt himself blush.

At the sound of a *ding* he took his hand off Kyle's shoulder and resisted the urge to look back at Vicki. He didn't need her approval to do what was right. "Son," he said, "it's important that you stop this. All right? It's not healthy. It's not wise. And really, I think something else is going on here, something you should probably talk to someone about. If it's me or" – here came his gesture to Vicki, he hoped she appreciated it – "your mom, that's great. But if you want to talk to someone else, someone professional, that's fine too."

"I don't want to talk, Dad."

Gerald nodded; this was a wave he was riding and he was still on the board, it was a bull and he still had the reins. "Okay, I understand. I get that," he said. "You're not ready to talk and no one's rushing you. But this betting is a problem, son. I need you to see that it's a problem. I" – Gerald touched himself on the chest, at his heart, even though his son wasn't looking – "I have a responsibility here, as a parent. So, listen, what if I asked you to stop what you're doing, right now, stop betting all your money away. Would you do that for me?"

"Why don't you ask me, Dad, and find out?"

"I'm asking, Kyle. I'm asking. Please stop betting."

"No."

"But this isn't like you, son. *What's gotten into you?*"

Kyle turned and shrugged, his hand still on the mouse. "I'm just trying my luck, Dad. It's no big fuckin' deal."

Now he looked back at Vicki, for help. But Vicki didn't appear to be listening to what Kyle was saying, she was surveying the room, with her hands on her hips.

"Vicki?" he said. "What do you think?"

She faced him, her eyes sharp. "I think it's not important what I think, Gerald. And as I've told you before it's not important what you think, either. How old is our son? Twenty? Did you know that he lived in Afghanistan? For nine months?"

She seemed to be waiting for an answer. "Yes," he said, helpless.

"He's old enough then to do whatever makes him happy, and our job is to support him." She spread her hands. "This is Kyle's room. You have no business being in here, trying to impose your wishes, and neither do I. Do you see me standing here telling Kyle it's time for new window treatments? I'd like to, Gerald, believe me. But I'm not."

What was left to him? When reason and concern couldn't penetrate, what could he do? Gerald heard scrabbling and looked at the window in time to see a squirrel's black tail brush the glass. He turned back to the computer and stared, not at the images on the screen, but at the physical thing itself, the box through which the images came. The box, he understood suddenly, was not the problem. It was only the venue, the intersection where two problems met. And if he couldn't get through to Kyle, and it wasn't right to impose his will in his son's room . . .

"You win, Vicki." He turned and strode past her to the door.

"Oh, Gerald, it's not about winning."

He was in the hall, heading for their bedroom. The sound of Vicki's footsteps followed him but he didn't care. He reached under his pillow and pulled out the red-handled shears, then headed out of the bedroom past Vicki, toward the stairs.

"What are those?" she said as he went by. "Why were they in our bed?"

His feet drummed down the stairs and took him through the centre hall, into the kitchen and on to the mud room that led to the back porch. Outside, the trees at the edge of the ravine displayed budding leaves of a milky, naïve green, a green unprepared for August, with no concept of October. Gerald headed around the house, to the side where the Linders' shagbark hickory loomed over the fence. He saw Tracey Linder at the edge of her flower garden, clutching her housecoat close as she bent to pick the morning's bagged newspaper out of the recently tilled soil. And when she saw him and waved a greeting, he carved a hello wave in the air above his head as he went straight to the side of his house, where the aluminum ladder lay.

It was an extendable ladder, and it felt light in his hands. He stuck the shears in his back pocket, gripped the base section of the ladder and released the spring-loaded catch, then he slid the extension to its clacketty limit. When it banged to a stop, he hoisted the ladder vertical, leaned it against the wall, and began to climb up.

Mounting a swaying ladder typically gave Gerald pause, typically triggered a flood of plunging-related imagery, but that was when his objectives were mundane – examining the flashing around the chimney, clearing vegetation from the eaves – but this time his objective pushed him through all his misgivings, until he could see his son, still at his computer, through the leaded window. He watched him for a moment, the light of the screen pale on his face. Then he plucked the shears out of his back pocket, reached up and, doing in a second what might have taken the squirrels months, cut the cable to Kyle's room.

5

E dward Caughley swept back his blond wisps of hair, leaned over the display table, and picked up a small tin car. It was about the size of a whisky flask and painted a gas-flame blue. It had a metal key in a slot in its trunk, just above an outside-mounted spare tire the diameter of an old silver dollar. He held it so that its wheels rested on the platform of his hands, and presented it to Vicki.

"This just came in on Tuesday," he said, his voice a reverent murmur. "It's a J. Distler clockwork sports coupe. Circa 1949."

She picked it up and turned it over in her hands out of a sense of courtesy. The morning was ruined – she had planned to spend a good two hours searching all of her Yorkville shops for the crucial elements of the Lightenham boy's room, while Hella worked at the house, supervising the last delivery of furnishings and accents, and beginning the final stage of setting tables and making beds. But after the ridiculous business with Gerald and having to drive him to work, she had been left with time to visit only one of the stores, and so of course she chose her favourite. It was at Caughley Antiques, some years ago, that she had found the set of three stone bisque-headed dolls from Sweden, with their lovely, almost marbleized finish, that were such a popular addition to her young girl's rooms. And it was Edward who had researched Russian samovars for her and found a wonderful silver one with bone handles from the late 1800s, which she often used as a focal point on the William IV mahogany side table (and was in fact having delivered today).

Though he was a slightly tremulous man with long fingers and limp hair that was forever falling into his eyes, Edward Caughley was the dealer she most trusted. He was one of the few who seemed happy to pursue her tastes and not his own, and he was the only one to whom she had confided her method, an act of faith she had never once had cause to regret.

She handed him back the Distler car. "It's charming, Edward. Really very sweet, but I don't think so."

"Too young?"

"Perhaps." She scanned the table of toys. "I'm just not sure."

"That's all right. It's a bit expensive anyway." He replaced the car amongst an array of shiny trains and tin money boxes. Then he clasped his fingers under his chin and gave her a probing look. "What can you tell me about this boy? What are his interests?"

She gave a weak little laugh. "I'm at a bit of a loss, actually."

"Well, let's start with his age. Middle school? Slightly older?"

He was trying so hard, and she was failing him. "Frankly, Edward, I'm struggling with this one, I don't quite know why.

But I guess I was hoping to find some inspiration here. It's happened so often before."

It was a small thing she could do for him, and he seemed delighted.

"You know," he said, touching her arm, "I almost didn't open the shop today – I had a bit of a headache this morning – but now I'm so happy I did. Do you know that no one has . . ." He stopped, with a far-off look, and waved the thought away. "Never mind. Of all the things to talk about." He seemed to have an idea. "Victoria, would you like some tea? I have a pot steeping."

In the back of the store, where the space was cluttered with old wooden filing cabinets, broken-limbed hat stands and dusty stacks of magazines, and where the ancient linoleum was chipped and worn away in a trough, exposing subflooring all the way to the rear door, Vicki sat on the edge of a bentwood chair and sipped too-strong tea from the cup that Edward had given her.

He rolled up a tippy wooden office chair that was missing one of its casters and slid into the low side. "I've been meaning to ask," he said, "how's Kyle? Have you heard from him lately?"

Vicki stared at Edward, not quite comprehending.

"He's in Afghanistan, isn't he? Among the dunes?"

"Oh." She smiled and looked down at her cup. "No, he's home, actually. He flew home last week."

"Well, that year went by quickly, didn't it? I remember you telling me –"

"No," she said. "He came home early."

"Oh, I see."

"There was some problem."

Edward's pale green gaze seemed to search for a place to land. "Well, I'm sorry to hear that." He pushed the hair back from his forehead. "Is he all right?"

Vicki shook her head as she beamed. "Completely," she said. "He's taking some time to think about what he wants to do now that he's home. I expect he'll go back to school."

"Pick up where he left off," said Edward.

"Exactly."

"He's quite the science whiz, isn't he?"

"Oh, yes." She wanted to set her cup down, because the tea was too acidic for her, but there didn't seem to be a handy surface. She began to reach with it toward the shelf of a dilapidated cabinet that held what Edward called his "undecidables," which included a nineteenth-century silver-mounted French violin bow that had belonged to a renowned local prodigy named Stephan Brunett. The odd thing about the bow was that the bow hair had been severed cleanly, as with a pair of scissors, at each end. What made it an undecidable, in Edward's eyes, was that a few months after the bow had come into his possession, Stephan, then a young man in his twenties, had committed suicide by jumping into the path of a subway train. In the view of some collectors, that raised its value, and Edward was disinclined to profit from tragedy, or allow anyone else to.

"Here, I'll take that," he said, reaching out for Vicki's cup.

"Thank you." She rose and smoothed her skirt over her hips. "That was lovely, Edward. A lovely break in a hectic day."

He was hunting for a place to put both cups down and finally cleared a space on his desk with an elbow. "I left the tea steep too long, didn't I?"

"No, no. I just have to get back."

"I'm always doing that." He put a palm to the side of his face. "I get talking with elegant women, you see. And then things like tea just . . ." He filigreed the air with his fingers to show the thoughts escaping his head.

Just now, looking at Edward's shy smile, a boy's smile, Vicki felt a terrible sadness wash over her. "It was very kind of you, Edward. And just what I needed. Thank you."

She turned and began to walk back through the store.

"So it's that gorgeous Lightenham Avenue house you're working on now," he said as he followed.

"That's right." She opened her purse and rummaged for a Kleenex. "The builders want to list it on Saturday, and Avis has a private showing tomorrow, which gives us no time."

"And it's only the one room you're having trouble with?"

"Just that one."

"Well, when you've got some ideas, please call, all right? And I'll do —"

She had turned at the door, just to say goodbye, and the sight of her had stopped him. His hand went to his mouth. "Victoria?"

She swept a thumb under her eyes and chuckled. "I'm being silly. Everything's fine." The heavy iron door latch seemed to be sticking.

His eyes shone with alarm. "Are you sure?"

"I think I'm just feeling a *lot* of pressure to get this house ready." She opened the door and then, with a smile, touched the air between them. "Thank you, Edward. I'll come back as soon as I know what I'm doing."

He held on to the edge of the door with both hands as she left. "I know it's a ridiculous thing to say, but I want you to call me if there's anything I can do."

At the moment the brick steps took her into the sunshine, she turned and lifted a hand.

Where was the box of artificial fruit?

"Hella?" called Vicki. She was in the kitchen of the Lightenham house, well over her little moment in the doorway of Caughley Antiques, and the Peruvian fruit was missing. Hella was outside, on the front steps, having one of her cigarettes, but Vicki was sure she could hear.

"Hella! Hella, sweetheart!" She heard the front door open.

"Sorry?" came Hella's voice.

"The fruit," she called. "Where have you put the box of papier mâché fruit?"

She heard a sigh and the sound of the door closing, and then Hella appeared under the arch between the kitchen and hallway, binding her dark, shoulder-length hair with a thick elastic band. "You're missing what? The fruit?"

"Yes, all of it." Vicki stood at a kitchen island whose marble surface should have been polished and blank, save for a reticulated Worcester basket in white porcelain filled with a bounty of oversized artificial apples and rustic pears, but which was instead laden with four heavy but decidedly fruitless cardboard boxes. "I've looked in every one of these," she said, lifting cardboard flaps at random, "including the one labelled 'fruit,' which I gather is old, and I can't find them anywhere."

"They should be there."

"Yes." Vicki nodded. "They should be." She told herself not to worry, that Margeaux was not one to fuss over a thing like artificial apples and pears handmade by artisans in Arequipa and she could easily send Hella out to buy six pounds of real fruit if it came to that. But the trouble was Avis would be arriving in half an hour expecting the main level to be ready and this was bad timing for a setback.

"Well, I don't know," said Hella.

"Hmm," said Vicki with a nod and a tight pursing of her lips. "What do you think we should do?"

"What do you mean?"

She set her hands on her hips. "Well, only that we're expecting Avis at one, aren't we?"

"I think so."

"Yes. And she's going to want to see how we've set everything up, and if we can't find the fruit, I have nothing to put in the Worcester basket."

Hella stared for a moment at the porcelain basket sitting empty on the counter. Her eyes brightened. "We have that extra set of linen napkins, right? You could put them in there and it could be like a napkin server."

Vicki offered a thin smile, like a gift. "No, I don't think so."

"Why not?" Hella folded her arms and seemed slightly hurt. "I think it's a good idea. It's kind of fun."

Vicki closed her eyes and shook her head as her smile held fast. "It's not a napkin server, Hella, it's meant specifically for fruit. And the point, let's remember, is colour."

"Okay, well . . ." Hella looked off and shrugged. "I don't know what else to suggest."

There were days when Vicki wondered whether Hella really enjoyed her job, days when she found wrinkles in the bedspreads Hella was paid to make smooth, when bathmats failed to line up square to the flooring tiles and now when boxes of artisan fruit disappeared without explanation, and without any sense that Hella understood why it mattered. Vicki took these events as proof that, even when one made the best choices available, things didn't always work out as planned, because when Hella had started with her three years ago, she seemed to have such potential.

"Anyway," said Hella, "I don't know why we're so worried about a bowl of fake fruit when there's a whole bedroom upstairs that's hardly been started."

Vicki dropped her head without a word, then picked up a box filled with Longton Hall china and took it into the dining room, where the drapes and the Matthews series of wood warbler illustrations had been hung (as per Margeaux's affection for northern hemisphere perching birds), but the table and sideboard had yet to be finished.

She began unpacking the plates and stacking them at the head of the dining table, and kept at it when Hella came in.

"I can do that," Hella said, wadding up a handful of packing paper.

"Actually I'd prefer it if you located the papier mâché fruit," said Vicki, her eyes on the plates. "At the moment that's where you could be the most help to me."

"But I looked. I don't know where they are."

Vicki lifted her head. "Exactly where have you looked?"

"Well" – Hella waved an arm behind her – "this whole floor to start with. And some of the boxes upstairs too."

Vicki exerted the great energy to smile. "Then why don't you try looking in the boxes that you haven't checked?"

"There's no point, they're not up there. I think we should just try some –"

"I can't *tell* you what a tremendous help it would *be* to me," stressed Vicki, her jaw as tight as the fist she was butting against the table, "if you would just look *high and low* for the artificial *fruit*."

For a moment Hella, who was already a thin, wiry woman, seemed to become thinner and more wiry. She dropped her eyes to the balled paper in her hands and began pulling at its edges. "There's probably a better use of my time, though, Vicki," she said quietly. "Because I know I'm not going to find them."

Vicki forced the muscles of her neck and jaw to ease, but she still found it necessary to keep her fist pressed against the table. "How do you know, Hella? What are you not telling me about the fruit?"

Hella's chest rose with a deep breath and fell. "I feel really stupid, but" – she looked up – "you know how one of the apples was chipped on the top?"

"Yes, we always put that one at the bottom of the bowl. It's never a problem."

"Well, I was telling my husband about it. He's a wood guy, you know? Refinishes wood? Mostly pine stuff, for cottagers." Hella was making intermittent eye contact with Vicki, but most of the time kept her eyes on the ball of paper, which she was now turning in her hands. "And he said he could probably fix it. And I thought that would be a nice thing to do for you. And then, so, I brought the box home with me, because it was easier than searching through the whole thing at the warehouse. And while it was at home with me, my kids got into it." She paused and looked up, as if to gauge Vicki's state of mind, then continued turning the paper ball. "I was in the basement, doing the laundry, and I don't know where the heck my husband was, but anyway my, well, one of my kids got into the box. You know Jeremy."

Yes, she knew Jeremy. He was Hella's little terror. A product, Vicki suspected, of inappropriate habits during pregnancy, though her other two children had turned out all right.

"And he started throwing the apples and pears around and, see" – Hella looked up again – "we have a dog."

Vicki closed her eyes.

"Normally he's not like that, really. Like, he doesn't wreck things? He's really a good dog? But something got into him. I don't know what, but he just went to town and by the time I came upstairs it was like, wow, crunchy bits of fake fruit everywhere."

Hella stopped for a moment, and in the silence, Vicki thought she could hear the shush of a car outside, driving too quickly down Lightenham Avenue. The new owners of this house, whoever they turned out to be, would probably not like that very much, though Robert and Margeaux were the kind of people able to tune out that sort of thing.

"I see," said Vicki.

Hella stared down at the ball of paper, her angular face taking on the wide-eyed look of someone reliving a bad memory. "For a while I was really worried, you know, that maybe he'd eaten a lot of it, because that wouldn't be good for him, all that glue and varnish. I was going to take him to the vet, but –"

"Actually," said Vicki, "it's fairly edible." She could feel herself giving Hella a reassuring smile, though the muscles of her face seemed to be functioning without her having to be very much involved. "It's really just flour paste and paper, and the type of varnish most of these artisans use isn't poisonous once it's dry. I'm sure your dog will be fine."

"Yeah, that's what my husband said."

"Well there, you see?" Vicki looked down and discovered a pretty Longton Hall dinner plate in her hands, its delicate bouquet garni pattern seeming quite pale against the creamy background. She wondered for a moment whether this pattern, so faint and frail, was really the sort of which Margeaux would approve. It was possible, thought Vicki, that she had made a terrible mistake, and with Avis arriving in twenty minutes, it was one she had no time to repair.

"Anyway," said Hella. "I'm really sorry. I thought I was doing something nice, and it turned out really shitty. And I'm really, really sorry."

"Yes," said Vicki.

"Are you upset?"

It was clear she had to make the best of things with the china, she had to move on because it was too late, and there was nothing to be done. She set down the plate in her hands and reached into the box for another. "There should be a set of side plates to go with these," she said to Hella. "And a sauceboat. Do you think you could find them for me?"

Hella reached back and lobbed her paper ball through the doorway toward the sink in the kitchen, and seemed chagrined when she missed the mark. Then she turned and faced Vicki with her arms crossed. "Do you want me to, you know, repay you for the fruit or anything? I don't know how much they cost, but I could. I could pay you back in, like, instalments. If you wanted."

Vicki shook her head. "No, Hella. These things happen. I've lost a number of fragile items over the years and it's always unfortunate, but you can't dwell on it." She unwrapped a plate and folded the paper into a tight package. "Now listen," she said, looking into Hella's eyes and gripping the paper hard, "let's try to work very quickly over the next twenty minutes, so that we have the downstairs as ready as possible when Avis arrives. All right?"

Hella sighed as she checked the band in her hair and then sang out an "Okay" that suggested she was far from convinced. "What'll we put in the bowl in the kitchen?"

Vicki reached across the table and handed Hella the wedge of folded paper. "Why don't I leave that up to you?"

At five minutes after one, Avis trilled a sweet "Halloo" when she opened the door. She had slipped off her shoes and was setting them beside Vicki's blue pumps when Vicki entered the foyer from the library.

"Have you seen what they're doing to that beautiful Georgian on the corner?" she asked, stretching to her full height to meet Vicki as Vicki leaned down to kiss her on the cheek.

"You're warm," said Vicki as she straightened.

"Oh" – Avis fluttered a hand – "there's something wrong with the air conditioning and Peter refuses to lift a finger about it and I've been in the car since about nine this morning. Anyway I'm furious. You know the one I'm talking about?"

"Where they've added an addition and covered the whole west side with stucco?"

"Can you believe that?" Avis's fury sounded like the caroling of meadowlarks. She pulled the silk scarf from around her neck and pushed it fiercely through the handles of her purse. "I sold that house two years ago, and three years before that. It was simply gorgeous. The stone work! And now they've really made it a dog's business."

"It's a shame."

"It's a shock. I hate what's become of that whole end of the street, all those stucco additions spreading like disease."

"They finished the one on the corner about two months ago."

"Well, I hadn't noticed. I hardly ever come up that way." She was pressing the hair at her temples into place. "Anyway, dear, let's see what you've been up to!"

She stepped forward into the circular foyer and Vicki felt her heart quicken as Avis passed her eyes over the flanking oyster-veneered mirrors, up to the Viennese chandelier with glass pendants, and down to the fresh flowers exploding from a coppery Pilkington's vase set on an enormous tripod table with a piecrust top.

"I'm never disappointed," Avis said, "to see that table in one of my houses."

Vicki smiled.

"Cherry, isn't it?"

"Walnut," said Vicki.

"But I don't think you've ever used it with that particular vase before."

Vicki crinkled her eyes, because she had.

"Well, whether you have or not," said Avis, "it's lovely. And the flowers."

As she continued her tour of the main level, Avis seemed pleased, even delighted, by nearly everything Vicki had done. In the grand living room, she cooed over Vicki's juxtaposition of swooping Regency curves against straight-backed Edwardian rigour, appreciated her medley of silk cushions and admired each of the topiaries she had placed in majolica jardinières. In the library, she paused for a moment when she spied the thin, tapered legs of what Vicki thought of as Robert Lightenham's Carlton House desk, before pronouncing the desk – and Vicki's arrangement of a bound leather journal, a blue-and-gold Sèvres inkstand and several loose tea-coloured papers featuring her own impersonation of a man's dashed handwriting – "inspired."

She approved of the kitchen counter arrangements, which included a set of buttery glazed Savoie pottery jugs under the window and a Victorian syrup dispenser in the corner, and said not a disapproving word as she passed by Hella's concoction of dried flowers in the porcelain Worcester basket.

In the dining room, she seemed to hesitate over the George III drop-leaf table, and bent down to peer closely at one of the

Longton Hall plates. It was then that Vicki had an urge to admit
to Avis that these particular plates were not ideal, that in fact she
would probably change them before the weekend, to bring in
something more appropriate (though of course she would not
say "appropriate for Margeaux"). But before she could say a
word, Avis straightened and proceeded to purse her mouth and
lift her eyebrows in a way that suggested she was calculating the
outcome of an intricate equation. And she said, "The couple I'm
bringing tomorrow – he's in tire manufacturing, and she's on a
huge number of committees – and of course I've been to their
home for dinner many times . . . unless I'm mistaken" – she bent
down again to examine the plate's pattern – "I think they have a
set with this exact design."

When she straightened again, she squinted an eye at Vicki.
"There are times, Victoria, when I think you're either a genius
or some kind of clairvoyant."

Vicki brought a hand to her forehead and touched the soft
place where her brow met the bridge of her nose. "Actually,
Avis, I was thinking of replacing those tomorrow, possibly with
a Chelsea set, or something a little more . . ." She waved her
fingers in the air.

"Vivacious?"

"That's a good word."

Avis shook her head. "Don't – these people are not the
slightest bit vivacious."

"Oh."

"They are grim and disheartened people, quite frankly. It
takes everything I have to get through dinner with them." Avis
tilted her head toward Vicki. "Just between us."

"Of course."

Avis, lost in thought, shuddered at some memory.

Vicki clasped her elbows as though she was cold. "Do you think, Avis, they would be happy here?"

The agent surveyed the room and inhaled as though she were standing in a field, savouring the perfume of mown hay, and when she looked at Vicki she gave a wry little tilt to her head and showed her palms to indicate their generalized surroundings. "I think they will give every appearance of being happy."

Vicki smiled to signal that she understood and moved away from the table to the window. From here only a stretch of ground and a tall cedar hedge could be seen. She let her hand fall against a drapery panel of clay-red damask and felt at her fingertips the small imperfections in the weave that gave the fabric texture, that made it seductive.

"I just don't know why," she said, almost to herself, "you would want to bring people like that here."

Avis's phone twittered in her purse. "Excuse me one moment." She plucked it out, looked at the caller, and placed it against her ear. "Avis!" she barked. "No, that's ridiculous and I'm in a meeting." She closed the phone. "I'm sorry, darling?"

Vicki's face was to the window. "This is a happy house," she said. She turned back to the agent, who was showing the beginnings of a frown and seemed to be leaning over to one side. "Doesn't it feel happy to you?"

"I'm not following you, Victoria."

It seemed to Vicki almost as if the drapery panel were electrified; she could not let go. She felt the damask crunching in her hand. "I work so hard," she said.

"Of course you do."

She knew that it was wrong to give Avis trouble over the sorts of clients – the "clee-on-tell" – she cultivated. Their personalities, their behaviours, weren't really in her control. But this house, Vicki thought, this home she had made, was meant for joyful, contented people. Unhappiness had no place here.

"What are their names?" she asked, still facing the window.

"Who?"

"The grim, disheartened people you want to bring here."

Avis cleared her throat precisely. "I shouldn't have said that, Victoria. It was unkind. I hope you won't repeat it." She opened her purse and began to shuffle through its contents.

Vicki held tight to the damask as she faced out the window. "It wouldn't even occur to me," she said. She wished she could see trees from here. She wished Margeaux had not been so stubborn about the light.

"Victoria," said Avis behind her, "I still have some time. Would it be possible to see the upstairs?"

Though she could not place when it had happened, the discomfort under her ribs that she hadn't felt for several days had returned, a constriction that made it difficult to breathe. She felt the ridges in the damask weave chafing under her fingers. "But who are they?"

She heard Avis sigh. "Mildred and Alan Webb."

Vicki repeated the names silently and thought for a moment, trying to attach faces and facts to the blank substructure of "Mildred and Alan Webb." She turned partway toward Avis. "Aren't they quite old?"

"Late sixties, more or less."

"She has very hard features." Vicki searched her memory. "I can't picture him, but I've seen her somewhere. I remember her face looked grey and set, like a plaster cast." She tried to imagine Mildred Webb's plaster face smiling to put guests at ease, Mildred Webb staring at her plaster face in the mirror of the Empire dressing table, with the light streaming unwanted through the bedroom windows behind her.

Avis took her hand out of her purse; she seemed to be breathing more calmly. "You don't see him I expect because he spends his evenings holed up in his den, so far as I know. Kept company by big-shouldered bottles of gin. Well, of course it's been very hard for them, but I think Mildred is functioning rather remarkably. At least she puts herself out there and gets involved. You have to admire that, even if it gets a bit morbid, all the frenetic activity." Avis looked around the dining room. "Anyway, I think they *could* be happy here. They still have lots of visitors, children with grandchildren, people who care about them. The main thing is for them to get out of the house they're in now."

"Why?"

Avis blinked, as if startled by Vicki's innocence. "Because of their daughter, the one they adopted."

Gripping the damask as if she might otherwise sink, Vicki shook her head.

"She was a bit of a hellion, as I understand it. Gave them a lot of trouble. And I don't know the whole story but one night she brought someone home with her, and he was a bad sort — I gather there were drugs involved — and she wound up dead. Really very tragic." Avis snapped her purse shut. "So. Shall we go upstairs?"

As she stood at the window, feeling the speculative warmth of April sunshine on her skin, Vicki began to see things in a way that perhaps she hadn't before. There were fresh colours and details in her awareness, and the discomfort under her ribs eased a little, as if it were being pushed aside by the arrival of a new acceptance of what she must do. She had always known that happiness was the product of wise choices, something a person, or a family, built and shaped from within. She saw now that once it existed, once it was alive, it needed to be protected. In that way, she saw, happiness was like a fire, fuelled by diligence and hope. She saw that unhappiness came from outside, like rain.

She loosened her fingers and released the damask curtain, then tried to pull the panel smooth where her grip had left creases in the fabric.

Avis lifted a hand and pointed. "I think that may need the touch of an iron." She turned and rounded the dining table on her way to the arc of stairs. "Just a quick peek at the bedrooms and then I'm off."

"They're not finished yet, Avis."

The agent hesitated, and blinked. "It's Thursday." For a moment this fact seemed sufficiently weighty to Avis that it was possible she might say nothing more. Then, for extra heft, she added, "I'm bringing the Webbs tomorrow."

Vicki left the window and started through the dining room toward the foyer. "There's still one room I need time with."

Avis was frowning as she whipped the scarf from the handles of her purse. "Houses this expensive don't have streams of potential buyers, which I know you appreciate."

"I do."

She arrayed the scarf in a haphazard tumble around her neck and gripped the clasp of her purse as Vicki passed silently across the guilloche tiling on the way to the front door. "Tomorrow is when I'm bringing the Webbs," repeated Avis. "They have been expecting to come that particular day. Mildred made space in her schedule."

"What time?"

"Two," she said, her face full of concern. "That was the opening she gave me. It was two and nothing else. It doesn't matter to Alan, he's like the last buffalo roaming the plains, but Mildred has a schedule. Aren't you afraid, Victoria, that you might be cutting it rather fine?"

The door, as it opened, produced the suckling sound of air-tight seals temporarily letting go, which Vicki always found one of the great comforts of a new home.

"It has to be right," she said, standing aside to give Avis room to leave.

Avis was again shuffling through her purse. When she seemed to find what she was after, she lifted her head and turned as if her intent was to enter the small bathroom tucked away to the right of the stairs. Then she shook her head at an unspoken thought and murmured, "I have water in the car."

Near the entrance way she wedged her stocking feet into her shoes, then faced Vicki at the door.

"Two, tomorrow," said Vicki, smiling.

"*Two*," emphasized Avis. She stepped out into the sunshine and turned to face Vicki as if she had one more thing to say. Then something pulled her gaze downward. "You still have Hella working for you?" she said.

"Yes."

Avis directed a finger at the ground. "There's a cigarette butt."

Vicki, standing on the threshold with her thoughts cast forward to a more distant hour, didn't watch Avis bend to pick the cigarette up. But she heard her gasp and saw the new distress on her face when she straightened. Wordlessly, Avis placed the flattened butt in Vicki's hand. Then, her mouth set at a tormented skew, she reached into her purse, pulled out a narrow leather folder, flipped its plastic pages and produced a tan card.

"My pedicurist," she rasped, suddenly hoarse. "Do you never look down?"

6

In his office, Gerald dialled extensions one by one. It was extraordinary –

"Trick? Hi. Like to meet with you in the boardroom in about ten minutes. Bring your market percentage projections. Yup."

– it was extraordinary how invigorated he felt after taking decisive action with Kyle. One snip of a cable, and suddenly anything –

"Sandy? I want you to come to this meeting with Trick. Bring all your papers from our talk last night. That's right."

– suddenly anything seemed possible. He tried not to think of all the times in his life he'd worried himself into paralysis in the face of a challenge, because today he was making things happen.

"Hi, Doug. I want you in on a meeting in the boardroom at nine-thirty. We'll probably get into budgets a bit, so bring all your numbers. Thanks."

One snip of a cable. And Kyle hadn't even flinched. That was surprising. Gerald had half expected an explosion of pent-up something – anger or grief or whatever had gotten stuck inside him over there, before the military had washed its hands of him. Part of Gerald, while he was climbing up the ladder, had fervently hoped for it. But it hadn't happened, and he chose to believe his son had not been indifferent but rather had measured the fatherly resolve Gerald was discharging like sparks and understood it was game over! and nothing could be done. Regardless, the best result was not that he'd put an end to the betting spree, but that he'd prodded his son out of his chair, out of his room, and into the light. Kyle had walked down to the back porch while Gerald was putting the ladder away. He was still there when Gerald returned, eating half a bagel trowelled with cream cheese that Vicki had evidently given him. And instead of blasting anger or noise at Gerald, his son had simply held out his hand.

KYLE: Good work on cutting the cable, Dad. But now I need to borrow your car.

Under the circumstances, having taken his Internet away, and being pleased to see him breathing outdoor air for the first time in a week, it had seemed petty to quiz Kyle over what he planned to do with the car. Though in hindsight, after he'd handed over the keys, while he was sitting in the passenger seat of Vicki's Camry as she grudgingly drove him to work, Gerald had suffered through a pang of doubt so strong it made him see colours.

But that was momentary. That was behind him. Now he was back on the determined track and rustling up a strategy session of potentially company-shaking proportions. As he thought about who else to include, Gerald's finger hesitated over his phone's grey-gumdrop buttons. In a situation like this protocol dictated that he call Bishop, but Bishop was sinking deeper into his Susan fog. Just minutes ago, Gerald had glanced out his window and discovered his boss standing at the edge of the grass that stretched from the main Spent building to the ditch next to the Service Road, looking as lost as if he'd forgotten where he'd parked his car.

He punched in Phil Barbuda's number. "Phil, it's Gerald. Sorry for the late notice. I'm getting a meeting together in the boardroom at nine-thirty and it'd be good to have finance there. . . . Great."

At 9:35 in the main boardroom, as he waited for the last of his invited attendees (Trick Runiman) to arrive, Gerald stared at Bishop's empty chair and imagined himself being purged.

This was his great career-related fear. Often, when he sat with the business pages in the breakfast nook at home, he wasn't reading whole stories, he was focusing on one word: purged. Someone had been purged. Someone would be purged. There were rumours of purgings to come. It happened every time a CEO was fired. Gerald read the stories as he ate his breakfast and imagined the new board-appointed chief executive spreading around sweet jammy gibberish about getting to know the current team before making any snap decisions, about relying on the current team's expertise to persevere through the challenging times ahead, when everyone knew the current team was as gone as fuzzy milk, and the most gone of all, the dead body most dead, was the second-in-command, the CEO's right hand man, no matter what cinnamony claptrap was being sprinkled. Gerald saw in Bishop's empty chair intimations of performance reviews and emergency board meetings, he saw the founder of Spent Materials, its heart and soul, being ousted and publicly shamed, thrown from a figurative roof, sucked down a figurative drain, and he saw the inevitable news item to follow, the insignificant inch of type on the business section's third or fourth page, he saw the words in his head – *Reports surfaced yesterday that Spent Materials' Gerald Woodlore would be purged* – and he smelled toast.

"Sorry. Sorry I'm late."

The arrival of Trick Runiman, flushed and carrying a laptop that trailed its cord along the floor, offered Gerald the chance to refocus. Everyone was here: Doug Allsop in tie and short sleeves, setting up a series of pens, points aligned, on the table in front of him; Sandy at the end of the table, near the projector, clasping the leading edge of her notebook as if it buoyed her; Phil Barbuda, slumped in the chair opposite Sandy, drumming the edge of the table in a jouncey hip-hoppish rhythm; and now Trick, looking for a place to plug in his laptop.

Trick pointed to Phil Barbuda. "Can I sit there?"

"Why?" said Phil, continuing to drum.

"There's an outlet behind you."

Phil lifted his right hand off the table – but maintained the beat of the left – as he bent around to look for the outlet.

"There's one over here," offered Doug, from the other side of the table.

"This one's closer to the chair though," said Trick. "My cord isn't very long."

Sandy seemed to examine the leather grain of her notebook and shook her head almost imperceptibly.

"Those things work off batteries you know," said Phil, drumming.

"I know. I didn't —"

"Thought maybe you didn't know that."

"Yeah, thanks," said Trick. "I forgot to plug it in last night, that's all."

Gerald cleared his throat pointedly. "Can we get started? Phil, can you stop that? Trick, can you find a place to sit? Thank you all very much for coming."

He stood up and walked to the front of the room. The projector screen was lowered into position and he tugged on it to make it roll up and out of the way to reveal the large whiteboard mounted on the wall behind it. When he turned around Trick Runiman was still standing.

"Trick, please."

"But . . ." Trick extended a hand to indicate Phil's continuing illegal occupation of the outlet-handy chair. Then, sighing loudly, he bent down to plug his cord into the outlet, and made his way to the seat at the centreline of the table.

"Okay, thanks everyone. I know this was short notice. But something's come up and I thought we should all be here to discuss it."

Doug Allsop, cleaning his glasses, gave a small wave to catch Gerald's attention. "Where's Bishop?"

"This is preliminary," said Gerald. "It's too soon to involve

Bishop. As soon as we have a sense of direction, then of course I'll be taking it to him for approval."

"See?" Trick held his laptop at table height but an arm's length away from the edge. "The cord doesn't reach."

Sandy raised a hand and showed Gerald a surplus of teeth. "Did you want me to say anything?"

"Not yet."

In the midst of bending over to set his laptop on the floor, Trick suddenly surfaced and looked over at Sandy. "Why would you be saying anything?"

Sandy managed to smile broadly, shrug innocently and avert her eyes toward Gerald in a single, balletic motion.

Beside her, Doug swivelled left and right in his chair, surveying the cabinet acreage along the wall, then exchanged glances with Phil Barbuda and mouthed the words "No doughnuts."

"Can I get everyone looking up here? Trick?"

"Sorry," called Trick, once again below the table, "this is how I have to work now."

"Well, I'll let you know when I need your data, all right?"

"Sure." Trick sat up, red-faced from the pressure of being doubled over, and set his eyes on Sandy.

Gerald found a blue marker along the whiteboard's ledge and picked it up. "Now, can I say, first of all, that what I'm going to talk about here is not meant to reflect negatively on any one person, either in this room or outside of it."

"Uh, oh," said Phil, giving the sides of his chair a foreboding thumpa-thump.

"I have been made aware of something pretty shocking – shocking to me, anyway. It's the fact that Spent Materials, in terms of its window-screen market share, is now at its lowest point ever, in its history." He paused to make sure he had everyone's attention. When he focused on his sales and marketing director, Trick hesitated, then startled into life.

"Did you want . . .?" He made a move toward his laptop.

"No. I think what you're going to tell us, Trick, is that our market share percentage is around three something."

Trick was caught halfway between the table and his laptop. "Close, I mean, if I could look here I could tell you exactly, but once our Q-three spending kicks in, it should be up near four. But let me just —"

"What I'd like to know," said Gerald, "is what our share is at this moment. Do you have that?"

"I'll see," called Trick, his voice sounding squeezed. Bent over and tapping away on the floor, he appeared to be tying his shoes. When he straightened, his chest heaved. "Whew! Hard to breathe like that." Then he turned his chair back to the table. "Sorry, that number must be in another file."

Sandy gave a short, specific cough.

"Well, it doesn't matter because I already know the number," said Gerald. "It's two point five."

There were no audible gasps from either Doug or Phil, the only two people in the room who should have been surprised. Each of them, looking at Gerald, appeared unfazed. Gerald turned and wrote the number 2.5 on the whiteboard behind him. He tapped it with the marker.

"Am I the only one who's astounded by that number?"

Around the boardroom table, faces moved. Doug regarded

Phil and Trick. Phil looked at Trick and Doug. Trick focused exclusively on Sandy. Sandy kept her eyes to the front.

"Phil," said Gerald. "Did you know we were at two point five?"

Phil placed his hands on the armrests of his chair, and pushed himself into a fully upright position.

"Yes."

"What about you, Doug?"

Doug appeared to suppress a burp. "I had an idea."

It seemed to Gerald the only solid thing in his life, the only thing he could count on, was the blue whiteboard marker in his hand. At least Sandy had come to him with the truth; where had the rest of them been when the company that kept them alive was sliding into the crapper? Where had *he* been? And where was the loyalty to Bishop? In the fist that hung at his side, next to his pants pocket, Gerald squeezed the blue marker as if he could choke answers out of it. And he reached for the granite strength of will he'd showed just a few hours before, in the face of the forces overwhelming his son. It was a cable of apathy that had them all in its grip, and he was going to frigging well cut it.

"Here's what I think," said Gerald. "I think this company's headed for trouble. *Big* trouble. Okay? I think that because we make window screens and furnace filters a lot of you" – he looked at the men – "have the idea we don't need to be creative and energized and strategic. And that's the kind of attitude that's made us eleventh out of eleven. Or let's make that eleventh out of ten. Because we're now actually *behind* a company that's out of business." He reached and tapped the number on the board with his marker. "Two point five. I don't know about you" – he looked at the men – "but to me that's obscene. And we should all be disgusted with ourselves."

He searched for signs that Phil, Doug, and Trick were adequately disgusted. Each of the men was looking into a middle zone of nothingness somewhere above the table, which could have been read as either dawning shame or insensate lethargy. Gerald, reaching for optimism, chose shame. In contrast, by the oddly flat set of her mouth and the way her eyes seemed to be bulging, Sandy appeared to be wrestling mano-a-mano with a writhing gator of mirth. Well, that was fine, thought Gerald, because as the one Spent employee with a fresh idea in her head, she'd earned a moment of self-regard.

"So," he continued, "what are we going to do about it? What are our options? I guess one, the one we seem to like around here, is to do nothing and let Spent Materials, the company that feeds our families, and Bishop Spent, the man who gave all of us our jobs, just slide into oblivion like a cardboard box you toss into the recycling bin."

"Mr. Woodlore?" chirped Sandy, pushing her chair back from the table's edge. "Gerald? Do you think this might be a good time for me to come up?" She edged her chair one anticipatory inch farther.

Gerald shook his head as a frowning Trick raised his hand halfway in the air.

"Yes, Trick?"

"Why is Sandy asking if it's time to go up?"

"You'll find out in a minute."

"Well" – he looked hurt – "she's *my* assistant."

"I was wondering the same thing," said Doug. He looked over at Phil. "Weren't you?"

Phil, dab-dabbling the table with an oscillating thumb and fourth finger, nodded to the beat. "Uh-huh."

Gerald breathed noisily to convey his irritation. He'd planned a whole lot more chastising about the systemic infection of inertia at Spent before getting to Sandy's idea. He'd also planned to do the presenting himself, while giving Sandy full credit, because he had more presenting experience than she did and knew exactly how to use her idea to spark a productive brainstorming session. On the other hand, he understood that delegating – the Prime Instrument for Executive Success ("PIES") according to every leadership training workshop he'd attended – was something he needed to work on. And he recognized that meetings were living things, that they couldn't always be contained and controlled, and that thanks to Sandy's over-eagerness his grip on this one was slipping. So he decided, just this once, to take his hands right off the leash.

"Sandy," he said, "why don't you come on up here. Now people" – she was already at his side – "I want to preface what Sandy has to say by telling you that we have put ourselves in a position, all right?, where we have to consider the unusual, we have to be prepared to take a bold step outside our comfort zone and take a chance. So now, let Sandy give her presentation, and then we'll get into some discussion. And keep in mind that I'd like to come out of this meeting, at the end, with some kind of action plan." He turned to Sandy and offered what he hoped was an encouraging smile. "Okay, Sandy?"

Sandy, it was quickly apparent, had no need of his smile. She swept her eyes from Gerald to the men seated around the table and opened her folder like wings. "People," she said, "get ready to have your worlds rocked."

It was at 10:13 a.m., by Gerald's watch, when Sandy lost the group. There'd been a few moments, while she was talking about uncontrolled incursions of potentially deadly viruses and bacteria riding into homes on the backs of Algerian dust particles like suicide bombers ploughing through unarmed checkpoints, when she seemed to have them in thrall. There'd even been a glimmer of admiration in Trick Runiman's otherwise hooded-with-suspicion eyes. But the window filter idea itself met with incredulous squinting all around. And when Doug Allsop averred that it might be a tad harder than perhaps Sandy realized to convince residential building contractors and housing material resellers to stock up on a lot of washable furnace filters repurposed to function as view-blocking window screens — and Sandy responded by grabbing her throat and making wet gagging noises to suggest their lack of courage — it became obvious to Gerald that he needed to step in.

He lifted a hand. "Let's hold off on making any quick judgments."

"If you don't have those contractors and resellers onside," warned Doug, "then you're pissing up a dead tree."

"Thank you," said Sandy. "Great universal metaphor."

"I'm *telling* you."

"What I wanna know," said Trick, "is when she had the time to put all this together when she was supposed to be working for me." He spread his hands imploringly. "Like, was she doing this when we were supposed to be making trade show calls?"

"I did it after hours," said Sandy. "I stayed late. Do I have any witnesses? Uh, *no*."

"What's that mean?" said Doug. "No one else works late?"

Phil Barbuda fired a quick drum roll and jabbed a finger at Doug. "That's it."

"I stay late sometimes," Doug insisted. "When it's necessary."

"So do I," said Trick.

Sandy shuffled her papers and sniffed. "Not since I've been here."

"I think," said Gerald, "we may be losing the thread."

Trick thrust out an arm and pointed to a symbolic region in space. "I take work *home*."

"Can we get back to the idea?" pleaded Gerald. "Sandy's at least trying to make a contribution."

"Thank you," said Sandy, offering him a solemn smile.

"I'll *show* you," grunted Trick, who was now bent over, clicking on the floor. "Here! Look at the modification times on all these newsletter files. Like twenty of them. Look at this, eight-seventeen p.m."

"That's fine, Trick."

"Ten-forty-one."

"Phil, did you –"

"Some of these I wrote in *bed*."

"We believe you," said Doug. "Everybody here works hard."

Trick sat up red-faced, gasping for air. "Anyone wants to look, it's right there."

Phil brought his hands down flat on the table. "I'm willing to talk money issues whenever you want."

"Yes!" exclaimed Gerald. "Please, Phil, what are the money issues?"

Phil turned his palms over. "We have no money."

"I'm sorry?"

"No money to speak of. We have debt. We have *a lot* of debt. And we have assets. But something like this, new product development, needs cash, of which we have none."

Doug shook his head as though greatly saddened. "Well, that sounds pretty final to me."

"No," said Gerald, "we can reallocate money. When Phil says we have no cash, he means we have no cash reserves. It doesn't mean we can't push money around."

"Not mine," said Doug. "Bishop told me my budget was untouchable."

"Our R&D money's already tied up in maintenance over-ages," added Phil.

"My department's barely scraping by as it is," said Trick.

At the front of the room, Sandy pressed her hands to her ears. "Everybody's just protecting their turf here. No one's talking about the actual idea!"

"We're being polite," said Trick.

"Oh?"

"Opaque window screens?" He made a face of distaste. "I don't think so."

"Trans*lucent* window *filters*."

Trick shaped a newspaper ad in the air. "'Block Out the Sun with Spent Window Filters.' Oh yeah, *that's* a grabber."

"'Stock Up on Building Materials No One Will Buy,'" offered Doug.

"Try 'Keep Your Family Safe' or 'Guard Your Family's Health.'" Sandy threw up her hands. "I mean, I could be just as negative as you if I wanted to be. How about 'Let Every Invasive, Deadly, Evil Particle Known to Science into Your Home with Spent Window Screens,' or 'Spent Window Screens – the Next Best Thing to Doing Nothing.' Or, hey, 'Want Your Family to Get Sick? Get Spent.'"

"Okay, Sandy." Gerald knew he had to grab hold of the meeting before it rolled away, beyond his reach, but he was battling waves of disappointment. He'd wanted keenly to believe that a daring business idea could invigorate a static mindset, that risk could spur real change, that a bolt of innovation could trigger creative aftershocks that would wipe out the impediments to industry, in the fundamental sense of that word – energy, diligence, devotion!

And he'd wanted to prove he could lead, that with a light touch he could steer a company clear of the black waters, the way a chief executive was supposed to.

But he was starting to think it wasn't that easy. Or maybe not easy for him. He'd been willing to try delegating. He'd been willing to hope for the best. But he had the sense now that allowing Sandy to present her window filters idea had made the task of getting people onside and focused a whole lot tougher. And so, when Gerald rose from his chair, he was triply angry, at the inability of a daring idea to engender yet more daring, at the failure of the delegating approach, which he'd never had any faith in no matter what the workshops said, and at himself, for having faint-hearted instincts that twittered when they should have shouted, and for leaving himself bereft of anything remotely like a Plan B.

"You know," he said, walking slowly to the front of the room, "I'm hearing a lot of unconstructive whining and ass-covering going on here and I'm a little sick of it." He picked up the blue whiteboard marker and circled the 2.5 he'd drawn. "This is the problem." The misgivings shouting at him now, he decided, were too late to do him any good. "This member of our team" – he pointed his marker at Sandy – "has tried to solve the problem by contributing a bold, imaginative idea. And because none of you has offered an even slightly better one, this is what we're going to do."

Gerald wrote *Window Filters* on the whiteboard, then he underlined it, twice, and turned. "This is our new product initiative."

Trick raised an index finger. "Yeah, but shouldn't –"

"Tomorrow afternoon," continued Gerald, "I want all of you to come in equipped with some serious, constructive thoughts on design and production, on sales and marketing, on customer support and anything else you can think of, so that we can shape and implement Sandy's idea."

Sandy's hand shot up like a flare. "Gerald, do you want them to report to me?"

He tossed the marker onto the whiteboard ledge. "No," he said. "I'll be directing this."

7

There were other places, closer to home, that I could have gone. But I didn't care about convenience; I didn't care about saving time or money or gas. Niagara Falls was the place that I thought of as soon as the image on the screen seized up and the clicks stopped getting through, and so I just went with it. I was adapting to circumstances, you know? Being equa-mouse.

As I drove along the QEW, around the toe of the lake, I hit the scan button on Dad's radio and just let it run the dial. After the third or fourth pass through all the six-second fragments, it was obvious that all the stations were playing garbage, nothing you could really listen to. I mean, unlike Dad, I can't get all caught up in talk and traffic reports and weather. So I turned off the radio and gave in to the music in my head. Sometimes in camp you could hear songs coming from the tent with the Kurdish workers. You could hear flutes and drums that rose and fell like wind sliding over the dunes. A couple of times during the water run in Balakhet I heard music that was similar coming from the mud-wall buildings. So I just let that run in my head while I drove, and it made me think of other things.

"You playing or what?"

It was my first night of cards with Legg and his buddies: the big warrant officer named Tanner, the sergeant Joe Leunette, and another corporal they called "Wedge," maybe for the shape of his chin, although Legg didn't seem to know him as well as the others. It was ten or so at night and we were sitting around an end table under the hanging fluorescents of the Camp Laverne kitchen, me beside Leunette, Tanner and Legg across from us, and Wedge on the end, dealing.

Tanner had already folded his cards and Wedge was staring at Legg, who was leaning forward onto the back of his turned-around chair, the curved edges digging into his chest. "I said, you playing?"

Legg frowned up at him. "Whaddaya mean am I fuckin' playin'? That's my money already in there. You raised, I fuckin' called."

"You haven't even looked at your hole cards."

"What the fucksit matter to you if I look at my cards? It's not gonna change 'em. They're still gonna beat your fuckin' shit."

"So you're in."

"I'm in, I'm in! Let's play!"

Wedge turned to me. "What about you?"

All I had was a pair of sevens — one turned up and one in the hole — but it was early and we were just playing for quarters. And to be honest, I'd never played a lot of poker. "I call."

Wedge lifted his eyebrow at me. "You sure about that?"

"Yup."

Wedge seemed unhappy. He waited for Leunette, who'd bet first with two nines showing. Leunette folded.

"You guys keep bulldozing right over my fifty cents," said Leunette. "Like to see a little more respect for your elders."

"Okay," said Wedge. "Last card down." He dealt cards to Legg, me and himself, and gave his new hole card a look. Then he glanced around the table. "My pair of sixes bet. I check."

Legg flicked in two quarters from his pile.

"You still haven't looked," said Wedge.

"Are you gonna fuckin' hound me all night?"

It was my turn next and I called.

Wedge smiled. "Looks like both you fairies have fallen into my web." He tossed two dollars into the pot. "Raise a buck fifty."

"Limit's a buck," said Leunette.

"You're not playing."

"Still a buck."

"Just take 'em back, asshole," said Legg, and he slid two quarters out of the pot toward Wedge. Then he looked at his hole cards, shrugged and tossed them into the discard pile.

"Finally," muttered Wedge.

I started to reach for my quarters.

"Hoo hoo," said Tanner, rubbing his hands. "Action's heating up."

"Watch it – what's your name, Kyle?" said Wedge. "I'd be careful."

"Why?"

Wedge seemed to think this was funny. "Why? I just checked and raised. That's not telling you something?"

About a dozen stupid responses to that question came into my mind, but I was surrounded by guys I didn't know that well, and I was playing a game I'd only ever played with my cousins, so I decided to keep my mouth shut for once. I looked at my cards again and at the pair of sixes showing in front of Wedge, then I tossed in a dollar to call and showed my pair of sevens.

"Fuckin' hell!" Wedge whipped his cards across the table.

"All he had were the sixes," giggled Tanner.

"Yeah," said Legg. "We got that."

Wedge glared at me. "What the fuck were you doin' calling a check-raise with a pair of sevens?"

"I dunno." I shrugged. "Winning?"

"No way. No *way* you should've called that with sevens. You keep playing like that you're gonna lose a lot of fuckin' money."

I scraped up the quarters from the pot and glanced around to try and figure out where everybody else stood on this whole calling-with-sevens issue. The face I really wanted to read was Legg's, but he was resting his chin on his arms folded in front of him, and he had his eyes on Wedge.

When it was his turn to deal, Legg swept up the cards and started shuffling with a loony kind of grin.

"Okay ladies, we're playin' Butcher Boy."

Sergeant Leunette leaned back in his chair in disgust. "I hate this game."

"Ah, shut up."

"There's no skill, it's a luck game," he said. "You watch, Kyle." He waited until Legg started to deal the cards, face up.

"See? There's no hole cards; everybody sees what everybody's got. And when a card gets dealt that somebody else has, like you get a ten, say, and I already have a ten, the card goes to me."

"Then we bet," said Tanner.

"First hand with four of a kind wins and splits with the low hand. All you're doing is betting on probabilities."

Legg followed each round of cards he dealt with a fist on the table. "Good fuckin' game," he said. "Like slots. Closest thing to pure chance in the fuckin' desert."

Wedge straightened his cards in front of him and muttered, "Says the guy who turns his back on the ghosts."

"What the fuck you care." Legg slapped the table. "That's my queen. Fifty cents."

"Ghosts?" I said. Quarters were flying into the pot from all sides, so I tossed some in too.

Legg kept dealing. "Ghosts is what the Soviets called the Pashtos."

"You take too many chances, that's all. It's risky for everybody. You can't trust those militia assholes."

Tanner opened a pack of gum. "They're okay around here, most of 'em. If they look like they might be trouble I just give 'em cigars."

"What'd we find in that basement yesterday," said Wedge to the sergeant, "like six thousand rounds?"

"Close."

"And some 107s, and a bunch of grenade launchers."

"Most of that shit's old."

"But a lot of it's from these militia fuckers spreading stuff out to their friends in the jihad who are just waiting for somebody wearing CADPAT to cross their eyes at them and then it's 'God is great!' Boom!" Wedge pounded the table. "Hey, kid, wake up! Are you betting or what?"

I looked at my cards; the betting patterns were so irregular I had no idea what I was supposed to be doing. Legg wasn't giving me any clues; all his focus was on Wedge. So I took a guess and slid in two quarters.

"It's up to seventy-five," barked Wedge. "Fuck, stay with us or get out of the hand."

"Lay off," said Leunette.

"I'm telling you," said Wedge. "They're just squatting there, waiting for some excuse."

Legg went back to firing cards around the table.

"Ace! That's mine," said Tanner.

"If you were them," said Wedge, "wouldn't you be?" He watched Tanner reach over to the pile of cards in front of him and take up the ace of diamonds, then he plucked at the sleeve of Tanner's fatigues. "I swear, they see these colours, we're like a splinter under their fingernail or something. American, Canadian, I don't think it matters." He nodded at Tanner. "You think they like you because you hand out cigars?"

"No," said Tanner, smacking on his gum. "'Cause I give 'em Cubans. They *love* me."

"They smile to your face. What are they saying behind your back?"

Legg leered and sniggered. "'There's that dumb mother-fucker hands out Cubans for *free*.'"

The sergeant was shaking his head. "Most folks around here – I mean besides the ones whipped up by that Mullah Dashti character – they're devoted to their families." He examined his cards. "The main trouble is these people have been through too much . . . all the wars, they're practically in shock. Some look at me as if I'm going to open fire on them. That can complicate things. Kyle?"

I was lost. "Yeah?"

"Bet's to you, son."

"Sorry." I shoved in three quarters.

"What," said Wedge. "Are you raising?"

"No."

"Bet's fifty cents then, it's a new round. *Jesus.*" He picked a quarter from the centre and pitched it across the table. It stung me on the cheekbone.

Before I could react, or even understand what was happening, I saw Legg move. When I look back on those months at Camp Laverne, it seems to me Legg was always doing that, flashing through my vision, pushed by something I never fully understood. That time, I watched him jump out of his seat, grab the top of Wedge's chair, and tip it backward – "Hey! Fuck off!" – then drag the chair clear of the table. While Wedge was caterwauling and struggling to get out, and Tanner and Leunette were hooting at the table, Legg steered the chair on its back legs like a wheelbarrow across the floor and spilled the corporal over the threshold into the hot dirt outside.

When Legg came back in, alone, he didn't look at me. Just climbed onto his chair, restacked his quarters, and muttered, "Not playing with anybody whose aim is that fuckin' bad."

It was almost lunchtime, the sun making a rainbow arc in the crests of mist from the Falls, when I pulled into the old casino's parking lot. I didn't have any particular plan, other than to keep doing what I'd been doing, because it seemed to be working fine. But I was hungry – that was one thing that never changed – so after I parked Dad's car at the far edge of the lot and made my way around all the fenders and hoods, and past two police cars that were sitting under the canopy of the building's entrance, my first stop was the Market buffet.

In the big all-you-can-eat room, I loaded up on fresh-made pasta with oyster mushrooms and stood at the roast beef table as a thick-chested chef who looked a bit like Tanner carved off glossy slices of prime rib. There were lots of tables empty so I carried my plate over to a spot near the food display tables, ate what I had, and went back for more. Most of the people in the restaurant were aging couples in pastel sweaters; they hovered nervously by the heaped-up serving bowls as if they weren't sure they were entitled to all the choices laid out for them, like there might be some mistake. Besides the old people, there were four young guys about my age seated behind me at a corner table. They had buzzed hair and they were wearing long, industrial-league hockey sweaters, and when I got up to get another helping I could see them filling their faces and laughing while they eyed the room.

Eating in that big space, surrounded by strangers, reminded me a lot of eating in the kitchen tent at Camp Laverne. When I was finished, I picked up my plate and turned left without thinking, the way I'd done after every meal for nine months, and for a second it was confusing not to see the dirty dishes counter where we were supposed to scrape off the scraps and leave our plates to be washed. It was strange not to see soldiers hunched over the tables, and sunlight forcing its way in through dusty windows. But then I snapped to, and sat back down hoping for a waitress so I could pay my bill.

She finally came and took the money – never looking at me, looking over my shoulder the whole time – and when I got up to leave I saw one of the hockey sweater guys standing in the aisle, next to the dessert station. He wasn't holding a plate, which was weird. I had to go past him to get out, and when I tried, Hockey Sweater Guy leaned a shoulder into my path.

"Hey, kid," he whispered, looking into my eyes. "You got anything?"

I didn't know what he was talking about, so I said, "No" and shook my head and tried to keep going. But Hockey Sweater Guy got in my way.

"Come on, you got *something*, man. I *know* it." Hockey Sweater Guy seemed all fired up and eager, as if he was pretty sure something good was coming to him right there beside the black forest cake in the all-you-can-eat buffet.

"I'm sorry," I said, feeling equa-mouse. "Are you one of the unfortunate deaf?"

Slowly Hockey Sweater Guy's antsy fervour dissipated, replaced first by confusion and then hostility. I seemed to be ruining his day.

"Are you messing with me, man?" He nudged my shoulder with the heel of his hand. "I asked you a question." He nudged me again. "What's this fucking bullshit?"

I tilted my head to the side. Just a few feet away, near the bean salads, two older people held salad plates piled with greens and dotted with croutons. They were watching us, concerned. Way off in the distance, I could hear the jangly sound of the slot machines I'd come to play.

I shook my head. "Sorry, I misheard you. I didn't realize you wanted me to identify your bullshit."

Hockey Sweater Guy narrowed his eyes. He looked over at his friends in the corner and back at me.

"I'll do my best," I said. "Do you have the bullshit on you?"

Hockey Sweater Guy scowled and shoved me again in the shoulder. "What the fuck you talking about?"

Another time maybe I would've explained about my sense of humour, but I could tell he wasn't in a receptive mood. And there was a security guard eyeing us from the front of the restaurant. I nodded for Hockey Sweater Guy to look. "Probably we should do this later," I said. "Maybe I'll see you."

His eyes were like pins and he punched my shoulder one last time as he left. "Count on it, fuckhead."

In the casino, by the slot machines, I felt jazzy. It was partly the light. It was like being sunk in champagne bubbles; all these scattered rays reflected off a zillion shiny surfaces kept fizzing into my eyes. But mostly it was the sound, shushing and howling around me like I was deep in an electronic jungle, the air filled with the cries of techno toucans, battery-powered acajous, and mechanized screech monkeys. I found an ATM, pulled money out of it, and sat down at a slot machine next to a fake waterfall. I almost felt happy. Then I started feeding the bills into the machine's mouth and let the numbness of losing begin.

Gradually the sound faded away, and what I thought of first was the cold. I remembered how it seemed crazy to me that a desert world could be so wintry. When Legg had woken me early that morning and I'd tumbled outside, what had struck me, besides the embarrassment of keeping the military waiting, was the slap of ice in the air, the pills of frost on the canvas that covered the trucks, the clouds the men breathed.

Despite the cold, the dust still kicked up off the truck tires. It blew into the cabs through the spaces between the window frames and glass, and up through the vents that sucked and heated the air from outside so that as I bounced on the vinyl seat, I had to pull my undershirt up and over my nose to breathe. The rifleman sitting in the seat beside me turned his head and hacked into the crook of his arm. "Jesus, eh? Like to know whose bent idea this was." I just grimaced and rolled my eyes, and he went back to looking out the window.

Every stop at every building and well until the end was a torture of nerves, an opportunity for delay; the kite fighters could be gone by the time we arrived. Why did I have to suggest treating five wells? Why not four, or three? Why twelve water deliveries? Why any deliveries at all? None of it mattered anyway, it was all just camouflage. There was only one stop that counted.

As we approached the final well, I glimpsed the kites through the gaps between buildings and felt a surge of relief. I wondered whether Legg, in the truck behind, had seen them too. Even if he hadn't, I figured he'd know we were getting close to the kite field from the landmarks we passed – an empty lot turned into a graveyard for rusted orange and white minivans; one solid building topped with a satellite dish painted black, red, and green for the restored Afghan flag; a bombed-out mosque, nothing standing but its gold minaret. If he was really doing his job, though, he wouldn't be thinking about the kites at all: the D&S guys had been briefed on Operation Slaked Thirst along with everybody else, but they'd had their own briefing too, about Mullah Takhar Dashti, who'd been released from ISAF custody and was already whipping up animosities against foreign forces in the country. So Legg would've been keeping his eyes on alleys and doorways; he wouldn't even have been looking at the sky.

At the slot machine, I pulled the lever until my arm burned; after that I just pushed the button. And I thought about the moment we arrived:

Our three trucks pulled up to the edge of the trampled field, and as we climbed down onto the scrub grass and dirt, thirty or forty turbaned men wrapped in patou blankets watched us while the small boys at their feet, or clinging to their necks, cheered on the *gudiparan*. I wanted to see the kites with burning strings, and the look on Legg's face when he saw them too, but Nila the language assistant had to show me the hotel that wasn't there.

I went to the well and faked testing the water, held my breath against the chlorine sting, and poured half a pound of calcium hypochlorite tablets from the bag. Then they called me to the edge of the field, to see the man with the scar-tissue hand, and I

left the kit and the bag at the side of the well, rounded the platform of bricks, and rushed over.

It was amazing, the waxy hand, and the look on Legg's face
too – his awe at the tangible proof, that you could live a lifetime
of "whatever."

Then the *gudiparan* fighter came over.

"What's this fucker want?"

"We're done. We should get going."

But we didn't leave. Because of me. We could've done what
Jayne said and gotten out of there. But I had to care about something, I had this thing I had to make happen.

"I think Legg wants to try."

His face always comes back to me, the way his eyes opened
up as he looked over at Jayne. This was the one thing he couldn't
help but want.

"That mother's gonna scar up!"

"Gate duty. Count on it."

Except Legg wasn't satisfied; he wanted me to try. He pulled
the kite against the wind, held the glass-covered string, made me
reach out my hand.

"Come on, asshole! Don't be a pussy!"

In the casino, at my slot machine by the waterfall, something
momentous was taking shape, the reward for hours of work.
Whooping sirens, clanging bells, and clattering coins – I could
hear it all around me, the inescapable clamour of winning. But
if there were flashing lights I didn't see them; my fragmented
memory was feeding me the visuals.

I reached out for the string Legg held, with the anxious
gudiparan fighter watching. I closed my hand around it as Legg

let go, and I felt the glass shards cut. And because it hurt, I flinched, and that was all it took. The wind lifted the prized kite away before the fighter, or Legg, could grab it.

Both of them scrambled after the string while I stood dumb and the spectators shook contemptuous fists. Then something made their expressions change and their faces turn, and I followed their stares.

The sirens whooped, the coins poured down. I was a winner! Big winner here!

On the far side of the well, there was a man, kneeling. I caught a glimpse of his face and I began to run across the dirt and sand. It wasn't until I rounded the well that I saw.

A little boy. Two years old, or three, his head in his father's hands. A little boy with fat cheeks who'd wandered to the well, who'd seen the tablets that looked like mints. He'd wanted just one, and he didn't care about the smell; in Balakhet, even strange candy was precious. So just one, into his small mouth. And the tissues of a kid's throat swell so fast.

But the coins didn't stop coming. And the bells wouldn't stop ringing. Because here was a jackpot winner!

I could see the father, his face broken in two, making a sound I couldn't hear. And because I couldn't stop the images, and I couldn't turn away, I saw his dark eyes open, and the recognition in his face of who and what I was. I saw him set his little boy down and rise up, to take the neck of his son's killer in his hands.

And then, from somewhere hidden, almost quicker than I could see, came Legg, not knowing why I was being strangled by the Pashtun, only that I needed help. He exploded into view and brought the man down, before anyone could stop him or explain.

One other thing I remembered seeing – it was slid toward me across a table – was the press release the military issued two days after the "off-camp event." I think they meant it as a comfort to me, that's the only thing I can figure. All it said was that Corporal Marc Sebastien Leggado, rifleman, had been shot in the midst of an Afghani riot, and investigations were still underway. There was no mention made of the little boy I had killed, or that I had been there at all.

At the casino, I was taken under the wing of a jolly woman with chestnut hair and a casino name badge, who would not let me leave the coins where they were.

"You're the day's big jackpot winner!" she exclaimed. "You are a *very lucky man!*"

She hoisted a walkie-talkie to her mouth and pressed the talk button. "Hassan? Yah, gonna need some help at number fourteen-ought-three. It's a nice one."

At the cashier's counter she stood at my side, scraping the tip of her finger with a thumbnail, as the teller counted out my winnings. "Glad to see a young person win for a change," she said, seeming genuinely pleased. "So often it's some blue-haired, nicotine-stained old biddy who wouldn't know what to do with the money if it bit her. 'Cept smoke it. Oh, there you go!"

The teller had pushed a stack of bills toward the window. "Eighteen thousand, four hundred and twenty-six dollars."

"I don't want it," I said.

The chestnut-haired woman, whose name badge said Jo-Anne, put a firm hand on my arm and looked straight into my eyes. "It's the shock," she said. "It's a wild thing, winning at the slots. Almost crazy. You think you haven't earned this money. You don't deserve it. Maybe there's some mistake." She looked at me like she was trying to go deeper with her eyes. "It's a natural reaction, hon. But I saw you — you were at that machine a long time. Since before I came on shift. So you darn well earned it."

"Sir?" The teller was trying to get my attention.

Jo-Anne looked down. "Oh, you have to sign the receipt."

"I don't want the money."

"No, but you have to sign the receipt." She patted the piece of paper being pushed under the glass. "That shows we fulfilled our obligations. Everything has to be clean and legal. You don't want us to get in trouble." She pointed a silver fingernail at the line. "Right here, dear."

I took the pen being slid under the glass and signed the paper.

"Now," said Jo-Anne, "since you've signed that paper, you have to take the money."

Why couldn't they hear me? "I don't *want* it."

"Understood, hon. However, the law states that once you sign that paper, that's your money. And we have a responsibility as a respected gaming establishment to protect you and your money as long as you're on the casino premises. So we can't leave this lying around." She took the stack of bills off the counter and slapped them into my right hand. "There you go, young sir. Your hard-earned winnings." She patted me on the shoulder and winked. "Go and buy your mother something nice."

I walked in the direction I was pointed, across the casino floor, between the rows of slots, past the crowded restaurants and T-shirt shops, carrying the money like a rock I meant to hurl through plate glass. It was dark when I made it outside but that didn't surprise me; my legs felt heavy with blood from sitting, and my head was fuzzy from not having eaten since lunch. I stood at the entrance under a blanket of bulbs, as people came and went around me, and I tried to think of what to do.

"Car, sir?"

A black limousine had pulled up to the curb in front of me, and a uniformed driver held open the door. I shook my head and began walking to the parking lot, and as I did the driver called after me, "You might want to put that away."

I considered going to the edge of the Falls and dumping the money over the railing; there was a pleasant symmetry in the idea of water sucking away whatever prosperity I had. For a while I thought about releasing the money, bill by bill, into the evening breeze. But halfway to where I'd parked my dad's car, I knew what I was going to do.

At the quiet edge of the lot, Hockey Sweater Guy was leaning against a fence with his friends. They were nudging each other like boats tied to a pier. As I tacked a diagonal course through the parallels of cars, I sensed them becoming aware of me, and by the time I left the last pool of light, they were moving.

Their jabbering sounded like carny noise as they rolled closer, along the fence; ahead I could see the outline of Dad's GS 450. There was a chance I could have made it inside and locked the door before they reached me, and if that's what I'd intended I would have felt for my keys. Instead, when there was just the space of an open lane between me and the car, I stopped and turned toward them.

"Hey, fuckhead," Hockey Sweater Guy called. "That's right, motherfucker. You and me, we got unfinished business." He laughed in a jagged way that made the others join in. "I told my boys about you, man. All about you, motherfucker. How you were fuckin' with me? 'member that? 'member that? Yeah, you do, asshole. Now we're gonna teach you respect."

I felt no urge to run as they bullied toward me. When they were two car lengths away and one of them pointed to my hand, what I did was tighten my grip.

"Ooo-hoo, what's that?" Hockey Sweater Guy crouched as he came, the fingers of his hands reaching out like he was approaching a toddler with a shell on the beach. "What's that you got, motherfucker? You been holding out on me?" I waited as he came in low with a grin, waited still as he rose with a fist. I heard him say one more word – "Jackpot" – and then he came down on me like a wave.

As I lay on the pavement, while they pummelled and stomped, I put everything I had into my hand. I made them use their heavy boots to crush the knuckles and fingers, made them use the sharp edges of their heels. Because this time, I told myself, I wasn't going to flinch. I wasn't going to let myself care.

THREE

1

"That's a stop sign coming up, Bish. Right there, straight ahead."

Bishop, behind the wheel, was lost somewhere deep. Already this morning, since picking up Gerald at the house, he'd missed a crucial left turn, overestimated to a fair degree the duration of two yellow lights, and failed to make his Lincoln Town Car straddle or evade any number of potholes. Even the Lincoln's bathwater ride could no longer keep Gerald from tensing up at the sight of the slightest depression in the road ahead. But right now he'd have traded for a good-sized pothole and been thankful for it.

"See the sign? Coming up in two secs."

Gerald had been put in the position of getting a lift from Bishop because Kyle had called late the night before saying he was tired and didn't think he should drive home. And Gerald, resisting the powerful urge to quiz his son on where the hell he was and what the hell he was doing, told him that sounded wise. Then this morning Vicki had driven off without a word before he woke up. Now, having missed the first exit off the highway, he and Bishop were being forced to double back through regions of industrial parkland Gerald had never seen before. It was all god-forsaken, treeless, and drained of any breath of life, a lot like the affordably leased acreage Spent Materials called home. There was only one benefit to industrial parkland that Gerald could see as he pressed back, rigid, into his glove-leather seat, and that was the complete absence of foliage that might obscure the presence of cars travelling along perpendicular roadways one was *about to cross without stopping —*

"Son of a bitch." He tried to relax his fists and let his breath out slowly, but it got held up somehow and came out in a gust.

"Sorry, Gerald, what?"

"Missed the stop sign back there, Bish."

"Did I?" Bishop examined his rear-view to see if he could spot the sign to which Gerald referred. "Oh yes."

"You're having a bit of trouble concentrating."

"Am I?"

"Yes," said Gerald. They were half a minute away from another crossroads and he was already working on the problem, scanning the horizon as he imagined water buffalo watched for moving cheetah spots amid the tall grasses. "If you don't mind me saying so, Bish, you don't seem really with us these days." Between the car and the intersection ahead, the road dipped and he could see a coffee shop elevated on the right. There was no visible driveway for the coffee shop, which de facto meant the driveway was hidden in the dip and any kind of vehicle of any shape or size – a tanker truck seemed the likeliest possibility – could be pulling out of the driveway at any moment. "Hey," said Gerald. "Do you feel like a coffee?"

"Feel what?"

"Feel like having a coffee, and maybe a doughnut. Boy, I could sure use one." White hair or no, it was all Gerald could do not to knock Bishop out with some kind of karate chop and take hold of the wheel.

Bishop appeared confused. "You want to stop?"

"Yes," said Gerald. "Slow down and pull in there. Slow down and, slow down and pull in – see where the *truck* is coming out?" He flicked a glance at Bishop hoping to see recognition in his eyes. Bishop was looking in his side mirror. "Up there, Bishop. Up ahead!"

"I see it, I see it." The car began to slow down, though not as much as Gerald would have liked, and Bishop turned the heavy Lincoln into the coffee shop drive with a NASCAR-like drift of all four wheels, clearing the tail light and bumper of the exiting pickup only by dint of its scooting out into the road. He pulled the car into a space dead ahead, turned off the ignition, and sat for a moment, still. Then he turned to Gerald with a look of perplexity. "Why are we here?"

Inside, the two men smoothed their ties as they slid into a booth. They gave their orders to a tall, aproned waitress and, after a quiet moment, as they were stirring their cups, Gerald took delivery of a cream-filled chocolate-glazed.

"Didn't know you liked doughnuts," said Bishop.

"Vicki doesn't like me eating them." The way the doughnut sat like a dark satin cushion almost perfectly centred on its clean white plate gave Gerald a good feeling about the coffee shop. "But I've decided it's all right once in a while."

"Good for you." Bishop lifted his cup and took a delicate sip. His thin, aging lips pulled back tight from the heat. "Have to enjoy what we can on this earth while we're here."

"Yes indeed."

"How is Victoria?"

"Oh, fine." He picked the doughnut up off the plate and liked its weight. "More to the point, how's Susan?"

"Well, I'm afraid" – he sighed heavily – "she may be dying."

In the briefest moment after asking about Susan, about the time it takes to step on an antique Christmas ornament your wife has treasured for years, Gerald had given himself to the doughnut – he'd bitten deep, with gusto – and already begun to see what a mistake that probably was. Now he had a mouth full of glorious cakey chocolate and sweet custardy filling at the precise moment when he should have been expressing his heartfelt horror. He saw that Bishop, having shared his terrible news, was now watching Gerald eat his doughnut in the face of it. And he felt unsurpassably guilty, because the doughnut was superb.

"Bishop," he managed through his mouthful, "that awful."

"I don't actually know she's dying," his boss clarified. "But given what the doctors in Denver are saying I'm starting to think the worst."

Gerald, swallowing, thought it best to set the doughnut down. "What are they saying?"

"The worst kind of nonsense." Bishop watched two men in construction vests settle on stools at the counter. "They're talking about 'amplifying the fields of opportunity.' 'Exploring discretionary scenarios.' Which all sounds like 'Expanding our paycheques' to me. But it's clear enough they're mystified. They're talking, if you can believe it, about sending her to Phoenix."

"Phoenix," said Gerald.

"What the devil Phoenix has to do with anything I have no idea." He grabbed his cup by the handle and then slammed it down again. "I told them on the phone, if you people in Denver can't fix the problem what makes you think it's going to be any better in Phoenix?"

"What did they say?"

"They said Phoenix has a new clinic with new equipment."

"That sounds good," said Gerald.

"So I called the damned doctors in Cincinnati." Bishop had sloshed coffee onto his saucer and the laminate table around it, and Gerald slid his napkin across the table and cosied it around his boss's dish as he talked. "I said to them, 'Why the hell did you send my wife to Denver when they've got a new clinic in bloody Phoenix?'"

"I'll bet that felt good."

"Hell, no," Bishop grumbled. "I felt like the most impotent fool. And the Cincinnati doctors said the Phoenix clinic specializes in something entirely different from the problem my wife has, and they can't understand the Denver doctors' thinking." He shook his head as if all doctors and the medical system itself had gone mad.

"What problem is it exactly? If I'm not intruding."

"Hmm?"

"Susan's problem," said Gerald. "We've never actually talked about it."

Bishop sighed even more heavily than before, as if a great sacrifice were being demanded of him. He glanced up at Gerald and then focused on his two furrowed hands, the fingers of which he began to entwine. "It's a kind of . . ." His face grew strained and pink as he knotted his hands tighter and made faint, throaty sounds of struggle, until Gerald reached out and laid a hand on his wrist, and Bishop's shoulders slumped. He looked up, helpless. "It's hard to explain."

For a while, the two men drank their coffee, and accepted refills when the waitress brought a carafe to the table. Then Bishop set his cup down with finality.

"So I've decided to go," he said. "I'm heading to Denver first thing tomorrow and then flying with Susan to Phoenix." He looked at Gerald with a face so vulnerable it was as if he expected some rebuke. "You'll wonder why I didn't go before, to be with my wife."

"No." Gerald shook his head. "I wasn't thinking that."

"Somehow I had it worked out that leaving the office and flying down there made it official, that things were serious." He turned his face to the window, and his voice seemed to choke and submerge. "And so she's been traipsing thousands of miles, from one set of doctors to the next, facing it all alone, while I've been here keeping myself comfy and safe like a goddamned mouse in the wall."

He glanced back at Gerald and gave him a rueful smile. "And I've been letting the company go to hell while I'm at it."

"No, Bish. That's —"

"Goddamned market share's pissed down to nothing."

"That's my fault," insisted Gerald. "I should have been on top of that sooner."

Bishop seemed to absorb that notion and twitched his mouth as though he thought it might be true. "You're operations though. Wasn't really on your plate."

"Still, I should have seen what was happening and come to you. If as you say . . ." Gerald stopped himself from completing the thought, *If as you say I'm CEO material*, because now wasn't the time to throw his own ambitions into the mix, and he didn't want Bishop, in his disappointment, to contradict him. *Sorry to lead you on there, my friend, but . . .*

"Well, whatever the case," said Bishop, "the board's not happy about it."

"What are they saying?"

Bishop looked down at Gerald's doughnut and pointed. "You going to finish that?"

Gerald glanced down at the bitten doughnut. He associated it with shame now, guilt over putting his own trivial needs first, and it was ruined for him. He pushed the plate across the table. "Be my guest."

The older man broke off a peaty hunk and lifted it to his mouth trailing a primordial ooze of cream filling. "It's good," he said, after a minute. "Sure you don't want the rest?" When Gerald shook his head Bishop pulled away a second bite and held it ready as he washed down the first.

"What did the board tell you?"

"Well, it's Gwyn, really."

Gerald had never more than shaken hands with the board's short, stocky chairman, but Gwyn Doremond's reputation as a humourless Welsh prick was firmly established. Bishop had brought him in as a director three years ago, hoping his experience in fasteners manufacturing (high tensile nuts and bolts, pop rivets, and socket screws) in Cardiff during the downsizing phase of the early nineties would improve Spent's image among materials industry analysts. Within fifteen months, Doremond's coal-browed ferocity had overawed enough of his fellow board members to get him nominated as chairman. After that he'd become an ever-tightening band around Bishop's neck.

"I'm told Gwyn's been on the phone to a number of the board, saying if we don't get the market share up to double digits by the next quarter, he's going to call for a vote on me."

Gerald worked very hard to keep the involuntary thoughts of purging at bay. It was like walking along the curb of a busy roadway and trying not to think about tripping and falling into the path of an onrushing truck. In other words, nearly impossible. "I'm sure you'd win that," he said.

For a moment there was a stillness to Bishop as he studied the dregs of his coffee. He seemed more saddened than angered. "I don't know that I care," he said finally. "I think this company needs somebody to take it by the scruff of the neck and shake it hard. But this thing with Susan . . ." He rubbed the rim of his cup with a puckered finger. "Not sure I'm that somebody any more."

Gerald distracted himself with motions – he pulled a napkin out of the tin dispenser and pressed it to the corners of his mouth, then laid it on the table and began to fold it into progressively smaller halves. There were coffee spots on the laminate that needed his attention, and he worked against them with the dry corner of the tight napkin bundle he'd made.

"What do you think?" Bishop asked.

"Well . . ." He attempted a chuckle, to suggest how much less than seriously he might be taking the notion of Bishop leaving the company he'd founded and built. But to his chagrin the chuckle came out somewhat squeakily, somewhat tiny chipmunkily, which seemed to signal to a precise degree how very seriously he took it, in fact. "That's hard for me to answer, Bish," he said. "Only you know how you feel, but, I think the company needs you."

"Company needs somebody," said Bishop. "Doesn't have to be me."

The purging fears that had been creeping up the walls Gerald had erected began to trickle over the top. He caught his first glimpse of a headline: CHANGES COMING AT SPENT. Ghostly images started to form of board-appointed auditors trooping in to examine books in search of excuses to "achieve economies" in the costs of personnel.

"What would you say," Bishop continued, "if I were to recommend to the board that we begin a succession process with a view to naming you chief executive within the year?"

Suddenly the purging waters receded. The spectres vanished. The newsprint under the headline began to fill up with type in which the name "Gerald Woodlore" appeared in the vicinity of adjectives such as "capable" and "promising." He searched the older man's eyes to make sure this idea of *succession* – which as a word sounded remarkably close to *succeed* – was not some ephemeral fancy akin to "What if the sky were orange?" but actually something thought through and solid. He tried to think of the most ideal response to a hypothetical question that used as its central assumption the idea that he, Gerald Woodlore, was so well-regarded as an executive that he could be considered a viable, indeed, the *preferred* leader of a nationally traded company.

"Are you serious?" he said, regrettably.

"Absolutely." Bishop's weary face acquired a new keenness. "I've been meaning to talk to you about this for a while, Gerald. It's hard to find executives who are committed to the slow climb in an old industry. You're what I like to call 'a good soldier.' Most talented people want the quick splash, big money, star-making jobs." Bishop snapped his fingers at each kind of job Gerald evidently didn't want, or have. "Hard to find smart, experienced, trustworthy people like yourself willing to attend to the small stuff and wait for their opportunity. How long have you been chief of operations now?"

"Four years," said Gerald.

Bishop smiled warmly. "There, you see? In a company like ours, most people can't handle more than two years at that job. They get bored. They want new challenges. I went through five operations men in eleven years before I found you."

Gerald nodded, not sure whether he was supposed to respond. It hadn't sounded like the sort of thing to which a person said "thank you."

"Yet, somehow, you manage to stay engaged in the every-day details." Bishop seemed as perplexed by this as he was impressed.

"It's because I'm a worrier," said Gerald.

"A what?"

"A worrier."

Bishop's hearty eye contact faltered a little, and Gerald reviewed some of the many things he might have said that wouldn't have involved giving his trusting, succession-recommending boss insight into one of the primary flaws in his character.

"Well," said Bishop, finding his smile. "I guess I knew that about you." Then he turned serious again. "As we go forward, that's not something I'd let on to Gwyn."

"No."

"He's more of a jam-on-the-helmet, charge-over-the-ramparts type."

"Understood."

Bishop smiled, and patted him on the arm.

Once they had arrived safely at Spent, Gerald climbed the stairs to the second floor as if new super fibres had been grafted into his quad muscles. He took the steps two at a time, hardly noticing the effort, and gripped the railing with a new superized grip. When the receptionist, the lovely, stalwart Mary, greeted him with a cheerful "Good morning," he said, "*Very* good." And by the time he had walked the length of the hall, past the land of offices and open-concept cubicles that would be his to lead, his newly super brain had found and prioritized all the reasons he couldn't possibly handle the job Bishop was trying to bestow on him, and why Bishop was sure to realize it soon.

He rounded the corner with his lack of leadership expertise and found Sandy waiting for him next to the bank of filing cabinets, outside his locked office door.

"You need to move me," she told him before he had his keys out of his pocket. "I can't work with him any more."

"One second, Sandy." He jammed the key into his inability to delegate and entered his office, his assistant sales and marketing director riding his heels. She closed the door behind them.

"He says I can't be trusted. He says I went to you behind his back."

Gerald pointed to the guest chair with his already proven failure to respond to warning signs in ways that might have prevented the market share fiasco. "Have a seat." He took off his suit jacket and hung it on the wooden coat rack next to his complete dearth of strategic vision.

Sandy lingered in the undefined region between Gerald's desk and the table by the window, but when he rolled back his chair and dropped into it, she appeared to latch on to some new resolve and grasped the back of the upholstered guest chair with both hands as if it were a lectern.

"It's an impossible situation," she announced.

"Would you please have a seat?"

"He won't even look at me."

Gerald sighed with a full day's worth of weariness, and waited. Finally she rounded the chair, drew it closer to his desk, and slipped in.

"I need my own office," she said.

He wondered why he had deluded himself all these years,

believing that he had CEO potential, when now, with the opportunity at hand, it was obvious he was barely competent at the job he already held, let alone ready for the ultimate step. Every occasion of hesitation and miscalculation in his past seemed fresh to him. He was being pelted with mistakes, including the time the cutting machine went down two days before a big shipment to Alberta and the plant manager Ned Mattick called him from the site:

> NED: There's something balled up here, Gerald. It's the feeder assembly, I think, but the whole business is seized and I don't know how long it's gonna take to fix. Prob'ly days.

And what did he do? He paced. He swore. Son of a bitch, he said. Holy shit. What the fuck. He couldn't get past the problem to the solution. The problem waggled its grotesque haunches in front of him and it was all he could see! It had taken Mattick himself to remind him that their closest competitor, in Oak Ridges, had not long before shut down an old cutting machine and that maybe they could buy some time on it until they got theirs fixed. Ned Mattick had more CEO potential than he did.

"Isn't there an office in the sales area that isn't being used?" Sandy was saying.

He reached forward and turned on his computer.

"You don't need your own office, Sandy. I'm sorry. You and Trick are going to have to work this out."

"We can't," said Sandy. "I don't see how."

He heard a knock on his door and called "Come in" before he registered Sandy's desperate flurry of *No! No!* waving. A large figure appeared in the doorway.

"Oh, I see," said Trick, setting his hands on his hips.

Sandy slammed her forehead into her palm.

"So this is the way it works now," said Trick, adopting a louche air. "I guess I should start scheduling my own private grievance sessions."

Sandy seemed to make a point of turning only halfway around and speaking to the wall. "Isn't that why you're here?"

"Ha! No, it isn't. I'm here about the strategy meeting." He lifted his chin at Gerald. "When's the strategy meeting?"

Sandy pushed herself back in her seat and rolled her eyes for Gerald's benefit.

Here was a problem, thought Gerald. Here was his very own personnel crisis. He allowed himself the luxuriant, excruciating irony of wondering how good ol' Ned Mattick would solve it.

"Trick," he began, wondering whether it was better to attack this head on or wait to see if it would erode naturally, over time, like the pyramids. "Sandy tells me you think she came to me behind your back with her window filters idea."

In the doorway, Trick wobbled his head. "Well, something like that."

"Okay. Did you make it clear to her you preferred that she go to you first with new product suggestions?"

Sandy mouthed a big *No* at Gerald.

Trick's arms flew out from his sides. "Since when is it our job to come up with new products? Isn't that Allsop's job?"

"So the answer would be *no*," said Sandy, to the wall.

"Okay, what about this?" said Gerald, leaning back in his chair. "When were you planning on coming to me about the real market share numbers?"

For a moment Trick seemed undecided about arms-folded or hands-on-hips. He chose arms-folded. "Market share numbers fluctuate, Gerald, you know that. They're a snapshot. They're history. I prefer to look at projections."

"Did you project two point five?"

Trick's head bobbled and swayed. "Hard to remember all the scenarios."

In her seat, Sandy sputtered the sound of uproarious laughter barely suppressed.

"Look," said Gerald, glaring at her. "You two are going to have to figure out how to get along. Any company staring at a two-point-five share has enough to worry about." He held up a hand as they both tried to speak. "Trick, from now on, Sandy will come to you first with any new product innovations she comes up with."

"Yeah, and then I guess I'll just schlep them over to Allsop's office where they belong."

"No. If they sound good, you'll bring them to me."

Trick found a new and apparently more comfortable arms-folded position. "Fine."

"Sandy," said Gerald.

"Yes." She had folded her arms Jack Benny-like, her deflated cheek laid against her peevish fist.

"If you feel Trick is not giving your bold new ideas their due, you can tell me so during one of our monthly meetings together."

"Monthly meetings?" She straightened her head. "You meet with him once a *week*."

"Right, because he's the sales and marketing director." Through conscious effort, Gerald managed to keep a note of incredulity out of his voice. "You and I will meet on the third Wednesday of every month," he said. "Eleven o'clock."

"But," she was calculating something, "we just *passed* the third Wednesday."

He looked innocuously at them both and picked up the handset of his phone to indicate their time together was over. "See you at the meeting at three."

2

Sitting in the boy's room of the Lightenham Avenue house, Vicki could hear Hella in the next bedroom, chopping at the Yves Delorme sheets. She could picture the fierce hatcheting of Hella's hand as she jammed edges *down* between mattresses and headboards and *flat* between mattresses and box springs. She could imagine the stabbing of her blade fingers into tight corners and the winching taut of pretty coverlets. Even at her most laissez-faire, Hella was a demon of bed making; it was the thing that had impressed Vicki most. And now that Vicki had angered her, she was making the bedding suffer.

The chopping sounds stopped, and Vicki could hear Hella's feet pounding down the hall. When she appeared in the doorway, she seemed out of breath, and her face was flushed from her effort.

"So that's the *third* bedroom done," she said. "Do you need more time to sit here? You want me to keep going?"

Vicki pressed her back flat against the headboard of the mahogany sleigh bed. "Yes, Hella, I do need a bit more time. In fact I wondered whether there might be something left for you to do downstairs, or perhaps in the basement. I'm finding the noise up here a bit distracting."

Hella folded her arms and nodded with an apparently grim appreciation of the state of things. "The noise of my working is distracting you," she said. "You know, I'm not used to having to do *all* the finishing work."

Vicki drew her hands into her lap. "You don't have to do all of it, Hella. Most of the downstairs is done. The window treatments are properly arranged, the floors are clean, and the tables are all beautifully set. We've both worked very hard. I've simply asked you to finish the beds, which you do so wonderfully well, and see to whatever details we might have missed downstairs."

Hella regarded her for a second or two, then took a crisp step into the boy's room and swept her gaze around. "Oh, look. Here's a detail we missed. *An entire room.*"

"Tell me," said Vicki, "have you ironed the beds you've made?" Ironing the sheets and coverlets once they were on the beds helped fix the folds of the turn-downs and gave a bedroom an almost subliminal polish. And as a task, it had the advantage of being relatively silent.

"No," said Hella. "That's always the last thing. And I like to do all the beds one after the other so I don't have to keep waiting for the stupid iron to heat up." She spread her arms. "And I can't do this room."

"Well, I'm sorry." Vicki turned her face away. "I'm not ready to do this room yet. Maybe you could run out for some more fresh flowers."

"Avis is going to be here for her showing in, like, two hours."

"The white callas in the foyer," said Vicki, "are looking a little wizened."

Hella sighed as she reached back to yank her dark ponytail tight. "Well, I'd go, but I don't have a car today."

"Take mine." Vicki felt beside the bed for her purse, but it wasn't there. Where had she left it? "I think my purse should be sitting in the sink of the guest bathroom downstairs. My keys are in there." Her assistant persisted in the doorway like a cloud of cigarette smoke. "I would get enough for the foyer and dining room, if they have them."

After another moment, Hella shrugged her bony shoulders and gave a sigh. "All right," she said, heading down the hall. "I just hope Avis is taking her pills today."

Vicki leaned her head back against the scrolled top of the headboard and waited for the sound of Hella leaving. Seated this way, with her legs stretched out before her along the bed, she could clearly see the toenail that had caused Avis such distress. It wasn't clear to her how the nail had been mutilated, though she had her Geraldish suspicions. But even now it was as though the nail, the toe beneath it, and the foot itself, belonged – or should have belonged – to a different person. Lately (perhaps, she thought, it was age) her body and the things she covered it with were becoming less important to her. In the mornings, it was only habit that pushed her through the motions of putting on makeup, and getting dressed. Looking at her toes now, she was faintly irritated that she'd even been made to consider them. It should have been someone else's concern. What she needed — here she smiled — was a Hella of the toes.

When she heard the front door open and close she was able to relax and think about what really mattered. For a long while she sat on the unmade sleigh bed, watched the occasional shadows of birds pass through the circle of light from the bull's-eye window, and listened to the room. She tried to keep her breathing steady, but that was something of a struggle, because never before, never in all her years of staging had it taken so long to decipher what she was meant to do in a single room. She had already considered the possibility that she was trying too hard now, and that she was blocked, the way artists were sometimes said to become. But it didn't feel that way; it felt as though she wasn't trying, or listening, hard enough.

She worked to get a picture in her mind. She pressed her temples and tried to see the child as an extension of Robert and Margeaux, as an amalgam of their contentment. A boy from those two should be fearless, she thought, and of the world, born into trust and steadiness, into impetuous joys and a flood of light. A child like that, it seemed to Vicki, should be *easy* to see.

When that didn't work, and it hadn't before, she tried to see the boy through his parents' eyes. She strove to know Margeaux's expectations and intuit what kind of boy she would love. In an effort to jog her inspiration, Vicki did silly things. She got off the bed and roamed the room carelessly, as she imagined Margeaux might. She walked partway down the hall, turned, and came racing back, as if she had wonderful news, in the desperate hope that when she arrived at the doorway, the boy would appear to her, surrounded by his things. But it was a futile effort that only made her breathe all the harder.

There was never any thought, however, of giving up and filling the child's room with make-do delight – a ball and a base-ball glove on the side table, an encyclopaedia on the revolving bookshelf, open to the page on grasshoppers, and a framed picture of the space shuttle mounted on the wall – except to acknowledge how desolate the idea made her feel. And she knew anyway that she had more time, that the deadline was not as imminent as Hella believed. Because when two o'clock arrived, Avis would not be walking into the house, bringing her sorrowful couple with her. Vicki had a plan to see to that.

When she heard the sound of her own car pulling into the driveway at half past one, Vicki went downstairs to meet her assistant at the door.

"I got all they had," called Hella as she came in, her arms loaded with linen-white callas. "I'm sorry it took so long. And it came to over two hundred dollars!"

"They're lovely," said Vicki as she walked barefoot across the foyer tiles.

Hella kicked off her shoes in a rush and started to make for the kitchen, but Vicki greeted her with her arms outspread.

"I'll take them," she said.

"Don't you want me to put them in the vases?"

"No, it's fine." She received them into her arms the way she would a newborn, protecting their fragile blooms. "Now, Hella," she said, "you've done so much, and I'm very grateful because I know it's been frustrating for you. Why don't you consider your work done for the day?"

"But there's still tons more to do!"

"Well, as you made clear it's time I did my share."

Hella frowned as if she was confused, and when Vicki turned with the flowers she began to follow. "What about the boy's room? Is it done? Can I see?"

Vicki stopped and faced her again. "I'm quite serious, Hella. I'd like you to go home now. I'll pay you for a full day."

"Well" – Hella blinked – "my husband's not picking me up today. I was hoping I could get a ride with you."

"Take my car."

"But what –"

"Please." She stared at Hella until the angular woman seemed to settle back on her heels. Then she smiled. "All right now, off you go!" And she turned and took the flowers into the kitchen where she stayed, tense at the sink, until she heard the shuffling of shoes, and the closing of the door.

Quickly she cut the tips off the flower stems – because the callas *were* lovely and it would have been a shame to waste them – set them in the sink and ran enough cold water to cover their severed ends. And when she was sure that Hella had driven off through the arbour of Lightenham Avenue's shapely oaks, she hurried back across the polished floor to the front entrance, drying her hands on her dress as she went. With the practice of years she slipped on her pumps without looking, took the house keys from her purse, which Hella had left on the floor, and went outside.

There were three doors to worry about: front, rear, and the

access from the garage. The front was most important, but all three had to be addressed.

She slid in her key and secured the front door's dead bolt, but she knew it wasn't enough merely to lock the doors, because Avis also had a key. And, under the assumption that Vicki had finished the staging and gone home or back to the warehouse, she would be expecting to need it.

Nor could there be any obvious signs of tampering – nothing jammed into the keyhole and broken off – because her relationship with Avis was important, and Vicki couldn't be seen to be trying to jeopardize a sale. Which was, of course, exactly what she intended to do. Jeopardize it. Kill it. Because the home she was creating, had nearly finished, was not meant for stricken, woeful people, and they could not be allowed inside.

A plan had come to her the night before, as she was drifting off to sleep. Kyle hadn't returned home and wouldn't, according to Gerald, until the following day. And as she lay in bed she thought about him and tried to imagine, as she had sometimes during the months he was away, the strange, far-off place to which he had bravely, though inexplicably, gone. And the image that had appeared to her most vividly was of her son on a field of blowing dirt and sand.

Vicki looked down. With the exception of the drive, and the flagstone path on which she stood, the ground surrounding the house was the dry, sandy soil of a construction site. Weeks ago the landscapers had shaped the grounds, and seeded them. But the grass seed they used was slow to root, and what threads of green did show seemed, where she stood, more like the sparse hairs on a child's arm.

This plan wasn't tested, there was no way of knowing if it would work, but she kneeled, scooped up a handful of the loose dirt and carried it to the door. The latch — she checked to be certain — held firm. With her mound of dirt cradled in her palm she bent close to the brass plate of the keyhole. Then she blew.

The dry granules lifted off her hand like a tiny sirocco. Many of them scattered, useless, against the brass plate but some, she could tell, flew into the jagged slot. So she kept blowing. She blew across her mound of sand and dirt until her hand was empty and her lungs were sore. Then she tried her key.

It caught and grated against the sand inside, but made it all the way in with a shove. So she went back to the edge of the flagstone and brought back a second handful. She blew until she couldn't any more and then pinched what was left between her thumb and finger and tried to push the last of it in the slot. And this time, when she tried her key, it made it halfway and wouldn't budge a millimetre more.

Madly, Vicki fell onto her hands and knees and brushed the scattered sand and earth, the visible evidence, off the front steps. Then she ran to the rear entrance and did the same to the lock there, this time making sure to keep the rear door open, so that when the lock had been fully sabotaged, she was able to slip inside the house, and shut the door.

In the basement, she found the circuit box, located the switch that controlled the sliding garage doors, and knuckled it down against its hard spring. Then, just to make sure, she came back upstairs, veered through the kitchen and pantry, entered the garage, and walked across the cool concrete floor to take hold of one of the inside handles. And she wrenched.

The metal door rattled upward.

Pulse racing, she shoved it back down. There was no time left to stop up the lock of the door leading from the garage into the house. Even if she could, it would be one thing to attribute two sand-stuffed exterior door locks to a freak swirling wind, quite another to explain how such a wind made it into the garage. She scanned the doors' inner workings, and her eyes went to the clean metal runners that the wheels of the doors travelled. It might work, she thought, to jam something in there. In the kitchen, from a box under the sink, she fetched two silver serving forks left over from the dining room setting. She rushed with them and a dining chair to stand on back into the garage, and rammed the forks home between the wheels and the runner of each door. Stepping down off the chair, she nearly tripped in her haste and took a moment, in the cool concrete room, to breathe.

Inside the house, Vicki ran the water in the kitchen sink, took one of the crystal glasses she had set out on a Tunbridge ware tray, and held it under the tap with a trembling hand. She brought the glass with her into the living room and set it inside the brass railing of a rosewood side table she adored, which would have featured the Meissen candlestick figures, had they survived Hella's misguided packing. Then she sat in the mahogany-framed Edwardian armchair with string inlay, which kept her hidden but provided a view through the front windows to the driveway and Lightenham Avenue beyond. And she waited.

It didn't take long. Within a few minutes, Avis Nye's bronze Jaguar emerged from the mottled shade of the street and turned into the sunshine of the drive. Behind her came a black Mercedes sedan bearing Mildred and Alan Webb. When the car first came to a stop, the two of them seemed frozen in their seats, staring at the house through the windshield of the car, watching it as if they thought it might do something, as Avis, in the middle of a call, hopped from her vehicle and made her little black purse swallow her keys.

Whether by decision or accident of routine, the doors of the Mercedes opened together and the Webbs issued from the car in synchrony, though Vicki's vantage point gave her a better view of Alan. He was tall and patrician, as she'd expected, and tailored in fine charcoal wools, and the features of his face looked to Vicki to bear the wonderment of a man who'd just been struck, and was confused as to why. He walked tentatively past the Mercedes' fender, looking up at the house all the while, and converged with his wife at the hood ornament in the middle, as Avis put away her phone.

"The landscaping," Vicki could hear Avis trill through the window, "was done, from concept to execution, by Tallis and Mauvrey. I mean you can just tell, can't you? The plateaus are so distinctive. And it should all be grown in by July."

As they proceeded toward the house, Avis talked about the pale gold bricks, imported from Portugal, about the reputation of the builders, and the desirability of their signature roofing slate. Neither of the Webbs seemed to hear the specifics of what Avis was saying, in that they gave no nods or glances of understanding, as if a pane of glass far thicker than the one through which Vicki peered separated them from the living world. They held on to each other as they walked toward the house, almost as if it terrified them. But Vicki could see that Mildred, in a dark blue sheath dress that exposed her pale arms to the sun, made an effort to smile as Avis spoke. As a smile, as an expression of pleasure or warmth, it failed. It was no more than a stretching of lips. But Vicki felt a kinship with Mildred Webb in that moment that she hadn't expected, and couldn't have explained.

Avis had made it to the front steps, and Vicki took a calming sip of water from her glass. She heard the muffled jangling of the house keys outside the door. "When you step inside," Avis was saying, "I want you to notice the breadth and sweep of the staircase; it's quite unusual." Vicki could no longer see Avis or her clients from where she sat, but she could hear the scratching of Avis's key as she attempted to insert it into the lock. "The tiling too," Avis continued, "in the foyer, is something the builders are particularly . . ." The scratching in the lock grew more insistent, and then came a sudden silence when Avis wrenched the key out.

"I'm sure this is the right key," she said, sounding confused. In it went again, and to the grinding and scraping sound was added an intense joggling of the latch. "I don't understand." Joggling. Scratching. "It worked just yesterday!"

"Is there another door?" This was Mildred Webb's voice, sounding flat and lifeless after Avis's fluty variance.

"Oh yes, oh yes, there's the rear entrance," said Avis. But she seemed intent on making the front one work and attempted to wedge the key in again.

"Perhaps we should try the back door," said Mildred.

Avis, on the steps, sighed. "Yes, of course. That makes much more sense. I'm sorry about this. But luckily there's a lovely stone path just . . ." Her voice faded out as she led the Webbs around the side of the house. Vicki, careful to stay hidden, rose out of her chair and walked through the living room to the hushed foyer, past the sweeping stairs on the left, the hall to the pantry on the right. She walked by the door to Robert's library, where only one of the Chinese folding chairs could be used (the other having indeed been ruined, as Hella had indicated, by a mysterious split in the seat), and entered the family room. Here she stationed herself in a niche behind a towering dieffenbachia that she'd set next to the window, which allowed a discreet view of the back porch.

". . . of this entire area, which is so exciting," said Avis, as she rounded the corner of the house and passed by a large window that looked out onto the rolling steppe that stretched to the edge of the property. The three figures made their way to the porch, with Alan Webb a doleful presence in the rear, and Vicki watched them, through a smaller window, climb the steps to the rear entrance.

"Isn't that a delightful ancon above the door," said Avis, motioning in an abstract way to the carved s-scroll that seemed to spill from the top of the moulded casing like a tiny waterfall. "You don't often find a detail like that at the rear entrance, but these builders . . ." Avis was not looking at the ancon as she spoke, her efforts and attention appeared to be entirely focused on the keyhole of the door, the key in her hand and the successful merging of the two, and her patter died away as she tried once and then again to push the key into the lock.

"Damn," she said. "Damn!" She gave a tiny, furious stomp of her foot, and then turned and looked at the woeful Webbs, helpless. Vicki couldn't help feeling guilty for the trouble she was causing her.

"I just don't understand," said Avis, her face blank with disbelief. "This *is* the key."

Alan Webb stepped forward with an outstretched hand. "Maybe if I gave it a try." He accepted the key without enthusiasm and attempted, as Avis backed away, to do what she could not. And then he lowered himself onto one knee and examined the keyhole.

"There appears to be something here."

"Something . . ."

"Sand or soil it looks like," said the grave Mr. Webb. He tried to push the key in again with a barely audible grunt. "It's no good," he said finally, and rose from his knee. "I expect these locks will have to be replaced."

Avis looked from the lock to her clients to the lock again and gave a tiny cough of astonishment. "I don't know what to say," she said, sounding fragile and possibly on the verge of tears. "I mean, there must be an easy way to fix this. I'm sure there's someone I can call —"

"We won't be able to wait, I'm afraid," said Mildred, giving Avis another of her pleasureless smiles.

"I understand. But is there . . ." The agent couldn't seem to find the spirit to continue and simply watched as the Webbs began to move away from the porch.

"At least look in the windows," she said suddenly. "I mean, it's not the same, but you'll get some sense."

Mildred Webb hesitated on the steps that were taking her away from the house and then moved toward the nearest window, where Vicki stood only partly obscured by the dieffenbachia's broad leaves. She leaned tentatively toward the glass and

shielded her eyes with a lined hand, and Vicki, pressed tight
against the wall but watching, thought she saw in the woman's
face a flash of something she recognized. Mildred Webb, it was
obvious to Vicki, felt forsaken by the world. That portion of
contentment that should have been part of her life, that allot-
ment of joy that was rightly hers, was missing. And nothing
warming had taken its place. Not even the sense, or the faith,
that the emptiness and disillusionment that overpowered her
could be accepted or understood. When Mildred looked through
the glass into the Lightenham house, it seemed to Vicki that the
woman was searching for what she didn't have, without any
hope of finding it.

And when Vicki saw the loss and despair in Mildred Webb's
face, and recognized the look from, of all things, the face of her
own son . . . she felt a pain under her ribs that made her gasp and
bend into the leaves of the dieffenbachia. She was still there,
struggling to breathe, when the Webbs drove away, and Avis
marched back to the door to give it a kick.

3

Authority, Gerald had once been informed, went to those with a knack for dispassion. The authoritative, he was told, conveyed indifference. Did they do so because of talent? Money? Title? Was disinterest a rare and innate gift? And how was it distinct from apathy? He didn't know, and he suspected there were nuances to not caring that would always be beyond him, that would keep him, as a leader, from ever being great. But if there was even a chance that he was going to be a CEO, Gerald thought, it was time he started acting like one. And so, though it took an extraordinary act of will, he managed to hold on as the meeting time approached, not arriving five minutes early as he typically did but waiting until an almost blasé five minutes past, before he rose out of his chair and headed down the hall to the boardroom.

He took the long way past the photocopy station, where Monik was wrestling with a toner cartridge, and beat back the impulse to stop and help her, because he was already engaged in an important activity and Monik was perfectly capable.

He passed the small lunch room where someone had left the coffee maker unattended and found the strength to do nothing about the scorched arabica stink.

He continued through the sales area where three of the five salespeople were sitting at their desks not taking calls and not drumming up business. And instead of expressing his irritation by blurting out something pointedly ironic ("Everyone on target for this month? Terrific!"), he made a mental note to have a sit-down with Leslie Morton, the chief sales rep, in the very near future.

But his stamina for high-level disinterest was nowhere near CEO grade, and before he made it out of the sales area he found himself turning and asking, in a voice more plaintive than he would have wished, "Did anyone here leave the coffee on?" And so, after a general mute shaking of heads, Gerald was able to savour the sour taste of his inability to maintain even a pretence of chief executive nonchalance all the way to the boardroom entrance.

He entered the room angry. He tossed the leather portfolio he was carrying on the end of the table and when it landed with a slap loud enough to make everyone in the room jump, he liked it. A quick scan around the table told him everyone he expected to be there was, and they all looked anxious, and that suited him. He sat with a whump.

"All right, everybody, let's get started." He glanced at Sandy on his left. "Sandy, why don't you go first."

"Um . . ." Sandy leaned forward, over the table, and appeared to be trying for more intense eye contact. "Do you think I could go last? What I'm doing needs a bit of set-up and I don't want to delay things too –"

"Fine. I don't care. Trick, you go first."

Trick, who was sitting across from Sandy and maintaining extraordinary focus on the pad in front of him, looked up, wide-eyed. "I was thinking I'd go last." He glanced at the others, and back at Gerald. "You know, as sales and marketing director."

"Well, as sales and marketing director," said Gerald, "why don't you go first and set the standard."

"Sure, but –"

"That's what I'd like," said Gerald. "We'll go around the table, starting with you. Then Phil –" He noticed Phil, who was abnormally still, had a tensor bandage around his left wrist. "What happened to you?"

Phil raised his wrist. "Squash with my kid. Hit it with a fore-hand."

"Ouch," said Doug, wincing. "Hurt?"

"Like a mother."

"Ouch," Doug said again.

"Okay," said Gerald. "So the order's Trick, Phil with the sore wrist, then Doug, then we'll break so Sandy can set up, and then she'll go. Sound good?" He leaned back, set his eyes on Trick, and waited.

Trick had a pen in his hand and he began to wobble it between his thumb and his index finger. He looked at Gerald and wobbled his pen and swallowed. "Yeah," he said. "That's good." He firmed up the grip on his pen and rapped the pad in front of him. "I didn't make up any slides, you know, because I couldn't be sure of getting the outlet, so" – he rapped the pad again – "I just jotted down some thoughts here." He cleared his throat and edged his chair away from the table.

"It seems to me," he began, "you know, we want to be open to good ideas. And Sandy's got a really interesting one here, with the window filters."

"Thank you," said Sandy, giving him a trim smile.

"Yeah, but there's a lot of issues." Trick drew his pad close as if to review the many issues. "Acceptance. You know, that's a big one. How do you make people accept the idea of a window filter that won't let them see outside? Right? That's something we have to work on, acceptance. Okay, uh, pricing. We have to figure out, vis-à-vis our regular window screens, do we charge more for a window filter because it filters out stuff, or do we charge less because it won't let you see outside?"

Across from him, Sandy emitted a long, loud sigh.

"Well, you know, hey, it's an issue. So, okay . . ." He drew his pen down the list on his pad. ". . . acceptance . . . pricing . . . Next one, customer service. I think we should plan on establishing a toll-free customer service number, and staffing up with call-centre people, to take the calls from customers who've had the filters installed and want to know how the hell they're supposed to see outside."

Sandy had begun to agitate in her swivelling chair like the vanes of a washing machine. "Thank you, Mr. Negativity!"

"Once we solve those issues" – Trick made his face and voice sunshine bright – "I think we got a winner!"

Sandy stopped hard and faced Gerald with a hand pointing at Trick. "You see?" She turned on her antagonist. "This is supposed to be a 'how to' meeting, not a 'why not' meeting."

"What's that?" Trick glanced around sunnily. "I don't even know what that means."

"Go to school," she muttered.

"Okay, enough," said Gerald. He looked at Trick. "Is that the extent of your contribution?"

Trick set his head at a reflective angle and shrugged. "Important issues."

"Well, we need to do more than raise issues, we need solutions." He pointed at Phil. "You're next."

For the next twenty minutes, Phil detailed the financial picture of Spent Materials, including the trends in its debt-equity ratios, its profit and loss ratios, and its inventory turnover ratios. He presented numbers showing the historic performance of new product launches within the building materials sector, indicated what revenues would be required from a new line of window filters within the final three-quarters of the fiscal year to offset increased development and marketing costs in the first. And he presented compelling evidence to support the two-pronged conclusion that Spent Materials (a) desperately needed a new product launch, and (b) would find a new product launch all but ruinous.

Pink Fiber Glas insulation, according to Phil, was the model to shoot for. "Basically," he said, "either we do a Pink Fiber Glas right out of the box, or we're screwed." He underlined his point with a sharp patty-pat of the table, and grimaced.

"Ouch," said Doug.

Gerald opened his portfolio and wrote, *Discuss debt numbers with Bishop.*

"Hey," piped Trick. "Maybe we can come up with an animated character. Like Pink Fiber Glas has the Pink Panther, right? So maybe we could have, I dunno, a blind mole."

"Oh," said Doug, "I like that."

"Put little dark glasses on him," said Trick with a smirk.

"Give him a cane," cracked Doug.

Trick spread his hands to make a banner above him. "Slogan could be 'Who needs to see outside anyway?'"

Sandy's chin dropped to her chest. "Hopeless," she muttered.

Review salary structure re Sandy/Trick, Gerald wrote. "Doug?" he said. "What have you got to offer?"

Doug was still having a chuckle over the blind mole idea. "I don't know if I can do any better than that!"

Gerald flashed him a look. "I hope you can."

Like water down a clogged drain Doug's grin died away. He rustled some papers in a cardboard folder in front of him and his expression became strained. "As you know, Gerald, I'm not big on making presentations."

"Doesn't have to be a presentation," said Gerald. "Just tell us what you've been thinking about."

"Well, I've put some thoughts down on paper." Doug patted the folder fondly. "If it's okay with you" – he leaned over the table and began sliding the folder toward Gerald – "I'd prefer to just give you that."

"Why don't you summarize —"

"No. Here you go." Doug sent the folder skittering down to Gerald with a shove.

Gerald opened the folder to a scribbled note on the first page — *Please don't make me* — and he remembered the first time Doug Allsop had been asked to give a monthly operating report. It was back before Spent had digital projectors and Doug had stood at the front of the room fumbling acetate sheets and reading so softly he could barely be heard above the overhead projector's humming fan. The more he handled the acetate charts and summaries, the more the sweat on his palms mingled with the blue and green inks, until every new page laid on the glass bore an abstract watercolour smear. When Doug had finally retreated to his seat, Gerald had reached out to see if he could look at one of the pages again, and Doug, perhaps thinking he was being congratulated for surviving his ordeal, had grasped his hand in a cold, damp grip that left a turquoise stain.

"Okay, Doug," said Gerald. "Thanks." *Presentation training for Doug.*

"I think we should all have to present," sniffed Sandy. "That way we know how to evaluate everyone's contribution."

"Don't worry," said Doug, nodding down the table. "It's all there. Cost projections, equipment requirements, what-have-you."

Sandy smiled cleanly. "I'll just assume it's negative."

Gerald rolled himself away from the table. "Okay, Sandy, how long do you need to set up?"

"Five minutes."

"Let's break."

In his office, Gerald sat at his desk and called home. The main house number was set to go to voice mail at three rings, and it took four tries of calling and hanging up before someone finally answered.

"Yeah?" said a hazy version of Kyle's voice.

"Hey, you're home!" Gerald hunched over the phone as if he had to protect it. "Everything all right, son? Any problems with the car?"

It took a while for Kyle to answer. "No," he said. "I don't think so."

"Can I ask where you were, son?" Gerald looked up to see Bishop standing at his door. He waved him in. "Kyle?"

"Yeah?"

Gerald couldn't be sure but he thought Kyle might be drunk. He sounded half asleep. Near his desk, Bishop lifted a tentative finger. "One second, son." He covered the mouthpiece and looked at Bishop.

"Everything okay at home?" Bishop whispered.

"I don't know," said Gerald. "Probably."

Bishop had the tight, suspended body language of someone tiptoeing over delicate ground. "Well, I just wanted to say that I'm about to give Gwyn Doremond a call, you know, to fill him in on what's happening here. He hates surprises." Bishop grinned sheepishly. "Always manage up, as they say. Anyway, I thought I'd set up a meeting with you, me, and him for when I get back. Couple of weeks, I'm thinking. You'll be around?"

Gerald nodded. "Should be."

"That's fine," Bishop whispered. "Well, I'll make that call

and then I'm off." His eyes flicked toward the phone. "Sorry to interrupt." He raised a palm in farewell.

Gerald stood up and grabbed his boss's hand. He shook it firmly. "Good luck in Phoenix."

Bishop gave him a fragile smile but a sturdy thumbs-up. "Hope for the best."

As he watched the older man make a quiet exit, Gerald took his hand off the phone. "Kyle? You still there, son?" He heard the sound of something being dragged over the mouthpiece, or vice versa. "Kyle?"

"Huh?"

"How are you doing, son? Is everything all right?" He heard a kind of chuckle on the other end of the line.

"Just taking it easy, Dad. Just being equa-mouse, you know? Me and Rumsfeld."

"Kyle, stay away from that cat. It's not —"

"Hey," said Kyle, "you wanna hear it purr?"

"No, son, listen . . ." But he could tell Kyle wasn't there any more. He heard the rustling of cat fur against the mouthpiece, and the muffled drone of feline ease, then the sound of Kyle hanging up.

As Gerald marched back down the hall toward the boardroom, he caught another whiff of burning coffee, and this time, without thinking about it, he veered left into the kitchen. Two of the salespeople were there, chatting. He pointed to the coffee maker on the counter.

"Can you not smell that?"

They looked at him dumbly.

"That coffee has been sitting there, reeking, for nearly an hour."

They seemed incapable of speech – remarkable for sales-people – so there was no point in waiting for an answer. He pushed past them, grabbed the half-full carafe and poured its rancid contents into the sink. "If you're not going to go out and make calls," he fumed, "the least you could do is help out around here." Then he stuck the carafe under a rinsing stream of cold water and instantly there was a loud snap.

"Uh oh," said one of the salespeople.

He could see it: a clean crack, north to south, right along the dirty bottom of the carafe. "Yes, *uh oh*," said Gerald. He flipped the lid of the garbage can and banged the carafe in. "*Uh oh. Right*," he said. "Well done." He stormed out of the kitchen. "Good work!"

In the corridor, before he made the last turn for the board-room, Gerald slowed himself down and stopped next to a framed illustration of mallards floating amid marshy grasses. Hands on his hips, he breathed deeply and tried to regain his balance, and as he did he looked at the mallard print, which had hung on the wall at this particular corner for as long as he'd been employed at Spent. He thought about the fact that some-one – possibly Bishop's first secretary, Gita, whom Bishop often spoke of with fondness – had selected the picture of mallards from a catalogue of reliable office art, and that this decision had affected the lives of hundreds of people for untold years in subtle, unknowable ways. He considered the possibility that whatever beneficial influence the picture had once had was now long gone. And he decided that his first delegatory act, if he became CEO, would be to ask someone to do something about the mallards.

When he arrived at the boardroom entrance, the others were already inside, and Sandy was standing impatiently at the door. She thrust a sealed white envelope at him.

"Now don't open that," she warned, "until I say so."

Gerald squeezed the envelope in his hand. "Sandy, how long is this going to take?"

Her eyelids fluttered and she looked briefly wounded. "I haven't timed it," she said. Then she pushed a smile through. "Don't worry. However long it takes, it'll be worth it."

He took his seat and saw that everyone else had been given an envelope too; Doug had placed his squarely on the table in front of him, Trick had shoved his to the side and seemed determined to ignore it, Phil held his in his good hand and hatcheted the table with it to a steady beat.

When everyone was settled, Sandy switched off the lights without warning.

"Oh boy," muttered Trick. "Here we go."

She was a silent sylph as she moved through the murk to the back of the room and pressed the button of a digital music player. Slowly an ominous wind effect built up around them, interspersed with sporadic discordant organ notes and menacing, arrhythmic drums.

"Ooo, spooky," said Trick.

Sandy's exasperated sigh marked her passage to the head of the room in the dark. When she reached the front she pulled down the projection screen, wheeled and flicked on the projector in one practised motion.

"This," she announced, "is the world outside your home."

On the screen in front of them bloomed chaos and mayhem. Pictures of war and upheaval, of bombed-out cities and wave-battered coasts, of burning buildings, swastikas, assault rifles in raised fists, and skies filled with smoke. Gerald pressed back in his seat, and his retreating feet rolled him to the edge of the room. "Look at it," she commanded them, and they did, they watched, as Sandy showed them death and destruction, terrorism and madness, while the music and sound effects played.

"What can you do about this?" she asked as the images came. "Nothing," she told them. "These threats exist beyond your control. If the forces of nature or evil or God above decided time was up for your town, your home, your family, there is *nothing* you could do. Because against powers like these, a man's curse is his helplessness."

The wind effects kept coming while the music changed, turned fervent and hip-hoppy as the images on the screen began to morph too. "But some threats," said Sandy, "are more our size. And those we *do* have the strength to fight." Scenes of horror and devastation gave way to more personal terrors. Masked criminals on the attack, fanged pit bulls on the loose, the eyes and wounds of impoverished children teaming with larval incursions. Gerald, gripping the vinyl armrests of his chair, watched the images flash by until they began to merge, until they became elements of the same unifying peril.

"And when there's a chance these threats can be overcome," said Sandy, "isn't it your obligation, isn't it your *duty*, to try?"

They saw pictures of doctors bent over bloodied torsos, of small boys standing up to schoolyard bullies, of smoky streets alive with protest, citizens with placards in their hands and cloths over their mouths, and mothers in rags shielding children from rain that was undoubtedly acidic.

"Now think about this," Sandy told them as they watched. "What if these dangers were right outside your door?" The wind kept blowing while the music took on a synthy sci-fi throb, all digital flutters and searing strings. And on the screen they saw blown-up images of horror-film creatures, grotesque viral monsters and slavering bus-sized bugs. "What if these beasts were trying to get inside your home, trying to attack your family?" Sandy wanted to know. "What if there was just one thing you could do to protect them?"

Suddenly the screen went dark, and the music stopped. "What if all you could do," Sandy whispered in the darkness, "was bargain for your loved ones' safety?"

It seemed for a moment, at least to Gerald, as if Sandy was all around them, bodiless. So it was a shock when a high-powered flashlight came on at the front of the room, and Sandy pointed its ferocious, pencil beam at Trick. "Your wife is being held at knifepoint."

"What the hell?" said Trick, shielding his eyes.

"Your wife!" shouted Sandy. "A home invader's got her! The only thing you can do to save her is give up your SUV! Will you do it?"

"Well, sure," said Trick, squinting manfully. "I guess so."

Sandy turned the beam on Phil. "Your son's being attacked by a giant cockroach!"

"No problem," said Phil. "Beat it off with his squash racquet."

"What if he was asleep" – Sandy crept up to him, her voice low – "and the cockroach's pinchers were about to chop off his head, and all you could do to stop it was give up all your passions, your entertainments, your music." She shone the light down on top of him. "Would you do it?"

"How fast is a nanosecond?"

She aimed the flashlight at Doug, who shrank back. "Your daughter's contracted a deadly virus! Will you give up your sailboat to save her?"

"Well," Doug cringed helplessly, "I don't own a sailboat, but –"

"Your cottage!"

"Okay! Yes, I would, of course!"

Gerald braced for the flashlight's beam to fall on him. He had his answer ready: *Yes!* But Sandy had other ideas. She charged to the front of the room, slammed on the overhead fluorescents, and strafed them with a lunatic stare. "What if you didn't know for certain that someone in your family was in imminent danger. What if it was only probable? Even just *possible?* Would you be willing to give up something you didn't absolutely need to keep them safe?"

She grabbed an envelope from the edge of the table and held it up. "In each of the envelopes I've given you, there is a tool for calculating something no one else has been able to quantify before. It's a finely calibrated instrument, and what it measures . . . is love."

Like a lioness pouncing on injured prey, Sandy lunged

forward and stabbed a button on her laptop, and up on the screen shone an image of a father, holding a newborn child.

"The world," she said softly, "is a threatening place, full of frightening things. And right now, at this moment, your family is vulnerable." She began to walk the perimeter of the board-room, around the table, pausing as she passed by each man. "As we speak, as you sit here, your wives, your daughters and sons, are being exposed to perils they don't understand. Dangers they can't see or touch. What are you going to do, before it's too late?" She came to Gerald's chair, stopped and gazed down with what seemed to him a knowing empathy, almost pity. She put a hand on his shoulder. "How are you going to protect them?" Then she turned away, and four precise steps took her to the front of the room.

"Each of you loves your family," she said. "The only ques-tion is, how much?" She held up her envelope. "What's in here, and how you use it, will tell you."

Then Sandy smiled, sweetness tinged with triumph, switched off the projector, and clasped her hands in front of her. "That's the marketing campaign, gentlemen. Any questions?" None of the men in the room answered Sandy. They were all staring at the envelopes in their hands. "We can do a thirty-second and a sixty-second version for TV," she continued, "and a full version like this for trade shows and product knowledge semi-nars. We could even videotape it for smaller markets. And this" – she flapped her own envelope as she walked to her seat – "is the perfect direct-mail component. What we do is run regional teaser ads that talk about the envelope just like I did, and then we send it out to targeted households."

At the table she sat and looked around at the men in their apparent stupors. "Come on, open it up! It's only a flyer."

Gerald was looking at his envelope, but he wasn't thinking about it. He was thinking about Kyle and the way he sounded on the phone. There was something odd about it, there was a mistiness that frightened him. As he heard the sound of ripping paper around him, he pushed himself out of his chair.

"Nice presentation, Sandy," he said.

His sales and marketing director, which was how he now thought of her, beamed.

"I'm afraid I have to go." He looked at the men around the table. "Boys? For the next hour or so, Sandy's going to lead a discussion on how we implement this plan. Get other people in here if you need to. Work out the details and we'll go over them on Monday." He looked at Sandy. "All right?"

"Yes, sir!" she said.

Trick and the others nodded in silence. Gerald started for the door.

"Wait!" Sandy rushed his envelope to him. "Don't forget the payoff."

He took it without a word.

During his taxi ride home, as interminable traffic light delays and poor shortcut choices killed him incrementally, Gerald kept thinking about one thing. He kept revisiting in his mind the nights of Kyle's childhood, when he would look in on his son, hours after he'd gone to sleep. Of the time he shared with Kyle, this was his favourite, because it entailed none of the erratic moods and movements of a child's waking hours. There were no unexplained crashes in the basement, there was no absurd bouncing in the hall. No need to order an end to a ten-year-old's frightening, drunken joy at being allowed to play with one of his rowdier friends. No inevitable anger to regret.

It was as pure a moment as he could find, in any of his days. Not that he ever came away unscathed. When he crept into the plum-stained dark of Kyle's bedroom – and it didn't matter what age his son was, two, eight, fifteen – the pattern of feelings was always the same, a sequence that came at him in waves. He'd see his boy's pudgy fist tucked into his neck, or his fingers, wet with spit, half in, half out of his mouth, and he'd feel the first one roll into him – that rush of joy, and then awe that he was allowed such joy – that he assumed was any father's privilege and due. He handled the first wave just fine; he cherished the first wave. But he could never enjoy it for long, because the second wave came fast. That white crest of fear – the certainty that he would screw it up, that it would all be snatched away – crashed down on his joy and pulled it out from under him every time. Vicki once asked him, as he was closing the door to Kyle's room, why he looked so upset.

"Ach!" The taxi driver hit the wheel with the flat of his hand as they pressed into the back end of another slowdown. He turned halfway around: "Everyone getting a start on the weekend, I think."

"Can't you take Merrivale?" Gerald asked.

The driver shook his head in disgust. "Merrivale is no good! It's all construction!"

Gerald felt the clench of rising panic in his chest. To distract himself, he dug into his pocket and brought out the envelope

Sandy had insisted he take with him. Inside was, as she'd said, just a mock-up of a flyer she'd roughed out on her computer and printed on orange paper. Her love-measuring instrument, folded into three panels:

1

HOW MUCH DO YOU LOVE YOUR FAMILY?

THIS MUCH: {——MORE THAN THE MOUNTAINS——}

THIS MUCH: {——————MORE THAN THE SKY——————}

2

DO YOU LOVE THEM ENOUGH TO PROTECT THEM
FROM THE AIR'S FEARSOME PARTICLES?

3

THEN YOU LOVE THEM THIS MUCH:
{————————SPENT WINDOW FILTERS————————}

SPENT WINDOW FILTERS:
IF YOUR FAMILY MEANS MORE TO YOU
THAN A PRETTY VIEW

Maybe it was a little over the top; Gerald couldn't be sure. It was situations like this when he didn't trust his instincts. That was the problem with having no strategic vision; you were lost in the forest and you couldn't tell the way out from the path that took you deeper in. But he liked the fact that on the back of the flyer, Sandy had drawn a rough facsimile of a $50-off coupon (good for orders of twenty filters or more). He trusted a sales and marketing director who hedged her bets.

For a while he studied the flyer, or maintained the posture of studying, as the cab crawled like sepsis from the fingertips of the city to its residential heart. But there was only so long he could stare at the flyer before the staring became as obsessive as the worrying it was supposed to forestall, and eventually he let it slide from his hand to the seat beside him and made do with noting all the roadside signage he would never have had the opportunity to read if his cab driver had made better off-ramp decisions.

Finally, when it was almost five by Gerald's watch, the car turned onto Breere Crescent. The driver looked back.

"What's the number?"

"Ninety-*three*," stressed Gerald. "It's around the curve."

The cabbie took them at an unnecessarily solemn pace past the stucco-smooth Victorian townhouses with their sunken garages that Vicki had once reliably clicked her tongue at, and past the pair of Hall & Ehrlich-designed French Country houses she'd transformed three years before. They skirted properties hemmed with shrubbery and properties walled with brick, and it was taking so long Gerald wanted to toss all his cash into the front seat and run the rest of the way.

"It's right there," he said, pointing over the driver's shoulder to the turreted house beside the Linders' shagbark hickory.

"Which one?"

"Just stop the car."

He paid the fare and opened the door at the same time, and he told himself as he ran through the tender spring air, down the sidewalk and up the drive, that he had no earthly reason for running. Out of breath, he went to the garage first, saw Vicki's car was still gone and surveyed his own for ominous indications. He found, to his scant relief, none; it was parked in its proper spot, if a little off-line, and there were no marks on it that he could see. Which meant nothing.

The door from the garage led to the mud room, and he wiped his feet out of habit. "Kyle?" he called, expecting no answer. "Son?" He found the kitchen empty, the breakfast nook hollow, and abandoned further downstairs searching. It was a straight path up he needed to take, to the door of his son's room, and though he tried to stay calm as he climbed the stacked staircase, he still hated each landing and turn.

Outside Kyle's door, he forced himself to slow down. Even if his son seemed fine, he really wasn't, and no good could come from bursting in. He took a breath and flattened his tie, then called in a soft voice, "Kyle?" His son didn't answer, but it wasn't for that reason he pushed open the door. It was because he heard something else. A meow.

He saw Kyle lying on his back, on his bed, over at the far side of the room. He was apparently asleep. And for a minute it all seemed normal, the old joy wave came rolling in, except the damned cat was there too, sitting on the bed beside his son. It was licking the outside of what appeared to be a bag of candy, butterscotch and grape and cherry sweets, that Kyle was holding on his stomach. Gerald went in quietly like he always had, this time to shoo the cat away. When he got close enough to see it wasn't a bag of candy at all, a surge of dizziness knocked him to his knees.

He was suddenly swimming. It seemed he was swimming across the floor, through a tide that kept pushing him back. He was required to swim against the current to his son.

"Kyle!" he shouted.

He grabbed hold of the side of the bed and pulled himself up. The hissing cat he swept away. "Son!"

Kyle opened his eyes sleepily. "Dad," he said. "Don't."

Gerald's response was to grunt, because he was trying to pick his son up. It was clear to him what he needed to do. But his legs weren't working, he couldn't get leverage, and his son was so much heavier than he looked. "I need your help, son," he gasped, in between his attempts to shove his arm underneath Kyle's shoulders. "We're going to the hospital."

"No," said Kyle.

"Come on, son." He felt strangely calm. "Can you stand?"

"Stop," yelled Kyle. Gerald thought he yelled *stop*. Which made no sense so he kept working. He kept trying to lift his little boy.

And then Kyle started flailing with his good hand. "No! Let me go!" He started to push and to hit. Gerald took a popping fist on the ear and began to understand something else was wrong. He backed away so that his son's mangled hand wouldn't be hurt any more.

"Kyle," he said from his knees, his chest heaving, "we have to get you to the hospital." He spoke slowly, in case his son was drugged or drunk, though no signs or smells told him that was

true. He began to see that Kyle had other marks on him, bruises
and cuts to his face and neck. It occurred to Gerald – it seemed
logical, it seemed complete – that here were the effects of the
unexplained off-camp event, the physical manifestations, that
they'd somehow been delayed until now. His son had been in a
war. And though he tried not to see the hand, its dried blood and
swollen flesh, the knobs and crooks of broken bones, he couldn't
help but look. And when he looked he couldn't breathe.

"I'm not going," said Kyle. "You can't make me go." He said
it in a way that seemed rational, not crazy. Which made it harder
to comprehend. Kyle pushed himself up with his good hand until
his back was against the wall. As if his father were the enemy.

Gerald's mouth hung open but he was having trouble
getting air. It didn't matter what had happened; he had to think
about what was next. He pressed his skull with his hands to quell
the panic, so he could figure out how to speak, to make his son
understand.

"Your hand, son." He had to do better. Had to try again.
"Doctors have to see to your hand."

"No!"

Oh, lord, these *no*'s and *not*'s were making him queasy. It
was probable he was going to throw up. "It could be infected,"
he whimpered. "The bones . . . need to be set."

"Don't worry," said Kyle, full of anger, contempt. "I ran it
under the tap."

It was then Gerald heard the clack of heels on hardwood,
and he knew he had to stand and get to the door. "Vicki," he
called out, "don't come in." He stumbled across the carpet she'd
chosen. "Please . . ."

She peeked in the doorway as if unsure whether to intrude. When she came in and saw him flopping about, her eyes brightened as if she might laugh. He found his footing just as she looked over his shoulder, as she coughed and crumpled as though she'd been punched.

What parents they were, Gerald thought as he went to her. In a moment of crisis they couldn't even stay on their feet.

4

Everybody was freaking out so much – Dad running around, Mom sort of catatonic – I decided I had to get out of there. As soon as Dad was busy trying to carry Mom into their bedroom and make sure she was all right, I grabbed a sweater and eased down the stairs and out the back door. I thought for a second about taking the cat with me, but that just seemed like too much to deal with.

My hand hurt like hell, of course. The fact that it was useless didn't bother me, but if I let it hang at my side the throbbing was so intense it got hard to see for all the sparks in my eyes. It took me a while to figure out that if I kept it above my waist, the hand stopped feeling like it was going to explode. So as I walked to a street where I knew I could get a cab, making sure to take the back lanes and cutting through some properties so Dad couldn't follow, I held my hand up over my heart, like I felt really deeply about something. And I wrapped it in the sweater so people wouldn't stare.

When I was finally able to get a cab, I asked the driver, a dark-eyed young guy who looked almost Pashtun, to take me to a hotel with Internet service.

"They all got that," said the cabbie, looking at me in the rear-view mirror. "You got a computer?"

I looked around the back seat. Under my armpits. "No."

"Then you have to use the business centre." The cabbie seemed to study me through the mirror. "They might not let you, though."

"Why not?"

"You're a kid." The cabbie grinned. "They might think you want to use it for porn or something." He shrugged as he made a turn. "Which, you know, I'm not saying is bad. People should do what they want." He looked back at me again. "So, any place in particular you're thinking of?"

I shook my head.

"Someplace cheap though."

"Doesn't matter." I still had money in my account, and the military was paying my full salary until the end of my COF-AP contract.

"You have some way to pay? Credit card?"

I still had my wallet with about three hundred dollars in my back pocket – the guys at the casino were probably so excited about the eighteen thousand in cash they forgot to look for it. I took it out and held it up for him.

The cabbie bobbed his head from side to side. "Okay," he said. "I know where."

We drove for a few blocks. Sat at red lights that wouldn't turn. The cabbie must have had his air conditioning on high because I was starting to shiver. When I unwrapped the sweater and pulled it on he looked back again. "Whoa, you hurt yourself or something?"

I laid my hand in my lap, out of view. "It's all right."

"What's it, like, cut or something? You need to see a doctor?"

"No."

"What did you do to it?"

He was bugging me, so I just stared out the window. If Legg had been in the same situation, he would've probably told the driver to fuck off. But that wasn't necessarily one of his better qualities. I looked up at the driver. "Are you from Afghanistan?"

He laughed as if I'd said something funny. "I'm from Oakville," he said. "My parents, though, they're from Iran originally."

"Have you ever heard of the *gudiparan*?"

The driver looked back at me through the mirror. "No, I never heard of that. What is it?"

I stared out the window again and pulled the sweater tighter. "Doesn't matter," I said.

5

Gerald was a good husband. Not exceptional. Not award-winning on a grand scale. But better than most, Vicki suspected. And she found the realization warming, even after twenty-odd years, despite the events it had taken to make her see. Over the weekend, practically every hour, he'd come into the bedroom to check on how she was doing and to give her reports, though at first she hadn't been fully able to respond. Why that had been so still wasn't entirely clear, but it was as if a heavy blanket had been laid over her, and everything that had once come easily – speaking, thinking, getting out of bed – seemed suddenly to require a preposterous effort. She was in the clutch of some sort of anxiety crisis, Gerald said he'd been told. It was connected to the pains and shortness of breath she'd been experiencing, and what she needed was quiet and rest and calm. And Gerald's presence, after what she'd seen in Kyle's room, had helped a great deal. Surprisingly so. That was something she wanted to tell him, now that she was feeling very much better.

As for Kyle, Gerald had insisted the whole weekend that he was fine. And when she'd asked about his hand, and what could possibly have happened, and for heaven's sake what was being *done*, he'd been very firm. It was all under control; she was not to worry – that, Gerald had said with a half smile, was his job. And at the time, without the energy to argue, she'd chosen to believe that what Gerald meant was that Kyle was receiving treatment and getting well.

But now that she was here in his room, sitting on the edge of his bed, now that she saw the touches of dried blood on his duvet, which Rosary had neglected to launder, she could sense that Gerald had not been telling her the whole truth. That he had been trying to protect her from facts she had a right to know. And so she was angry at Gerald and needed to tell him that too. She would have to make it as clear to him as it was to her that, when it came to painful truths about their children, mothers should not be protected.

The spring light coming into the room, through the leaded glass windows, gave everything in it an elevated glow. The encyclopaedias and textbooks, the pieces of furniture she'd selected over the years, the Persian carpet in reds and golds – all these things seemed strangely vivid, as if she'd never seen them before. From the bed she looked up at the antiquated periodic tables she'd given to Kyle when he was much younger, when his growing love of science seemed to define him the way hockey or video games or practical jokes served to define other boys, in a kind of characteristic shorthand that was useful in any conversation that began "My son. . . ." She remembered how pleased she was to be able to give him these old musty tables, framed and flattened under glass, which showed only the elements that were known and understood at a time when science hardly knew how to look.

Then she pulled Kyle's duvet in bunches into her lap. She drew her fingertips across the coin-sized stains, and bent to press them against her cheek, and lips.

Somewhere in the room, she remembered, there was a plastic model of a man, with transparent skin that revealed all his inner workings. When Kyle was nine it seemed nothing could make him happier than painting the veins and arteries, the liver and lungs, giving shape to what was inside. It was surely proof, Vicki and Gerald had agreed, that he was a doctor, a researcher, some kind of scientist in the making, and it had stood on his desk, with pride of place, ever since. But now she couldn't see the transparent man there or on any of the shelves.

It became very important to find the transparent man. And after some minutes spent shifting boxes and searching among the detritus of Kyle's closet, Vicki saw its veined plastic legs peeking out at her. The man had fallen or been thrown into a corner and become buried under an accumulation of old shoes and books.

When she pulled it out, the sudden thrill she'd felt at recovering it fled. Although its organs were intact, one of its fragile outstretched arms was broken off at the shoulder. And despite falling to her hands and knees and pawing for the missing piece through paper clips and balls of dust, it wasn't to be found. So, for a time, until the sainted light in the room had dimmed, Vicki sat on the floor of Kyle's closet, holding the transparent man to her chest, and the shirts and pants hanging from above absorbed the sound of her unrestrained weeping for the man and his lost plastic arm.

A call late on that Monday afternoon determined that Hella was not at home, and she still had Vicki's car. So after she'd washed the dust and salt from her face in the ensuite, and dressed for what was left of the day, Vicki ordered a taxi to take her to the warehouse. With the twisting chain of rush hour traffic headed in the opposite direction, it was an easy drive downtown along the sweeping road that tracked the edge of the ravine, and she was able to roll down the window and let the breeze swirl through the cab until it tossed the driver's fine hair and fluttered the pages of the clipboard beside him. He turned it over on the seat without a word.

As the cab pulled into the alley next to the warehouse entrance, she saw her car parked across the street, where it was sure to get a ticket, and she allowed herself a sigh at Hella's lack of care. After she paid the $12.80 fare with a twenty-dollar bill, insisting the driver keep the rest, she went to the car and found it unlocked, with assorted sticky Popsicle wrappers on the back seat. She set down the large fabric bag she was carrying, opened the door, and gathered them up, one by one.

Rather than take the freight elevator to her floor of the building, which would have announced her presence, Vicki walked up the four flights of dimly lit wooden stairs, her shoes falling softly on old iron treads embossed with the name GateHouse Ltd., the long-dead cardboard maker whose plant the building used to house. As she ascended the last few steps, she was met with the sound of children.

She pulled open the heavy, paint-chipped door.

"Nooooo! Dooon't!"

Although her view was blocked by the first of two wide warehouse shelving units that spanned two-thirds of the cavernous length and bore the majority of her smaller pieces and boxes of accents, she could tell that the sound was coming from the northwest corner.

"Jeremeee!"

Vicki made her way quietly across the width of the old plank floor, following the path that separated the bulky main-level furnishings (dining room sets, cabinets, upholstered sofas and chairs) from bedroom and auxiliary room pieces. She rounded the end of the first shelving structure and saw at the far end largely what she expected to see.

Hella was there, her thin frame doubled over a slat wood box, searching – for what, Vicki could hardly imagine – and behind her were her three small children: Peter, Jeremy, and Erin. With Hella's attention diverted, they were down on the floor, playing with Vicki's small collection of seventy- and eighty-year-old German and British-made toys.

"Jere*meee*! *Quiiit* it!"

Erin, eight, was happily engaged with examining a Kestner "character" doll and making it dance from knee to knee. A short distance away, Peter, barely five, was making putt-putt noises and attempting to push a yellow-painted tin Dinky van in a continuous path, unmolested. Seven-year-old Jeremy, however, appeared determined to thwart this effort, by using a 1930s torpedo-shaped Güntherman landspeed-record car, worth approximately eight hundred dollars, to ram the Dinky van repeatedly.

"Jere*meee*! *Stoooop*!"

Vicki had covered half the distance to them when Hella looked up.

"Oh, shit! Kids! Jeremy! Put those toys away. You *know* how I don't like you playing with Mrs. Woodlore's things." Hella left the box she'd been hunting through, skipped around her children – "Now!" she ordered, snapping her fingers – and intercepted Vicki as she approached with a stream of goodwill: "How *are* you? I was really worried. I called your house on Saturday and Mr. Woodlore said you were knocked flat by something. Did you hear about Avis not being able to get into the house? Oh, boy, she was furious. There was something wrong with the locks so she had to get them all changed on Sunday and then she asked me, because we weren't sure how long you were going to be sick and I didn't want her bothering you, I said I'd try to finish the boy's room, you know, just add a few sportsy things? So that's what I'm doing here. I was looking for football stuff but . . ." She gave Vicki a desperate smile. "Do you mind?"

Vicki looked past Hella to the children behind her, reluctantly returning the toys to a pile near the box.

"I'm really sorry about that," insisted Hella. "I know some of those things are expensive but the kids were just going squirrelly waiting for me and I didn't think they could really hurt anything."

Jeremy, his head dominated by a thatch of his mother's dark

hair, was still in the process of putting his toy back where it belonged, the delay caused by the fact that he'd chosen to return the car by kicking it half-heartedly across the floor.

Hella turned to see what Vicki was watching. "Jeremy!" She ran back and hauled him away from the car by his elbow.

Vicki stepped forward and picked up the slender blue Güntherman car. Then she crouched down with it in front of Jeremy.

"Jeremy, you're such a little monster sometimes," said Hella. "Say you're sorry to Mrs. Woodlore."

Vicki looked up. "It's all right, Hella. I don't want an apology." She lowered her gaze back to the boy. "This is an interesting car, don't you think, Jeremy? So long and thin."

His angry eyes wouldn't connect with hers. He shrugged.

"You don't have to like it," Vicki assured him. "Tell me what you really think. Is it sort of old and dumb?"

Jeremy flicked a glance at Vicki. "It's stupid," he sneered. "It doesn't work right. The wheels don't turn properly."

"Jeremy!" huffed Hella. "He doesn't mean it, really."

Vicki waved her off. She focused on Jeremy, on his down-turned eyes and curled-up mouth. "What do you really want to do with this car?" She waited. "Do you like to smash things?"

Jeremy's face popped up. "Yeah," he said, tentatively.

Vicki grinned at him. "Well, if your mother will let go of you, it would be okay with me if you gave this car a good smashing."

He brightened as if he couldn't believe his luck. "Really?"

Hella was shaking her head. "You don't have to do that, Vicki – Victoria. Mrs. Woodlore. Really, I don't think –"

She stopped when Vicki glared up at her. Then Vicki set the car against Jeremy's stomach, and held it there until he cradled it in his hands. "All right now," she said. "I'm going to give you one minute to play with that car the way you really want to."

He stared at her with a dark gleam. "One minute? Are you going to time me?"

Vicki tapped her watch. "I'm going to time you. But the rule is you can't touch anything with the car, except the floor and the walls. Otherwise the fun's over. Okay?"

"O-*kay*!" He raced off with the car toward the north wall and rammed it straight in. He dive-bombed invisible enemies by flinging the car repeatedly into the floorboards, the sounds of his explosions dissipating into the aching hollows of the warehouse. He mashed the tin tires with his heels as Vicki watched, and kicked the Güntherman like a football halfway to the murky rafters.

"Time!" she yelled.

Jeremy stopped his assault, and returned to Vicki with the battered scrap of tin borne proudly in his hands. She thanked him, took the car and placed it in her voluminous fabric bag.

"Wow," said Hella, seemingly in shock. "That was . . ." She gathered Jeremy in. "I don't know what to say."

Vicki smiled slightly. She held out her hand. "Could I have the keys now, Hella?"

"Oh, the car keys, right!" Hella ran back to get her purse, and returned rifling through it. She pulled out the car keys and handed them to Vicki. "Do you think we could –"

"Also the new keys for Lightenham Avenue," said Vicki.

"Okay, I have them here." Hella searched and handed them over. "We could go over now, if you wanted."

Vicki held out her hand once more. "And the warehouse keys," she said.

Hella blinked. "The warehouse keys?"

"The ones you use to get in here."

"Oh." Somewhat less energetically, Hella hunted through her purse until she came up with the warehouse keys. "How am I going to –"

"You're not," said Vicki, taking them. "I've come to the conclusion, Hella, sadly, that this sort of work is not really suited to you. It may seem silly, but someone doing what we do really must have an appreciation of things. Must want to take care of them. Must want to understand what they represent."

"But . . . I do."

Vicki shook her head with genuine sympathy. "No."

Hella's face took on a hardness. "What about severance pay?"

"You were a casual employee working by the hour. You were paying no taxes. I don't really think severance is required. But I will give you the equivalent of twenty hours."

"I think it should be at least forty."

"I could give you forty," said Vicki. "But then I would be inclined to bill you for the destruction of the papier mâché fruit, which will cost about three hundred dollars to replace, and the four-thousand-dollar Chinese folding chair that you allowed your children to ruin." She cast her gaze around the warehouse. "And I suppose I should do an inventory soon to see what else is damaged or missing."

Hella narrowed her eyes at Vicki. "You know, they're just kids. You can't blame kids for what happens."

Vicki felt her store of patience coming to its end. She breathed out slowly into the cool warehouse air and gave Hella one last smile.

"I don't," she said.

On her way to the Lightenham Avenue house, Vicki made two calls. The first was to Edward Caughley; she knew he was about to close shop for the day and wondered whether it was possible to have an item delivered. He said he would bring it personally.

The second call went to Avis Nye. For several minutes, Vicki apologized to the agent for having been out of touch for the previous two days, assured her all was well, and consoled her over the trouble with the locks. It was, indeed, a mystery. Then she shared with Avis the brighter news that the Lightenham house would be finished within the hour, and invited her to come by for a look.

She drove through the curtains of evening being spread across the city, past stores in which she had never shopped, and neighbourhoods whose homes she was never likely to enter, and she wondered whether the path of Kyle's life from this point on would take him into homes like these, beyond her reach, where no one knew the comfort of surroundings designed to keep incivility at bay, and where the happiness she had always assumed was appreciated, instead, as luxury.

When she arrived at the door of the Lightenham house, she thrust a new key into a different lock, and walked into a home she barely recognized. It contained all the same things set pre-cisely the same way, under ceilings too high to touch as before. But she saw them now as the belongings of a family she had to admit she hardly knew. Margeaux and Robert Lightenham were not the people they had appeared, in her imagination, to be. The responsibility for this, Vicki accepted as her own; certain aspects of their lives she had simply been unwilling to see.

She waited for Edward with her fabric bag on a cream upholstered Regency settee, in the transition area between foyer and hall, and met him at the door when she heard him pull in.

"You're a dear to come, Edward," she said as he arrived on the front steps bearing a thin mahogany box. "I'm lucky you close at six on Mondays."

He looked up at her gravely and blushed, from under wisps of hair. "I would have closed if it were the middle of the day."

She held the box as he removed his shoes, then took her bag and led him upstairs. "I'd only ever seen pictures before, of what you do," he said, admiring it all. "I'm agog."

Together they walked down the hall of the second floor, past the open den that featured the Georges Jacob chairs in cross-hatch blue, into the boy's room that, until now, had given her such trouble.

"Oh, I love those," said Edward, pointing to the *oeil-de-boeuf*, glowing tangerine from the sunset beyond. "When I was eight we lived in a house that had one."

"What did you imagine it was?"

Edward thought for a moment, and brought a hand to his cheek. "I wasn't very popular at school," he said. "It was my looking glass onto all my tormentors, something like the witch's in *The Wizard of Oz*."

"Well then," she said quietly, "you were lucky to have it." And she watched Edward raise his eyebrows and nod against his hand, and his memories.

Then she took the thin wooden box to the revolving bookcase. On the broad, low top of the bookcase she laid a square of blue silk, and across the far third of this square she set the box. Then she opened it, and lifted out the silver-mounted violin bow with its severed hair, which Edward had long been so reluctant to sell. This she laid in front of the box, on the middle of the silk, where an anguished prodigy might have placed it before closing his instrument forever in its case.

"There," she said, with approval. Then she went to her bag and retrieved the battered Güntherman landspeed car, and took it to the bookcase, showing it to Edward as she went. "You may not recognize this, but you sold it to me years ago."

"I do, vaguely," said Edward. "What *happened* to it?"

Vicki crouched in front of the bookcase. "It sacrificed itself for a worthy cause." She turned the revolving compartments of the bookcase until the one left empty of books was revealed, and placed the car there.

Then she took her bag to the *bonheur du jour*, where an angry young boy might have sat for hours after school, struggling with his homework. She pulled out Kyle's wounded transparent man, and placed it in the corner of the padded writing surface.

Finally, she went to the mahogany dressing table and laid across its top a simple panel of sand-coloured felt. At either end of this, she set the pieces of her broken Meissen candlesticks.

"Oh," exclaimed Edward, a hand across his mouth. "You loved those."

Vicki touched the face of each innocent *putto*. "I still do."

Avis arrived twenty minutes later, and Vicki called out for her to come up. She entered the room and surveyed Vicki's work with fading excitement until her face settled into a frown.

"I don't understand, Victoria," she said. "I thought you were done."

"I am."

"But what are all these broken things?"

Vicki picked up her bag. "This is Kyle's room," she said, and turned for the door. "You can let the Webbs see it now."

6

It was as though the city was keeping his son from him, hiding him away under the flare of its long coat. Gerald did his best not to imagine that it constituted a personal indictment, a clear impeachment of his abilities and conduct as a father, but every phone call he made that yielded no information or leads on Kyle's whereabouts confirmed his suspicion that "Kyle Woodlore: better off on the streets" was the pervasively held view.

He was into his third day of making calls when Bishop's wifely secretary, Sylvia, arrived at his open door. She leaned across the threshold and knocked.

"Are you in?" Sylvia asked, as if it were entirely optional.

He doused the list of regional hospitals showing on his computer screen with a mouse click. "Yes."

"I would have buzzed you," said Sylvia, approaching his desk, "but your line has been skipping straight to voice mail for the longest time."

"I'm sorry."

"This is why you need an assistant, Gerald." She picked up the glasses that were hanging by a chain around her neck. "Someone to manage incoming needs. Voice mail is only useful to a point."

"I'm sort of – what can I do for you, Syl?"

"I have a message here from Gwyn Doremond." She studied a small piece of paper in her hand. "You've met Gwyn, have you?" she said, speaking to the paper.

"A few times, yes." Gerald's eyes moved back to the computer screen.

"Very competent, very direct," she asserted.

Gerald's hand inched toward the mouse.

"Now it says here that Gwyn is coming in at three to meet with you. And he wants a full rundown on your plans regarding the drop in market share."

Gerald pressed a thumb into his temple. "Are you sure that's right, Syl? Bishop said he was going to set up a meeting with Gwyn for when he came back."

Sylvia regarded Gerald from on high. "This is the message I took from Deirdre, who is Gwyn's assistant." She removed her glasses and let them, once again, dangle. "If this is, indeed, a surprise visit, it's perfectly in keeping with Gwyn Doremond's modus operandi, which is to throw challenges out to people to see how they respond. I should think he wants to see how you react to a sudden change in plans."

He sighed and checked his watch. It was one o'clock. "Well, fine, we'll see what we can do." He watched Sylvia begin to leave. "Syl, could you do me a favour –"

She turned like a ship in the harbour.

"Could you let Sandy Beale and, uh, Trick Runiman, know that I'll need to see them in a few minutes? Please?"

Sylvia smiled as if deciphering a complex puzzle of words. Finally she said, "Of course."

As she left, he restored the list of hospitals with one hand and picked up his phone with the other.

He was done with the hospitals and midway through his rounds of the hotels when Sandy and Trick arrived at his door. Sandy entered first, with Trick tailing in behind her with a clipboard and a pen and the face of a dog who had lost track of the slipper he liked to chew.

Gerald held his hand over the phone as the day-shift man at the Moonlight Inn in Wexford grumbled into his ear. "You keep calling, mister, and I keep telling you. Nobody named Kyle Woodlore here."

"I'm in the middle of something," he said to Sandy.

"You said you wanted to see us."

He had called the first-class hotels first, because talking to efficient, well-spoken desk clerks made the outlook seem less bleak than it would have had he begun with the flophouses. But getting to the fifty-dollar-a-night hotels was a disheartening stage, and it took all his effort to fling handfuls of air at the door until Sandy's eyes lit up and she laid a hand on Trick's wrist and began to back them both out through the doorway, holding a shush finger over her pursed lips.

"I don't know what you expect me to do," the man was saying.

"I don't want you to do anything," stressed Gerald, "except call me if you see a twenty-year-old boy with light brown collar-length hair and a *broken hand*."

"Wha'd he do, get in a fight?"

"I don't know, it's not important. I just need to find him."

"What's a broken hand look like anyway? What if he sticks it in his pocket?"

"It won't fit in his pocket," said Gerald, hardly able to spit out the words. "It's too swollen."

The man made a noise like a tire leaking air. "Sounds more than broken to me. Sounds infected."

"Yes," he breathed. "It's possible. Do you still have my number?"

"Lemme look, lemme look," said the man. Gerald heard the sound of the phone being dropped onto a hard surface. He heard a conversation taking place between the day-shift man and someone else, a conversation that *had nothing to do with his son*. Finally he heard the phone being picked up again. "Yeah, I think this is it. I scribbled 'Wood' but it's Woodlore, right? Six, three –"

"That's it. Now, this is important," he leaned into the phone. "Sir, if – what's your name? I should have asked you before."

"Me?" said the man. "Mike. I'm Mike."

"Mike," said Gerald, like an old friend, "if my son comes in, can you please not scare him. Just act normally and call me without making him suspicious."

"Look, I'm not some friggin undercover cop here. If he comes in, I'll call you."

"Fine. Good. And, one more thing!" He heard Mike sigh through the phone and he cringed. He did not want to make

Mike angry – please don't be angry, he thought – just conscientious. "Can you leave the number, with a note, some place obvious for the next person who comes on shift? Mike?"

Mike sighed again. "Sure, yeah. Okay?" He hung up.

Sandy sat down in the seat opposite Gerald's desk and motioned for Trick to drag over one of the chairs by the window. Which he did. Then she turned her attention to Gerald.

"Is there anything that, you know, we can do?" she said, pressing her skirt down across her knees.

Gerald was only half aware of their presence; he was concentrating on the check marks he'd made on the Yellow Pages ads of all the hotels he had called. Those with only three checks, instead of four, he needed to call again. Then back to the hospitals.

He glanced up at her. "What do you mean?"

"Well, you seem to be in the middle of some sort of . . . problem." As she said this, she brought her hands up and agitated them in the air, little facsimiles of commotion.

Gerald was thinking about hotels and hospitals. It seemed to him as though he was missing something, as if he had cast out a net that had gaping holes through which entire groups of buildings could swim. "No, it's under control," he said. "But here's the thing." He dragged his eyes off the Yellow Pages to look at her. "Gwyn Doremond is coming here at three and he wants a rundown on our plan to attack the market share. I need you to give me what you've worked up since Friday."

"Gwyn Doremond?" said Sandy.

"The chairman," offered Trick, at her elbow.

Sandy turned her head with a frown as if to speak sharply to Trick, but resisted the urge. "Gerald," she said, "do you want me to give the presentation?"

He stared at her for an extended moment, until she sat back in her chair. "If you wanted to stay somewhere in the city for a few nights," he said, "where would you stay?"

She blinked. "You mean if I was visiting?"

"Sure. But not a hotel. Somewhere else."

"Uh." She glanced over at Trick and then back. "With friends?"

"No," muttered Gerald. "Tried that."

"You can rent condos," offered Trick. "Down by the water. Place is teeming with them."

Gerald shook his head. "No. That's not it." He flipped pages.

"I'm sorry, I don't know," said Sandy, and she gave a stoic laugh. "I hardly ever travel anywhere. I'm always *working!*"

He turned the pages of ads and circled the ones with only three checks and nodded at the words coming out of Sandy's mouth. And the whole time he tried not to think of Kyle's hand, festering, and the bones setting into contortions, because whenever he did, his head started to spin and he accomplished nothing. When he picked up the phone to make his next call – university housing, that was something he hadn't tried – he barely noticed that Sandy and Trick had gone.

Gwyn Doremond was a short, brick-shaped man with a head of wavy black hair who would have struck some observers as handsome in a threatening, bar-thug sort of way were he remotely interested in their opinion of him. But an expression of barely suppressed contempt for anyone he spoke to tended to erase the handsome from his features.

Gerald, on his way to the reception area to meet him, found him in the corridor, staring into the sales area with his legs set wide apart and his dark suit jacket flared back from the hands on his hips.

"Mr. Doremond," Gerald said, extending his hand.

"You hear that?" Doremond grumbled as a greeting, his Welsh accent knuckling each word as it emerged. He shook Gerald's hand as an afterthought and folded his arms. "What's that telling you?"

Gerald looked where Doremond was looking; tried to understand. "I'm not following."

"This is your sales department, correct?" He leaned forward and cupped a hand to his ear. "Don't hear a fucking thing, do you?"

"They're probably all out on sales calls."

"Stand where I'm standing," he said. He backed away and pointed to the spot. "Go on. Stand right there."

Gerald took his position and stared where Doremond had stared. From there he saw two sets of salespeople feet, crossed at the ankles and propped up on salespeople desks, the way Kyle had once studied for his exams, lying with his back on the padded carpet in the living room, a textbook suspended over his head, his feet propped up on the edge of a sofa.

"So," Doremond said. "What are you gonna do about it?"

What could he do? Could he restore those days? Could he

take back every moment of thoughtless neglect, rescind every overbearing command to shape up or buckle down? He remembered seeing Kyle study that way, and because it made him seem careless, he'd once actually told him to stop:

GERALD: That's no way to study for an exam, Kyle. I never would have gotten away with that. You're just reading. You can't learn that way. You have to take notes. You have to get the whole body engaged in absorbing the information. Come on, sit up properly! Use your logic!

Could he take that back? Could he find some way to patch all the rents that were showing now in the fabric of his son? Before he could do that, he had to find him, and more than anything he wanted to get back to the phone. But Doremond was talking about something else, he knew. Gerald turned to him. "I've been meaning to have a talk with Leslie Morton."

"You've been *meaning* to," repeated Doremond. He chuckled with apparent disgust. "Man of action, eh?" He glanced up and down at the figure in front of him, taking in the vision through narrowed eyes. Then he turned his square shoulders and signalled for Gerald to follow him. "We can use Bishop's office."

Gerald walked with Doremond partway down the hall and stopped outside the sales and marketing department. "Be right there, sir," he said and for a moment watched Doremond carry on as if he hadn't heard. Then he looked in as Sandy met him at the door with a file folder thick with papers.

"I think everything's here," she said in a half whisper. "You've got the market share figures for the last three years, and then I've sketched out the marketing plan, including the trade shows and the direct mail and the distribution, and I have cost projections from Doug and –"

Gerald took it from her. "Thanks, Sandy." The folder felt heavy, but no more than he'd expected; it had the heft of hard work. "Could you let the woman at reception – what's her name?"

Sandy stared at him. "You mean Mary?"

"Mary, right." He tapped his forehead with a knuckle. "Could you ask Mary to monitor my line, and let her know where I am, and ask her to" – he tried to breathe deep, but his lungs seemed to resist the air – "to let me know if any calls come in about my son."

For a second, Sandy's eyes searched his. "Yes. Of course."

She said it so firmly, so precisely, his knees almost buckled with relief. He set a hand against the doorframe and managed a better breath. Then he thanked her and pushed off down the hall.

"I'll be close by," she whispered after him, "if you need me."

For the first few minutes Doremond didn't bother with a chair in Bishop's office of walnut and dark leather. He stood at the window looking down on the movements of men and trucks at the loading dock.

"How many shipments out today?" he said as Gerald stepped into the room.

Gerald had to think for a minute. "Six," he finally said. "Four to western Canada and two to the States."

"And tomorrow?"

"Let me – uh, four, I think."

"You never think of piggybacking your shipments to regions?"

"Yes, all the time."

"What I'm looking at here," said Doremond, jabbing a hand toward the scene below, "is two teams of men filling two mid-sized trucks going to the same goddamn place." He glanced scornfully at Gerald. "Am I right?"

"Actually no," said Gerald. "One of those is going to Edmonton, the other's going to New York State."

"Did you have two trucks going west this morning?"

"Yes. To Winnipeg and . . . " – he had to think – "Saskatoon."

"So. Same fucking difference. You could've combined those two into one, saved yourself a truck and a driver, half the men, and cut your fuel costs thirty per cent."

None of that was true, because the trucks in the morning had been full-sized rigs, completely filled. But Gerald didn't have the heart to argue. He wanted this to be over, and he watched Doremond finger the change in his pocket until he turned his attention back into the room.

"Bishop thinks highly of you," Doremond said, not looking at him.

"And I think the same of Bishop."

That seemed to pique the chairman's interest. He glared at him, jangling his change. "Some friend you turned out to be then, letting him step knee deep into the muck."

Gerald hesitated. "You're talking about the market share?"

Doremond played his tongue along his lower lip. "If you can call it that. 'Market sliver,' I'd say. Bloody shame the way the people in this company, yourself included, let it wither up till there's almost nothing left." He brushed his hand through the air, as if to show the weightlessness of the company, or the effort made. Abruptly he turned and strode to the corner of the office, where he claimed a stuffed armchair, leaving the low leather sofa for Gerald. "All right then," he said. "Sit down and let's hear what you have to say about it."

If a man could become attached to an open, empty space, Gerald felt nailed to the doorway. The doorway opened onto the hall, which led to his office and his phone, and his only chance of finding Kyle.

"Well?"

He thought of Bishop in Phoenix, leaving him with this opportunity. Counting on him. And it was true what Doremond had said; he had already let the man down. He forced himself to the sofa and sunk to its edge, telling himself there was nothing he could do for Kyle just now, and not believing it for a second. He opened the folder, set it onto the glass-topped coffee table in front of him, and tried to make sense of what it contained.

"There's been a trend . . ." he began. But the knowledge of what sort of trend it had been seemed to slip away from him. He picked up the first set of laser-printed pages to get a better look, saw the names of companies, the numbers in rows, nothing like phone numbers. The image came to him, without warning, of five-year-old Kyle wanting to be picked up. He had gone running through the grass in his bare feet, and he'd stepped on a sharp pebble. It obviously hurt, but there was no cut. Why all the fuss? Gerald had given him a pat on the bottom, no comfort, and told him to go on and play. But he was here to talk about his plan. He tried to set himself to the task. "The market share has been, um . . ." He had to keep going, had to throw some words out there, keep talking. "Not what, really . . . it hasn't been." He cleared his throat, tried to focus. But he was shivering from memories . . . Kyle pleading to be taken into his arms . . . places he hadn't thought to call.

"Mr. Doremond," said a strong voice. "I'm Sandy Beale, from the sales and marketing department."

He looked up from the confusion of pages in his lap and saw his rescuer taking Doremond's thick hand into her firm, cool grip.

"Mr. Woodlore asked me to present you with our strategy to turn the market share of this company around."

"Saw you outside there," said Doremond, watching his hand being shaken. "Wondered what was going on."

Sandy nodded and winked at Gerald. "Just waiting for Mr. Woodlore's cue."

He threw water on his face in the staff washroom and came back damp to his desk, breathing again, everything clear in front of him – his telephone, his phone book, his plan. The numbers were screaming at him from the page. He'd begun dialling hospitals again when Mary the receptionist peeked into the room.

"Oh, Mr. Woodlore, I didn't realize you were here." She showed a pink slip of paper in her hand. "I was just going to leave this on your desk."

He watched her come forward. "What is it?" he said, his finger and his faint hopes frozen above a nine.

"I don't think it's important," said Mary. "Sandy told me you were expecting a call about your son. I would have put that through. This was just some woman from a bed and breakfast in Oakville." She held the pink slip out to him, across his desk. "She didn't say what it was about."

He took it from her as he hung up the phone and stared at the name written in Mary's crisp hand: *Meda Ghaemi, Gooseberry B&B.*

Bed and breakfasts, Gerald thought. People stay in them.

"Okay?" chirped Mary, on her way out. "Do you want me to keep watching your line?"

He pressed his thumbnail under each written number as he dialled it, for fear he would mix up the order because of the swirling in his head. "Thank you," he mumbled over the kettle-drums in his chest. He sealed the phone to his ear through two rings . . . three.

"Hello?" said a woman.

"Is this Gooseberry Bed and Breakfast? Are you Meda Ghaemi?"

"Yes, hello?"

"This is Gerald Woodlore. You called me just now."

"Oh, yes," she whispered. "Thank you. I am sorry to call you."

"That's fine. Just –"

"I want to ask, are you in the family of Kyle? He is a young man, a boy –"

"What is it!" barked Gerald. "Is Kyle there?"

"Yes," she whispered. "At the computer of my son. His hand is not good. I think maybe he was in an accident? And

more now – he is sick, I think. He shakes from cold. I gave him
a coat. I said to him go to a doctor but he said no. So I went to
his room to look inside his wallet, I am so sorry, forgive me, but
it was good because I found the card for you."

"Where are you?"

He wrote down the address and the directions she gave
him.

"Don't let him leave."

"Yes, thank you," said the woman. "Are you coming?"

"I'm coming now. It will take me twenty minutes."

"Thank you," said the woman.

The hall he raced down took him by Bishop's office. No
light showed from under the closed door and as he ran past he
heard Sandy's voice, shouting, "They've got your wife, Mr.
Doremond! Will you give up your wine cellar to save her?"

He never heard Doremond's answer.

The way was miraculously clear, as if the whole city, instead of
trying to get an early start on the traffic, had decided to put in a
full day's work. Or maybe it was just his instincts that enabled
Gerald to weave from the express lanes to the collectors and
back again, avoiding every possible delay. He didn't even need
to turn on the radio.

Gooseberry B&B was housed in a large white-brick split-
level sitting on the edge of a small park that overlooked Lake
Ontario. He would have missed it except for a discreet, goose-
berry-shaped sign the size of a mailbox at the end of a broad
drive with three cars. As he ran between them up to the house a

small, elegant woman in her sixties, wearing a dress of lavender silk, opened the door, her dark eyes full of worry.

"You are Mr. Woodlore?"

"Yes!"

"Thank you please come," she said, straining to keep to a whisper. "He is upstairs, he saw you drive in."

She pushed open the screen door for Gerald and turned to hurry ahead of him across a tiled foyer and up a set of wide, carpeted stairs.

"This is the way for my guests," she whispered, gripping the railing with a veiny hand and climbing as fast as she could. As he started to pass her she gave him a pained smile. "Your son is no trouble. He pays every day in cash."

He reached the top before she did and found himself helpless in a warren of closed doors.

"This one!" she said, pointing as her small, urgent steps took her to a door halfway down the hall. "This is for my son's computer."

Gerald tried the brass knob and found it locked. "Kyle, it's Dad!" he shouted. "Let me in!"

"No," yelled Kyle from the other side.

"Come on! We've got to get that hand looked at."

"Stay the fuck out."

His son's voice sounded weak. He sounded in pain. Gerald joggled the knob again and turned to the woman. "Do you have a key?"

Her dark eyes filled with apology. "No, this is my son's room. He has a key, but he is working in the taxicab." She lifted a purposeful finger. "I will call him. He may be able to come."

She waggled her finger like a banner in the air as she hurried along the carpeted hall and back down the stairs.

Gerald pounded on the door. "Kyle! Son! You have to let me in."

There was a pause. Then he heard: "I don't have to do anything, Dad."

This was no way to negotiate. He had to try something different. "I don't understand, son, I don't get it. Why don't you want to see a doctor?"

He waited.

"Kyle!"

The silence stretched, and standing in this stranger's house, under a dim ceiling fixture, on a thick, champagne-coloured carpet, Gerald thought of all the times he'd failed to act boldly even when he'd suspected boldness was required. All the times he'd been afraid to reach for what he hoped for, even when it was his responsibility. "A man of action," Doremond had sneered, and rightly so. But Gerald knew that behind the wooden door his son was in danger, and if he was ever to find the will to do what was necessary, it was now.

"Kyle," said Gerald, "move away from the door."

"My son," called the woman as she climbed back up the stairs. "He is not far away. He is coming."

He heaved his shoulder into the wood.

"Don't!" called Kyle.

He backed up a step, trembling as much from the shock of action as from the impact itself, and slammed into the door again. The blow jarred his jaw and made him dizzy, but he could tell the wood was giving.

"Stay out," yelled Kyle, sounding far away. "I don't want you here!"

His heart thudding, his thoughts hectic, Gerald pressed up against the opposite wall to give himself the room to build momentum, and as he did he saw the woman in the lavender dress standing at the head of the stairs, her hand across her mouth as if she were witnessing a horror. A man breaking in on his child.

"I only want to help him," he said. He turned again toward the door.

"Just leave me alone," Kyle moaned.

Something about that voice made Gerald hesitate. Something about its frailty and its remoteness sucked the certainty he'd conjured out of him. His sudden, brief surge of will dissipated, and in its place came fear.

He found that he understood that feeling. Its familiarity calmed him. He knelt onto the carpet in front of the door.

"Kyle," he said, just loud enough to be heard. "I'm not coming in."

Silence.

"I'm not going to make you do anything you don't want to do."

"Good."

Gerald pressed his palm against wood that would stay unbroken. "But Kyle," he said, "can you do something for me?"

After a second his son said, "What?"

"Can you tell me what's important about the hand? Can you explain to me why you don't want to get it fixed?"

For a long time Kyle said nothing. And though Gerald listened hard through his own ragged breathing for any sound or movement behind the door, none came. It was only when he'd begun to think that his son had fallen unconscious that he heard him say, in a voice so much like a child's, "You wouldn't understand. It just has to stay this way."

"But you'll lose the use of it, son!"

"I don't care," Kyle said. "I want it to stay like this."

"Okay," said Gerald, his mind still working. "But son, your hand is infected. The lady here says you were cold, and I think that means the infection is spreading. If it isn't treated, it could get very bad. Are you listening? You could go into shock. You could get gangrene." He thought of his son slipping out the window before he could reach him, lying in an alley somewhere, his flesh going putrid. "And if that happens the doctors" – if they could even find him, if they weren't too late – "the doctors would have to cut off your hand to save your life. And you wouldn't be able to stop them. Do you hear me? Nothing you could do."

He waited for that to sink in.

"So Kyle," he said, and took a breath. "Here's what I'm willing to do." All of the years Gerald had spent in want of faith, all the boyish possibility he'd squandered imposing his need for certainty and control, the ease with which he'd surrendered his son's right to risk, to err, to be trusted – the essential nature that had guided him so long, and so woefully – all of it echoed for Gerald as he knelt on the carpet, in this stranger's house, where his son had sought refuge. He didn't understand what he was about to do, not entirely, but that was all right. He realized it was time to take a chance. To let go. And hope for the best.

He closed his eyes and laid his spinning head against the cream-painted door. "Kyle, I'm willing to take you to the hospital, and tell the doctors to treat the infection, but not the hand."

He remembered, as he waited for his son to answer, the September day when Kyle turned four. It was a lucid day, summery and so bright the sun seemed to rise from the sidewalks. And because of this, and the specialness of the day, and the fact that as he passed them on his way to work the maples on their street were still green, Gerald had contracted the idea of playing catch with his son in the yard. His own father – always too busy, or too angry, or too drunk – had never done that with Gerald, and Gerald would not have his son say the same. Through meetings, lunch, and a two-hour conference call with Edmonton, he'd kept a loop running in his mind, the coming scene of him tossing his son the ball, getting him to throw it back, and tossing it to him again. It wasn't a rubber ball he imagined his son catching, but a serious ball. A softball. Kyle was four now, so he had the necessary coordination.

He'd left work as early as he could and stopped on the way home to buy the softball he needed (leather, with red stitching) and a small boy's baseball glove. And when he arrived home he found his son happily playing in the kitchen, and learned that Kyle didn't want to come outside. Gerald showed him the ball, showed him the glove, and still Kyle was unmoved. But Gerald had been looking forward to this for so long, was so infected with his idea, that he took Kyle by the hand and led him out onto the lawn. He pushed the baseball glove onto his son's left hand,

and crouched down a few paces away. Then he tossed the ball the way he'd imagined he would, in a parabola that was crisp and true, and the ball sailed through the air, through Kyle's reaching hands, and crushed his four-year-old lip.

"Do you hear me?" Gerald leaned against the door. "They'll give you antibiotics to take the swelling down and get the infection out of your system. But they won't set the bones. They won't do anything else to fix the hand, if that's what you want."

And after the blood had been cleaned from Kyle's mouth and the ice had been applied, it was Gerald's face Vicki had had to wipe dry, his head she'd had to hold to her chest. Because in the replays in his mind, of what actually happened, he could see that his son was never ready to catch, his hands were not close enough together. And yet with all the will in the world he could not, in his mind, keep himself from throwing the ball.

"I won't let them, son." He listened, and swallowed through the rock in his throat. "I won't let them."

From somewhere downstairs came the sound of a door opening, and a man's voice. "Mom?"

"My son," whispered the woman. "He has the key!"

Gerald held up a hand to warn them off. "Kyle," he called. "Someone is here with a key for this door. But I'm not going to use it. All right? No one is going to come in. If you want to save the hand, if you want to keep it the way it is, then you have to come out of the room. It's up to you. And I promise not to try to force you into something. I promise not to do anything."

He pressed the heels of his hands against his eyes, and waited.

"That's the bargain," he said.

When finally, after hours that might have been minutes, he heard the sound of movement from inside the room, he stood up and backed away from the door. At the edge of his vision he saw the woman and her son, below her on the steps, with the key, and he gestured for them to get back downstairs, out of sight.

From behind the door he heard the soft groan of a floor-board giving, and the catch of a lock being released. Then slowly the brass knob turned, the door began to open, and Gerald saw his child come into view.

His eyes were black with mistrust, and still some indecision. As he inched forward, through the doorway, Gerald didn't move. Not to touch his son's face, not to hold him, save him, not even when he saw his swollen hand, and the scarlet streaks running up his arm.

"You promised," said Kyle, as a warning to his father.

"Don't worry, son," he said. Though it killed him. "Don't worry," Gerald said. "I won't help you."

7

A week later, on a clear-skied May morning, Lorie Campeau arrived on the front steps of 93 Breere Crescent. When Gerald opened the door he found her beaming and holding a small white box tied with a gold elastic string.

"Mom's all set," Lorie announced. "We've got her into a really wonderful retirement home with a view of the mountains. She's going to be so happy there." Smiling, Lorie shook her head as if to express how quite incredible her mother's good fortune was. "Anyway, I wanted to thank you so much for taking care of Sprinkles while we were gone. I hope he wasn't too much trouble." She handed Gerald the white box and tapped it with a fingernail. "That's marzipan from Victoria. It's one of my favourite things and I wanted you to have some." Her eyes crinkled up with thanks for a moment, and then gradually went smooth. She cleared her throat and leaned slightly to peek around the sides of Gerald's form in the doorway.

"Sprinkles?" said Gerald, blinking against the daylight.

The woman on his front step hesitated for a moment. "Oh, that's right!" she exclaimed. "We hadn't named it when we left. Well, it's so sweet. While we were there in the hospital, waiting for Mom to come out of surgery, Jewels came up with the name Sprinkles. And she would not be deterred." Lorie tilted her head and rolled her eyes, a face of good-natured parental tolerance. Then she brought her hands together lightly. "So."

"There's no cat named Sprinkles here," said Gerald. "Our cat's name is Rumsfeld."

He handed the box of marzipan back to Lorie Campeau, and softly closed the door.

Acknowledgements

For their support during the writing of this book, I owe thanks to the following: My wife, Krista, for all she does to keep me real; the Canada Council for funding assistance; my editor, Jennifer Lambert, for her love of craft and her trustworthy ear; Nicole Winstanley, who launched the boat with such verve, and captain Bruce and the crew at Westwood, who kept it on course.

I'm grateful to the military and civilian personnel I met and played poker with in several Canadian Forces camps in Bosnia-Herzegovina for offering a glimpse into life on an armed forces base. Thanks also to Major Richard Sneddon, Captain Mike Mailleux, and particularly journalist Les Perreaux, for sharing their Afghanistan experiences. Most of the details of water treatment in a hostile environment I learned from John H. Schnieders, a specialist in the chemistry and microbiology of potable water. My understanding of staging owes much to the time I spent researching the world of luxury real estate for *Report on Business Magazine*. I also found *Miller's International Antiques Price Guide* a valuable resource.

Finally, I owe belated thanks to Patricia Best, for seeing the writer in me, and to my mother, Hilda Mason, for offering unflagging encouragement and modeling a work ethic second to none.

Mohan Juneja

Trevor Cole's second novel, *The Fearsome Particles*, was a national bestseller and a finalist for the Governor General's Award. His first novel, *Norman Bray in the Performance of His Life*, was also a finalist for the Governor General's Award and earned him the City of Hamilton Arts Award for Literature. In addition, it was named a regional finalist for the Commonwealth Writers' Prize and longlisted for the International IMPAC Dublin Literary Award. He is also a multiple-award-winning magazine journalist.

Trevor Cole lives in Hamilton, Ontario, where he runs a web site dedicated to audio readings by Canadian writers, authorsaloud.com.